Patricia Grey was born in Highgate, went to school in Barnet and college in London, and now lives in South Hertfordshire. She became a secretary and worked in all manner of companies from plastic mouldings and Japanese banking through to film production and BBC radio, eventually ending up as contracts manager for a computer company. The background of GOOD HOPE STATION and her two earlier novels, JUNCTION CUT and BALACLAVA ROW, was in part supplied by her parents, who grew up in Kentish Town.

Good Hope Station

Patricia Grey

HEADLINE

First published in 1997
by HEADLINE BOOK PUBLISHING

First published in paperback in 1998
by HEADLINE BOOK PUBLISHING

10 9 8 7 6 5 4 3 2 1

ISBN 0 7472 5495 8

Typeset by Avon Dataset Ltd, Bidford-on-Avon, Warks

Printed and bound in Great Britain by
Clays Ltd St Ives plc

HEADLINE BOOK PUBLISHING
A division of Hodder Headline PLC
338 Euston Road
London NW1 3BH

For my mother – with much love for always.

To the women of the Auxiliary Fire Service – I'm sure you worked far harder (and with far less time off) than my AFS girls but I had to take certain liberties with their working hours otherwise there would have been no plot!

I should also like to send my grateful thanks to Mrs Wyn Hordern for providing me with such detailed information on conditions for female officers in the Metropolitan Police during the War and to Mr A. I. Rose for his description of his mother (Hilda)'s service in the wartime police force.

Chapter 1

September 1940

'*I'm in Hell*,' was Betty Shaw's first thought. This was swiftly followed by the more mundane: *It's not supposed to be like this*.

'It' in this case was the blaze resulting from a major air-raid, not Betty's vision of the Underworld.

She'd always imagined the fire vehicles would rush swiftly through deserted streets with just the exploding bombs for company. Instead here she was stuck on the back of a traffic jam that made Piccadilly Circus in rush hour look like a quiet Sunday on Hampstead Heath.

'Go round, woman, go round,' Superintendent Bailey ordered. He'd been puffing and snorting angrily in the back seat for the past half-mile.

She forgave him his abrupt tone; it wasn't rudeness, just an overriding impatience to reach the fire appliances under his supposed control. Well, he was just going to have to fume a bit longer, she decided. There was no way she could get the car down the narrow gap between the queue of pumps and trailer units and the row of two-up, two-down houses bordering the gates to the docks.

It was a wonder they were still there; they had already passed rows of streets blown to unrecognisable piles of brick, timber and twisted metal.

'For heaven's sake,' Bailey muttered. 'Is nobody in charge? Where are the police? Where's the traffic control, for heaven's sake?'

In response to his unheard complaint, a uniformed figure appeared, briefly silhouetted by the vivid orange light from the

1

docks behind him. He paused, and they sensed his bewilderment as he regarded the jam of vehicles all trying to get into the one dock gate. Then, as silently as he'd come, he disappeared down a cobbled street that ran adjacent to the one they'd become trapped in.

'Very helpful,' Bailey snorted. 'Remind me to ring the Police Commissioner and complain when I get back to the station, Firewoman, um, er . . .'

'Shaw, sir,' Betty reminded him again. 'Firewoman Betty Shaw.'

She'd been on duty in the watchroom when the call had come through from the district control room. Their superintendent's car – and driver – had become one of the first casualties of the Blitz. Could the auxiliary station supply a replacement?

The mobilising officer experienced the same problem that every other station had encountered that night. He certainly had a car, but for the first time since it had been mobilised, every driver in his station was off the premises.

Betty had seen her chance. 'I've passed fit to drive. One of the other women can take over my watch here.'

She'd seen the hesitation in the man's face, and had sympathised. She knew the reason behind it, but didn't intend to back down. Ten minutes later she'd been speeding through the blacked-out streets to collect her passenger from Euston and carry him on to the Thames docks, which had already sucked in most of the appliances from his region.

Swallowing hard, she concentrated on keeping the car moving. Ahead of her the queue of vehicles was inching forward at an agonisingly slow pace. The need for their pumps was obvious. The whole of the docks seemed to be ablaze with a steady, intense heat that hurt the eyes. Occasionally a blanket of thick smoke swirled over the scene, obscuring the vehicles and tiny figures. Then another stack of wood would catch, exploding in a shower of dry, bright red heat.

Through the smoke and showering sparks, she could make out a turntable ladder. A hundred feet above the ground a solitary figure at the top played a pitiful stream of water into a blazing warehouse.

Don't let it be Len, she prayed silently, finally managing to bump her own vehicle into the dock yards.

'Which way, sir?'

Bailey's breath sounded harshly in her ear; his wheezing speech a legacy of too much smoke inhalation. 'God knows. This is chaos.' Winding down the window, he hailed a passing AFS dispatch rider. 'Hey, boy. Where's the control point?'

'Isn't one, sir, best find your own way.' His final word was already a distant wail as he sped away, his narrower motorbike swerving easily between a taxi-cab pulling a pump and the posts of the dock gates.

'Damned lunacy,' grumbled Bailey. 'Excuse my French, young woman. Pull over and park.'

Betty did her best to comply. It wasn't easy. The yard was crisscrossed with hoses, stretching from the river to clusters of firemen struggling to support the business ends. Eventually she managed to back into a deceptively safe gap between the outer wall and an empty delivery lorry.

The superintendent had already left the car. Joining him outside she became aware of the incredible cacophony of noise: straining pumps, roaring updraughts, collapsing buildings and exploding incendiaries were all crashing against her ear-drums.

'Shall I try to find our appliances, sir?' she yelled, ending on a choke as a gust of tar black smoke passed over them.

'No. I'll go and look. You stay here with the car. And listen to me, Firewoman . . .'

'Shaw,' Betty reminded him automatically.

'Well, Shaw, see that stack of timber there . . . ?'

Squinting through the heat, Betty made out a pile higher than a three-storey house.

'If that catches, it's your cue to get yourself and this car out of here. Go to the nearest fire station and I'll find you there. Understand?'

He was gone even as she was assuring him she did.

Left alone, she felt oddly bereft. Which was stupid really, since every fire engine in London seemed to be packed into the East End tonight.

A sudden backwash of water cascaded over the ground in a

3

wave, soaking her to the calves. Startled, she stepped backwards. Her ankle bone collided with a hose turned stone-hard by hours of pressure. With a gasp of pain, she sat down heavily.

'Steady on, love, you'd best take more water with it in future,' a laughing voice told her.

A strong grip hauled her to her feet. Tilting her head upwards to thank her rescuer shifted the deep shadow of her tin helmet off her face and illuminated her features. She could only make out the whites of the eyes in the smoke-blackened face, but she saw recognition dawning.

'Blimey, it's Station Officer Shaw's missus, ain't it?' The tone instantly became more respectful. She was no longer 'love', she was Mrs Leonard Shaw.

It was almost impossible to distinguish his features beneath the thick layer of black grease.

'Tanner,' he prompted. 'Marty Tanner. Me and Len served at Soho together.'

'Yes, of course. Stay safe, Marty.'

'You too, Mrs Shaw. Your lot's down the far end. I'll tell Len I seen you.'

'No. Don't do that, Marty. He'll only worry if he knows I'm down here. It's better he keeps his mind on the job.'

'Fair enough. Best get back to me pump. You take care now. Can't say I'd want my missus out in this lot.'

Neither would Len, that was the problem. She'd joined the Auxiliary Fire Service with the intention of becoming a driver. But Len had had other ideas. He'd pulled strings at headquarters to ensure she was assigned office duties. Now here she was right in the thick of it.

Even the air was burning. It lay against the exposed skin on her face and hands like a scorched sheet. It didn't matter which direction you looked in; the whole world seemed to be on fire. Even the ships on the Thames had caught; amongst the drifting palls of smoke she could just about see a solitary fire boat battling valiantly to bring its pumps to bear on a blazing cargo ship.

A shout, followed by a shower of water, brought her back to her senses. Startled, she looked upwards. The blaze had jumped

4

across the stacks and the pile of timber Superintendent Bailey had indicated now had a fringe of flames leaping from its crown. A hose had been brought round to play on it and the furthest arc of its spray was raining down on her.

Belatedly remembering the car, she ran back and wriggled into the driving seat. Leaving the docks proved an even bigger problem than getting in in the first place. The stream of vehicles still trying to enter had to have priority, meaning she was forced to lurk a few yards to the side, waiting her chance to slip into a lull in the flow.

A new problem occurred to her. How was she supposed to drive to the nearest fire station when she hadn't a clue where it was? Winding down the window, she called out to a running figure: 'Excuse me, the fire . . . oh, lord . . .'

Despite the grime, she recognised this one. Leading Fireman Patrick O'Day belonged to her husband's watch. He'd stooped to the window before he registered her identity.

'Is my husband all right?' she asked quickly, before he could say anything.

'He's fine, Mrs Shaw. We're down the far end.' He lowered his voice slightly. It was an unnecessary precaution, since you couldn't have heard a double-decker bus drop ten paces away, much less the proverbial pin. 'It's hopeless, Mrs Shaw. Nobody seems to know who's in charge of what. We don't reckon they even know how to call up more pumps.' Despite the grime and smoke, his face suddenly split into an attractive grin. 'So the guv'nor's sent me to commandeer us a bit of help. Watch this . . .'

With a wink he was gone, before she could warn him not to mention her presence to Len.

A red London Fire Brigade engine was just nosing through the gates. She saw Pat spring up next to the driver's window and say something. Next moment he was pulled inside the cab, and the vehicle turned sharp left and disappeared into the shimmering curtain of heat.

Seizing her opportunity, Betty gunned her own engine and shot back out into the street.

The press of traffic in the road directly opposite the gates was still heading into the docks. Rather than try to force her way through, she turned left again, down the narrow side street that the policeman had ducked into a while before.

At once she had a sense of being in another world. The glow from the docks still lit up the scene, the reflection of tangerine skies flickering spitefully in the upstairs windows, but the street was deserted. After the bustle of the last few hours, to suddenly be confronted by an empty world was unnerving. Slowly she crawled along the cobblestoned street, her eyes alert for anyone who could provide directions to the fire station. The occupants had obviously taken cover in the air-raid shelters. But there ought to be an ARP post somewhere.

The street gave on to other identical terraces of two-up, two-down cottages. Miraculously, these too were untouched, despite their proximity to the blazing dockyards. Betty stared at them in frustration. She didn't know this area of London at all; her life had been spent in the west and north of the city. 'And at the rate you're going, woman,' she informed her reflection in the driving mirror, 'you're going to spend the rest of this war driving in circles.' A small voice in her head added: 'If you don't get blown to smithereens any second.'

She tried another right turn. And then stood on her brakes in total disbelief.

A woman was standing in the window of one of the houses, a small child clutched in her arms, staring out at the scene as if it were a pleasant summer's afternoon rather than the middle of the worst air-raid London had ever seen.

For a moment the three of them stared into each others' eyes. The woman was indifferent; the baby wide-eyed with the novelty of it all. Betty just had time to register the crude number 14 painted on the wooden door, then the woman stepped back into the room and calmly flicked a blackout curtain across.

'Wait, you can't . . .' She'd got the car door half open before she was aware of the policeman sheltering in a neighbouring doorway.

'There's a woman,' she called across. 'In there . . .'

'I know that, love. But if Myrtle don't fancy the shelters, I'm blowed if I'm gonna drag 'er. You lost?'

'Is the fire station around here?'

He nodded back the way she'd come. 'Straight down there, take the fourth left. There's a substation in the old infirmary building.'

The substation's yard was empty, its appliances already deployed in the docks. Inside the gloomy hall, a rudimentary first-aid post was being manned by a couple of female auxiliaries, whilst two others answered the telephones and chalked up the situation boards. The only other fireman present was an elderly sub-officer who was moving pinned flags around a local map.

Betty's presence was accepted with a casual 'Stick a bandage on that one, will you?'

Swallowing her nausea, Betty applied cold water and bandages to blackened hands. The blistered skin came away as she touched it.

'Sorry.'

'It's OK, miss. Can't hardly feel a thing. Better off than Toby at any rate.'

For the first time Betty noticed the silent figure, covered by a blanket, lying under a deal table in the corner of the room.

'Leg blown off,' her patient continued cheerily.

'Oh.' Her eyes met another girl's over the man's head.

'Ambulance is coming,' the girl said. 'Oh, so . . .' The expletive was drowned by the sound of an air-raid siren, and a minute later the scream of descending bombs sent them all diving under the tables.

'There's a cellar,' the other girl shouted. 'If you fancy it. Full of rats, though.'

'Thanks, I'll stop up here,' Betty bawled back.

The image of the woman and child swam into her mind again. 'The houses along by the docks, do they have cellars?'

On her knees, hushing the legless patient, who was showing signs of coming round, the girl shook her head. 'No. Lot of them go down the Tube, I heard, though you ain't supposed to. Why?'

Betty told her about Myrtle and the baby at number fourteen.

'Sounds like Florizel Passage.' The auxiliary seemed as

7

indifferent as the policeman had been. 'I'm surprised she hasn't caught a packet already. Still, some folks just can't be told.'

The all-clear sounded after forty minutes. Making her way to the door, Betty scanned the houses between the station and the docks. There was no tell-tale smoke or rising dust from the direction of Florizel Passage.

'Another lot for Thames-Haven, I reckon,' the other girl remarked at her elbow, indicating the fiercer glow staining the eastern sky. 'Here's the medicals at last.'

An auxiliary ambulance bumped into sight and two Home Guard members jumped from the back. The unconscious Toby was swiftly removed, together with a couple of walking wounded. Within minutes others had taken their places. Despite their injuries, they all seemed remarkably cheerful.

'Where you from then, gorgeous?' one enquired.

'Kentish Town,' Betty informed him. 'What about you?'

'Upminster. Know it?'

'Can't say I do.'

'Thought not. I'd have spotted a little cracker like you soon as she set foot in the place.'

Despite herself, Betty couldn't help laughing. He looked about nineteen to her thirty-five. 'I'm old enough to be your mum, you cheeky devil. And I'm a married woman I'll have . . . Oh, lord!'

The windows on the upper floor blew out in a rush of glass and wooden frames as a delayed-action bomb roared into life. Instinctively Betty identified the direction of the sound; it had come from the rows of terraces by the docks.

'Hey, gorgeous, where you going . . . ?' The young fireman's plaintive cry followed her into the deserted street.

'Florizel Passage, the baby . . .' she shouted at the startled girl auxiliary, who was grabbing a stirrup pump to tackle a shower of burning fragments splattering down into the yard.

She found the street more by luck than judgement. The adjacent rows had already collapsed, spilling bricks and twisted timbers across the road and tainting the air with clouds of choking dust and cordite. Stumbling over the rubble, her ears

8

straining for the scream of a descending bomb, she mentally counted: '*Two, four, six* . . .'

Number fourteen was on fire. Its roof had collapsed in on the upper floor; the lower floor looked relatively intact.

Grabbing the latch, Betty pushed. The light from outside was enough to show her the hall was deserted. A gust of thick smoke rolled down the stairs. Crouching to find the freshest air, she called into the stillness: 'Myrtle? Where are you?'

An ominous crash from upstairs dislodged a shower of plaster from the hall ceiling. She smelt singed wood.

'Myrtle!' Perhaps the woman had gone to a shelter when the last raid started?

The room Myrtle had been watching from was to the right. It was sparsely furnished and obviously empty. There was a closed door ahead. Betty hesitated. The smoke was already growing denser and the creaks and groans from above became more violent with each second.

Returning to the street, she snatched a deep breath, then ran forward in a crouched position.

The scullery window had been blown in; the tattered remnants of flour-sack curtains flapped inwards in the draught from the blazing docks. At first glance the room seemed deserted. Then she saw the huddled figure in one corner.

'Myrtle? You must get out. Please. Come to the fire station with me.'

Pulling at the woman's clothes, she tried to drag her upright. Myrtle flopped awkwardly. Her head dropped forward; blood poured from her nose, ears and mouth. Betty stared aghast. She'd heard that people could be killed by blast, but this was the first one she'd ever seen. Without thinking, she took Myrtle's limp hand in a futile gesture of comfort. Part of her mind registered the lack of a wedding ring, whilst the rest of her senses probed the smoky hell, trying to locate the baby.

A whimper claimed her attention. It was coming from under the upended tin bath on the floor. Levering it up, she peered underneath.

The baby lay curled on its side, one fat thumb in its mouth and wide-awake eyes regarding Betty solemnly.

'Come on, darling, let's get you out of here.'

The back door was unyielding. The reverberations of wood on stone told her that something had fallen against it outside. Turning, she blundered out into the hall passage again. A cloud of heat and choking smoke met her. All around the horsehair infilling between the cheap lath and plaster walls was burning merrily. Unconsciously she took a breath, and felt her head start to spin dizzily.

The baby, her mind whispered. *Must save the baby.*

Fixing her attention on the open street, she plunged forward.

A tall figure filled the outline of the door. 'Missus Shaw? For God's sake, get out of there.'

Pat O'Day's firm hands grasped her shoulders and urged her along. The sound of wood wrenching from brick filled the air. Looking up, Betty saw a burning joist plunge down in slow motion, releasing the rest of the burning first storey on to their heads.

Chapter 2

'Blimey, that was close!' Pat exclaimed, picking himself up from the rubble.

Betty struggled to her knees too. The baby was worryingly silent. Looking over her shoulder, Betty found number fourteen was well ablaze, the shell of the walls turning the inside into a gigantic blazing chimney.

'His mum's in there. Oh Pat, she was dead.'

'Then whichever way she went, she's probably cooler than we're gonna be in a minute. Can you walk?' Without waiting for a reply, he hauled her to her feet. 'Honestly, Mrs Shaw, you're a fireman's missus. Even me little brother knows better than to go into a burning house without any back-up. What if I hadn't come by?'

Trying to retain her dignity in the face of fright, tears and the horrible suspicion that she looked like a chimney sweep, Betty asked him how come he had happened to 'come by'.

'Brought one of the crew into the first-aid station,' he replied, marching her in that direction. 'They told me some stupid female from Kentish Town had gone looking for casualties in Florizel Passage. I guessed it was you. Ain't that many of you down here tonight.' He gave her arm a stern shake. 'Don't you ever do that again, Mrs Shaw. If you'd caught it out there we might never have known what 'appened to yer. 'Ow d'you reckon that would make the guv'nor feel?'

They were almost at the substation again. An ARP warden was helping to load another fire casualty into the back of an ambulance. The injured man's waving hands signalled to the world even more effectively than the white bandage round his eyes that he couldn't see.

'Best give the baby to them, Mrs Shaw. The ARP will sort him out.'

She wanted to keep the sturdy little body clasped protectively to hers, but she knew Pat was right. With reluctance she surrendered him to the ARP warden, giving as many details as she could about his background.

'I've gotta get back,' Pat said.

'Pat.' She caught his jacket arm. 'Don't tell Len. About the house and the baby. Just say you saw me down here at the station if you have to. Please, Pat.'

Their eyes met and locked for a moment. She knew she was asking a lot of him. If Len found out some other way, he could make Pat's life very uncomfortable indeed.

'Make a deal with you,' Pat said finally. 'If you see my mum, you don't tell her what it's really like down here. And I won't say nothing to your old man. Deal?'

'Deal,' Betty agreed, relieved. 'Take care, Pat,' she called after his disappearing figure.

He raised one hand in casual salute and then was gone.

The demand for first-aid remained steady throughout the night, although there were no more casualties as bad as the young boy with his leg blown away. Most of the string of exhausted and dirty men dashing in once they could be spared from their pumps and branches were suffering from embedded splinters of wood and metal which had been sent into the air in lethal showers by exploding bombs. As soon as the splinter was drawn, and the wound disinfected and dressed, they dashed back out to their posts again.

Throughout the night, air-raid sirens signalled further incoming waves of bombers. The infirmary substation shook with each blast, sending great chunks of plaster tumbling to the floor, but the heavy walls stayed more or less intact.

After each 'raiders passed', Betty went out to check on the staff car. Apart from a thick film of black wood ash that had settled over it, it seemed unscathed.

Returning from her last inspection, she said worriedly to the other auxiliaries: 'I think I've lost my superintendent.'

'Careless that,' one of the telephone operators called across. 'Fran there lost a whole clutch of stirrup pumps once. And I misplaced the gas masks. Can't say we've ever lost an officer, though. Wonder if they'll make you pay for him. What d'you reckon the going rate for a superintendent is?'

'About tuppence 'a'ppenny,' yelled across one of the firemen, whose eyelids, swollen to the size of pigeons' eggs, were being bathed in cold water.

The auxiliary administering the first-aid peered closer and gave the opinion that she couldn't do much else. 'Me mum always used cold tea for swellings.'

'Hot tea wouldn't come amiss, ducks. I'm spitting feathers out there. We all are.'

'Control say they're sending canteen vans down.'

'I could make tea,' Betty offered. 'If there is any.'

'There's a kitchen back there. If the gas is still working . . . Make us all one, will you? Me and Fran been on for . . .' She checked the yellowing face of the ancient clock that had been loudly clicking away their watch all night. 'God . . . twelve hours without no break.'

Betty made her way down the corridor indicated. Ancient iron beds and dusty curtaining gave off an aura of rust and mould which suggested the infirmary had been abandoned long before the fire service commandeered the building. A yellowing calendar in the small kitchen was open at 1924.

There was no blackout in this room. Looking upwards to the high barred windows, she was startled to see the first streaks of a rose-coloured dawn beyond the smoky pall that hung over the whole sky.

The gas, miraculously, was still connected. The water pipes, however, banged, coughed and rattled in protest when she spun the taps on. She should have realised; the fire pumps had drained the pipes and reservoirs dry.

Eventually, after much protest, the cold tap disgorged a thin trickle of suspiciously coloured water. Praying that she wasn't about to bless the whole station with Lipton's *à la* cholera, she filled an ancient flat-bottomed kettle and set it to boil. In doing so, she caught a glimpse of her reflection in the metal sides.

Goggle eyes in a distorted face the colour of road tar, framed by a halo of erratically spiked locks, stared back at her.

'Oh, no. Why didn't somebody *say*?'

The tap had given up, so she had to tip tepid water from the kettle over her handkerchief. A vigorous scrub removed part of the mess. Using her fingers as a rake, she attempted to tame her hair. Knots, tangles and lumps of ash frustrated her. Eventually she admitted defeat, and found a greening mirror in the cutlery drawer to check the results.

Sometimes she didn't recognise the woman who looked back at her these days. The round face with its large brown eyes and soft cloud of curly chin-length chestnut hair was the same one in her photo taken the day she'd wed Len. But now there were fine lines she didn't remember between her nose and mouth, and a plumping and slackening around the jawline that hadn't been there before.

'You're getting old,' she told her reflection. 'Now when did that happen?'

A shrill whistle jerked her out of her brooding. She was about to fling herself to the floor when she identified the sound. The kettle was boiling. She found half a packet of tea and filled the enamelled teapot. Dividing the liquid between the station's assortment of mugs and cups, she added milk and then found a tin box of thick arrowroot biscuits.

'No food in the control room,' the sub-officer growled, abandoning his maps and pins for the first time when she reappeared.

'We'll come back to the kitchen with you. Two on, two off, OK, Sub?' Fran asked.

'Suppose it will have to be. Don't take all day.'

Two of the girls went back with Betty, together with three grateful firemen who'd come in for first-aid.

'I couldn't find any sugar,' Betty apologised as they all squeezed round the tiny table.

'Isn't any. Meant to go up the market today, if it's open.'

'It'll be wide open, I reckon,' one the men remarked.

The girl giggled loudly. Others joined in. There was a note of hysteria in their laughter. Gulping down hot tea, they rocked with a mixture of light-hearted relief that they were alive and sheer tiredness now they'd passed the sleep threshold.

'Well, this is a fine carry-on, I must say,' boomed a voice from the doorway.

Choking on their tea, they struggled to their feet as Superintendent Bailey inserted as much of his bulk into the room as the furniture would allow.

Ignoring a clamour of explanations, Bailey addressed Betty.

'It's all right for some, isn't it, Firewoman, um, er . . .'

'Shaw.'

'Quite right. Well, while you've been sitting around at tea parties all night, some of us have been up to our necks in it. And now we'd like to get back to our office, if you could tear yourself away from your social engagements.'

The tone was stern, but Betty caught the glint in the old boy's eye. After years of being desk-bound, he'd finally found an excuse to be in the centre of the action again.

'I'll get the car, sir,' Betty said meekly.

She'd forgotten the wood ash. It was lying three inches deep over the vehicle. A nearly bristleless broom dealt with the worst of the dirt and added a few scratches to the paintwork as a bonus.

Returning breathless to the hall to collect the superintendent, she was hailed by him with the news: 'There's another one of your lot over there. We'll be taking an extra passenger back to base.'

Her heart gave a lurch. She half expected to see another member of her husband's watch, if not Len himself. But it was a slim female in an auxiliary uniform who rose to meet her.

'Oh, hello, Nell.'

'Good morning,' Nell De Groot replied.

'Firewoman De Groot has been unhorsed, so to speak,' Superintendent Bailey boomed. Eight hours of fire, smoke and imminent death with every explosion had put new heart into him.

'My hose lorry was caught in a blast,' Nell elaborated, seeing Betty's blank expression. 'It's being towed back to the workshops.'

Her uniform looked neat and uncrumpled. Her silver-fair hair was swept smoothly back off her pale oval face. Anyone who didn't know Nell de Groot would have assumed she'd spent the night in a comfortable, well-furnished bomb shelter.

Betty felt obliged to ask if she was hurt.

'I'm quite well, thank you,' Nell replied.

Her brittle air of composure didn't invite any further conversation. Not that the superintendent didn't try. As Betty drove slowly back through a flattened and smoking city, Bailey made an attempt at a little gallant flattery. Nell responded coolly: 'Yes, sir' . . . 'Thank you, sir' . . . 'I'm sure that's correct, sir.'

Eventually Bailey gave up and they both stared moodily through the windows at the stream of dazed pedestrians emerging from the shelters, and the clusters of rescue services picking over the collapsed buildings.

At Euston they delivered Bailey back to his office.

'Thank you for your sterling assistance, Firewoman, um, er . . .'

'Scarlett O'Hara,' Betty said sweetly, letting in her clutch and gliding away from the steps.

She caught Nell's eye in the rear-view mirror, half smiled, then changed her mind. It was hard to say why it was so difficult to communicate with Nell. It seemed as if she had an invisible fence around her marked: 'Keep out – trespassers will be frozen to death'. It was a relief to turn into the yard behind the disused factory that now served as the auxiliary station and see the cheery faces of the two Millers. Well, Ruth at least was cheerful. Hatty was her usual slow, amiable self. Both had obviously taken the opportunity to slip outside and have a quick smoke during a lull in the proceedings.

Parking in the designated slot was difficult. One of the heavy pump vehicles had already returned and the yard was criss-crossed by snaking hose, laid out for inspection and cleaning. In the end Betty squeezed into a corner under the faded and sooty sign that had given this station its name. At some time in the past century a former tenant of the building had had a contract to supply beer and ale to Her Majesty's Capetown and

Natal garrisons. The brewer had long since gone out of business and been superseded by numerous tenants since, but a remnant of his painted advertisement still obstinately blazed from beneath layers of railway engine soot, announcing to passing trains that this was the premises of 'The Good Hope Brewing and Bottling Company Limited'. The station might be known by a collection of numbers and letters to Fire HQ in Lambeth, but its inhabitants – with a mixture of irony and wishful thinking – had christened it 'Good Hope Station'.

Climbing stiffly from the car, aware for the first time of the bruises she'd collected after her adventures in Florizel Passage, Betty called across to Ruth, who'd been on duty in the watchroom last night: 'Many calls?'

'Fiftyish, I reckon,' Ruth shouted back, passing the cigarette back to her cousin. 'Couldn't do nuffing about most. Our boys got sent down the City. Bartholomew and Busby got it, they reckon. Where'd you go?'

'The docks,' Betty said. 'The regulars are there.'

'Is Station Officer Shaw all right?'

'Last I heard, thank you, Hatty.'

'Oooh, will you look at that!' Ruth squealed.

'That' was two firemen descending from the upper storey that housed the living quarters. Both were dressed solely in their underpants, vests and boots.

'You've forgotten yer trousers, fellahs!'

The younger one flushed at Ruth's shout. The older flashed her a wink that was swiftly extinguished as the sub-officer came down behind them. Since he was similarly under-dressed, he managed a credible attempt at authority, delivering orders in his crisp Knightsbridge accent.

'Aren't you other ladies due to go off at this watch changeover?'

Murmuring agreement, Betty and Nell provided brief reports of their night's activities and then joined the Millers, who were hovering in the yard and, in Ruth's case at least, embarrassing the half-dressed firemen trying to clean and check their equipment. Above their heads, sodden tunics and trousers had been shut in the sash windows in an attempt to dry them off.

17

'Seems a pity to leave when the view here's so smashing, don't it?' Ruth giggled. 'What d'you reckon, Nell?'

If she was hoping to disconcert the normally icy Nell, she was out of luck. Calmly remarking that she thought it a pity the government hadn't taken notice and issued the auxiliaries with spare uniforms, Nell wished them all good morning and left.

'Snooty Miss Grooty,' Ruth said without heat, as the blonde crossed the road and turned left up the hill towards the Archway.

'She's just a bit shy,' Hatty said with the sympathy of a fellow sufferer.

'She's been here for months. What's she got to be shy about? No, she just reckons she's too good for the likes of us. Well . . .' Ruth said, resettling her cap, 'her loss. You walking down the road, Betty?'

'I think I'll just stop by the station. See if the crews are back yet.'

The regular station was scarcely a few hundred yards from the auxiliary. 'Nice and 'andy for Hitler to get both with one bomb,' an old hand had remarked sarcastically when the factory had been requisitioned. It had, however, led to a degree of sharing of personnel between the two, and a somewhat warmer relationship than that which existed between a lot of regular and auxiliary stations. Today it also meant that the women could legitimately claim to be 'just passing' on their way home.

The yard was empty. The doors to the vehicle bays gaped widely. There wasn't even a stand-by appliance in evidence.

'Let's go in and ask,' Ruth suggested.

'No.' Betty forced herself to move a few steps away from the yard gates. 'None of the men want a fussing woman under their feet. Len wouldn't thank me for it. They'll be back when they're ready.'

A small corner of her mind pushed away the pictures: the legless fireman; the blinded crew member; the three-storey stacks of timber that could bury a whole engine in seconds if they toppled.

'I'm just popping to the shops up Leighton; the tobacconist said he'd try to get me some of Len's mixture,' she said, swallowing a lump in her throat. 'I'll see you both tomorrow.'

She turned off down a side street, leaving the other two to make their way down the main road.

'It's not as bad as I thought,' Hatty said after a few moments.

'No,' Ruth agreed. ' 'Ardly any damage at all.'

Some shops had lost windows. The crash and tinkle of broken glass being swept up acted as a counterpoint to the rumble of the first morning trains rattling along the tracks at the top and bottom of the street. But apart from that, Kentish Town seemed relatively intact.

It was a different story to the south-east. In the distance the pall of smoke over the still-smouldering City hung between the earth and the sky like a solid sheet. By unspoken consent, the cousins stopped to stare.

Suddenly Ruth let forth an ear-splitting screech. ' 'Atty! Look down. Look!'

Chapter 3

Hatty followed the direction of the pointing finger down the hill.

After the violence of the previous night's raid, few vehicles were moving around yet. At the bottom of the near-deserted high street, where the road split into two, a red escape was trundling up the right-hand fork. A few more yards and they could see the pump unit following behind.

'It's them,' Ruth squealed. 'It's our lot.' Snatching off her cap, she leapt up and down, waving it vigorously.

With teeth flashing in unrecognisable black faces, the passing crew acknowledged the women. One doffed a tin helmet in their direction, revealing a pale border of skin just beneath his light-brown hair.

'That's Pat O'Day,' Ruth announced to Hatty and everyone else in a fifty-yard radius.

The last of the shelterers were just emerging bleary-eyed from the Tube stations and making their way home clutching piles of blankets, Thermos flasks and sleeping babies. Intermingled amongst them were the day's first workers, stepping over glass and sweeping brooms as they hurried to catch buses and trains. Ruth's pronouncement brought several of them to a halt. After a moment one of the women jiggled her toddler on to her hip, dumped her blankets on the pavement and started to clap loudly. Several others spectators joined in. The two fire appliances swept up Kentish Town Road on a ripple of appreciative applause.

'Well, that makes a change, doesn't it?' Ruth remarked as the vehicles disappeared from their sight. 'Last week nobody had a good word to say for the fire service. Now everyone wants to be matey. Hypo-whatsit, that's what it is.'

Marching on down the road, her nose in the air and her cap replaced at a jaunty angle, Ruth reached the entrance to Bartholomew Road. And came face to face with her first bomb incident.

Prior to today it had all been theory and training. Now she was confronted with reality. Where two houses had once stood, two partial side walls were all that was left. The rest had collapsed into a pile of bricks and timber. Somewhere in the top of the pile a brass double bed was sticking up like a flagpole, its gleaming knobs reflecting the rising sun.

'Oh, Ruth, how horrible,' Hatty breathed in her ear. 'I hope they weren't in there.'

' 'Spect they went down the shelter,' Ruth said robustly. Then, in a smaller voice, 'Hat, d'you reckon our house is all right?'

'Why shouldn't it be? There were no calls to our street, were there?' Hatty's attempt at morale-raising was somewhat marred, however, when she added that if there had been no fire, they might have just called out the Heavy Rescue Unit.

'Oh, shut up, Hat. Nothing's happened at home.'

Ruth started forward again. At first they walked briskly. Then, without meaning to, they speeded up to a trot. Within a minute they were both flying down the road. Startled pedestrians leapt out of the way. The sight of two auxiliary firewomen in such a hurry convinced some that something dreadful had happened.

Ruth overtook Hatty as she darted across the street to tear down Hawley Road. They took the final turn together, and sped down the short row of terraced houses neck and neck. Reaching inside the letter box, Ruth flicked out the key on the dangling string with one finger, inserted it in the lock and thrust the door open.

'Dad!'

'Ye loaves and little fishes, Ruthie, what d'you come crashing in like that for? I've cut meself now.'

Emerging from the back scullery in his vest, with his braces dangling to his knees, Duggie Miller dabbed a couple of fingers at the red tributary flowing amongst the white lather covering his chin and cheeks.

'Sorry, Dad,' Ruth gasped, leaning against the hall wall and panting loudly. 'We were scared you'd got bombed.'

'Nothing come down near us. Thank the Lord.'

'Amen,' Hatty responded, before going through to the outside lavatory and tearing off a sheet of paper. 'Here you are, Uncle Duggie.'

'Ta, Hat.' Slapping the temporary patch over the cut, Duggie thanked the Lord that the funeral parlour had no internments that morning. 'It don't do to wear sticking plaster. Looks sloppy, and that's disrespectful to the departed. Here's the post.'

Rattling the knocker of the still-open door, the postman wished them good morning, adding: 'One for you, Ruth.'

'Ta.' Without looking at the envelope, Ruth thrust it into her trouser pocket and dimpled at the young man. 'Miss seeing your smiling face them mornings I stop up the fire station. D'you miss me?'

Stuttering and stammering his assurances, the postman was gently guided outside by Duggie's hand and deposited firmly on the doorstep.

'Stop leading the poor lad on, Ruthie. You know you got no serious intentions. You'll be getting yourself a reputation. There was another one of your collection round asking after you on Saturday night.'

'Which one?'

'Bus driver.'

'Oh. Stan.'

Ruth turned and leapt upstairs, calling back that she was starving and could eat a horse.

'Probably will be if we get the meat ration up the market again. You had breakfast, Uncle?' Hatty asked, following him back into the scullery.

'An hour ago. I'm off.'

'Did you get the rations?'

Splashing copious quantities of cold water over his head and neck, Duggie Miller swept up the remnants of shaving lather and blood with the scrap of towel round his bare neck.

Somewhere in the midst of this performance he could just about be heard to mutter that Saturday had been a particularly busy time at the parlour. Which was a partial truth. The rest being that he hated standing in shopping queues. It was, in his estimation, 'woman's work'. With the doors firmly shut and the curtains drawn, he might just contribute to the war effort by pressing his trousers if it was needed, or peel a few vegetables if necessity – and hunger – dictated. But there was no way he'd be seen in public between a string of housewives queuing for the bacon ration.

'Leave your book,' Hatty instructed. 'I'll go up the shops today.'

'You're a good girl, Hat. Twin diamonds, the pair of you. Always said so. I must depart.'

Slipping on the shirt, striped waistcoat and coat that were swinging on a hanger behind the scullery door, he slicked his sandy, thinning hair to one side, carefully covering the gleaming pink scalp, and knotted a black tie into place.

Before Hatty's eyes the cheerful round face rearranged itself like melting wax. The undertaker's assistant who left was a walking embodiment of steadfast sympathy and respectful firmness.

Making her way upstairs, Hatty joined her cousin in the back bedroom. Ruth's uniform hung over the end of her bed. The letter was still folded into her pocket; temporarily forgotten. Lying flat on the bedspread in her knickers and brassière, Ruth was dangling a black suede shoe from one raised foot.

Taking off her own jacket and shirt, Hatty slipped a flowered dress over her head and then wriggled out of her trousers, grunting and puffing with the effort. 'There's a part-loaf in the bin. Shall I do fried bread for breakfast?'

'If you're offering.' Ruth continued to admire the shoe clinging to three rosy toes. Hatty knew what was coming: 'I bought these the day after that Mr Chamberlain said we was at war.'

'I know,' Hatty said, inserting her feet into a corset and jiggling it to thigh level.

As if her cousin hadn't spoken, Ruth continued: 'Been watching them for absolutely *ages* in Selfridges. I said to Dad, if I'm gonna get blown to bits I just got to have something lovely. So I took all me savings from the post office – three quid nearly – and Dad give me the rest.' She waved the high heels in a gentle sweep, admiring the way the light caught the sprinkle of fake diamonds embedded in the heels. 'Genuine French design. Five guineas. Just think, Hatty, that's more than our wages fer a fortnight.'

Groaning and puffing, Hatty succeeded in heaving the corset to her waist. The exertion had turned her skin pink and sweaty.

Ruth yawned loudly. 'I'm tired. Let's get some sleep.'

'Best try and stay up until tonight. Otherwise we'll be nodding off on duty. And there's washing ought to be done.'

Ruth wrinkled her nose.

'And we need shopping.'

Ruth brightened. Scrambling to her knees, she took a hairbrush from the shelf next to her bedhead and dragged it vigorously through her long hair, pulling out pins with the other hand and clamping them between her lips.

Hatty found her own brush and joined her cousin on the bed so that they could both peer into the only mirror in the room; a free-standing oval one that lived on Ruth's shelf amongst her collection of cosmetic boxes, bottles and tins.

They made a strange contrast. Ruth was scarcely five feet tall; a small, well-proportioned package, with an oval face, long, naturally curly black hair and sparkling blue eyes. Hatty, on the other hand, was a good ten inches taller; a large-boned, square-faced young woman with straight chestnut hair that hung in a plain bob to her shoulders, and a pair of hazel eyes that peered shyly through a heavy fringe.

'I fink I'll put me blue blouse on,' Ruth remarked, squinting critically at her reflection. 'With that grey and blue check skirt. And me little jacket. That one I got up Blustons sale summer before the war.' Finishing her inspection, she opened a box of Bourjois rouge and flicked a dab expertly on each cheek.

Long experience had taught Hatty that it was useless to point out that they were only going to do the household shopping.

Ruth never left the house unless she was, in her own words, 'Turned out fit to be seen. After all, you never know who yer might meet, do you?'

In Ruth's case, she lived in the hope of tripping over a rich, titled dreamboat somewhere in the middle of Kentish Town High Street. Just lately she'd taken to endowing the man of her dreams with a commission in the armed services – preferably the RAF, since she found the pilots' uniforms the most romantic.

Leaving her cousin carefully pinning and twisting her hair back into place, Hatty went to slice up the remains of the loaf. On the way out of the bedroom, she automatically picked up Ruth's discarded uniform and hung it in the wardrobe. The letter fell unnoticed to the floor.

The shopping took three times longer than usual. That weekend had brought the first major raids on north London, and the whole area was abuzz with news, rumour and a sheer desire to expiate the experience by talking it out. Returning home, they found a visitor hovering by the gate.

'Oh. Hello, Stan.'

Unabashed by this lukewarm welcome, Stan whipped off his cap and bent forward to claim a kiss.

Ruth side-stepped and asked him what he wanted.

'Got a bit of news. Ain't you going to ask me in?'

'We got a lot to do. Washing and like. Me and Hatty's been at work the past couple of days, yer know.'

'I know. Saw yer dad. So don't you wanna know me news?'

'Go on then,' Ruth invited without enthusiasm.

'I joined up. Army.'

'I thought they wouldn't take yer. Thought you failed yer medical.'

' 'Ad another one, didn't I? Fit as a flea the doc reckoned. First one must have been a mistake. Anyhow I'll be off soon. Can't 'ave our Lulu the only one in uniform.'

The mention of his sister reminded Ruth of something. 'I 'ad a letter from Lou this morning. Where'd I put it, Hatty?'

'I don't know.' Retrieving the key from her pocket Hatty opened the front door.

'That's where it got to then,' Stan remarked. 'I was gonna let meself in, but the string was empty.'

'Well, I'll thank you not to walk into our 'ouse uninvited, Stan Wilkins,' Ruth snapped, tossing her head but, in a reflex action, softening the words with a saucy dimple.

Seizing his chance, Stan suggested they invited him in then.

'I told yer. We're busy.'

Darting in after Hatty, Ruth shut the door in his face. Being made of sterner stuff than the postman, Stan bent to the letter box and shouted through an invitation to come up The Castle tonight.

'We'll be down the shelter, same as all normal people, thank you very much, Stan, not in some public 'ouse,' Ruth called back before flouncing down the hall and into the scullery.

'Will we?' Hatty asked, unwrapping the stewing steak Ruth had managed to charm out of their elderly butcher when his wife had been safely engaged adding up dockets in the cashier's box.

'Will we what?'

'Be down the shelter?'

It was an interesting question. The house had no cellar, and the narrow garden backing on to the railway arches was deemed too small for an Anderson shelter. So during the first false alerts of the war, all three of them had trooped down to the communal street shelter when the air-raid sirens had sounded.

After her third visit, Ruth had rebelled. 'It stinks, me backside hurts from sitting on them slats, and if I 'ave to listen to her from number three clicking her false teeth one more night, there's gonna be murder done. I'm stopping home.'

Since all the alerts were false anyway, her determination to remain in bed hadn't mattered. And during the past two nights of heavy raids, they'd both been in the relative safety of the auxiliary fire station, with its cellar shelters.

'We could go down the Tube station,' Hatty suggested.

'The posters say you ain't supposed to. Anyhow, it'll be just like the shelter, I 'spect. Let's stop here. We could get under the beds or something.'

The image of the destroyed house in Bartholomew Road, with its crowning brass bed, came to them both.

'Or maybe we could shift the beds down here?' Ruth said hopefully. 'Stick them in the parlour?'

'We'd have to move stuff out first.'

'Let's try then.' Ruth scrambled upstairs. Prior to her furniture removing, she changed back into her AFS uniform. 'No sense spoiling me own clothes,' she explained, thrusting a hand into her trouser pocket. ' 'S funny.'

'What?'

'Thought I'd put Lulu's letter in 'ere.'

'Maybe you left it downstairs.'

'Maybe,' Ruth agreed, rolling up precious rayon stockings and stowing them carefully between her underwear. 'Won't be nothing in it anyway. I mean, what can you say when you're living in the middle of a field? Shift the mattresses first, shall we?'

It took most of the afternoon, but when Duggie Miller returned that evening, he was confronted by a parlour stuffed full of two single beds and the mattress from his own double bed, and curtained off by dangling blankets hanging down to floor level.

'What on earth . . . ?' His exclamation was cut off by the rising wail of the air-raid siren.

Ruth face peeped up at him from beneath one of the beds. 'Under here, Dad, it's a shelter, see?'

Hatty appeared at the scullery door with a steaming saucepan. 'I'll put the stew on the plates and we can eat it under the beds.'

'We'll do nothing of the sort. Now shift those things . . .'

The distant 'crump' of a falling stick of bombs cut Duggie short. Today the funeral parlour had had to deal with its first air-raid victim. Perhaps, in the circumstances, looking stupid wasn't such a bad thing.

'Shift up then, Ruthie love,' he instructed.

After fifteen minutes of lying flat on their stomachs, balancing on their elbows whilst they tried to eat from the dishes under their noses, Duggie announced that his name was

Duggie Miller, not flaming Jack Russell. 'I'm not eating like a dog, bombs or no bombs.'

Backing out, he sat on the bed, the plate on his lap. The two girls joined him. 'I don't think it's us anyhow,' Ruth said, cocking her head. ' 'Spect they're bombing the docks again, don't you?'

'I daresay,' Duggie agreed, chewing on a lump of gristle. 'Not much of what you might call strategic importance up this way. 'Cept the railways, of course.'

On cue, the house shook as a train thundered along the line at the back of the garden. A second later it shook with even more ferocity as the blast from a distant bomb swept through the neighbouring streets.

'Gawd!'

As one, all three of them dived back under the beds.

'Shift up, Hat, you fat pig.'

'I can't.' Her bottom outside the bedframe, Hatty scrambled to get further inside. The action bumped Ruth against the bed legs.

'Yow, that was me head, the clumsy lump.'

'Well, get your elbow out me eye.'

'Girls, girls,' Duggie scolded. 'Don't fight. You could get blown to bits any minute. Think of what's important to you.'

He'd intended to turn their minds to family affection, or one of the other equally uplifting themes that often featured in his employer's speech to the deceased's frequently feuding relatives. His reminder didn't have quite that effect in this case.

'Me shoes!' squealed Ruth, wriggling backwards again.

'My pictures,' wailed Hatty, struggling to extract herself from the space where she'd become wedged like the filling in a sandwich of bed springs and parlour carpet.

Ruth squirmed free like an eel and was already in the bedroom, collecting up an armful of cosmetics and clothes, when Hatty puffed her way up the stairs. Scooping up the collection of framed family photos from her own shelf, Hatty swung round and nearly fell straight over Ruth, who was now on her knees extracting the box with the precious five-guinea shoes from the floor of the wardrobe.

'Look at that,' she exclaimed, picking up something from under the box. 'That's where Lulu's letter went.'

'Come on,' Hatty urged. 'Before they drop another lot.'

' 'Ang on.' Ruth turned the envelope into the light. 'That ain't Lulu's writing. Who else would be writing me?'

'Open it and find out. Now come *on*.'

' 'Old your horses.' The sound of the ack-ack guns had ceased abruptly, and in the silence there was no drone of bombers overhead. Running her thumbnail along the envelope, Ruth said: 'Take the rest of me powders and stuff down, would you, Hat?'

'I haven't got three hands,' Hat grumbled. But she thrust a handful of photoframes into her brassière and scooped up the rest of the cosmetic boxes in one arm.

'Now for heaven's sake, Ruth, let's get . . .' Her voice died away. Even in the fading twilight she could make out the pale oval of Ruth's face. At present it was drained of colour, apart from the two bright circles left by the pink stain of rouge.

'What's the matter? Is it bad news? It's not Lulu, is it? Her poor mum.'

'It's not Lulu. I mean, it's nothing.' Thrusting the letter into the pocket of a coat still hanging in the wardrobe, Ruth pushed Hatty towards the door. 'Let's get down quick before the blighters drop annuver lot.'

Her fast, shallow breathing and heightened colour gave her away. 'What's up, Ruthie?' Duggie demanded.

'Nothing, Dad. Stick this lot under the bed, would ya?'

'She's had bad news in her letter,' Hatty explained in answer to a raised eyebrow.

'I ain't.'

'Well, something's up,' her father said. 'Who was your letter from, then?'

'Nobody.'

'Nobody don't write letters that I know of.' He put an arm round the resisting shoulders and continued: 'I'm your dad. I'm here to share yer troubles, Ruthie. That's what family's for. Now you tell your old dad, what's up?'

Ruth was saved the necessity of answering by a salvo of

ack-ack guns to the south. Their ferocious challenge announced that they had raiders in their sights, a fact confirmed a moment later by the roar of exploding bombs. Once more the three Millers hurled themselves flat under the beds.

It was another two hours before the all-clear sounded again. If Ruth had hoped that the possibility of being blown to pieces was going to divert her father's attention from the letter, she was out of luck. During every lull in the raid, he returned to the subject, like a tongue probing at a throbbing toothache.

'Give it a rest,' she pleaded. 'It's my letter. Ain't I entitled to a bit of privacy?'

'Not when you're living under my roof, my girl. Now if you won't show us, I'll go look for myself. Where is this famous letter, Hatty?'

'I, um, er . . . I'm not sure,' Hatty muttered.

'Oh, all *right*,' Ruth snapped. 'I'll fetch it meself.'

Grabbing her torch, she flew upstairs. After a few minutes she came slowly down again.

'There yer are.' She thrust the crumpled sheet into her father's hand. 'Read that then!'

Chapter 4

'Don't, Dad, please. Leave it be, for Gawd's sake!' Ruth pleaded rushing along two paces behind her father's right shoulder.

'Leave it be? Leave it *be*?' Duggie Miller snarled. 'Just you wait till I get my hands on . . . The ungodly deserve to be struck down, Ruthie.'

'Amen,' Hatty gasped, struggling to stay two paces behind his left shoulder.

'I shall be the instrument of God's wrath. Leastways, this lot will be,' Duggie concluded, marching past the copper on duty outside Agar street police station.

'But Dad,' Ruth wailed, catching up just as he arrived at the reception desk. 'I expect it's a joke.'

Duggie slapped the sheet down on the oak counter, instructing the desk sergeant to 'Read that. Filth. It shouldn't be allowed.'

The sergeant quickly read the letter. 'That's dreadful, sir,' the sergeant said. 'But this lady's first. Now, love, you want to get yourself down the assistance office soon as they open.'

Clutching a birdcage to her breast and a wicker basket to her hip, the recipient of this advice informed him stiffly that she wasn't a beggar. 'I've been bombed out. I don't want no hand-outs. I just want the lend of my train fare to get to my sister's place.' The patient, precise recitation was delivered in a placid tone that suggested it had already been said a dozen times before. 'My little girl needs a bit of fresh air. Country will make her better.'

'Yes, love, but . . .'

Reluctantly Duggie let himself be guided to a wall bench. Flanked on either side by Ruth and Hatty, he reread the offending letter. In large pencilled capitals it announced:

JEZEBEL!
YOU ARE THE WHORE OF BABYLON
EVERYONE KNOWS YOUR KNICKER ELASTIC
GOES UP AND DOWN
LIKE A YO-YO RUTH MILLER

'Dad, please. Don't,' Ruth hissed, pushing the single sheet of paper back on itself. 'Don't show everyone.'

'I'm not showing everyone. I'm just showing these here coppers. There must be laws against sending filth like this through the post. And if there isn't, there ought t'be. The meek may be going to inherit the earth, girls, but in the meantime they're going to be back of the ration queue, just remember that. I'm having this sorted out.'

Hatty and Ruth exchanged resigned glances across Duggie Miller's waistcoated chest.

Thin, pale and slightly dishevelled, the girl at the counter stood her ground. 'I want to go to the country,' she repeated. 'To my sister. She'll know how to make my baby better, you see.'

'Yes, miss,' the sergeant agreed, lifting the counter flap and stepping out. 'And I expect she'll be glad to lend you this 'ere train fare.' Taking her arm, he gently chivvied her towards the door. 'You get yourself down the post office now, love. Send your sis one of them tellygrams. Tell her how you're fixed.'

Attempting to resist the sergeant's urging, the girl pulled back towards the counter. The action dislodged the blanket over the wicker basket.

'God save us,' the sergeant breathed. The blood drained from his face until it was pale greenish-white, dissected by two flashes of mauve veins across his cheekbones.

'Now look what you done,' the girl scolded, setting the basket to the floor and tucking the blanket back into place with sharp, jabbing movements. 'She'll get cold. There, darling, Mummy make it better.'

She bent forward and pressed a kiss to the tiny fist that was curled into the ribbons of a white cotton smock.

'All better now.' Smiling serenely, she lifted the basket back on to the counter and met the frozen stares of the police sergeant and the three Millers.

The baby had no face; just the blackening mess of its remains thrust through the pie-crust frill of the spotless baby dress.

The sergeant recovered his wits first. Steering the girl to the bench seat, he called through to a uniformed constable to 'Get us one of the women, quick.'

The three Millers had stood up and moved away with one movement, as if they were frightened that a touch from the girl would infect them with her madness. With the ridge of the reception desk pressed into their backs, they watched wide-eyed as a female police sergeant came through from the back section and spoke in low tones to the desk officer.

Only the mother seemed unaffected by the horror. When the woman sergeant moved across to sit by her and asked to see the baby, she calmly lifted the blanket back and cooed happily, retying the ribbons at the neck of the smock.

The woman sergeant's long face paled beneath her coil of brown hair, but her voice was steady as she said: 'What lovely smocking. Did you do it yourself?'

'Oh, yes. I've always had a knack with a needle. Me mum always said I could set a stitch better than any of me sisters. I changed her into this gown special this morning before I come out. I wanted her to look pretty for going visiting her auntie.'

'Do your sisters live around here, Mrs . . . ?'

'Lester. Elaine Lester.'

'I'm Sergeant Sarah McNeill.'

'Pleased to meet you, I'm sure. This is Tilly. Called after her Auntie Matilda, my big sister, see?'

'And where does Matilda live, Elaine?'

'Carlisle. That's in the country, isn't it? She said I should fetch little Tilly to the country. But we don't like to, do we, darling? In case Daddy comes home and can't find us.'

'Right.' Taking the woman's elbow, Sergeant McNeill urged her to her feet again. 'Let's go see if we can get in touch with Auntie Matilda, shall we?'

The girl's face lit up. 'She could come down and fetch us, couldn't she? That would be better, wouldn't it, darling? We've never been on a train on our own before, have we?'

'I feel sick,' Ruth hissed. 'I gotta get out of here, Dad.'

Her urgent request brought attention round to the trio huddled by the desk. The desk sergeant seemed to come out of a trance and focused on Duggie properly for the first time since they'd entered the station.

'It's Mr Miller, ain't it, sir? Mottram and Cropper's? The funeral parlour?'

Drawing himself a little taller, Duggie composed himself into a walking advertisement for his employers.

'That's a bit of luck, in a manner of speakin',' the officer said with some relief. 'Only we'll be needing someone to deal with the remains.' He jerked a head in the direction of the door through which the deranged mother had been gently guided. 'Best to get them laid out decent soon as possible, eh?'

'You may rely on Mottram's for a discreet and efficient service, Sergeant.'

'Sure we can, sir.' With a slightly shaking hand, the sergeant lifted the desk flap and stepped back into the safe and familiar office. The experience seemed to steady him. 'Now, sir, if you was wanting to use the phone, perhaps? Get 'em to fetch something up to put the baby in? Don't suppose they'll be bothering with no inquest on this one. It'll be the bombing, you see, terrible things, bombs, not that I ain't had much experience so far, but they showed us pictures, you see, sir . . .'

The sergeant came to an abrupt halt, apparently conscious that he was rambling. With an effort he took a deeper breath. 'Now, was there something you was wanting, Mr Miller?' He seemed to have forgotten the letter.

'Dad!' snapped Ruth, before Duggie could answer. 'It ain't right, not after . . .' She gestured desperately to the back of the station. 'It ain't nothing . . . not after . . . Tell him, Hatty!'

34

But it wasn't necessary for Hatty to say anything. Duggie was used to dealing with death; 'almost a way of life' was his own little joke about his occupation. But he'd never seen anything like the past ten minutes. Infant deaths, yes. Plenty of them. Kids did die, didn't they? Measles, scarlet fever, whooping cough, diphtheria, tuberculosis; there was plenty to carry 'em off. But a sudden and violent death; that was another matter. Despite the many earnest government warnings that had been impressed on the population over the year of the 'Phoney War', this was the first time the reality of the horror had really struck home with Duggie.

He suddenly saw himself, with dreadful clarity, going to wake Ruth one morning and finding her like that; with half her face blown away and nothing left for him to recognise.

The letter accusing his little girl of being a common whore was no longer important. She was alive, she was here with him. Nothing else mattered.

So thanks to a dead baby and her poor, mad mother, instead of being filed in the Agar Street CID office, the first anonymous letter ended up in a dozen pieces fluttering through the drain grille in Kentish Town High Street.

'That's that,' Ruth said, rubbing her fingers to dispose of the last clinging fragments of paper.

'You could have put it in the paper salvage,' Hatty reproved.

'And 'ave 'em all reading that muck about me? Not likely. You all right, Hat?'

'No,' Hatty wailed, turning green. 'Oh, Ruth, wasn't the baby horrible? I think I'm going to be sick.'

'Breathe deep, quick,' Ruth urged, sucking in several huge lungfuls of air herself.

Ignoring the startled looks from passers-by, they gripped each other's hands and squeezed until the pain brought tears to their eyes. Finally the nausea subsided. Swallowing the last of her bile, Ruth said: 'Let's not think about it no more, Hat. Let's not say nothing to them up the fire station. We'll just pretend like it was a bad dream. Come on, let's get to work.'

By the time they both rushed into the auxiliary station, the mess manager – who answered to the nickname of 'Snakey' –

was already banging around in the kitchen in a pointed manner that clearly said: 'You're late, miss.'

'Sorry,' Hatty panted, answering the unspoken criticism. 'We had to go up the police station. Ruth had a letter.'

'Criminal h'offence now, h'is it?' asked Snakey, stirring a bubbling cauldron of porridge. 'H'a good morning, my lovely. Will you be gracing h'our breakfast mess?'

This last remark was addressed to another AFS female, called Adele, who'd just entered the room. Shaking her mop of curls, she declined the invitation. 'I just came across from the control room to collect some returns from your watchroom.'

'H'our loss,' Snakey said gallantly. 'You'd best cut h'along to the watchroom, Miss Ruthie. H'unless you got a parcel and want to call in Scotland Yard?'

'It was one of those anonymous letters,' Hatty explained, lifting down a much-blackened cast-iron frying pan from the shelf.

'Who sent h'it?'

'What did it say?'

Snakey and Adele spoke simultaneously.

'I don't know, do I?' Ruth pointed out. 'It wouldn't be 'nonymous if they'd have signed it.'

'What did it say?' Adele repeated.

Ruth would have told the girl to mind her own business, but Hatty had paused from slicing cold lard into the gently steaming pan to give their audience the gist of the letter.

'Some people h'is terrible h'ignorant,' Snakey sympathised.

'Ain't they just?' Ruth agreed. 'Don't save us nuffing for breakfast, Hat. I . . . I don't feel very hungry.'

Hatty's 'All right' didn't quite drown out Adele's murmured remark that the letter-writer was being unfair to yo-yos.

Snakey's sniggers followed the red-eared Ruth along the corridors until she reached the inner room which had been converted to take the watchroom phones and maps. She was surprised to find Betty Shaw manning the post.

'Thought you were off until today?'

Betty gave an enormous yawn. 'Two of the women reported

in for sick parade, so they sent someone down the house to get me. Anyway, it's all yours now. Pump's out at Holborn, damping down. I don't know when it'll be back. It's been gone nearly ten hours now. They couldn't send us a stand-by.'

'OK,' Ruth said, sliding into the still-warm seat. 'Hat's just starting the breakfasts.'

'I'll not bother,' Betty said, hitching gas mask case and tin helmet over her shoulder. 'I'm off to get some sleep. I've got something important to do this afternoon.'

There was a sparkle in her brown eyes that startled Ruth. For a brief moment she entertained the notion that Betty Shaw was going to meet a lover. Then she dismissed it as ridiculous. You could see by the way she looked at Station Officer Shaw that she was dopey about the bloke. The idea of her going off to meet another man was just plain daft. Personally Ruth thought it was quite touching, really, people that old still being in love.

Five hours later, Betty was on her way to do exactly what Ruth had first suspected: meet another man. Or at least that was what he would be in another twenty years or so. At present she guessed he was no more than nine or ten months old. Remembering the warmth and smell of the baby's body as she'd pulled him from under Myrtle's tin bath sent a twist of excitement spinning around her stomach and made her wish she'd waited for breakfast.

During the first few years of their marriage, the lack of children had been seen as a blessing by both Shaws. They hadn't wanted or needed anyone but each other; a third person would have been an intrusion rather than a blessing. There had been financial advantages too; despite Len's objections, Betty had kept on her job after marriage. With two regular wages coming in, she'd managed to put a goodly sum into the post office book each week.

Gradually, however, a yearning to hold her own child in her arms had started to creep over her, startling her sometimes with a sudden intense pain when she passed a sleeping child in its pram.

'Plenty of time yet, old girl. Who wants some screaming kid smelling the place out?' Len had said when she tentatively broached the subject one summer's evening on Parliament Hill Fields. 'Had enough of that with my mum. Never had a baby off her breast when I was growing up. Sucked her dry they did. Got old before her time, me mum. Don't want you going that way.'

'Yes, but . . .' She couldn't put it into words; but with each childless year she'd felt less of a proper woman. Other wives got pregnant with no trouble at all. There wasn't one of her own or Len's sisters who hadn't had a baby within a year of her marriage. And who weren't full of sly digs and hints as to when Betty would be producing another little Shaw to add to the clan.

Len wouldn't hear of adoption. 'It's our own kid or nothing,' he'd said firmly. 'I don't want some other man's kid in this house. I'm sorry,' he'd added, seeing her tears. 'But that's how I feel. Wouldn't be fair to the kid, would it, bringing it here if I don't want it?'

So she'd sought help elsewhere. Quacks in back streets and refined women in walk-up flats had taken her pound notes and sold her odd-tasting drinks that she'd known in her heart of hearts wouldn't help.

Oddly enough, the only person who'd ever given her hope had been a gypsy fortune-teller at the Hampstead Heath fair. She'd spent her last half-crown that Bank Holiday on having her fortune told.

'What'll be, me dear? Cards, hand or crystal ball?'

'Whichever's truest.'

'Hand, then. Give it over here, m'lovely.'

The teller's own fingers had been rough and dry as a bird's claw. With one finger she'd traced the lines in Betty's palm, whilst Betty herself had inhaled the stuffy odours of stale tobacco and scented spices that emanated from the woman's skin.

Winter's dampness, still trapped in the Heath's fields, had seeped up from the grass floor of the tent and through her leather shoes. Impatiently she'd started to shuffle them beneath the tatty velvet tablecloth. The silence had lasted so long she'd become uneasy. 'Look, I've changed my min . . .' she'd started to say, trying to withdraw her hand.

The claw had closed so fast she'd cried out with pain.

'You want a child, m'dear,' the soft voice had whispered, whilst black eyes glinted in the tent's gloom.

'Yes.' Betty tried to twist her fingers free. 'I do.'

The claw had become even tighter; like a bird hanging on to its prey. 'You'll have one, m'dear. A fine boy. But not from here.' The other claw had patted the shawl knotted across her own stomach. 'You'll know him for your own when you see him. And he'll know you as his mam. You remember that, m'dear. Here, this is yours. For luck.'

Something hard and cold was pushed into Betty's fingers, and abruptly the claw released her.

Outside in the sunlight, she'd discovered it was a charm made of some kind of cheap yellow metal. Its four bent legs seemed to chase each other in a circle. It had looked like a swastika, that crawling, spider-like symbol of the Nazi party. And once war was declared she'd known she ought to destroy it. But something had made her cling to the tawdry token. It had become a symbol; her lifeline to her son.

Touching her breast now as she climbed off the bus and made her way through the shattered debris of the East End blitz to the East London Hospital, she felt the charm's edges pressing into her skin.

A few strictly illegal calls on the watchroom telephone last night had traced 'her' baby to this hospital. At first the crisply efficient voice on the other end of the receiver had refused to divulge any information about a patient, but after Betty had identified herself as a member of the Auxiliary Fire Service a certain warmth had crept into the distant sister's tone. 'Baby Gibson', she was informed, was well, but being kept in until they could find him some kind of place in a children's home. No next of kin had claimed him yet. Visiting hours were between two and three if she wished to call at the hospital.

Her watch said ten minutes to two, but a crowd had already

39

collected in the tiled corridor and all the wooden benches were taken. A stout woman, overly blessed with rolls of flesh, shopping bags and whining children, made room for her against a wall.

'Lean here for a bit, love,' she invited. 'Get a bit of the weight off yer plates. Leave off, Alfie,' she added, aiming a vague smack in the direction of one of her offspring, whose whine was reaching the decibel level of a diving Hurricane fighter. 'Drive yer bleedin' doolally, don' they, kids.'

Betty smiled thinly as she slipped into the proffered gap on the wall. She could just make out rows of cots and beds through the glass panels of the ward doors. A small face was peering through the bars of the nearest cot, its features framed by the two rosy fists that grasped the iron bars.

It was 'her' baby, she was sure of it. Raising himself on his toes, he was struggling to bite the cot bars. Betty half raised her hand to wave and then dropped it to her side before anyone noticed. It was a stupid gesture. He wouldn't remember her. He wouldn't know that she planned to take him home and love and cherish him.

Would they let her take him today? Probably not. There would be formalities, adoption papers to sign. But there wouldn't be any problem about that, surely? The authorities would see that she and Len were a respectable couple with a good home and regular income. What more could they ask for?

And once he'd held the baby and seen what a bonny little boy he was, Len would come round, she was sure of it.

What would they call him? She rather fancied John herself. John Leonard Shaw had a good ring about it.

She was jerked back out of her day-dream by an exasperated command to 'Shaddup, will yer' from the stout woman. Alfie gulped down his last whimper. And promptly stamped hard on one of his sister's feet. With a shriek she grabbed his ears and they both fell on the floor, thrashing wildly.

'Gawd, I should 'ave left the both of yer on the orphanage steps, and I will if yer don't leave off,' their harassed mother groaned, dragging them apart by their hair.

A nursing sister, starched to crackling crispness, announced in clipped tones that children were not permitted as visitors: 'Kindly remove them from the hospital.'

'Hear that?' their fond parent snapped. 'Lady's gonna call a policeman to yer if yer don't hold yer noise. Here, Maisie, take 'em out front and don' let 'em go under no buses. I'll come get yer once I seen to our Tommy.'

The tallest girl wiped a sleeve across her permanently dripping nose, seized a couple of hands at random, and hauled her siblings away down the corridor.

'Makes you sick, don' it?' The woman continued releasing the buttons on a coat that was several sizes too small. 'Fourteen of 'em I've had, and all healthy, worse luck. Thank Gawd for the brewery, I say.'

'Pardon?' Betty said blankly.

'Made sure me old man turned his toes up before he could give me number fifteen,' her new friend explained.

'You mean he drank himself to death?'

'No, ducks, they dropped a barrel of stout on him.'

'Oh?'

'Here we go, then. 'Bout time too.' The woman surged forward as the double doors were flung open.

Betty followed. Little 'John' was on his feet, milk teeth gnawing the cot bars, bright eyes watching the newcomers with interest.

Still talking, the woman waddled in front of Betty. 'Got no 'elp, you know. No one to give me a hand with 'em 'cept me old man's sister. And she was as much use as a chocolate fire guard. Gone now, Gawd rest her. Left me youngest wiv 'er while I went to fetch our Alfie back from the evacuee lady, on account of her not being able to stand the little sod no more, and what does our Myrtle do but go get 'erself bombed. Well, there you are then, your old mum thought she'd seen the last of you.'

Finally recognising someone he knew, Tommy Gibson abandoned the soothing comfort of metal bars against his sore gums, and lifted his arms. His mum swept him up in a fierce bear-hug and squeezed the smelly bundle to her shoulder. ' 'Ere you all right, ducks?' she asked over her youngest's head.

'Yes. Yes. Thank you,' Betty whispered. She knew that tears were pouring down her cheeks, but somehow she couldn't summon up the energy to wipe them away.

Chapter 5

December 1940

It had been brewing all day. A poisonous cloud that pressed low over the fire station's mess room. Pretending to be absorbed in mashing down the pulp of boiled turnips, Pat O'Day glanced up quickly from beneath dark lashes. He caught Frankie watching him broodingly across the table. The other man looked away quickly.

Sighing inwardly, Pat forked up a mouthful of turnip and wondered what he should do. He'd seen Frankie nearly kill a watch-mate that morning. Frankie had claimed it was a mistake. He'd thought Steve had shouted for 'water on'; with all that racket going on round them he'd misheard, hadn't he? The rest of the crew had, reluctantly, agreed it was the sort of mistake anyone could make. Only it hadn't been a mistake, and Pat knew it. And Frankie knew he knew it.

Pushing his plate away, he drew the dish of rice pudding towards him and took a spoonful. He caught a movement out of the corner of his eye and saw Adele, one of the control room girls, passing the mess door.

'Tea's on,' he called, nodding towards the large metal pot.

'No, no thanks,' she gasped. 'I'll . . . I'll . . . get mine later, thanks.' She melted into the dim corridor like a ghost.

And she's another one, Pat thought grimly, ploughing to the end of the glutinous pudding. When she'd first arrived at the station, Adele had been a sparky bundle who was only too ready to bring out the violin she'd played professionally before the war. With feet tapping and eyes sparkling she'd fiddled enthusiastically through many an impromptu singsong in the recreation room.

Nowadays she scuttled out of rooms like a frightened rabbit if you tried to pass the time of day with her. Even worse, Pat had heard her several times weeping quietly in the outside lavatory that had been set aside for the women.

Lost in rice pudding and his thoughts, the eruption caught him unawares.

'You bastard, Frankie,' Steve Dawkins screamed. 'I'll wipe that smirk off yer stupid face.'

He'd dived over the table and smashed his fist into his brother-in-law's face before anyone else could react. Cutlery and plates went flying as the rest of the crew tried to separate the struggling men.

'What the hell's going on here!'

The stentorian bawl from the door froze everyone into statues. Frankie recovered his wits first. 'Nothing, sir,' he assured Len Shaw, stemming the blood dripping from his nose. 'I just . . . er, tripped over me own boots. Knocked the table flying. The others were just helping me clean up. Ain't that right, lads?'

There was a murmur of agreement. No one really expected the station officer to believe them. But providing he had a good excuse not to put them on a fizzer for fighting, they all knew he'd seize it. And he did.

'Right, well get this mess cleaned up. And Dawkins,' he added, 'scrub this deck until the wood's so thin I can see the joists underneath. Clear?'

'Aye, sir.'

'Good. This . . .' he jerked a thumb behind him, 'is Marty Tanner. Old mate of mine. He's joining your watch. I'll leave you to get acquainted.'

Marty acknowledged the muttered greetings with a conspiratorial wink and helped Pat heave the table back into place.

'And Leading Fireman O'Day,' Len Shaw said, turning back at the door.

'Sir?'

'Change that tunic. I'll not have my men improperly dressed on duty.'

Glancing down, Pat found that the remains of someone's

rice had spread down his front like an explosion of bird mess. He ran his fingers over the sticky mass and found it was adhering with all the strength of wallpaper paste. The tunic would have to be taken home and scrubbed clean, and in the meantime he was going to have to attend any further calls in his spare, which was already soaked through and had been steaming gently in the boiler room for the past hour.

That's it, Pat thought rebelliously. If Station Officer Shaw wasn't going to do anything about the situation in this flaming station, then he would!

Detective Chief Inspector Jack Stamford opened his door to Pat O'Day the following afternoon with some relief. He was bored and fed up with being on sick leave, and any diversion was welcome.

'Hello, Pat, come for a bath?'

As one of the few houses in the square with a plumbed-in indoor bathroom, he had – rather belatedly, he realised guiltily – extended an open invitation to the O'Day family to use it whenever they wished. Pat was the only one who ever took advantage of the suggestion. Mainly because Eileen O'Day considered it improper for her to take a bath in a man's house – even if she did clean it – and saw no reason why her two younger sons should go taking advantage.

'Maury works. Least he says he does, although I'm blowed if I know what he does,' she'd told Jack firmly as she vigorously buffed cream into the brass taps. 'But he's always got money in his pocket. He can spend some of it down the public baths if my house ain't good enough for him. Sammy can go in the tin tub. It won't hurt him. Older ones can make up their own minds.'

Since three of her older boys were away defending King and Country in the army, air force and navy respectively, only Pat, her eldest, had got into the habit of making the trek to the house opposite and sinking blissfully into a tub of hot water that didn't have to be lugged out into the yard and bailed out down the drains afterwards.

Sliding along the porcelain bottom now, he reached out with

his right foot and twiddled the tap, allowing a thin stream of hot water to trickle in. It was great this, he reflected. No shouting for the assistant to send down more hot, and no one yelling for you to get out 'cos your time was up, like they did down the Prince of Wales Baths. Maybe he could have a word with the landlord, see about getting a proper bath put into Mum's house. Cost a bit extra on the rent, of course, and they'd have to double up in the beds . . . still . . . Taking a deep breath, he ducked right under the water, letting it pour into his ears. Feeling blindly with his toes again, he ran more water before erupting upwards, spluttering and shaking droplets of water off. Opening his eyes, he watched small clouds of steam swirling from the sloshing water. They reminded him of white smoke, which very quickly led his mind back to the fire station; and the problem.

Climbing reluctantly out of the hot water into the unheated air of the bathroom, he hurriedly buffed himself dry and dragged on his clothes. Stepping on to the landing, he cocked his head, trying to locate his host. A muffled curse from the room opposite pointed him in the right direction. A sharp rap on the wood brought an invitation to 'Come through, Pat.'

Jack Stamford was sitting on the double bed that was a relic of his short-lived marriage. He'd moved into the Square twelve years ago after a legacy from a relative had allowed him to buy this property. For five years he'd lived alone in it, until a motorbike tour of the Netherlands one summer had introduced him to Neelie Deetman. It had been a disastrous marriage. By the time Jack had realised how unhappy Neelie was living in a strange country with a small child and a husband who worked long hours, it was too late to save the relationship.

He had a tie half over his head and was struggling to pull it down to his neck. As Pat watched, he dragged on the wrong end and succeeded in unravelling the knot he'd pre-tied.

'Oh, damn,' he cursed, thrusting a hand through his thick auburn hair and grinning ruefully at Pat. 'You never know what you need two hands for until you haven't got them, do you?'

'Arm no better, Mr Stamford?' Pat asked.

'Worse, if anything,' Jack said gloomily, cradling the useless limb to his chest.

He'd been shot in the course of an investigation a couple of months earlier. He'd just been congratulating himself on getting away with nothing more than a livid scar when he'd woken up one morning a fortnight previously to find an excruciating pain throbbing from shoulder to fingers and discovered he couldn't move the arm above waist level.

'Arthritis,' the police medical officer had diagnosed cheerfully. 'Bullet chipped the bone. Probably what set it off. That and the cold weather. Got to expect this sort of thing now. Not getting any younger, you know.'

Given that he was forty-one, Jack had found this remark unbelievably depressing. 'How long am I going to be out of action?' he asked.

'Couldn't say,' the relentlessly spry MO had beamed. 'Tricky thing, arthritis. Sometimes it just goes . . . pouf.' He'd flicked Jack's jacket with the air of an illusionist demonstrating there was no rabbit lurking within, before helping Jack back into the coat. 'Other times it gets a grip and there's no shaking it. It's like bloody deathwatch beetle. Get rid of it in one bit of the house, and you find it chomping its way through a rafter somewhere else.'

'Lucky I haven't got a wooden leg then, isn't it?' Jack had commented bitterly, struggling to get his overcoat on over the jacket.

'What? Oh yes.' The MO had laughed with the hearty enjoyment of one who did thirty press-ups before breakfast.

'Can you give me anything for it?'

'Not really. I should take a couple of aspirin if the pain gets bad. Come back in a fortnight. By that time we should be able to see whether you're going to recover or . . .'

'Be pensioned off as disabled?'

'Oh, I shouldn't think it would come to that, old man.'

Trying hard not to show his annoyance at that 'old man', Jack said: 'You think a full recovery's the most likely prognosis?'

'What?' The MO bounded across his own consulting room

47

to open the door and spare Jack the necessity. 'No. No idea what the prognosis is, frankly. But don't imagine they'll pension you off. There's a war on, you know. Expect they'll find you a desk job somewhere.'

Beaming with rude health, he'd stood with one arm fully extended to usher Jack from the room and into the Slough of Despond.

'You going into work, Mr Stamford?' Pat asked, taking the tie and flicking it over the other man's collar.

'No, I'm ordered off on sick leave. Can't fully perform my duties, you see. It's been a few years since I've had to chase a housebreaker up the back alleys, but I'm supposed to be in a fit state to do so if necessary. And I thought you were going to call me Jack?'

Pat flushed. It wasn't easy. He'd known the bloke since the year he'd gone into long trousers and started work. Still, he wanted a favour, didn't he?

'What kind of favour?' Jack asked.

'It's a bit difficult,' Pat admitted, tightening the tie's knot.

Jack waited. He was half expecting a request for a loan, whilst the other half wondered whether he was about to be consulted on the progress of Pat's love life.

'See, the thing is, we're having a bit of bother at work.'

Not lucre or love then. Jack raised one eyebrow, but kept his mouth shut.

Pat straddled the padded dressing table stool. 'If I was to tell you something, something that happened at work, you wouldn't have to do nothing about it, would you? As a policeman I mean?'

Jack hesitated. He didn't want to dissuade the young man from confiding in him; on the other hand . . . 'If you report a crime to me, Pat, I'm obliged to take action. On the other hand, I probably wouldn't proceed on just your word.'

He saw Pat's frown and elaborated. 'Supposing you told me you'd seen somebody take something from a locker, say? Well, unless there was other evidence – fingerprints, or the stolen property turning up in someone else's pocket, say . . .'

'It's nothing like that.' Pat sighed, bending his long legs into a more comfortable position on the insubstantial stool. 'See, the thing is . . . We've been getting letters.'

'We?'

'The crews.'

'At your fire station?'

'The auxiliary substation across the road have been getting them too.'

'What do they say?'

'All sorts, I reckon. I mean, I only ever seen one. But I know other blokes have had them. The women too, I think,' he added, remembering Adele's drained face.

'Whose letter did you see, Pat?'

Relieved to be able to talk about it at last, Pat eagerly poured the story out. The letter had belonged to Frankie Cole. 'He's all right is Frankie, good bloke on a shout,' Pat assured his listener earnestly. 'He's married to Steve Dawkins' sister. They've been mates for years, him and Steve. Used to be in the merchant navy together before they joined the brigade.'

'And now they're not such good mates?' Jack prompted.

'Now they're bleedin' trying to kill each other,' Pat said bitterly. 'And they're on my pump most of the time. So I'm supposed to keep them in order.'

Knowing Pat's mother's views on her sons using even the mildest swear words, Jack realised the situation was serious. 'Go on,' he said.

Pat did. He explained that during one of his early voyages, Frankie had acquired an Egyptian wife and daughter.

'And I take it the present Mrs Cole is unaware of this?'

'Yes. He and Steve figured maybe it wasn't legal anyway. I mean, it wasn't in a church or anything. So they thought they wouldn't mention it to Steve's sister.'

'And now someone's threatening to do just that?'

'Yeah. Sort of.'

'And Frankie thinks Steve's behind it?'

'Well, he's the only one who knows. And they had this row a few weeks back, about Steve cheating at cards.'

'You said others had received letters?'

Pat nodded.

'Does Steve Dawkins have any reason to dislike the rest of the crew?'

'Not that I know of, Mr Stam . . . Jack.'

'Isn't that likely to occur to Frankie as well when he calms down a bit?'

'Yeah. Trouble is, someone could end up dead before that penetrates Frankie's bone-head. He acts first, thinks later, does Frankie . . . a whole lot later.'

Taking his jacket from where it was swinging behind the door, Jack inserted his bad arm gingerly into one sleeve. 'I take it you're referring to this bother you don't want me to do anything about – as a policeman?'

Pat nodded. 'It was the night before last. Well, morning really time we got there.'

'Where?'

'Warehouses over Euston Road way. We were sent to relieve the crew that was damping down.' He went on to explain that the sub-officer in charge had ordered a hose on to the roof. 'Steve and one of the other blokes went up with the branch.'

'Not Frankie?'

'No. He was below on the pump. That was the problem.' Pat explained that the other bloke had left Steve alone holding the branch for a moment whilst he went across the roofs to see if there was a better position. 'Frankie turned the water on,' Pat said flatly.

'And?' Jack felt he was missing something.

'It was at one hundred and eighty pounds pressure, Mr Stam . . . Jack. You ever seen a hose under that pressure?'

Jack made vague noises. He'd certainly attended bomb incidents, but as to the mechanics of the firefighting . . .

'It's like trying to control a mad snake that's thick as yer waist and strong as an ox.' Steve Dawkins had been lifted clean off his feet and swept over the edge of the building by the thrashing serpent. 'Lucky for him there was one of them ledges 'bout two feet down,' Pat continued.

'Parapet,' Jack suggested.

'Yeah. Anyhow, Steve rolls into that and keeps his head down till we turn the water off. Otherwise he'd have gone forty feet into the street. Frankie said it was an accident. Said he'd heard a call for water.'

'And you don't believe him?'

'I was standing near where he was. I saw Steve was alone with that branch, so Frankie must have too. Mind,' Pat added fairly, 'Frankie looked pretty sick when Steve came off the roof. I reckon he was sorry then.'

'Mmm.' Jack fished for the other jacket sleeve. Pat held it still for him. 'Thanks. It sounds to me as if it's a job for your senior officer, Pat. Not the police.'

'I tried. Mr Shaw don't want to know nothing about it. I can't think why, he must know things ain't right in the station.'

'So what do you want me to do?'

Pat leaned forward, grasping the edge of the stool so tightly his knuckles gleamed. 'I thought you could ask around the station. Talk to people. Work out who's sending these letters. I mean, that's what detectives do, ain't it? Find things out.'

Jack's lips twitched. He had a mental image of himself standing in the middle of the fire station announcing to an admiring audience – *à la* Sherlock Holmes – that the letter-writer was a red-headed, left-handed man who smoked Black Cat cigarettes and went to chapel every third Sunday. If only most people knew the frustrating truth of CID work – that more villains got away with it than were ever caught.

Misunderstanding his expression, Pat said urgently: 'It ain't funny, Mr Stamford. You got to be able to rely on yer mates in this job. How would Mum manage if anything was to . . .'

His remark, even if it was a calculated bit of emotional blackmail, Jack thought wryly, had hit the right button. Eileen O'Day wasn't only his cleaner. She was also friend, nurse and part-time mother to Jack's small daughter.

'All right,' he said. 'Let's go pry. Discreetly, of course.'

51

Chapter 6

When they reached the end of the square, Pat turned right, intending to take his normal route up Queen's Crescent. Jack turned left.

'I want to stretch my leg, do you mind?' He felt unable to admit that he didn't want to pass the police station. How did you explain to a young, fit twenty-six-year-old that he was ashamed of being seen crippled with an old man's disease?

Since he couldn't avoid passing the end of Agar Street, Jack crossed to the opposite side of Kentish Town Road and feigned interest in the fishmonger's, stationer's, and Civil Defence notices outside the local rail station, until they were safely past on their way up Highgate Road and out of sight of the police station.

He'd always prided himself on his lack of arrogance. Now he realised that his reluctance to be seen by the rank-and-file of local coppers was founded on a fear of being regarded as a has-been rather than the all-seeing, all-knowing chief inspector from Scotland Yard. It was a salutary lesson to find out he was as egocentric as the next man.

Rather than taking him to the regular fire station, Pat headed further up the hill towards the auxiliary substation.

'Regulars might smell a rat. Showing visitors round ain't allowed. Well, ain't allowed in the AFS neither, really, but they aren't so particular. Probably think I got permission. This way.'

He led Jack round the back of the disused factory into the yards where the drab lines of grey vehicles were lined up under corrugated sheds or parked on the open cobblestones. Shining colourfully amongst them like a red dragon amongst grey beetles was a huge red turntable lorry.

Jack nodded in its direction. 'Isn't that one of yours? Regular requipment, I mean, not auxiliary?'

'Yes. But we couldn't get something that size in our station. So it's billeted over here.' Pat grinned suddenly. 'The crew too.'

'Is that a problem?'

'Not so much a problem, more a drop down the social scale,' remarked a light voice behind him. 'Red Riders have to mix with the hoi-polloi of the auxiliaries. Be dockers' tea parties at Buckingham Palace next.'

'We aren't that bad, Mrs Shaw,' Pat protested.

'Some of you are. But you're getting better. Bombs are a great social leveller, aren't they?'

Jack found a pair of chestnut eyes fixed on him in an enquiring fashion. Pat seemed oddly reluctant to make the introductions, so he was forced to do it himself, stifling a gasp of agony as he awkwardly proffered his right hand and quickly switched to the left.

'Betty Shaw,' she smiled, accepting his cack-handed shake.

'Mrs Shaw is married to Station Officer Shaw, my guv'nor,' Pat said, his voice firmer on the last two words.

Jack got the message. So, it would seem, did Betty.

'What are you up to, Pat?' She grinned.

'Nothing. Mr Stamford just fancied looking round a fire station. Said I'd give him a tour. Thought I'd best come up Good Hope. The guv'nor, you know . . .'

'Doesn't allow strangers on the premises,' the guv'nor's wife finished for him.

'No. I mean, yes.'

Lying did not come easily to Pat. His even-featured, open face hadn't been designed to hide the telltale flushes, and his straightforward nature hadn't given him sufficient practice in calling up a glib answer if the truth didn't suit. Jack knew he wouldn't last five minutes in a police interview room. He wasn't doing too well in an auxiliary substation's back yard, judging by the considering glance Betty Shaw was flicking in his direction. With wide-eyed innocence she asked if Jack were a German spy.

'Not guilty.' Jack smiled.

'Perhaps you want to join the fire service?'

'Perhaps I do.'

'I see. And in the meantime you're a . . . ?'

There was plainly no getting away from it. 'I'm a policeman.'

'He's on sick leave,' Pat interjected.

'And you want to convalesce in Good Hope?'

She was plainly teasing. She was equally plainly not likely to be fobbed off with an excuse. He could either brush her off or tell her the truth. He chose the latter option.

'Does Mrs Shaw know about the situation?' he asked Pat.

'I don't know really.'

'Sounds exciting,' Betty said. She checked her watch. 'I've ten minutes left of my break. Would you like to include the mess in your tour of the station, Mr Stamford? Or should I call you Sergeant, or Inspector or something?'

'I'm a chief inspector. But call me Jack.'

She led them through the back door and along a ground-floor corridor. Through a partially open internal door, Jack glimpsed an empty room which seemed to stretch the length of the factory. On the opposite side were two sets of big double doors that led out into the back yard. It had probably been some sort of loading or storage bay when the factory was in use. He was surprised to see a collection of auxiliary vehicles lined up in there; including a hose-laying lorry, a staff car, a canteen van and even two requisitioned London taxis with trailer pumps attached.

'You don't crew that lot, do you?'

Betty shook her head. 'Not regularly. We're a sort of pool. They're all standby vehicles. Sometimes our crews take them out. Or sometimes one of our drivers takes them over to another station where they're needed and they provide the crew. We're a bit of an oddity really; we're one of the few auxiliary stations that's bigger than the main station that it reports to.'

She pointed to another office, whose internal windows had steel shutters over them. 'That's where I work. They've bricked up the outside windows as well. It's like working in a coffin.'

'Is that the control room?' Jack asked.

'Watchroom,' Betty corrected him. 'Control room's attached to the main fire station across the road.'

'What's the difference?' Jack asked, in keeping with his role as tourist.

'Watchroom sends out appliances from this station. The control room oversees the main station and five substations. And they can request the divisional office to send assistance from outside the area if things get too . . .'

'Hot?' Jack suggested.

Betty laughed. 'Yes, for want of a better word.'

She opened another door and led the way down the stairs to a small basement room containing camp beds and metal lockers. Some attempt had been made to brighten it up by sticking pictures of film stars over the whitewashed walls.

'Women's locker room. It's every bit as uncomfortable as it looks. But luckily all the women at this station live within walking distance, so we can go home when we're off duty. The control room girls over the road are billeted in a house up the street.'

Shutting the door, she quickly showed him the strengthened cellar, which could be used as a bomb shelter, and then preceded him back up to the ground floor and along the corridor.

'The mess is in here.'

An internal wall had been knocked through with no attempt to make good. The bench tables and stools had an amateur carpentry feel to them. The pipes to the cookers crawled across the walls in a haphazard fashion that showed they'd been installed with more thought for speed than aesthetics. But despite its shortcomings there was a cosy feel to the room, which was helped by the aroma of cooking and the paper-chains which stretched across the room. The only other occupant at present was another firewoman. As they walked in she raised a pale face from her book and surveyed the trio with a complete lack of emotion.

'Oh, hello, Nell.' Betty waved a hand behind her. 'You know Pat O'Day, don't you?'

'Yes.'

'And this is Jack Stamford. Nell De Groot.'

'How do you do.' The voice was cool, its vowels betraying a middle-class background. The expression remained totally indifferent to his presence.

'De Groot? Dutch?'

'My great-grandfather was.'

'Oh. I see.' Hearing the disappointment in his own voice, Jack felt obliged to add, 'My wife was . . . is Dutch. Her family came from just outside Rotterdam. Do you know the area at all?'

'I'm afraid not. I believe the De Groots came from the Limburg region originally.' *But I really couldn't care less*, her tone implied. Her whole attitude screamed at him to stop probing and go away.

He took the hint and did so, following Betty and Pat to another table.

'I could scrounge tea, I expect,' Betty offered.

Both men shook their heads.

'So tell me all?' Betty invited. 'What is it that I might, or might not, know about?'

'Anonymous letters,' Pat murmured. 'Have you . . .' He broke off as a thunderclap echoed round the mess room.

'Sorry,' Nell apologised. 'My foot caught in it.' She righted the upturned chair and set it back on its legs before anyone could move to help. 'Sorry,' she repeated, before hurrying from the room. But not before Jack had glimpsed her eyes. He'd once seen the same expression on the face of a rabbit that had nearly twisted its own foot off struggling to escape from a wire snare.

'Letters?' Betty prompted.

'Apparently some members of this station and the regular station have been receiving anonymous letters,' Jack said. 'You'd not heard?'

'Well, yes. I mean, I did hear a couple of men joking about one.'

'When was that?'

Betty considered and decided it was probably about a month ago. 'But it's not a police matter, surely?'

'Who were the men? Can you remember?'

'Snakey was one.'

'Who?'

'Our mess manager. And talk of the devil.'

Jack swung round in time to see a thin, yellow-skinned auxiliary stagger through the door. He was holding the rope handle of a wooden crate stacked with mugs. The other handle was being grasped by a large female auxiliary, who heaved her end of the load on to a table with a relieved explosion of breath.

'Phew. That's better.'

'What's this then, a stranger h'on the deck?'

Betty made the introductions again. Snakey nodded a greeting. The woman, Hatty, blushed a rosy pink and said hello to Jack's shoes.

'I didn't know you were on duty today, Mrs Shaw,' she said, still avoiding eye contact as she started to unload the crate.

'I swapped with Ruth. She wanted to go and visit her friend. Lulu, isn't it? Didn't she tell you?'

'No. No. She didn't.' Broad, square-topped fingers lifted half a dozen mugs at a time on to the draining board.

'Here, I'll give you a hand.' Betty reached for a mug. 'Off the canteen van, are they?'

'Yes,' Hatty mumbled. 'I like to keep everything on it nice. 'Case I get to take it out.'

Snakey removed a jangling bunch of keys from his pocket, unlocked a padlocked meat safe and took out a tureen overflowing with sausages. The origin of his strange nickname became obvious when Jack realised that he expelled a hiss of air in front of most of his vowels.

'Not bad, h'eh? Pork. Mostly from the pig too. That what h'ain't from the baker's. Sausage h'and mash tonight. Peel the spuds for us, Hat?'

Jangling mugs into the sink, Hatty muttered that she was supposed to have gone off hours ago.

'Yeah. But help h'out a mate, eh, Hat?'

'I can't. I really can't. Not today, Snakey. Sorry.'

'Can't be helped, my lovely.' Spreading the string of sausages over the work counter, Snakey seized a cleaver and swept along

57

the links, the blade flashing up and down with the speed of a mechanical guillotine. 'Tell you what, Hat. Fishmonger's going to fetch us down some lovely sprats for breakfast, so you make sure you're in early to fillet them, eh?'

Hatty paused with an armful of dried mugs. A frown creased her square face. 'They're ever so little, Snakey. I'm not sure I can get all them bones out . . .'

Snakey raised his eyebrows and exchanged an expression of affectionate disbelief with Betty. 'It was a joke, Hat my love.'

'Oh, I see.' Hatty beamed, apparently without rancour at being the butt of their humour.

'Mr Stamford wants to know about your letter, Snakey,' said Betty.

'What letter would that be, Mrs Shaw?'

'You were joking about it with one of the others, I can't remember who. It said some daft things, you said.'

'Oh, h'aye. That would be Sid Halse and me. He had one. Said he had a secret life h'of sin h'and debaucher*eeee*. Well, chance h'ud be a fine thing, he says to me.'

'What did yours say, Mr, er . . .'

'Snakey, mate. Snakey by name h'and slippery by nature. Said h'as how h'I was fiddling the station rations.'

'And are you?'

' 'Course I h'is. Every job's got its perks, h'ain't it?'

'Er, Mr Stamford is a policeman,' Betty warned.

'So you said,' Snakey agreed, laying out rows of fat pink sausages on a baking sheet. 'Now h'if you want to see a body who really knows how to fiddle the mess supplies, you want to h'introduce yourself to the cook h'of the police canteen.' Snakey shook his head in admiration. 'What a woman. We could be the Fortnum h'and Mason h'of Gospel Oak if she'd a mind to h'it.'

Feeling that they were treading on dangerous ground, Jack returned to the subject of Snakey's letter and asked him what he could remember about it.

'H'in pencil it was. Just on regular paper, like h'anyone has.' And no, he hadn't noticed the postmark. 'Just had a laugh and used h'it to light the gas rings.' Sid Halse had thrown his into the rubbish.

'Do you know if anyone else has received letters?'

'H'I reckon.'

'Why?'

'Seen envelopes. In pencil. Most folks they use h'ink.'

'The letters are sent to the station?'

'H'I reckon.'

'Some men do get post here,' Betty explained.

'Do you remember who received them?'

Snakey ran a spill over the oven burners, lighting them with a row of 'pops' like softly shelling peas. A sour gas smell flooded the room. 'Can't say h'I do,' he said. 'Letters is either full of grief h'or full of boredom. Why should h'I want to hear how she misses him or that little Johnnie's first teeth h'is giving him gyp? Best to steer clear of h'others' correspondence h'if you can, h'I says.'

'And what about you, Mrs Shaw?'

'Betty, please. And no, I wouldn't, would I? I mean, I only live locally. There's no reason for anyone to write to me here.'

'I meant,' Jack elaborated, 'have you ever had an anonymous letter?'

'No.'

'What about your husband?'

'Len? Lord, no. He'd have told me.'

'What about you, miss?'

Jack had to repeat the question before Hatty realised she was being addressed. Lost in her own thoughts, she was washing, drying and stacking mugs with a dreamy contentment. Another one with secrets, Jack decided.

In response to Jack's question, she denied ever having received any strange letters. Stacking the last of the mugs back in the crate she added: 'Can you get someone to take this lot back to the van for me, Snakey? I . . . I have to go.'

'Just a minute.' Jack called her back. 'Do you know anyone else who might have got a letter?'

Belatedly Hatty remembered she'd promised her cousin she'd never again mention her letter. 'No, no, I don't,' she stuttered. The horror of that morning swept over her. The faceless baby that she'd so successfully tried to forget rose up into her head.

Her breakfast joined it. 'Excuse me.' And with a gasp she slapped a hand over her mouth and rushed from the room.

Betty hurried out after her, leaving Snakey to shrug philosophically and reflect upon the oddness of women. Hadn't young Ruth had a funny letter a couple of months back? Still, maybe it weren't like the ones the rozzer was talking about now. If Hatty didn't want to say nothing, it weren't any of his business, Snakey reckoned. 'Give a shout h'up the stairs for me, Pat. H'if they want their dinner tonight, they better lend a hand with these spuds.'

'I'll see who's up there,' Pat murmured. 'If the sub-officer ain't around maybe you could . . .' He raised his eyebrows to the ceiling joist in a conspiratorial fashion.

Even if he wasn't, Jack decided as he settled himself on a bench to watch Snakey peeling muddy King Edwards, he didn't really think questioning anyone else was going to help. It sounded like a malicious and spiteful prank that someone would eventually grow tired of.

The first brown curl of peel had barely dropped to the worktop before Pat was back.

'That was quick . . .' Jack began, before he noticed the figure behind Pat. He had never met the man, but one look at Pat's strained expression told him exactly who he was facing. 'Station Officer Shaw, I presume?'

'You presume right, mister,' said Len Shaw. 'I hear you're police. We don't need police to sort out fire service problems. We sort them out ourselves. Got that?'

He moved a few steps closer to Jack. The station officer was a good-looking man, dark-haired and eyed, with the muscular build of someone used to hard work. Only the slightest suggestion of slackness round the square jaw and chin showed that middle-age spread wasn't too many years away now.

'Right now I'll tell you plain not to come on to my station unless you've got permission from headquarters or a damn good reason. And I don't mean the fancies of some leading fireman. Understand?'

'Perfectly,' Jack said.

'Good. Now I assume you haven't got the sub-officer's

say-so to come on this station and start questioning his men?'

'No.'

'Then I'll see you off the premises. Stay where you are, Leading Fireman O'Day, I'll deal with you in a minute.'

He stood back to allow Jack to precede him to the door. They walked in silence through the yard, where auxiliaries were now hosing down and scrubbing the engines. As they reached the pavement, Jack turned back to face the station officer.

'Good afternoon, Mr Shaw.'

'Afternoon.' Len Shaw had planted himself foursquare in Jack's path, as if he half expected him to try and dash back for a spot of unauthorised interrogating.

Jack held his gaze. 'There is just one thing before I go, Mr Shaw.'

'Yes?'

'What did your letters say?'

Chapter 7

He'd denied it, of course. *But then*, as a small voice remarked inside Jack's head, *he would do, wouldn't he?* And the more Len Shaw protested, the more intrigued Jack became. What had started as a diversion on a boring sick leave suddenly took on an interesting dimension.

So absorbed was he in his puzzle that he forgot to watch where he was walking and ended up strolling down Agar Street. Too late he saw Detective Sergeant Alfred Agnew approaching from the opposite direction.

Every inch of the sergeant's body had been racked by disease; from dandruff in the north to athlete's foot in the south; with all possible variations in between. His limbs had borne their fair share of this suffering, and he was eager to share his experience of arthritis, rheumatism, blood poisoning, skin rashes and unidentified joint swellings which had baffled the best medical minds since the fledgling Constable Agnew had first trodden the metropolitan pavements in his size ten regulation boots.

Backing desperately down the pavement, his head reeling, Jack silently cursed the medical officer who had returned the sergeant to his desk at Agar Street CID after his encounter with an exploding incendiary in October.

'Nice to 'ave this little chat, sir,' the sergeant called when Jack had managed to increase the distance between them to fifty yards. 'It's cheered me up no end knowing there's someone out there worse off than myself.'

'My living has not been in vain then,' Jack muttered. Thrusting his bad arm into his overcoat, he cradled the elbow protectively against the jolts of each step and made his way home.

The December evening was falling fast. Without the pre-war glow of the street lamps and the cheerfulness of rooms warmed by blazing fires glimpsed through uncurtained windows, this cold, half-light time was a further drag on his spirits. By the time he turned into the square, the brief rush of adrenaline he'd got from his encounter at the fire station had trickled away like water from a cracked sink.

'Oi, Mr Stamford, come over 'ere, we got somefing to tell yer!'

The shout jolted through Jack's thoughts and caused a brief rush of annoyance that he'd been so rudely yanked from the self-pity that he'd been wallowing in for the past ten minutes. Before he could respond, another voice bawled:

'You're showing a light. Get it covered.' Jack couldn't see his small neighbour from this angle, but he gathered his response to this order from a further bark a second later: 'I saw that, Sammy O'Day. Just wait until I tell your mum.'

Prudently Sammy whisked back inside and banged the front door shut until the ARP warden had exchanged a wink with Jack and continued on his rounds. 'Cheeky little bugger,' he muttered out of the side of his mouth. 'Don't know where they learn these things.'

Jack had a fair idea where Sammy was learning them: from an East End kid who was currently being fostered by the teacher Pat O'Day was courting, and who seemed to treat the O'Day house as his own. Sure enough, when he stepped through the O'Days' unlocked front door, the first thing he saw was a skinny figure perched on the stairs, attempting to force up the locks on a large, battered brown suitcase.

'Is that your case, Nafnel?'

'No.' Unabashed, the boy continued to jiggle a hair-pin in the locks. 'You know 'ow to pick locks?'

Jack did, but he wasn't inclined to pass on the knowledge to an embryonic housebreaker. ' 'Fraid not,' he said.

'Why not?' Nafnel demanded. 'You could learn yerself all sorts of useful stuff being a copper.'

'I learnt other things instead. Like keeping my hands off other people's property.'

'I ain't gonna steal nothing. It's practice, ain't it? She said I could.'

She?

'Jack.' Eileen appeared in the kitchen door. 'Come through. Got someone you know here.'

Jack was conscious of a difficulty in swallowing. The palm that was nestling in his coat felt the increase in rhythm as his heartbeat accelerated. As far as he was aware, he and Eileen only had one female acquaintance in common who didn't live within walking distance. His wife, Neelie, had disappeared from Holland six months ago, just before the Germans had swept through the Channel coasts of France, Holland and Belgium. Was it possible she could somehow have . . . ?

He followed Eileen down into the back kitchen. And stopped.

Sergeant Sarah McNeill took her elbows off the table at the sight of a senior officer: 'Evening, sir.'

'Sarah's been bombed out,' Eileen said, squeezing past Pat to get to the stove.

'Last night?' Jack asked, while his eyes sought Pat with a question. He'd got home before Jack, so presumably the rollicking from his station officer had been short and sharp.

In confirmation of Jack's silent guess, Pat raised his eyebrows and shoulders in a resigned shrug.

'Not last night,' Sarah replied. 'The bomb came down a couple of months ago. Blew a bus into the house next door; they had to demolish it.'

The rest of the street had all been congratulating themselves on their lucky escape. Until today. Returning via Camden Town to the little street behind Mornington Crescent station where she'd lived for the past four years, Sarah had found her downstairs neighbours piling possessions into a carrier's cart. 'Here she is,' one called as Sarah's uniformed figure turned the corner.

'What's going on? Are you leaving?' It wasn't unusual these days. People had been moving out of London since the Blitz started, but the Johnsons had always vowed to stay, bombs or no bombs.

'No choice, my lovely,' Mrs Johnson said sadly. '*He* says we got to go.'

'He' was a slim, dark-haired man of medium height, whose thin face and pointed ears reminded Sarah irresistibly of a picture she'd once seen of some Greek god who was supposed to be half-man and half-goat. He answered to the name of Tobias Goole.

'Borough Surveyor's Office,' he explained, leaping daintily down the front steps in a manner that increased his resemblance to a goat. 'Have I the pleasure of addressing Miss McNeill?'

Sarah confirmed that he had, whilst strongly suspecting that the next few minutes weren't going to be equally pleasurable for her.

'I fear you must leave immediately,' Mr Goole informed her. 'At once,' he added, in case she should not grasp the meaning of 'immediately'.

'Other floors have already gone,' Sadie Johnson called across, heaving a coal scuttle into the back of the cart. 'Council put them in the emergency rest centre down the veterinary college.'

'But why?' Sarah asked.

'Danger. Subsidence. Imminent collapse.' Mr Goole rose on the points of his extraordinarily small feet to peer into her face. 'Let me show you.' Spinning round, he leapt back up the stairs, nimbly side-stepping the empty Great War shell case that the Johnsons had used as a front door stop. Sarah followed him to the top of the house.

The landlord described it as a flat. In reality it was just a large room with the kitchen divided off from the main living area by a curtain, and a bathroom that was shared with the tenants of the second floor. But it was the first place Sarah had ever truly thought of as her own, and she was damned if she was going to leave.

Apparently she was going to be damned if she didn't.

'The front wall of this property is becoming detached from the side walls,' Tobias Goole explained. 'They could part company at any moment.' He flung his arms wide to demonstrate just how aloof the two structures could be. 'Did you not notice . . . ?' With a half-pirouette, he skittered to the front wall and raised both hands, palms upwards. 'The cracks.'

Sarah admitted she had noticed one or two; well, half a dozen actually, but then you got cracks in old properties, didn't you?

Tobias fixed reproachful eyes on her; obviously there were cracks and there were cracks. And these were the sort of cracks that meant business. He clasped his hands together, at chest level in a gesture of prayer – whether for her or the crumbling masonry Sarah wasn't sure.

By now she was beginning to feel she was in the middle of a ballet performance. She wondered whether Tobias was expecting her to sink to the floor and flutter her arms to signify despair. She'd seen some girls do that in a dance class once and had only realised it wasn't supposed to be funny when the teacher had ordered her from the room. Dancing lessons had never figured in her family's budget, unless you counted a nimble sideways shuffle to avoid her dad's fists. Most of the money he'd earned had gone down his throat, leaving her mother, and latterly Sarah, to scrape together enough to pay the rent and put food on the table for the younger children. His death had been the catalyst which had split her family apart and left Sarah to fend solely for herself. As far as she was concerned, one of the advantages had been having rooms which she didn't have to share with *anyone*.

'The council will provide you with a temporary bed, Miss McNeill, although surely . . . don't the police have lodging houses of their own?' Tobias asked.

'Section Houses,' Sarah corrected.

'Or perhaps a relative?'

An even worse option from Sarah's point of view. Always assuming she could find any of them.

'So I hauled myself up here,' she explained as the O'Days finished laughing at her impression of Tobias Goole. 'I really do appreciate this, Eileen. I'll get myself fixed up in a couple of days, I promise.'

'No hurry, love, stay as long as you like. If Shane or Conn

get leave, they can always go in with Pat. Take Sarah's case up, will you, Pat? I'll get the table laid up in the front room, we'll never fit into the kitchen.'

'What's for dinner, Mum?' Sammy enquired.

'Bran tub pie.'

A suspicious expression flitted across Sammy's normally open face. 'What's that?'

'Dip in and see what you get,' his mother said tartly. 'Nafnel,' she shouted through to the hall. 'Go home.'

'Do I 'ave to?'

'Yes. Go on, run across now, in case the sirens start.'

Somewhat reluctantly, Nathaniel Starkey slouched towards the front door. Turning off the inside light, he pulled it open just as someone else was pushing in.

'Oi, watch it, you nearly had me flat on me face. Oh, it's you.' Maury O'Day finished on a squeal of pain. 'That was me fingers, you stupid little . . .'

'Sorry,' Nafnel yelled, sprinting into the darkness before Maury could gather his wits – and his fists.

'Shut the door,' Pat said, descending the stairs. 'I want to switch the light on.'

'Is the room all right?' his mother asked, bustling through with bouquets of cutlery in both hands. 'I've not had time to air it for weeks.'

'What room?' Maury demanded.

Pat explained about their unexpected house guest.

'How long's she staying?'

'As long as she likes,' Eileen informed her second youngest, flicking a chenille cloth over her dining table as she spoke.

Maury dug his hands into his pockets. As usual he was dressed in a suit, tie and trilby hat. The jacket sleeves hung to his knuckles, the trousers drooped on the front of his shoes and the hat balanced precariously on the back of his Brylcreemed black hair. Until his income stretched to bespoke tailors, Maury was forced to clothe his five-foot, four-inch frame in what he referred to as 'classy schmutter' from Mr Levy's Second Hand Clothes Emporium.

'What's that look for?' his mother demanded, adding a white

67

cloth and placing knives and forks with the speed of a poker dealer.

'I was thinking I'd move into that room.'

'You got a room.'

'But I have to share with 'im . . .' Maury scowled at his younger brother. 'And he kicks.'

'Least I don't stink. Cor . . .' Sammy held his nose. 'You don't half whiff.'

Eileen paused in her rush back to the kitchen. 'He's right,' she said, taking an inch of suit cloth between thumb and forefinger. 'Whatever you been doin', Maury? It's like . . .' She groped for a suitable description.

'Drains,' Sammy said gleefully.

'Stagnant water,' Eileen agreed. 'And this material's damp.'

'I was just helping a mate bail out their Anderson shelter, Mum,' Maury said. 'You know 'ow they get flooded.'

'Don't I just. Well, get out of them wet things before you catch a chill. Dinner's ready.'

She waited until he'd slouched upstairs before turning back to the kitchen. Jack had been lounging in the doorway, listening to this exchange. Her eyes met his and she half opened her mouth, changed her mind and said with a tight smile: 'Sit down, I can't get round this place with all you big fellas cluttering it up.'

Jack did as he was told, aware that they'd once again managed to avoid the unspoken question of exactly how Eileen's second youngest son earned a living.

Dinner was an uneasy affair. Maury was, as usual, monosyllabic in the presence of the police. Jack was aware of a certain reserve in Sarah's manner, for all her attempts to be the perfect dinner guest. His small daughter, Annaliese, had offered her cheek for her father's kiss and then settled herself determinedly on the other side of the table, keeping Eileen and Sammy as a buffer between herself and Jack. If he was truthful, Jack admitted later, his own behaviour hadn't exactly helped. Still frustrated by his handicap, he'd refused all help with his food with a snappish petulance. Determinedly he'd wielded his fork in a one-handed performance that had splattered Eileen's linen in gravy and left the slippery plate full of chopped mush.

'I'm not really that hungry,' he said finally.

'Pity you didn't say earlier,' Eileen replied. 'Saved me the bother of cooking it.'

Jack shrank. He felt relegated to the status of a six-year-old. As a consequence he excused himself early and made his way home, muttering about files to tidy up. He didn't bother to ask Annaliese whether she wanted to sleep in his house or the O'Days' any more. When Neelie had left him over two years ago to return home to Holland, she'd taken their daughter with her and flatly refused to come back to England even when the threat of a German invasion had become a distinct possibility.

He should have fought harder. But instead he'd relied on his father-in-law's promise that he would send them both to safety at the first hint of danger. And when the danger had come – overrunning the Lowlands faster than anyone had expected – Jack found the family had left weeks before to travel to unknown friends in France.

Annaliese had been brought to England by a group of refugees, but there had been no trace of Neelie or his father-in-law. They'd vanished in the mad scramble to get on the last boats before the Germans reached the channel coast and Annaliese couldn't – or wouldn't – talk about anything that had happened in that period. In fact she never talked about the past at all. It was possible, he supposed, that she didn't remember much about her earlier life in Kentish Town now, but it bothered him more than he'd care to admit that she never spoke about those two years in Holland with her mother and grandfather.

He'd looked across at the child silently chewing her dinner. This was a very different six-year-old to the five-year-old child he'd visited last Christmas in Holland. The sparkle had gone from her. Instead she was quiet and solemn and wary of men. The casual arrangement whereby Eileen had extended her charring duties to include minding the little girl while he was at work had rapidly become an almost full-time fostering. With each week his daughter seemed to become more a part of the O'Day family. Even her name had changed. He was the only one who called her 'Annaliese' now; to everyone else she was 'Annie'.

The lull in the nightly bombing of London was holding, and there had been no air-raid warning once again that evening. Nonetheless, he glanced upwards out of sheer habit. Above the blacked-out streets the sharp points of crystal stars twinkled with a clarity he'd never noticed before. Without the distraction of earth light reflecting into the atmosphere, he realised he was seeing the heavens as they must have been in the beginning, before electric lighting, gas mantels, candles or even those first primitive campfires.

He was so taken with his own sensitivity in coming to this conclusion that he totally failed to notice the man until he'd inserted his key into his front door and stepped into the hall.

'Detective Chief Inspector Stamford?' The caller was standing on the doorstep, one foot on the sill to prevent the door being closed. 'We'd like a word.'

'Who's we?' Jack asked. The key had caught in the lock. It needed another hand to hold the frame still whilst he released it.

'Allow me.' A black leather glove wrapped itself round the door's edge. The other reached over Jack and jiggled the key free. Wordlessly, his caller drew it past Jack's outstretched palm and dropped it in the pocket of his own raincoat. 'Shall we step inside?'

He was three inches taller than Jack and at least two stone heavier. And he was now standing foursquare on the door mat with less than six inches separating them, thereby frustrating any chance of slamming the door in his face. His attitude suggested he probably hadn't come to sell Provident cheques.

Possibilities scudded through Jack's mind. He could sprint for the back. But, he remembered, that door was also locked. Alternatively, he could throw himself forward and rely on the impetus to knock them both into the garden, where he could put up sufficient noise to attract help. His visitor solved his dilemma by stepping even closer and ensuring there was no chance of a rush attack.

'Let me get the blackout across.'

He chose the front room rather than the kitchen, on the grounds it might be easier to throw something through the windows if it came to that. The heavy drapes slid effortlessly closed. Without even the starlight to delineate vague shapes it was impossible to see what his uninvited guest was doing. He heard a shuffle of movement on the carpet and unconsciously tightened his stomach muscles to counteract a blow.

Light flooded the little room. His visitor moved away from the switch and stood in front of the door. For the first time Jack saw why he'd been using 'we' rather than 'I'. Of average height and medium build, the second man must have been completely hidden behind his bulkier colleague until now. Removing his bowler hat to reveal a tonsure of pepper-and-salt hair, he half bowed in Jack's direction and sat without being asked.

'I don't think I caught the names?' Jack said, seating himself.

'Unnecessary to toss them about,' the smaller man murmured. Compared with his colleague his attitude was reasonableness itself.

'Then perhaps you'd care to leave?' Jack suggested. 'I don't like anonymous visitors.'

'Oh no, sir. We couldn't do that. Not until we've had our little chat.'

'You do realise that it's illegal to detain someone against their will?'

'Oh yes, sir. We realise that. However, I wouldn't say "detain". Oh no. You did invite us in, if you'll recall.'

'So chat,' Jack invited. The swollen elbow was throbbing like hell and it took all his concentration not to wince with pain. Who on earth were they? Friends or relatives of someone he'd put away? Which of them would have the arrogance or stupidity to threaten a senior policeman in his own home?

'You've been asking questions, sir.'

'It's my job.'

'Not in this case, sir. Not in this case.'

'Which case?'

'The fire station, sir. Anonymous letters. They are not your province, are they, sir?'

It was the last thing Jack was expecting. Surely to God Len

71

Shaw hadn't been stupid enough to send a couple of heavies to threaten him? What on earth was the man hiding?

'Are you fire service?'

'Not exactly, sir. Although I suppose you might say that we damp down situations in our own way.' The smaller man exchanged a smile with the door guard. 'I should like your assurance that you will not investigate this matter further, Chief Inspector.'

'Would you? And what if you don't get it?'

'That would be unfortunate. Oh yes. Very unfortunate. We have our job to do, sir.'

'And what *is* that exactly?'

'To remove all obstacles that stand in the way of this country's victory, sir. No matter how painful such a task may be.'

'And I stand in the way of it, do I?' Jack asked. He was beginning to wonder if his two guests were escaped lunatics. Or someone's idea of an elaborate joke.

'You do, sir. We have come to give you fair warning. Everyone is expendable in pursuance of the ultimate victory. Drop your investigation, Chief Inspector, or pay the penalty.'

The room fell back into darkness again. Jack stood and flew sideways instinctively. The faintest chill across his cheek told him the door had been opened. It strengthened to a cold draught. Stepping through to the hall, he found the front door open. He was in the street in a second, but the small square was totally deserted.

Chapter 8

As soon as she was released from her duties at Good Hope Station, Hatty sped home, darting in and out of shops to collect the precious rationed goods as she made her way from Gospel Oak to Camden.

She eventually arrived in a breathless rush at an empty house. Tumbling the packages of meat and fat into the stone larder, she thrust the other bits and pieces haphazardly into cupboards. Lighting a gas ring she set the kettle on to boil whilst she padded through on sock-clad feet and propped a chair against the front door.

Collecting clean underwear, a towel, flannel and a small tin from the bedroom, she trotted downstairs again and stripped off her clothes in the kitchen.

Before the war she'd have kept a fire going in one of the rooms during the winter months so that Ruth and Uncle Duggie always came back to a welcoming home. But now . . . she gave an involuntary shiver and saw the flesh goosebump along her plump arms.

Taking a bowl from beneath the sink, she tipped hot water from the kettle and added a little cold from the tap. The lid of the tin had become stuck fast and she had to force her nails under the rim and heave. It parted company from the body of the tin with a loud 'plop' and released a perfumed fragrance into the gloomy kitchen. Closing her eyes, Hatty lost herself in the scent for a moment: Elizabeth Arden Geranium – bliss! Soaking the flannel and wringing it out tightly, she rubbed a thin film of the soap over the rough fabric and started to wash herself, sliding the wet cloth down her arms and into her armpits before massaging her heavy breasts. She really was getting huge, she decided, squinting downwards. Perhaps she ought to stop eating so much; but somehow she just always seemed to be hungry.

Rubbing off another layer of the precious soap, she worked her way across her stomach. Beneath her the floor reverberated with the rhythm of the goods trains clanking over the arches that abutted the back yard. Hatty didn't notice it. Like the rest of the street, she'd long ago 'tuned out' all the railway noises from her consciousness.

Dropping her dirty underwear into the bowl, she added more hot water, rubbed the garments against a bar of harsh yellow soap and rinsed them under the cold tap. Leaving them dripping with a tinny 'ping' into the bowl under the clothes horse, she tramped upstairs again. There was dust on the banisters and the carpets needed sweeping, but she firmly closed her eyes to her own slovenliness.

The girdle and stockings put up a bit of a fight, but the beige woollen dress and brown jacket slid on with relative ease. She didn't have a hat but she tied a pale-yellow scarf round her head in a snood style. Her toilette was finished off with a dab of powder from her cousin's box and – with great daring – a slick of red Coty lipstick. The final result of red and yellow against her pale skin made her look vaguely sleazy, but she hadn't the experience to know.

Unlocking the doors, she let herself out of the front. The rapidly descending twilight caught her by surprise. It had all taken longer than she'd realised. She started walking quickly, crossing into Chalk Farm Road and then following it northwards until she could turn left again and cross the canal and railway lines to enter the streets of small houses that nestled at the foot of Primrose Hill.

The barrage balloons in the Park hadn't been winched up, she noted; which meant no raiders had been plotted heading across the coast on a course that would take them over London. With any luck they'd have another quiet night.

The street she wanted was lined with rows of terraced brick cottages. In accordance with blackout regulations, they presented dark faces to the pavements. The one Hatty stopped at looked as deserted as the others. Nonetheless, she rapped hard on the knockerless door and stepped back to look up at the top windows. There was no telltale twitch of the curtains.

After a few moments, she thrust her hands into her pockets and started walking up and down the small street, pacing up the pavement on one side and down the other. It was a quiet road, but occasionally someone would hurry past, eager to get inside out of the December chill and into a warm room to a cooked meal. At each set of footsteps, Hatty stopped and strained towards the sound, trying to make out the walker's outline in the rapidly densing night.

Eventually she became tired and leant against the wall opposite the house, easing one foot up behind her as the pavement chill seeped through her shoes. She stayed there for nearly two hours. No one came. Eventually cold and hunger sent her trailing reluctantly back to Camden Town.

The front door of Mottram and Cropper had been locked for over an hour when she reached it, but a small printed card provided a telephone number which patrons were promised would be answered 'day or night' and an assurance that the caller would be met with 'a warm and sympathetic service that cannot be bettered in the whole of St Pancras'. Ignoring this invitation, Hatty made her way down a side alley and lifted the latch to the back yard. The three gleaming hearses were parked in the former stableyards to one side and – Hatty checked – the three 'luxuriously appointed' limousines which could carry mourners in 'the utmost comfort and dignity' were housed under the open sheds which had formerly contained the horse carriages.

A man was rubbing a cloth over the black paint of one of these vehicles, his slow, easy movements suggesting time-wasting rather than enthusiasm. He raised the yellow duster when he saw Hatty and called over: 'Mr Miller's in the chapel.'

Letting herself in through the back door, Hatty made her way to a small room, wrinkling her nose as the familiar smell of perfumed candles struggled to compete with the stink of formaldehyde and other embalming fluids. Duggie Miller was at the far end of the room, conferring over an open coffin with an odd-looking man she'd never seen before.

Hatty hesitated, not wanting to interrupt what might be a very private moment. She slid on to one of the chairs Mottram's had provided for mourners. The movement attracted Duggie's attention to her. He said something to the man, who nodded, picked up an attaché case and made his way to the back door. As he passed Hatty he doffed the hat to reveal black hair with a gleam of white skull the size of a boiled egg nestling in the centre.

She felt that politeness somehow obliged her to make a comment. 'I'm very sorry for your loss. Was it family?'

'Thank you, miss. But I was not acquainted with the deceased.' A half-regretful smile passed over his face, increasing its ugliness by the fleeting glimpse of twisted teeth. 'I have no family. Good evening.'

' 'Bye.' Hatty felt herself flushing at her own stupidity. She took a deep breath and gulped as bile rose in her throat.

'Everything all right, Hat?' Duggie leant over her. 'Nothing happened, has it? You look a bit funny.'

'No.' Hatty swallowed convulsively. She'd stopped at the public lavatories at the end of the street to soak her handkerchief and scrub the make-up off, but it wasn't that that was making her look so pale. 'I was just passing. I thought I'd see if you'd gone yet.' She heaved again. 'That smell makes me feel real queer, Uncle Duggie.'

' 'Ere.' He put a hand under her elbow and hauled her to her feet. 'Come down the basement with me. I got to get the lid for this one.'

Thankfully Hatty followed him down the stone steps into the large room that ran under the shop. Open coffins lined the walls, stretching away into a dimness that was hardly pierced by the two twenty-five-watt bulbs that hung from bare cords. Hatty suppressed a shudder. As little girls she and Ruth had often dared each other to come down here and brave the silent ranks of macabre boxes.

Duggie was oblivious to the ghoulish atmosphere. Cheerfully whistling the first few lines of 'Hark the Herald Angels

Sing,' he bounced down the room poking between the upright coffins, shouting back questions as he went.

'Ruthie OK?' *Hark the Herald Angels Sing* . . .

'She's gone to see Lulu.'

'Never said, did she?' *Glory to the newborn king* . . .

'No. She swapped shifts.'

'Wish she'd say. Might never know if she gets herself blown to smithereens in . . . where . . . ?'

'Bedfordshire.'

'Yeh. What you been up to today?' *Peace on earth and mercy mild* . . .

'I just went for a bit of a walk.'

Duggie emerged from the gloom, carrying a polished lid. 'Found it. Won't take a minute to screw him down. He's first out the trap tomorrow morning.' *God and sinners reconciled* . . .

'I've not cooked dinner yet.'

'Oh.' Duggie's sprightly step visibly faltered. Then he straightened again as a comforting idea occurred to him. 'Tell you what, there's no raid. Let's go along to Woods. Get some saveloys to take home. Or pie and mash if you like.' *Joyful all ye nations rise* . . .

'Can we afford it?'

' 'Course we can. The lord will provide, Hat.'

And just lately he'd been providing in spectacular abundance, Duggie might have added. The normal quota of infants and elderly customers that formed a steady stream of work once the colder months struck had been well supplemented by those who'd been hastened on their way by the bombing raids. Life for an undertaker's assistant was sweet indeed at present.

'Amen,' Hatty responded. 'I'll wait for you in the yard.' She followed her uncle's polished boots up the stair treads again.

'Right-o. If Jake's finished polishing, tell him to make sure he takes the keys out the carriages. We've got a flattie comes past here who's got a real bee in his helmet about immobilising vehicles. Though God knows why a German parachutist would want to go driving round in a bloomin' hearse.' *Join the triumph of the skies* . . .

The mention of the diligent constable reminded Hatty of her only bit of news. 'We had the police around this afternoon.' *With the angelic host proclaiii!!!* 'At the house? Why, what's happened?'

'Not at home. They came up Good Hope Station. This inspector bloke was asking about nasty letters, like that one Ruth got.'

'Oh, right, letters. 'Bout time too. Police ought to do something. Just give me a minute, Hat.'

He joined her in the yard five minutes later, seeing Jake off the premises and handing her two large lidded jars to hold before carefully padlocking the doubles gates to the vehicle yard. 'I'll take them back now.'

Hatty hefted the two vases back. Tucking one under each arm, Duggie set off again in the direction of his dinner.

The pie and eel shop was as dark as its neighbours, and a system of double curtaining enabled them to slip in without allowing a telltale beam of light to cut across the pavements. Delicious aromas of simmering meat and gravy and frying sausages tickled their noses as they made their way to the counter.

'What'll it be then, Hat?' Duggie asked. 'Looks like they got both in today. Pies and saveloys. Or eels if you fancy?'

'Yuck.' Hatty made a face. 'Pie, please, Uncle Duggie. Can I have two, I'm ever so hungry.' She dived into her bag and found a few coins. 'I'll buy the other one.'

'Rubbish. Put your money away. I'll have a pie too. Tell you what, we'll take a couple of them saveloys too. Pound to a penny Ruthie will be in time we get back.'

The ordered food was duly wrapped in newspaper.

'And we'll have some mash and liquor too, mate,' Duggie ordered.

'Got a dish?'

Duggie heaved the two vases on to the counter. 'Fill them up.'

Mounds of mashed potato were duly scooped into one, whilst steaming green liquid that released clouds of a pungent parsley scent filled the other. Tendering a pound note and collecting his change, Duggie took up his burdens once more and led the way home.

Sure enough, when they opened the front door they were both illuminated in an illegal bath of yellow light.

'Ruth,' Duggie bawled. 'Get this light off.'

'I'll get it, Mr Miller.'

A uniformed figure appeared briefly in the passage and clicked the switch. Momentarily dazzled, Duggie stepped inside. He heard Hatty follow, bumping the door closed with her rear. As the latch caught, the light flicked on again.

Duggie blinked and saw who his visitor was. 'Hello, Stan. On leave?'

'Twenty-four-hour pass, Mr Miller.'

'Did you go to see Lulu with Ruth?' Hatty asked, carefully depositing her parcels on the stairs whilst she wriggled out of her jacket and hung it over the banisters.

'Nah. Just got here. Thought maybe Ruth might want to come up the pictures.'

'I told him,' Ruth said, appearing in the kitchen doorway. 'I'm tired. The trains is dead crowded these days. You have to stand mostly.'

'Be thankful you got legs to stand on, Ruth. Some ain't.'

'Amen,' Hatty agreed.

Carrying his jars into the kitchen, Duggie set them on the table. 'Want to stop for a bite to eat, Stan? We got plenty.'

'Ta, Mr Miller.'

Duggie opened a cupboard and took out a china jug. 'Nip over to the pub then. Get us a jug of half-and-half.'

'Oh, right.'

By the time Stan arrived back, the plates were warming in the hissing oven and the table was laid.

'They only had mild. Bitter's out, Mr Miller.'

'Not to worry, son. Very kind of you I'm sure.' He reached into his waistcoat pocket. Stan's face brightened, and then fell again as Duggie pulled out a watch and examined the time. 'Best get this lot eaten before them darn sirens start.'

Obediently Hatty dished out the meat, leaving them to help themselves to mash and liquor.

'What are these?' Stan said curiously, twisting a lidded jar as he scraped out the last of the potato.

'Urns. For cremations,' Duggie added, seeing Stan's blank look. 'It's where they put the ashes after the dearly departed 'as gone up in smoke. Wash 'em up well before I take 'em back to the storeroom tomorrow morning, won't you, Hat.'

'Yes, Uncle Duggie.'

'Don't you want that saveloy, son?'

'No thanks, Mr Miller. Think I'd best be getting home. Me mum worries.' Looking rather green, Stan pushed himself away from the table.

'Fair enough. Ruth'll see you out. Thanks for the beer.'

After Stan had gone, the Millers ate the rest of their dinner in companionable silence. They played cards for a while and then went to bed for another miraculously peaceful night, for the Luftwaffe were still concentrating their attentions on Coventry. The following morning the two women made their way up Kentish Town High Street, both lost in their own thoughts. They didn't speak until they were almost at the bulk of St John's Church, when Ruth gave a gasp and seized Hatty's arm.

'Hatty. Look. Just *look*.'

Hatty stared round wildly. There was no new bomb damage that she could see. No parachutists dangling off the church steeple or invading tanks trundling down Highgate Road. Ruth drew short breaths of excitement. Her fingers locked into Hatty's arm with a force sufficient to disturb even the substantial layers of plump pink flesh her cousin had laid down over the years.

'What am I supposed to be looking *at*?'

'*Him*. There. Talking to Snooty Miss Grooty.'

Hatty refocused her gaze. Nell was standing outside the substation, bending forward to speak to the driver of a green two-seater car. Even Hatty, who knew nothing about cars, recognised that this was an expensive vehicle. Its long, lean lines hugged the road before the front wings swept up to end in huge round headlights. Despite the chilly weather, the convertible top was folded back, allowing the Millers a clear view of the occupant.

'God, isn't he *divine*?' Ruth breathed. 'Come on.' Her walk changed to a casual hip-swinging saunter.

He was the man she'd been dreaming about for years. Everything from the thick blond hair and chiselled features to the crisp RAF uniform was exactly right. It was as if he'd stepped down from the Gaisford cinema screen that she'd watch so avidly each week as she and Lulu wandered up and down the aisles with their usherettes' torches. She hardly dared breathe in case someone switched the projector off and he disappeared in a mass of flickering numbers.

As they got closer, Nell shook her head, replaced the tin helmet which had been dangling from her fingers and ran back inside the front door of the station.

'Nell!' Even his voice was right. Deep and well bred, but not too posh.

Nell didn't reappear. After a moment the officer pulled his cap on again and started the car's ignition. He was parked the wrong way round, but instead of moving across the opposite side of the road he allowed the car to freewheel a few yards. His eyes caught Ruth's. Deep sapphire blue with long dark lashes. Her toes curled in the front of her regulation lace-ups and the strangest sensation tingled down her stomach and between her thighs. One of his eyes closed slowly in a deep sensuous wink. She thought she was going to suffocate.

And then he was gone, swinging the car to the right side of the road and causing a motorbike carrying two army privates to swerve and deposit the pillion rider on the kerb.

'Sorry, Stan. You OK, mate?' The driver looked anxiously at his friend, who was struggling to his feet.

'Yeah. I reckon.'

'Bleedin' officers.'

'Yeah,' Stan agreed, flinging his leg over the seat. 'Bleedin' officers. Best put your foot down, Charlie, we'll be late back to camp.'

The bike roared past Good Hope Station. Neither Hatty nor Ruth noticed it. They had both stepped through the front door to find themselves face to face with Nell de Groot. The look of sheer hatred on her face had pierced even Ruth's delicious day-dream of true love.

Chapter 9

Running his finger and thumb along the inner seam to straighten it, Jack picked up the iron and pressed the hot metal over the cotton in smooth sweeps, leaving the sleeve flat and crisply pressed. *Nothing to it*, he thought triumphantly. Lifting the shirt one-handed, he twirled it to lay it across the board at another angle and saw with consternation that there was now a long, jagged crease ironed into the opposite side of the sleeve. Blowing out a large breath of annoyance, he jiggled the shoulder of the shirt across the board. It promptly slipped off and crumpled into a heap on the floor.

'Oh, blast and . . .' The sharp rap of the front door knocker saved the shirt from permanent damage.

The new lock he'd just had fitted resisted his fingers and the door displayed a tendency to stick that he'd never noticed before. Panting with the effort, he eventually managed to drag the damn thing open. His visitor turned back from his idle contemplation of the square.

'Morning, Stamford.' Chief Superintendent Dunn nodded.

'Good morning, sir,' Jack replied, standing back in an unspoken invitation to his boss to enter and concealing his surprise at the unexpected visit.

Before he stepped inside, Dunn turned and opened and closed the fingers of his right hand three times. The driver of a police Wolseley backed away from the kerb and started an awkward three-point turn.

'He'll pick me up in fifteen minutes. Just wanted to check you were in before I sent him off.'

'Come through.' Jack indicated the front room. He shut the front door and tried to fasten his top buttons before joining

Dunn. He wasn't wearing a tie because he hadn't wanted to ask Eileen or one of the younger children to help him with the knot. And he'd thrust his feet into a pair of carpet slippers since he had much the same reluctance regarding shoelaces. Feeling like a shambling old man, he asked Dunn if he could offer him anything: 'Tea, sir? Or something stronger. I think I might still have . . .'

Dunn waved him to a seat. 'Not for me, thanks. Haven't time. How's the, em . . .' Dunn nodded towards the injured limb.

'Oh, much better, sir,' Jack assured him. He laid his arm along the chair's back and choked back a gasp at the river of pain that swept from his shoulder to his fingers.

'Looks like it,' Dunn sniffed. 'Was some talk about pensioning you off.'

Gritting his teeth, Jack assured him there was no need for that. 'Just a temporary injury, the doctor said. Delayed reaction to being shot.'

'I read the MO's report. Arthritis,' Dunn said. 'Terrible curse. People don't realise. Crippled my mother. Poor woman's hands were like claws at the end. Couldn't do a thing for herself.'

'Did you just pop round to cheer me up, sir?'

'Eh? What? Oh, no. Came to talk about work, actually.'

Jack's ego, which had been contemplating the possibility of getting a bath chair and quietly freewheeling under the nearest tram, raised its fragile head over the parapet again. A case? Something that required his urgent return to his desk at Scotland Yard? Well, why not? It wasn't as if he needed to do much leg work any more. At his rank it was mostly just directing other officers' efforts. No reason at all why he couldn't get off his damn sick leave.

'Hear you had a couple of visitors the other day,' Dunn remarked.

For a moment Jack thought he was talking about Sarah McNeill. There had been an uncomfortable period on his previous case, investigating a death on Balaclava Row, when his insistence on having a woman assisting in CID work had led to rumours of an affair between himself and Sarah. But surely that idea had been well and truly squashed by now? He could hardly be held accountable for the sergeant's choice of lodgings across the road.

Then Dunn's words penetrated: *a couple of visitors.* How the hell did he know? Jack hadn't mentioned his late-night callers to anyone. There had seemed little point, since there was nothing they could actually be charged with. As they had pointed out at the time, Jack had, loosely speaking, invited them in; they hadn't uttered any direct threats; and the only thing they'd stolen was his front-door key – hence the new lock that he'd had fitted yesterday.

The obvious answer dawned as he looked at his boss's broad, imperturbable face. If only three people knew about the meeting, and he hadn't said anything . . . 'They were police?'

'Special Branch,' Dunn sighed, rubbing one finger down the side of his nostrils to deal with an imaginary itch. It was an unconscious gesture that he used when he was about to broach an embarrassing subject. 'Fact is . . . those letters . . . anonymous jobs . . . we already knew about them.'

'How?'

'One of the brigade officers had reported to his headquarters. Seems there had been a few nasty incidents. Bad for morale, that sort of thing.'

'Station Officer Shaw?'

'No. Don't think that was the name. Anyway, fire bods at Lambeth asked the Yard if they could do something. Not really our sort of thing. I mean, unpleasant for the recipients of course, but no demands for money or threats of violence from what we could ascertain. Not that that was much. Mostly hearsay, no actual letters. Still, we put a bloke on it to keep relations sweet. Make a few noises, you know? Look like we're doing something, then quietly let it drop.'

Jack nodded. He knew the scenario. Sometimes police work was more politics than law.

'First thing our bloke did,' Dunn continued, 'was ask for a list of names of those working at the main fire station and the substation. And that's when hell was let loose. Special Branch started jumping up and down, bleating on about national security and the war effort and insisting we drop the whole damn business.'

'And did you?'

' 'Course not. Damn it all, Jack, I'm not having some jumped-up pipsqueak inspector telling me what I can and can't do in my own office.'

Jack's lips twitched. He could imagine the scene. For all his stolid demeanour, Dunn could slice a junior officer into fillets with his tongue.

'Anyway, couple of days later the damn bloke's back again with Laurel and Hardy in tow.'

Jack recognised the description of his two callers.

'Accused me of deliberately drawing attention to the whole business by assigning a chief inspector to the case. Threatened me with all sort of poppycock, including the Commissioner. Told them to go ahead. Report me to the Home Secretary if they liked.'

'And?'

'Ended up having a little chat with the Commissioner.'

'I'm sorry.' Jack was seriously alarmed that a casual favour for Pat O'Day was rapidly turning into a major security incident.

'No problem. Anyway, upshot was, I was sent to have a talk with you. Debrief you, as Laurel and Hardy's boss put it. So kindly enlighten me as to your involvement in a nonexistent case during your supposed sick leave.'

As rapidly as possible Jack explained about Pat's worry that someone would end up seriously injured at the fire station, and his request for a little unofficial help. 'He didn't think any of his officers would take the matter seriously, otherwise I'm sure he would have gone through proper channels,' he concluded, anxious to keep his young neighbour as far away from any recriminations as possible.

Dunn grunted. He splayed square-tipped fingers across his knees, rubbing them slowly back and forth. 'There's a woman,' he said finally. 'At the auxiliary station. Name of De Groot. Come across her?'

'Nell,' Jack said instantly, remembering the pale girl with

the Dutch ancestry and the touch-me-not manner.

'Eleanor Margaret,' Dunn agreed. 'Suppose it might be shortened to Nell. File didn't say.'

'Special Branch have a file on Miss De Groot?'

'On her father. Dr Charles Wim De Groot. He's some kind of scientist, not a medical doctor.'

'Aaah.' A tiny gleam of enlightenment pierced the blackout in Jack's mind.

'Aaah indeed. Daddy is engaged in what is euphemistically known as "important war work". Don't know what, but since the fellow's degree is in chemistry, I don't think that I particularly *want* to know.'

Dunn's brothers had died from a mustard gas attack in the Great War. Presumably, thought Jack, he imagined that Dr De Groot was engaged in concocting some sort of equal horror for the present conflict. 'I still don't quite see Special Branch's interest in the daughter, sir. It's a bit . . .' Jack groped for the word, and was about to settle on 'obsessive' when his mind made another quick leap of deduction. 'They think she's involved in the letters?'

Dunn nodded wordlessly.

'She's done it before?'

'Eight years ago.'

'Where?'

'St Albans. The local police were involved at the time. The letter were . . . quite explicit.'

'Sexual?'

'Mostly, yes. But more than that, they contained threats of actual physical harm.'

'Against whom?'

'The mother received a fair few. Plus other local acquaintances. Vicar's wife got a couple. Owner of a tea shop was on the list too, far as I remember.'

'Was she prosecuted?'

'Lord no. The parents had her admitted to a mental hospital. That's part of the problem really. De Groot was so distressed by the whole business that he damn nearly ended up in the loony bin himself. And apparently they can't take the risk of that happening this time. His contribution to . . . whatever it is the man's doing . . . is vital.'

'So they're just going to ignore the matter?'

Dunn blew out a heavy breath. 'Looks like that isn't a feasible option any more, doesn't it? People are talking . . . Pretending it's not happening will just . . .'

'Fan the flames?'

Dunn permitted himself a small smile at the pun. 'No sense suggesting they transfer the wretched woman. She'd just start up her correspondence elsewhere. Wouldn't take long before some bright spark made the connection. Fire brigade's changing; auxiliary service is full of people with a bit of education and nous to use it.'

'Couldn't they ask for her resignation?'

'On what grounds? She's supposed to be sane. In fact, she's got a doctor's letter to prove it, which is more than the rest of us have. Anyway, what if they bring in conscription for women? She'd just be directed into another war job and someone else would get the problem.'

'They could refuse to accept her. Say she wasn't suitable.'

'They could. But she'd just try elsewhere, wouldn't she? She's patriotic. Wants to do her bit. Volunteered of her own accord. She's bright, apparently. Sooner or later she'd smell a rat. And if she starts believing people are persecuting her, she's likely to have another breakdown, which is precisely what we're trying to avoid.'

'So what's the answer?' Jack had a pretty shrewd idea that some course of action had already been decided upon, hence Dunn's unexpected call.

'Thing is, seems the real problem last time was the girl kept claiming she hadn't done it. Denial, the head doctors call it. It wasn't until they could actually get her to admit that she had written the letters that they could cure her.'

'I suppose there's no doubt that she *did* write them?'

'No. The evidence is pretty watertight on that one. Nevertheless, she still denied it for months.'

'Then I don't really see how you expect to convince her this time. I mean, if professional medical men couldn't before . . .'

'It's not her that needs convincing. It's her father. Listen.' Dunn leant forward, grasping his knees so firmly that Jack could see his knuckles glowing whitely through the skin. 'Last time she managed to convince De Groot that they'd got it all wrong. That his little girl was innocent. So then he started feeling guilty about having her locked up and treated, and that preyed on his mind until he was nearly fit for a straitjacket himself. This time we want him to be certain. We want you to find definite evidence that the girl's up to her old tricks.'

'And then?'

'And then we shall make a discreet approach to the De Groots and suggest that Miss De Groot be placed in a private nursing home. Nothing like the place she was in before. Just a pleasant country house . . .'

'With bars on the windows?'

'Possibly. However, she'd be allowed the freedom to do pretty much as she liked. Write letters to her heart's content, if that's what she wants. The staff would simply make sure that they were never posted.'

Jack shifted uneasily. 'I don't really like the sound of this, sir.'

'Well, we've all had to do things we didn't much care for in this job, haven't we, Stamford?'

The use of his surname warned Jack that this conversation was about to be terminated. In further confirmation, Dunn stood up just as a car horn sounded outside.

'There are those,' the Chief Superintendent pointed out, 'who might find the idea of spending their days being waited on hand and foot in luxurious surroundings with no responsibilities at all rather attractive.'

'But presumably you don't think Miss De Groot is one of them, otherwise you'd have invited her to step into the cage yourself?'

'There's no need to take that tone. I'm only obeying orders same as we all have to.' He waited until Jack had struggled to his feet and preceded him into the hall before adding, 'Look, it's thought to be best if the De Groot woman doesn't actually realise the police are involved yet. You'll have to find some way to do this that doesn't look too official.'

Jack paused with the door half-open. 'You mean you're officially telling me to conduct an unofficial investigation?'

'Got the target on the first shot, Jack. After all, can't put you on the case officially, can I? You're on sick leave. Keep in touch.'

He was halfway down the path before a question occurred to Jack. 'Sir! Where does Miss De Groot live when she's not on duty? Somewhere local, I assume?'

'She's got lodgings up by the Archway. Vorley Road, I believe. I can check the file if you wish. Why?'

'Well, she's more likely to write the letters at home than in the fire station. It might be a good idea if we could get someone close to her. Gain her confidence.'

'Yes, well, I suppose that makes sense. If they don't spook her.'

'Oh, I don't think they'll do that, sir.'

'You have someone in mind then?'

'Oh yes, sir.' Jack grinned. 'I happen to know someone who's looking for new lodgings.'

Chapter 10

Bridget O'Mara raised plump hands to the door lintel and blessed the luck that had caused her to have a vacant room just on the day that the young lady happened to be looking.

'Sure now, aren't the fates with us both today?' she twinkled, urging Sarah inside. 'There's you wanting a fine comfy room and me having just the thing and wondering where I could find a nice respectable young woman to grace me premises.'

The firmness of the hold on her arm wasn't lost on Sarah. Mrs O'Mara, she guessed, was having the same problems as many hoteliers, boarding-house keepers and landlords in London. The Blitz had made London a less than desirable address, and for reasons of family, business or sheer cowardice, those that could leave were doing so.

'I have full facilities,' Mrs O'Mara assured her, gesturing into a room on the first landing where Sarah caught a glimpse of copper piping and a claw-footed tub. 'Full facilities,' she repeated, opening what Sarah had taken to be a cupboard to reveal a lavatory topped by a cistern enclosed in dark polished wood. 'The other room there, now, is let to Mr Death. He's in cosmetics.'

Sarah grappled with a picture of the Grim Reaper in pancake and lipstick gliding around the first-floor landing until Mrs O'Mara stopped abruptly and asked: 'And what's your line of business, me dear?' She'd paused on the second flight of stairs. Since she was several steps ahead of Sarah, it meant that she could look straight into her eyes. 'You would be having a job, wouldn't you?'

'I'm in the police force,' Sarah said.

Some landlords wouldn't have police officers on the

premises, on the grounds that it gave the place a bad name, 'seeing coppers coming and going at all hours'. She held her breath, wondering whether Mrs O'Mara would march her straight back down the stairs again. Fate, however, was on her side this morning.

Mrs O'Mara's round face flushed with pleasure. 'Well now, and would you be knowing me brother-in-law, Danny? Sergeant Daniel O'Mara, that is. He's stationed up Kilburn. Would he be the one who put you on to me?'

Sarah mumbled vaguely as Mrs O'Mara continued her journey to the top landing, her breath coming in short, panting gasps.

'Well now, here we are.' Turning to her right, she opened a door and led the way into a room that faced the front of the street.

It was smaller than the Mornington Crescent 'flat', but it felt clean, and the walls looked as if they'd been painted fairly recently, though in a rather odd shade of light green.

'There's a little nook here for your washing and cooking, see.' Mrs O'Mara whisked aside a patterned curtain to reveal a small sink and two gas burners set on a shelf screwed to the wall. More shelves had been fixed across an alcove, and a small cupboard with a mesh front stood beneath.

Sarah examined the rest of the room. For her money she'd also get a large wardrobe, a bed that was currently stripped down to its mattress, a chest of drawers and a small folding table with two chairs.

Mrs O'Mara must have been following the direction of her gaze, because she announced at that point in the examination that she had no objection to visitors in rooms but she didn't allow overnight callers. 'No men, no pets,' she said firmly.

Fat chance, Sarah thought silently, whilst making a mental note to keep her eyes open for another flat. Given her previous luck, she was more likely to acquire a tabby than a man, but she might as well live in hope.

Mrs O'Mara completed the tour by pointing out the gas and electricity meters set high on the wall and drawing her attention to the small gas fire in front of the grate. 'Cleaner than all that nasty coal dust. Wasn't I forever washing my paintwork down when I had the coal? Well now, me dear, it's eighteen bob a week and a week in advance. Does that suit?'

'I work nights sometimes,' Sarah warned. 'In fact, I have to come and go at all sorts of strange times.'

'Sure now, that won't bother me. My other young lady is just the same.'

'Is she in the police service too?' Sarah asked artlessly.

'No, dear. Nell's an auxiliary firewoman. She has the room just across from you there. Always coming and going at night, especially in all that dreadful bombing.'

'I'll take it,' Sarah said.

Mrs O'Mara nodded as if she'd expected nothing less, and preceded Sarah back down the stairs. As they reached the ground floor, the door to a back room opened and a woman trotted into the hall, her high heels clicking against the black and white tiles.

'Ah, there yer are, Ruby. Here we are with a new top front.'

Sara extended a hand. 'Sarah McNeill.'

'Miss Ruby Rawkins. Pleased to meet you, I'm sure.' A birdlike claw touched Sarah's fingers briefly whilst Ruby peered out from the moth-eaten fur collar of her coat. Even in the high heels she was tiny. The feather dancing in the black hat perched on a cottage loaf of soft grey hair scarcely came up to Sarah's nose. 'Please excuse me. I must catch my bus.'

'Ground floor back,' Bridget O'Mara explained as the little woman hurried away. 'Ruby is a cashier. Ground floor front's Mr Butterman. Mr Butterman is . . . a disappointment. That room may be coming available soon. I could maybe let you have that one instead of the top if you like, although I'd have to be charging you more, lower rooms being in demand since the bombing started . . .'

Sarah hastily assured her the top floor was just fine. It left her better placed to initiate girly chats with Nell De Groot, although she could hardly tell Mrs O'Mara that.

'Just as you like, dear. I'm down in the basement myself and you're very welcome to bring your blankets down and sleep on my floor during a raid if you've a mind. That's what the rest of them do. Well now, shall we be settling the business then?'

The tour was plainly at an end. Sarah handed over her week's rent, collected a door key and told Mrs O'Mara she'd probably be moving in Sunday.

She emerged from Vorley Road just in time to see a number 27 bus disappearing down Junction Road. A quick glance at her watch told her it would be prudent to start walking if she didn't want to be late on parade. The main road was relatively unscarred by any bomb damage, apart from a few hastily repaired potholes, but from the corner of her eye she caught glimpses of the occasional boarded-up house or roofless property down a side road. By and large she knew this area had been lucky. Most of the damage had happened slightly further south, in the Euston and King's Cross regions, and even there, she knew from a recent trip to West Ham, the devastation had been only a fraction of what the East End had suffered.

But then, she thought, casting hopeful glances over her shoulder as she came to the next bus stop, suffering was a very personal thing. Would the young woman she'd had to deal with a few months previously consider her dead baby was worth less than a whole air-raid shelter of East End dead? Probably not, she decided, remembering the woman's mad crooning over the tiny faceless body.

Something about the memory nudged at her subconscious. It had somehow taken her thoughts full circle back to the reason for her sudden move to Vorley Road. But why should a dead baby make her think of anonymous letters at the fire station? DCI Stamford had explained his problem to her that morning when he'd called unexpectedly just after Eileen had taken the children to the shops. Given that Sarah had been using the time to catch up on her washing and ironing, she could have done without a visit from a senior officer. Particularly one with whom she might have become emotionally involved.

They'd worked together on two CID cases since his transfer to Agar Street Station the previous spring. The first occasion had been caused partly by her involvement in the investigation before Stamford's arrival and partly by a serious lack of man-power in the CID office at the time. The second time had been different. He'd specifically asked that she be transferred to the case. She'd been aware of feeling both professionally flattered and personally thrown off balance.

Ever since she'd met Stamford, she'd been conscious of an attraction on her side, which wasn't reciprocated on his. He liked her; he valued her professionally; but that extra spark wasn't there. And if it had been, she'd been unsure where any relationship could have gone. He was married. He was a superior officer. What could she have hoped for – a messy affair which might have led to one of them being transferred with a black mark on their records?

Taking a hold on her emotions with a firmness which she knew many people took for coldness, she'd decided to keep their association on the friendship basis that he seemed to prefer. But she was still feminine enough not to want him to see her looking like a charwoman.

Pushing back wisps of hair that had escaped from the scarf she'd tied round her head before giving Eileen a hand with sweeping and dusting the bedrooms that morning, she had tried to appear cool and collected as she entertained the chief inspector in the kitchen.

'I'm supposed to conduct an investigation without telling anyone about it in order to collect evidence so we won't prosecute the woman. Security has gone mad in this country, Sergeant.'

'Should you be telling me then, sir?'

'I need your help. It's all right, I've already cleared it with Chief Superintendent Dunn. He's agreed you can assist unofficially in an official capacity, so to speak.'

'How very kind of him, sir.'

The edge in her voice had not been lost on Stamford, who'd pointed out that refusing to co-operate in a CID investigation could be seen as cutting off her nose to spite her face.

'But sir, can Mr Dunn be sure this won't turn into one of those cases which might leave me vilely contaminated? I mean, considering that the less decent women see of these aspects of life . . .' she'd said, dredging up more or less verbatim the chief superintendent's objections to her – or any other female officer – joining the CID branch.

'Well, if you come out of this uncontaminated and with your maidenly modesty intact,' Stamford had said, 'it will be one more piece of ammunition in your battle, won't it?'

'I suppose,' Sarah had agreed. She knew she sounded ungracious, but was still smarting from this latest refusal. 'What do you want me to do exactly?'

He'd told her about Nell De Groot and suggested that Sarah might try to obtain a room in the same house. 'Might not have any vacancies, of course. But it's worth a shot.'

So she'd duly pegged her washing in the chilly back garden, where it would probably freeze rather than dry, pulled her coat on and walked up to the Archway, where Mrs O'Mara had fallen on her neck with delight. And now she was going to be late on duty, probably get a reprimand on her record, or a fine, and she couldn't even claim to be on official business.

The beat constable for Kentish Town Road was already lurking in a convenient shop doorway a few yards from the entrance to Agar Street. His breath rose in a frosty cloud on the air as he slapped his hands together and stamped his feet whilst he waited for his relief to pass and release him to return to the station.

Speeding into Prince of Wales Road, she swerved past several women wheeling pramloads of bedding into the laundry. A small queue had formed outside the licensed grocer's. They must have had a delivery of something scarce. She wished she could stop and investigate, but she didn't dare. Eileen was still out when she reached the house but the children had returned and had managed to collect on the way Nathaniel Starkey, the foster child who answered to the nickname 'Nafnel'.

'We been round the shops seeing what we want for Christmas,' Sammy explained, looking up from a sheet of paper. 'Now we're doing a list to stick up the chimney for Father Christmas.'

'I'm doing a real long one,' Nafnel said, firmly pressing a pencil into rounded letters. 'He never come to me other

Christmases, so I figure the bleeder stuck my presents in some other kid's chimney.'

'Good thinking,' Sarah agreed, reasoning that it wasn't her place to correct his language. 'Tell him he owes me a lot of years too.'

She sped upstairs, hurriedly scrambled into her uniform and dashed out again as Eileen rounded the corner laden down with bags. 'Can't stop, late, new digs, explain tonight,' Sarah shouted.

The station sergeant called 'Truncheons and Armlets' just as she slid in through the door of the parade room, trying desperately to merge into the walls. Which meant she was nearly twenty minutes late. Oh hell! The sergeant moved from behind his desk, eyes sweeping over the rows of striped armbands and truncheons presented for his inspection. Satisfied the relief was correctly turned out, he dismissed them to take up their duties and waited until they'd filed out before turning his attention to Sarah.

'Sorry,' she said quickly. 'I was fixing up new digs. My old ones were bombed out.'

The sergeant sniffed. 'You 'ad all morning. It don't set an example to the men for sergeants to be late on parade. Even a woman one. I'll have to report you.'

'I expected nothing less,' Sarah assured him. Mentally adding: *from a dyed-in-the-wool rule-book fanatic like you.*

Thwarted, the Sergeant muttered that she'd better get on then, he supposed. 'You've got to work a double shift, by the way. Inspectors' orders. They want you down the Tube station tonight. Had a bit of trouble. Thieving mostly. Women's stuff.'

'But isn't that Jeannie Crimmond's duty?' Sarah protested, referring to a WPC who was also stationed at Agar Street.

'Gone,' the sergeant said with a smug smile. 'Escort duty. Taking an absconder back to Cardiff. Won't be back until tomorrow.'

Sarah groaned. She hated shelter duties. They invariably stank of unwashed bodies, suspicious lavatory habits and stale cigarettes. As an added bonus, you could usually expect to collect a few samples of north London wildlife, particularly of

97

the bug and beetle variety. Feeling hard done by, she made a detour to the CID office on her way out. The solitary occupant of the gloomy room looked up as she entered and slid something out of sight up the sleeve of his jacket.

Sarah grinned. 'Afternoon, Ding-Dong. Practising for the children's party?'

DC 'Ding-Dong' Bell raised a face that would have looked good on a walrus with manic depression. Without rising from his desk, he reached up to flick a speck from the lapels of Sarah's uniform jacket and produced a bar of chocolate from thin air. 'Thought sweets would go down better than cards this year,' he said.

'You'll be a riot,' Sarah agreed.

'Shouldn't be at all surprised. I reckon some coppers breed delinquents special so they won't be out of work.'

'Are you busy?'

'Middling. Been giving Hoxton a hand tracing some air-raid victims they reckon might come from over this way. Don't like to bury what's left of them without a name, see. And then there's me poachers.'

'Poachers! In Kentish Town?'

'Up Hampstead really. But they lost the lorry down this way.'

'What on earth were they poaching?'

'Ducks, geese, whatever. Trying to lift them off the ponds. Or out of them.' He twitched his moustache in what might have passed for a smile in a light-hearted walrus. 'One of them went right in. If only the lads at Hampstead had a bloodhound they could have tracked him right to his door by the stink. What can I do for you, Sarge?'

'Would you look something up in the day book for me if you get time?'

She told him about the faceless baby. 'It was right at the beginning of the big raids.'

'What do you want to know?'

'Anything really. It might be connected to . . .' Just in time Sarah remembered the letter case was supposed to be confidential. 'Something else,' she finished lamely.

'Leave it with me,' Ding-Dong agreed.

He was gone by the time she returned to the station for a meal break, but a note in his neat script gave her details of the time and date of Elaine Lester's visit to the station, plus the information that her doctor had certified her. None of it seemed relevant to a spate of anonymous letters. Annoyed that she couldn't grasp the elusive memory that was sliding teasingly out of sight whenever she tried to stare it between the eyes, she folded the note into her pocket and went to collect a plate of corned-beef hash and carrots.

She managed to cadge tea and an acid drop from the shelterers that night, but by the time she made her weary way back to Eileen's on Sunday morning she was starving hungry and too tired to eat anything.

'On top of which,' she groaned to Eileen, slipping her shoes off, 'I've got to get the bits I left down Mornington Crescent, lug everything up to Vorley Road, and get back on duty by two o'clock. And . . .' She sniffed her sleeve. 'I need a bath.'

Eileen looked up from the pastry she was rolling. 'You go up. Get a bit of sleep. Leave those clothes off. I'll hang 'em out, let 'em air a bit. What's these things you left down Mornington?'

'Sheets, blankets, pots and pans. Mostly stuff I couldn't get in my case. A neighbour's storing them in their basement.'

'Write down the address. Maury can go fetch them.'

'No, no. Please don't bother, Eileen.' Sarah was ashamed to realise that her main emotion wasn't gratitude but alarm.

'It's all right,' Eileen said. 'He wouldn't dare thieve anything from someone stopping in my house.' Evidently Eileen wasn't quite as blind to her son's activities as she sometimes pretended to be. Draping the floury white pastry curtain over the chopped scrag end in her pie dish, she ordered Sarah upstairs.

Too tired to argue, Sarah made her way up to the chilly room, threw her uniform over the bed end, flopped under the covers in her underclothes, and closed her eyes.

When she woke up the uniform had gone. In fact all her clothes had disappeared, apart from a jumper, skirt and outdoor coat. She identified the noise that had woken her as a rhythmic 'slap-rattle' coming from outside. Sliding her feet on to the cold linoleum, she peered out of the window just in time to see a battered lorry with a torn canvas cover pulling around the corner of the square. Its scarred paintwork had probably been royal blue once, but now it had bleached to a washed-out pale eggshell. The rattling noise was coming from the badly secured tail-gate, which slapped back and forth with each bump in the road. Its visit was explained by the presence of various bundled and cardboard boxes tied with string that she found stacked at the bottom of the stairs.

'I've ironed your washing dry best I can,' Eileen said, bustling through from the kitchen. 'Maury's mate couldn't stop with his van but I reckon we can manage on the bus between us. I was hoping Pat would be home by now.'

'There's no need for you to come,' Sarah protested. 'I could get a lift from someone.'

'Well, I don't rightly know from who,' Eileen said, untying her apron strings. 'Won't be no delivery vans around on a Sunday. Tell you what,' she suggested. 'There's a taxi driver lives round Patshull Road. I'll get Sammy to run round, see if he's in.'

He wasn't, but his wife sent one of her own children round the pub to fetch him. However, by the time Sammy had ridden back in triumph and Sarah's worldly goods had been transported back up Junction Road, she was left with scarcely an hour to get herself unpacked, changed and back on duty.

Unpacking was simple. She threw everything into the room, dragged her uniform from the case, hung it behind the door, and unearthed a towel from one of the cardboard boxes. Her intention to take a bath was thwarted by a locked door and Miss Rawkins's apologetic trill from within. In the end she settled for filling the basin in her room with lukewarm water and washing in a haphazard application of soap and flannel. During this operation she became vaguely aware of voices from across the landing. The rhythm suggested two people, one male, one female, although their words were indistinguishable until the female voice rose sharply: 'No. I've told you. It's not possible. I've got to *go*.'

Me too, Sarah thought, struggling to pull on black stockings over damp legs. She shrugged on her tunic jacket and twisted her hair up underneath the helmet which was generally held to have been designed by a misanthropic sadist. It had gone quiet outside so she assumed that Nell De Groot's visitor had left, until she opened her door and found herself in the middle of a scene where three was going to be a crowd.

The woman – Nell presumably – saw her first. With a muffled cry she tried to push away the man, who was pinning her against the wall by her shoulders. For a second he resisted, then Sarah moved into the periphery of his vision. He glanced round, then straightened up, allowing Nell to slip free and pull her robe closed over her breasts.

'Sorry,' Sarah apologised. 'I didn't mean to interrupt.' She smiled at the other woman. 'I'm Sarah McNeill. New tenant.'

'How do you do?' Nell murmured. Making no attempt to introduce herself, she stepped back into the room and shut the door.

In the meantime, her friend had thrust his fingers through his fair hair and adjusted the jacket of an already immaculate RAF uniform. 'Well,' he grinned, 'mustn't keep the guardians of our law and order from their duties, must I, otherwise you might throw me in the clink. Good afternoon.' The handsome head nodded in an affable gesture as he flashed another boyish grin at her, then he was gone, bounding down the stairs with an easy, long-legged grace.

Sarah remained where she was until she heard the front door slam and the throaty roar of a car.

The landing was poorly lit, and the RAF officer had been the epitome of charm a second later, but just for a moment, when he'd first caught her eye, she'd had the sensation of gazing into pure evil.

Chapter 11

'Long time since you and me had a Sunday off together,' Len Shaw remarked, folding up his newspaper.

Glancing up from the ironing, Betty smiled at him. 'I know. It's nice, isn't it? Like before.'

She didn't say before what; it wasn't necessary. Everything now was defined as 'before the war' or 'since this lot started'.

'When you on again?' Len asked, sauntering over to casually lift the lid on a saucepan.

'Tomorrow. Doing-Her-Bit's on tonight,' Betty answered, referring to a Hampstead housewife who worked two days a week as her contribution to the war effort.

Len grunted, peering hopefully into the depths of another saucepan.

Betty suppressed a smile. For a man who expressed casual indifference to food, Len had always shown a healthy interest in whatever was going into his stomach. Watching him now continuing his exploration of the stove's contents, she felt a sudden rush of love twist in her heart and an increasingly familiar terror sweep through her. Like all firemen's wives she'd always lived with the possibility of a fatal accident whilst he was on duty. But prior to the war it had been easier to push it to the back of her mind. Now, thanks to her own job, it was always under her nose.

Her thoughts tumbled back to the young fireman who'd lost his leg at the docks, and the blinded one who'd be invalided out to live in a world of half-seen shadows. The terrible images wouldn't go away. In desperation, she cast about for something normal to say, and asked: 'What was in the post?'

'Post? Wasn't any.'

'But I heard the letter box go early. Just after you went down.'

'It wasn't for us. Addressed to number fourteen. I took it over.' He poked at a large china basin capped with linen which was bubbling gently on the gas. 'What's this?'

'Pudding. I got some syrup.'

'Shouldn't really,' he protested half-heartedly. 'Getting a bit of a belly on me.' He slapped two hands flatly over his broad leather belt.

'Rubbish. Who wants a man with less meat on him than a broth bone?'

'Daresay you're right. Still, not sure I can get through this lot.'

Betty folded the pillow cases, the warm scent of slightly scorched cotton rising up into her nostrils. 'I daresay I can find someone who'll be glad of the leftovers.'

'Like who?'

Busying herself with her sheets, Betty said briskly that she expected her on the top floor of number seven wouldn't refuse. 'She's four little ones, Len, and scarcely a few shillings coming in now her man's a prisoner-of-war. Except for what the public assistance hands out. And God knows that's not much.'

'Yeah, OK.' Len grinned. 'Didn't say you couldn't, did I? I suppose the meat ration's gone the same way?'

'Half,' Betty admitted.

'Anything else?'

'Bit of sugar. She wants to make some pink mice for their Christmas stockings.'

She gathered up an armful of the fresh ironing, and would have made her way upstairs with it, but he slid his arms round her, locking his hands in front and pulling her on to his lap. 'What a girl.'

'I'm hardly that any more, Len.'

'You'll always be the only girl for me, my love. Same little smasher I first saw on the Oxford Street tram in a daft hat.'

'There was nothing daft about my hat I'll have you know, Len Shaw. It was a cloche. Very fashionable. *And* from Madame Louise's Millinery in the West End. I saved up the half-crown my mum gave me back from my wage packet for weeks for that hat.'

'It was horrible. Hid your curls. Always fancied them curls.'

As proof, he buried his mouth in them and kissed the top of her head. At the same time he moved one of his hands in slow, easy circles, massaging the lower half of her stomach.

'Len,' she murmured, blushing pinkly.

'What?' The hand moved lower.

'Oh, Len.' She wriggled round, searching for his lips.

Hitching up her skirt, he found the flesh above her stocking top.

'Len,' she protested. 'We can't. It's Sunday morning.'

'So?'

'It doesn't seem right.'

'Does to me.'

She was pressed close enough to know exactly how it felt for him.

'Come on, love,' Len murmured thickly, dragging the pile of ironing from her arms and dropping it to the floor.

Betty pressed her lips more firmly on his. The rat-tat of the door knocker reverberated in time with her frantically beating heart.

'Leave it,' Len groaned. 'They'll go away.'

But the urgent tattoo on the knocker suggested the visitor had every intention of staying on the Shaws' step until he'd either beaten his way through the door panels or worn his arm out in the process.

'It might be the station, Len. Maybe you're wanted on duty.'

'Sodding hell,' Len muttered.

'*Len*. I won't have that language. Not in my house.'

'Sorry. But it had better be Buckingham Palace or Windsor Castle burning down at least.'

It was neither. It was, in fact, a small, untidy boy who wanted to know if Len could take a fare up the Archway right off.

'Fare?' Len repeated blankly. 'What do you think I am, son, a bus driver?'

'Taxi driver. Ain't that your taxi, mister?' He pointed to the black cab parked in front of the Shaws' house.

'Next door.' Len jerked an angry thumb.

'Oh, ta, mister.'

The boy skipped off, sunnily oblivious to Len's seething frustration. His wife pointed out it was all his own fault. 'It would be outside next door's gate if you hadn't told him not to park in front of the water hydrant.'

'Yeah, well, so he shouldn't,' Len grumbled, making to shut the front door again.

Before he could get it closed, Betty raised a hand in greeting to someone on the pavement. 'Hello, going visiting?'

Hatty Miller stopped by the front gate, twisting her handbag in her plump fingers. 'No, not exactly. Just a bit of a walk.'

'Ruth not with you?' Betty asked, since it was rare to see Hatty out without her cousin.

'No. She's having a bit of a lie-in. She goes on duty this afternoon.'

Betty waited for Hatty to move away. But the younger woman remained by the gate, hands rotating the handbag whilst she ground at the pavement with one toe. Betty was at a loss; it seemed rude to shut the door in Hatty's face. 'Have you got time for a cuppa?'

'Oh yes. Thank you.'

The enthusiasm with which her half-hearted invitation was greeted surprised Betty. But having offered she made the best of it, leading Hatty back into the kitchen and ignoring Len's furious look.

'Excuse the mess. I just . . . er . . . dropped the ironing.' She stooped to pick it up, but Hatty bent eagerly to the task, taking up each item and folding it with exaggerated care.

Filling the kettle and measuring out the precious tea ration, Betty was conscious of Len lolling at the kitchen table. His whole attitude radiated annoyance. Well, it wasn't her fault they'd been interrupted, was it? The remembrance of what they'd have been doing now but for the little boy's unexpected arrival caused a slight flush to stain her cheeks and a smile to curve the corners of her mouth. She tried to catch Len's eye and convey the sense of intimacy she was feeling, but Len's attention was firmly fixed on Hatty's intrusive figure.

One of his shirts was now folded in two across the large bosom, as Hatty lined up the two sleeves. 'You've forgotten to starch this one.'

'I haven't starched any of them,' Betty admitted. 'There's just no time these days to do a starch rinse.'

'What a pity. I think a starched shirt's much smarter, don't you, Mr Shaw?'

'Can't say I notice,' Len grunted.

'Oh, I expect you're just saying that. Men like to be looked after proper really. Uncle Duggie always has to have his collars starched right.'

'Yes, well, I daresay in his job it's necessary,' Betty said, setting down the teapot on the cloth rather more firmly than normal.

'Yes, it is,' Hatty admitted. 'But I'd do it anyway, even if he were a coalman or something. I like running the house properly.'

'How long have you been doing it?'

'Since I was fourteen.' Hatty spooned four large helpings of the Shaws' sugar ration into her cup and stirred vigorously. 'Well, since I was eleven really, when Auntie Doris died. But I had to go to school as well then.'

'I'd have thought it was rather boring, keeping house for your uncle.'

'Oh no!' Hatty was shocked at the suggestion. She'd never had the slightest wish to do anything else except have her own little house to look after. That first week after her fourteenth birthday, when she'd put the housekeeping money in her purse, closed the front door and set off up the shops like a real housewife, had been the proudest day of her life.

'Aren't you cooking for him today?' Betty asked, with one eye on the clock, which was ticking away this precious day that she'd planned to spend with Len.

'He's gone down the pub. He always has a pint Sunday mornings. I put our dinner in before I come out. Got a nice big piece of liver off the ration.'

'That was lucky.' Betty took a quick glance at the tea in Hatty's cup. She'd scarcely touched it.

'Yes. I'm stewing it, with a bit of onion. What are you having?'

'Steak and kidney pie. It's one of Len's favourites.'

'Is it, Mr Shaw? I didn't know that. I could make it for you sometime. I've a real light hand at pastry. Like my mum, Uncle Duggie says.'

'I doubt you could get enough steak to cater for the whole of Good Hope Station. Or even one watch, if it comes to that,' Betty pointed out. 'Excuse me,' she said, getting up and opening the oven as a warning scent of burning started to drift across the kitchen. The tray of tarts was already over-crisped round the edges, their thin layer of jam bubbling almost to a treacle-like consistency.

'Had some pastry trimmings left over,' she muttered, seeing the enquiring lift of Len's eyebrow.

'Top of number seven?'

'Yes.' She flushed and then, seeing the glint in his eye, giggled.

'Who's number seven?'

'Oh, nobody. Just some POW's kids Betty's lending a hand with.'

'Oh.' Hatty regarded the tarts with a look of such un-disguised hunger that Betty felt obliged to offer.

'Thanks.' Hatty bit into the hot jam with scant regard for her scalded mouth. Crumbs stuck to her lips and she greedily licked them off.

'How are they?'

'Bit tough,' Hatty mumbled, chewing steadily. 'Need more fat.'

'Yes, well, that's not easy these days, is it?' Betty bridled. It just wasn't done to eat other people's rations then criticise the food.

'Suppose not. I didn't mean to sound rude, Mrs Shaw, it's just I've always had a knack with pastry.'

'Like your mother. You said.' Betty tried to smooth the sharp edge from her tone and asked more pleasantly: 'What happened to your parents, Hatty?'

'They died when I was four. In a fire.'

107

'Oh. I'm sorry.' Betty had seen the devastated survivors of fires throughout her married life. Her annoyance at the implied criticism of her cooking melted. 'Did they live around here?'

Hatty gulped convulsively, sending the last morsel of hot pastry down her ample neck. 'No. They were in service. In Wales. Dad drove the car and Mum looked after this old lady, nursing and reading to her like. She was posh, my mum. Least Uncle Duggie says she was. I don't remember her much.' She eyed the rack of cooling tarts hopefully and smiled with gratitude when Betty got up and slid another one on to her plate. 'Oh, ta ever so much.'

'Were you in the fire too?'

'They said I was. But I don't remember that bit either. We had a cottage by the house. It was a big house, really posh. They put me in there with the cook after me mum and dad died. Only I didn't know they had. She said they'd gone off to heaven to live with the angels. I cried buckets because I wanted to go live with them too.'

Her tears had worried the elderly cook. She was basically a kind-hearted woman, but with little experience of children and a demanding household to cater for. So she'd offered the heartbroken little girl food as a consolation. It had worked. The tears had magically dried at the sight of a large slab of lardy cake. For the next month, whenever Hatty had wanted comfort, it had come via cakes, pudding and sweets. It still did.

'When Uncle Duggie come to fetch me,' Hatty explained, sliding a glistening tongue over the jam film, 'I thought me dad had come back from heaven. Me dad and Uncle Duggie were twins, see.'

She recalled with painful clarity the moment she'd flung herself across the vast tiled kitchen floor to hug her 'dadda's' knees. They'd gently disengaged her and explained that this wasn't her father and she was to call him 'Uncle Duggie'. She'd supposed at the time it must have something to do with him visiting heaven. Maybe they gave you a new name up there. It was only later, when he'd taken her on the train back to Camden Town and she'd found he lived with her Auntie Doris instead of

108

her mum, that she'd started to vaguely understand that this was a different person.

'Mind, they treated me the same as Ruth,' she assured Betty. 'It was just like I was their real daughter.'

'I expect they felt you were. I've heard people can love an adopted child just as much as if they'd had it themselves.'

She hadn't meant to say it, and the tightening of the muscles along Len's jawline warned her that she shouldn't have. Quickly she asked Hatty if her mother's family hadn't wanted her too.

'No. They didn't.' Hatty stared across the table with a hard expression in her normally placid brown eyes. 'They didn't want me mum, either. I wrote me grandmother once, asked if I could have a picture of me mum. I don't have none, see, and I thought they must have one they could spare. I got this letter back saying as how she didn't have no daughter and all photos of that person had been destroyed when she went against her family's wishes and married a member of the lower classes. And she said she wished to have no connection with me and I wasn't to attempt to contact her again. So I didn't, and I wouldn't, not if she begged me on her bended knees,' Hatty finished defiantly.

This speech, the longest she'd ever heard Hatty make, had left Betty at a loss for words. Luckily Len jumped into the silence.

'You know, love, I really fancy a pint. Don't mind if I pop down The Castle, do you?'

'Of course I don't. Half an hour?'

Standing, Len shrugged his jacket on. 'Walk you to the end of the road, Hat?'

'What? Oh yes, all right. Thank you for the tea, Mrs Shaw.'

'A pleasure,' Betty murmured, silently blessing Len for getting the woman out of her kitchen.

'I'll bring you a bottle back,' Len said, standing aside to allow Hatty to precede him out of the front door.

'Don't be long,' Betty whispered, standing on tiptoe to brush his lips. 'There's always this afternoon.' A brief squeeze on her bottom told her he'd understood, before he strolled out to where Hatty was waiting.

He waited until they were out of sight of the house before he gripped Hatty's elbow in a none-too-gentle hand and asked her what the hell she thought she was playing at.

'I'm sorry, Len. I didn't mean to come inside, honest. I was just waiting to see if you come out.'

'Waiting? Dear God, woman, how long had you been hanging around out there?'

'Not long. About ten minutes. Can I come to the pub with you?'

'No, of course you can't. I told you, we can't be together in public.'

'But I never see you in private no more. I went down the Chalk Farm house the other day when you was off duty in the afternoon. I thought perhaps you might . . .'

'My mate's coming back, needs the house again. You better not go there no more.'

'Oh? Well where, then?'

'I'll think of something. But don't go round my house again, understand?'

'Yes, Len.' They'd reached the junction with the high street, and despite the war and the lack of church bells it still had a Sunday feel about it. 'I could look after you better than her,' Hatty said, watching a family process past the empty shops in their Sunday-best outfits. 'I'd starch your shirts no matter how busy I was. And we could have babies too. Doesn't Mrs Shaw want children?'

'You leave Betty out of this. I've said. She's my wife. I'll tell her in my own time. These things have got to be done right. Now you go home like a good girl and get your uncle's dinner, all right?'

'All right, Len. But you'll tell her soon, won't you, promise?'

'Yeah, I promise. Get along with you now.'

For a dreadful moment he thought she was about to kiss him, but instead she smiled shyly and made her way towards the railway bridge. Len watched in despair as her ungainly figure swayed out of sight. He must have been mad picking one so close to home. But how was he to know she was going to take a few tumbles so seriously? He'd been giving her the cold shoulder for months in the hope the stupid woman would take the hint.

Why couldn't she go and get herself a boyfriend? Probably, he thought crossing the road and pushing his way into the public bar, because she couldn't find anyone who wanted to be seen with a mound of blubber. He couldn't think why he had now. Except he'd been bored that spring afternoon, and fed up because his wife was at work. And Hatty had been an easy conquest. It had never amounted to more than a few hours down his mate's house, and even that had been a bit of a farce. She'd actually turned up with a load of shopping one time and insisted on cooking dinner before they went up to the bedroom.

He certainly had no intention of leaving Betty for her, whatever the silly cow chose to believe. Because as he'd told his wife that morning, when it came to love, Betty was truly the only girl for him. He sipped his half in contented anticipation of the afternoon to come.

In the meantime, the only girl for him twisted the scrap of paper she'd found sticking to the lid of the dustbin. It looked like the torn corner of an envelope, and the smudged local postmark said that it had been franked at 7 p.m. the previous night. So it must have been delivered first post this morning. Yet Len had said the only post had been for number fourteen. Bending down, she poked amongst the debris at the bottom of the bin. Two more paper scraps were caught amongst the decomposing peelings. One said 'Mr . . .' and the other '. . . everyone . . .'. A bitter December breeze howled across the garden, sending up swirls of dust. Betty shuddered convulsively. Tipping the bin, she scrambled amongst the mess. She collected a palmful of paper confetti, but none of it was readable.

Returning to the house, she moved through to the parlour and stared through the windows crisscrossed with paper strips to protect against blast damage. The family at number fourteen were just going out, all ten of them erupting on to the street in a welter of kids, prams, pushchairs, adults, grans and bathchairs.

Taking a deep breath, Betty stepped into the hall and opened her front door.

Chapter 12

With a sigh, Hatty wandered home. Len was too kind for his own good, but that was one of the reasons why she loved him.

When she'd told Betty that all she ever wanted to do was keep house, she'd been speaking the truth. But over the past couple of years she'd gradually become aware that being a housekeeper for her uncle and cousin wasn't enough. She wanted her own home; with a husband and children in it that she could love and care for.

None of the local boys had ever shown any interest in her. Occasionally Ruth had made a boy who wanted to walk her home from a dance produce a friend for Hatty. But they'd been awful spotty, silly boys, with sweaty hands, who'd aimed slobbering kisses on her in the dark by the railway arches before muttering that they'd see her around. They weren't her idea of what a husband should be, and she'd begun to think she'd never meet the right man, until that day last spring when she'd gone for a walk up Parliament Hill Fields and run into Mr Shaw.

'What's this, Firewoman Miller?' he'd asked. 'They going hungry down Good Hope tonight then?'

Blushing because he was big and strong and she'd hardly dared speak to him when he took the women for hydrant practice, she mumbled that it was her day off. And then daringly confided that Ruth was on duty and her Uncle Duggie had gone to collect a body from Winchester and wouldn't be back tonight.

'It's the first time I've ever been in the house on my own all night, Mr Shaw . . . it feels ever so funny.'

'Really? Well, I don't like to think of you being lonely, Hatty. Tell you what, walk over the Heath with me for a bit. My Betty's

113

on duty too, so I'm at a bit of a loose end myself.'

So they'd walked and talked. At least he'd talked and she'd listened. And when it got dark, he'd taken her into the Bull and Bush and bought her cherry brandies. She hadn't much cared for the taste, but it had seemed rude not to drink them when he'd paid for them. Afterwards, when she'd begun to feel dizzy, he'd seen her safely home and helped her upstairs to lie down.

What had happened next had come as a surprise, but she hadn't liked to complain. He was, after all, a station officer and he seemed to think she ought to be enjoying herself. Managing a smile, she'd assured him it had been 'Very nice, thank you, Mr Shaw.'

'Good. Well, maybe we could do it again sometime. Not here, though.'

'Why not?'

'Well, em . . . your Uncle Duggie . . . and there's Betty . . .'

'Would she mind then . . . ?'

She knew from his expression that she'd said something silly. That was when he'd explained that what they'd just done was the sort of thing that only married people got up to normally.

'Shouldn't you be doing it with Mrs Shaw then, Mr Shaw?' she'd asked.

'Well . . . yes . . . but see, the thing is, Hatty, Betty's not that keen. Fact is, we don't really have a proper marriage.'

'Why don't you leave her then? I wouldn't mind having a proper marriage, Mr Shaw.' She'd snuggled closer, revelling in his strength.

'Yeah, well, I will. Later. I'd have to pick the right moment, Hatty. Meantime, promise me you won't tell anyone about us. It might get back to Betty, see? Before I can tell her myself.'

Reasoning that if they were doing something that only married people usually did, that must mean he intended to marry her sometime, she'd promised readily. And had been thrilled when he asked her to meet him at his friend's house in Chalk Farm next time they were both off duty. She'd even managed to keep back some rationed goods so she could cook him a proper dinner, just like a wife would.

She'd done her steamed pudding, which everyone said was

114

her best dish, and a big pork chop which had used up all her meat ration coupons for that week. She'd planned to do a cottage pie next time, but he'd become really busy at work and never seemed to have time to get to Chalk Farm. Still, it wouldn't be long, surely, before he found the right time to explain things to Mrs Shaw and get a divorce. And then they could be together all the time.

Cheered up by this heartening thought, Hatty hurried home. She opened the door to be met with a demand to know where the devil she'd been.

'Man, Hat, cannot live by bread alone. Or in this case veg. Especially when the taters are burnt and the cabbage is still raw.'

'Oh Ruth, you could have lit the gas under it.' Hatty flicked on a burner under the saucepan.

'Didn't have time.' Ruth shrugged, twisting combs into her hair. 'Must run, I'm gonna be late on duty. Some of us have to work.'

Hatty opened her mouth to complain about this unfair barb, but Ruth had already whisked out. Her sharp voice drifted back to them a second later, along with an icy blast from outside: 'Oh Gawd, it's you again. I thought there was supposed to be a war on.'

'Got to be back in camp at twenty-three fifty-nine. That's one minute to midnight to you.'

'I know what it is, thank you, Stan Wilkins. We ain't entirely ignorant in the fire service, you know.'

Hatty and Duggie both stepped back into the hall to greet their unexpected, if persistent, visitor. Duggie echoed Ruth's question about Stan's apparently limitless leave.

'Work in the office that issues the passes, don't I?' Stan said, taking their interest as an invitation to leave the step and come in. 'When I'm not scrubbing the blee . . . I mean when we aren't doing bull. Honest to God, Mr Miller,' he added earnestly, 'I thought the army would be dead exciting. Going abroad and fighting Germans and everything.' Instead of which he was stuck in an office not six miles from home, laboriously picking out letters on an ancient typewriter or scrubbing floors until they were fit for the officers to scoff banquets off.

'See yer then!' Ruth said.

' 'Ang on, it's you I come to see,' Stan protested. 'Thought you might want to come up the pictures with me or something.'

'I'm working.'

'Well, what about in the week?'

Ruth hesitated, one hand on the door latch. 'When in the week?'

'You say.'

'I ain't working Thursday night.'

'Thursday it is, then.'

'You that certain you can get the night off?' Duggie asked. 'Eh, that's a cushy billet you've found yourself, Stan Wilkins.'

Stan knew it was. But he didn't want a soft job, did he? He wanted to be a daredevil fighting hero just like them flaming film stars Ruth was so stuck on. In fact one of his favourite fantasies involved Ruth handing him a white feather and him – Stanley Wilkins – dashing off with a devil-may-care laugh to single-handedly defeat an entire regiment of parachutists and returning to a hero's welcome (medals and parades optional). At which point Ruth would fall on his neck, beg forgiveness, take back the feather and give herself to him completely.

This last scene in his fantasy was particularly gratifying and tended to feature a lot in his dreams as he lay wide awake listening to the twenty other blokes snoring in his barrack hut. But the way things stood at the moment, the only thing he could do to an enemy paratrooper was drop the damn typewriter on his toes or belt him with a floor mop.

He hastily assured the Millers that the adjutant was gonna put in a word for him and get him a transfer to a fighting unit.

'Well, make sure he don't do it before Thursday,' Ruth said tartly.

Banging the door shut, she pulled her AFS cap down more firmly against the breeze, which was becoming stronger and colder, with the icy threat of sleet to come. Head down, she hurried along into Kentish Town Road.

The engine caught her attention mainly because the road was virtually free of other traffic. For a second she mistook it for a fighter and glanced instinctively into the grey sky to see whether it was 'ours' or 'theirs'. There was nothing, unless it was above the clouds. Dropping her eyes, she found herself gazing at a green convertible which was hurtling down the street towards her. It was him, she was sure of it. Nell De Groot's RAF boyfriend.

The convertible's top was down again, giving her a clear view of the driver. Without thinking about it, Ruth raised one hand and waved as he swept past on the opposite side of the road. She'd expected a wave in return – or possibly to be ignored completely. But to her amazement he braked, slung the car into a tight turn, bumped up the pavement and came to rest by the kerb a few feet from her.

Ruth gaped.

'Hello.'

'I, er,' Ruth gulped. It was as if Clark Gable or Leslie Howard had stepped right off the screen and spoken to her.

'Fire station, wasn't it?' he said, taking off his cap and running a hand through his thick hair. 'Saw you up there the other day. With a fat girl.'

'Hatty,' Ruth said, recovering her voice.

'Short for Harriet?'

'Short for Richmal Harriet. She was named after her dad, me uncle. He was Richard Henry. Only me mum thought Richmal was too fancy for around here, so she said to use her middle name . . .' Ruth felt a hot flush setting her cheeks on fire. She could hear herself babbling but didn't seem able to shut up. It was as if her mouth had taken on a life of its own. Desperately she drew in an enormous breath of air and held it.

'Well, that deals with Hatty.' He grinned. 'Now how about you? What did your mum call you?'

The breath was released in an explosive gasp. 'Ruth.'

'Nice to make your acquaintance, Ruth. Would you like a lift?' He opened the passenger door.

Would she! She flung herself into the leather seat and directed a dazzling smile at him. 'Oh, thanks. Thanks a lot . . . Mr, er . . . I mean Captain, em . . .' She looked at his insignia in bewilderment. What rank was he?

'Call me Paul. It's easier.'

Ruth felt she wouldn't have cared if she'd had to address him as Nebuchadnezzar. Wriggling back into the seat with sigh of bliss, she stretched out her legs and regarded her navy trousers regretfully. Why had she had to be on duty? If only she could have been wearing stockings and maybe even the famous five-guinea shoes with the diamanté heels.

'Hang on!'

The car shot forward, slamming her back into her seat. A gust of wind caught her hat and would have whipped it off if she hadn't got there first. Thwarted, the gale dragged at her hair instead, sending locks dancing and slapping round her face. One of her combs spun out, hit the windscreen and dropped to the floor.

'Sorry,' Paul shouted. 'Should have put the top up. Only I prefer it down myself.'

So did Ruth. How else would anyone see her? Squinting against the icy breeze, she desperately scanned the pavements that were rushing past for a familiar face. Surely there must be someone she knew out and about? But there wasn't a soul. She could have cried with frustration.

He drew up outside the fire station and she glanced hopefully at the building. It was so still it could have been the *Marie Celeste* of the fire service.

'This is where you wanted to go, isn't it?' He was obviously waiting for her to get out of the car.

'Er, yes, it is. Ta ever so much.' She groped for something else to say. 'Me and Hat used to stand on the roof up there, watch you fighting in the Battle of Britain last summer.' A thought struck her. Maybe he had an office job like Stan. 'You do fly planes, don't you?'

'Spitfires.'

A Spitfire pilot! Ruth felt she could have died of happiness at that moment. She thought desperately for something else to say. Inspiration had deserted her. There was nothing to do but get out of the car.

'Ruth.'

She spun back so fast her heel caught in a hastily repaired

118

paving stone and nearly tipped over. Managing to save herself by grabbing the windscreen, she flushed with annoyance at her own gaucheness.

'You forgot this.'

'Oh yes. Ta.' She took the comb he was holding out and started to back away again.

'Ruth.'

'Yes?' Without thinking, she put her hand to her head. The other comb was still firmly in place.

He saw the gesture and half smiled. 'I was wondering if you'd care to come out with me sometime? Cocktails or something?'

'Cocktails,' Ruth purred, with the casual indifference of one who was in the habit of sipping them every night. 'How lovely.'

'It's a date then. I'll ring you.'

He was gone before she could shout out the station's number. But on reflection, she decided, making her way slowly inside, he'd probably called Nell here. The thought of Nell caused her no qualms of conscience at all. The icy female driver had never made any attempt at friendship with the other girls at the station. Well fair enough, Ruth thought, sauntering into the watchroom and exchanging a few minutes of light-hearted flirting with the male auxiliary who'd been manning the phones. If Snooty Miss Grooty thought she was a cut above them all, she was in for a nasty surprise. Come to think of it, she probably gave the poor bloke frostbite every time he stuck his arm round for a bit of a cuddle.

On this cheering thought Ruth checked her boards, found that all of her appliances and watch crews were on station, and settled down for the afternoon.

By six o'clock she was bored stiff. There had been no calls – not even a chimney fire – all afternoon, and the sub-officer had turned the crews out for yard exercises so that there was no one to chat to in the watchroom. The arrival of a stranger with two small boys in tow was a welcome diversion.

'Can I help yer?' Ruth asked.

He took off his hat and held it awkwardly whilst he used the same hand to thrust back thick auburn hair. 'We're just having a look round the station.'

'That ain't allowed . . .' Ruth began to explain, before he forestalled her by telling her the sub-officer had given the visit his official blessing.

'The boys are really keen on fire engines.'

'Want to be firemen when yer grow up, do you?'

Sammy and Nafnel nodded eagerly, their minds on the five bob they'd been promised to pretend they wanted to look round Good Hope Station.

'Well, it's nice of yer dad to give you a bit of a treat, ain't it?' Ruth smiled.

The larger one informed her his dad was dead. The smaller one thought his probably was too, but he wasn't sure because his mum hadn't ever told him. 'But I don't care anyhow, because I'm gonna get a new one.'

'This is Mr Stamford,' the first one explained. 'Me mum cleans for him. And does his washing and stuff.'

'He ain't her fancy man, though,' the second one told her as he pulled open drawers in the watchroom desk. ' 'Cos I asked. And she whacked me.'

'I hope we're not in your way, Miss, em . . .'

'Ruth Miller.'

'Jack Stamford.' He offered her an awkward handshake. 'Sorry. Arm's stiff. Old wound.'

'Dunkirk?'

'Er, no . . . I'm not in the army.'

'He's a copper,' Nafnel piped up again.

Which made him even less interesting in Ruth's eyes. Nonetheless she showed them over the small watchroom with good grace and suggested they might find it more exciting to go outside and watch the firemen drilling. 'They may let you have a sit in one of the engines and ring the bell. Bet you've never done that before.'

' 'Course I 'ave,' Sammy said scornfully. 'Me brother's a fireman.'

Jack caught Ruth's look of fleeting surprise. Behind her back Nafnel took hold of both his lips between forefinger and thumb and twisted them in a clear message to Sammy to keep his mouth buttoned. Obviously, Jack thought ruefully, the

120

quicker-witted little boy had realised that this was supposed to be an undercover operation.

He'd been wrestling for the past couple of days with the problem of how to continue with his 'unofficial official' probe into the anonymous letters. In the end he'd been forced to ring Superintendent Dunn and insist that at least the commanding officers at the fire stations must be told what was going on and allow him access to the station premises. 'I'll be discreet,' he said firmly. 'But I'm blowed if I'm going to hang around in pubs hoping to bump into off-duty firemen.' The fire service HQ had, surprisingly enough, raised no objection to allowing him to make free with their buildings. The magic words 'national security' were an open sesame these days.

'Is your brother stationed here?' Ruth asked, taking a sheaf of papers from Nafnel's hands and returning them to the drawer.

' 'Course not.' Sammy's chest swelled with pride. 'He's not an auxiliary. *He's* a Red Rider.'

Jack hastily made the introductions: 'This is Sammy O'Day. And this is Naf . . . Nathaniel Starkey.'

'Watcha,' Nafnel said casually.

''Lo.' Sammy grinned. The resemblance to his oldest brother was immediately obvious.

'You're Pat's brother,' Ruth laughed.

Sammy grew a little taller.

'He's nice, your brother,' Ruth said. He was nowhere near the demi-god who'd just invited her out for cocktails, of course, but you wouldn't mind being seen walking out with Pat, though apparently she wasn't going to get the chance. The smaller boy told her roundly that Pat was going to marry Mrs Goodwin, a teacher up Riley Street school, and he was going to live with them.

Startled that her face had given away her thoughts, Ruth tossed her curls, dislodged a comb, and said that she was spoken for, thanks.

'Is he a fireman?' Jack asked, trying to regain control of the conversation.

'No.' A self-satisfied tilt turned up the corners of Ruth's mouth. 'He's a pilot. Spitfires, actually.'

121

'Dangerous job,' Jack said.

'Yes. But Paul is ever so brave. And a wonderful flyer, of course,' Ruth sparkled, endowing the real-life Paul with all the qualities she'd wished on her dream lover for so long.

'I'm sure.' Jack looked round the gloomy watchroom with its smells of stale perfume, cigarettes and sweat and its perpetually burning light bulb. 'But then we all have to be brave in our own way these days, don't we?' He silently prayed that that hadn't sounded as patronising to Ruth as it had to him.

Her expression suggested she couldn't find anything very heroic about her own situation. 'I suppose so. I mean, there's the bombs and things . . .'

'Nothing easy about being a fireman these days,' Jack suggested.

'Oh, no.' Ruth's face cleared. Of course it stood to reason that Pat's little brother wanted to hear him praised a bit.

'So,' Jack ploughed on, aware that he wasn't handling this very well, 'it's a shame someone's out to make things even more dangerous for them.'

'Are they?'

'Well, these letters must have caused bad feeling. Not the kind of problem you want in a job where you've got to rely on your crew mates, is it?'

'What letters?'

'The anonymous ones. Don't tell me you haven't heard about them. I'd have thought most of the men around here wanted to chat to a pretty girl like you.' Inwardly Jack groaned. Now he sounded like an elderly Dutch uncle. If he stayed off on sick leave much longer he might as well take Dunn's advice and collect an early pension.

Ruth admitted she had heard of one or two. 'Did Pat report it to the police then? Are you going to arrest someone for writing them?'

'Good Lord, no.' Jack attempted a friendly smile which unfortunately turned into a grimace as a shaft of pain shot through his arm from elbow to shoulder. 'I'm on sick leave. Pat just asked me to ask around. Put a stop to them before they cause any more bad feeling. Have you had any yourself?'

Her 'no' was a bit too quick. Just like the other half-a-dozen.

After two hours of hanging around whilst Sammy and Nafnel watched ladder and hose drills and climbed over the engines, Jack found the recipients divided into two distinct classes: those like Snakey, the mess manager, who laughed the whole thing off; and the others with whom the letters, for whatever reason, had hit a target. One group cheerfully admitted to their receipt, the others denied ever having laid eyes on one. Both – for different reasons – had destroyed letters and envelopes. At present he was left trying to investigate a non-crime with zero evidence. It would have been easier trying to nail cobwebs to the ceiling, he thought ruefully, leading the boys home.

With his mind on his problems, he'd turned down Agar Street without thinking. A warning shout from Sammy jerked him out of his day-dream just as a car flew out of the yard behind the police station. Its unmasked headlights had already alerted his subconscious to its dispatch on an emergency call, before the driver switched the bell on and sped away at high speed.

'Cor,' Sammy breathed. 'Reckon they're gonna nick some-one, Mr Stamford?'

'I reckon,' Jack agreed. He was half tempted to go into the station and ask what was going on. *It's got nothing to do with you*, he reminded himself.

He was wrong.

Chapter 13

Pat was waiting for him when he returned the boys to the O'Day house.

'Any luck, Mr Stamford?' he asked as Sammy and Nafnel thundered down the passage to the back kitchen, attracted by the interesting scents of spice and treacle.

Wondering if Pat would ever get round to calling him 'Jack', he admitted no progress to date. 'And to be honest, Pat, I don't think I'm going to get much further with this unless I can actually lay my hands on some of the letters.'

'I could ask around,' Pat said doubtfully. 'See if anyone will let me have one. Trouble is, see, if it says something bad, they'd just think I wanted it to take the mickey. You know, have a bit of a laugh with the other lads. What would you be wanting it for, fingerprints?'

'Perhaps. Although there are other things. Postmarks, type of paper.'

He hadn't mentioned Dunn's visit to the O'Days, nor had he told them about Special Branch's theories regarding the probable author of the anonymous letters. Or, if it came to that, the real reason for Sarah's hasty departure to new lodgings. Pat still imagined he was going through this whole farce as a favour to himself. It made Jack feel uncomfortable. Whilst he'd never discussed a confidential case with the O'Days, he'd never actually lied to them either.

His discomfort was compounded by the presence of his daughter in Eileen's kitchen. The little girl was twirling round in a white robe whilst an insubstantial pair of wire and paper wings wobbled on her back. Eileen and a fair-haired young woman were watching this performance. Seeing the hungry expression in Pat's eyes as they fixed on the younger woman, Jack wondered just how much of Nafnel's confident prediction of a marriage between Pat and Rose Goodwin was wishful thinking on the little boy's part. Rose's first marriage had been violent and unhappy. And, as he knew from experience, a failure made you much warier of plunging into a close relationship again. It wasn't just fear of the unknown the second time around; there were the known-and-perhaps-to-be-repeated mistakes to be contended with as well. Looking back dispassionately on his own marriage, he could see now it had been based mainly on a mutual physical attraction. He and Neelie had very little in common once they got out of bed. After he'd got over the initial shock of outrage and loneliness when she had walked out on him, he had started to recognise that his main emotion at the split had been a growing relief.

'Here's your dad, love,' Eileen said. 'Show him what a lovely angel you make.'

Annaliese shuffled round, arms extended, her bare feet peeping from the bottom of a cut-down man's shirt. She watched for Eileen's reaction rather than her father's. Once again Jack was depressingly conscious of the lack of closeness between himself and his only child.

'What's this for then?' he asked. 'Fancy-dress party?'

'It's for the school Nativity play. I did tell you,' Eileen said. Her voice had a sharper edge than normal. 'It was just after you started . . .' She gestured towards the injured arm that he was cradling inside his jacket. Her expression, if not her words, said plainly: *just after you started feeling sorry for yourself.*

'Yes, of course you did.' He regarded his daughter beneath the wings which had slipped during her twirling to give her the appearance of a slightly disreputable cherub. 'Well, what a beautiful angel you make.'

Annaliese regarded him solemnly from between two plaits the colour of barley sugar. She wasn't fooled either. She knew perfectly well that he'd forgotten all about the play.

'Are you responsible for it this year, Mrs Goodwin?' he asked.

Rose nodded. 'Penalty of taking on the first year at Riley Street.'

'The little kids always do the play. I dun it when I was a little 'un,' Sammy informed the kitchen from the longevity of his eight years. 'I was a Wise Man. I had more.'

'More what?' Nafnel asked, lifting the muslin cover on a pudding basin.

'Myrrh,' Pat corrected. 'He was supposed to be carrying myrrh.'

'Is Naf . . .' Belatedly Jack remembered that Rose Goodwin preferred her foster child to be referred to by his given name. 'Is *Nathaniel* in the play too?'

'No. He's been put up a class, haven't you, Nathaniel?'

Nafnel shrugged. 'I'm smart, ain't I?'

'He's also older than he looks. And it wouldn't have done for his foster mum to be teaching him,' Rose explained. 'And he *is* bright,' she added under her breath, for Jack's ears only. In a louder tone she asked if he'd be coming to the play.

'I . . . er . . .'

'Thursday,' Eileen said, catching his eye. 'Day they break up for Christmas holidays.'

'Yes. Of course I'll be coming.'

'Oh good.' Rose smiled. 'I don't suppose we'll get many fathers there. Most of them are at work at that time. And of course this year a lot will be away in the forces.'

Jack felt himself ageing before their eyes. Once again he had become a useless creature, fit only to be included amongst housewives and small children. He was saved from total immersion under a tidal wave of self-pity by the violent crash of the front door on its hinges.

'What the he . . .' Biting back his curse in consideration of his mother, Pat shot out into the hall. Jack followed. They were both in time to see Maury start up the stairs.

'Oi,' Pat shouted. 'What's up with you?'

'Nothing.'

Jack hurriedly made his way down the hall and shut the door. He turned back at the sound of a muffled curse and found that Pat had gripped one of Maury's ankles through the stair

126

struts. Maury kicked out. It did him no good. Of all the O'Day boys, he was the only one to inherit his mother's small, thin frame. Pat, on the other hand, was a solid six-footer with muscles developed from holding hoses under pressure for hours on end.

'Get yer bleedin' 'ands off,' Maury yelled, sitting on the stairs and using the heel of his other foot to hack at Pat's hands.

'Maury!' his outraged mother snapped. 'I won't have language like that in this house.'

She was behind Pat, at the entrance to the kitchen door, and could only see Maury's lashing lower legs. From his vantage point at the bottom of the stairs, Jack had a clearer view. As Maury twisted, his face came out of shadow and into the dim light shed by the landing light. The brow and left side of his face had an angry redness that heralded a fine crop of ugly bruising by the morning.

With a frantic jerk, Maury managed to pull his ankle free from Pat's grasp. He started back up the stairs on all fours, but Pat was too quick for him. Grasping the stair rungs with both hands, he pulled himself up, vaulted the banister, grabbed the back of his brother's jacket and hauled him unceremoniously down the stairs.

'Now,' he panted, pinning Maury against the hall wall. 'What's going on?'

'Nothing, get yer hands off,' Maury snarled.

The white-eyed look flashed in his direction wasn't lost on Jack. Whatever had occurred tonight, Maury didn't want to discuss it in front of him.

'Whatever's happened to your face?' Eileen gasped.

'Nothing.' Maury aimed a kick at his brother's knees.

Pat responded with a forearm across Maury's throat and another demand to know what Maury had been up to.

'I told yer, none of yer business.'

'Oh, isn't it?' Pat leant more weight on his arm, causing Maury to give a choking gasp.

'Pat, be careful,' Jack warned.

'I want to know what he's been up to.'

'Well, I ain't saying. What's it got to do wiv you anyhow?

You ain't me dad. Tell him to let go, Mum.'

'Let him down, Pat,' Eileen said quietly. 'Come into the kitchen, Maury, I'll put some Lysol on those cuts.'

'I think we'd better be going.' Rose shrugged her way into her coat and tied a scarf over her hair. 'Come on, Nathaniel.'

Nafnel scowled. 'I wanna hear about the fight,' he said, going straight to the point.

'Come on,' Rose ordered. Recognising her schoolmistress tone as final, Nafnel sighed and scuffed his way along the hall with the air of the much put-upon.

'I'll see you Wednesday, air-raids willing,' Pat called after her.

By the time he and Jack returned to the back kitchen, Eileen was already dabbing at the raw redness with a pungent smelling milky liquid, whilst Maury winced and gasped at each contact.

'Now . . .' Pat advanced on his younger brother. Maury flattened himself against the wooden chair back.

Eileen patted the scraped face with a clean towel. 'Sammy, go upstairs and get ready for bed. Take Annaliese with you.'

'Aw, Mum,' Sammy protested.

'Do as you're told,' Eileen said. Her tight lips and sparkling eyes warned him not to argue.

'We going down the Anderson?' Sammy asked with an eye to delaying his departure until the grown-ups got to the interesting bit.

'No. But put your warm coats and balaclavas on the ends of the beds in case the sirens go. And don't come down again unless I call you, understand?'

'OK.' Taking the fledgling angel by the hand, Sammy trailed her out and up the stairs.

'You'll be wanting her to stop here tonight?' Eileen said, pausing in her nursing to look directly at Jack.

'I suppose . . . well, she normally does, doesn't she?' He'd become so used to his daughter's rejection that even he was beginning to find it normal. For a moment he couldn't understand why she should have bothered to ask him. Then he saw Pat and Eileen's faces. The dismissal in them was unmistakable. They wanted him to leave. Whatever Maury had done, they

128

would deal with it themselves; he wasn't wanted.

The rejection hurt him more than he would have thought possible. Without realising it, he'd almost come to think of himself as part of the family. Now they were clearly and unequivocally telling him he wasn't, and probably never would be.

His gaze flicked to Maury. The young man glared defiantly back from between clumps of Brylcreemed hair which drooped in an untypically messy fashion over his face. Watery disinfectant hung in droplets from his chin and dripped into a damp collar. Even as he took in the uncharacteristic dishevelment, the policeman part of Jack's mind noted that Maury's usual hat was missing, and the rough grazing of the face skin suggested contact with an uneven floor or wall rather than a fist.

'I'll wish you good night then,' he said.

He couldn't manage the front door catch one-handed and Pat had to come down the hall to help him.

'Pat,' he murmured, 'if there's anything I can do . . .'

'We'll let yer know, thanks, Mr Stamford.'

He held the front door open and Jack stepped out into the cold, unwelcoming night.

He told himself the only reason he made his way to Agar Street police station the following morning was to check in with Sarah McNeill and see if she'd managed to get anywhere with Nell De Groot yet.

'What a pity, sir,' Ding-Dong said brightly in answer to his casual enquiry. 'You just missed her. Been on shelter duty all night. Gone home to sleep the Sleep of the Just, as the lady wife would put it. What's that on your neck, sir?'

Before Jack could reply, the DC reached up and slid two fingers under his collar. He emerged with a playing card.

'Kiddies' Christmas party, sir. Always do a conjuring act. Will you be bringing your little girl?'

'I . . . er . . . I'm not sure.'

'Be five bob if you are, sir. Covers food provided by the lady wives and prizes for the games.'

Delving into his pocket, Jack found two half-crowns. If Annaliese didn't want to come, it could go into the kitty. He looked round the near-deserted CID offices. 'Much on?'

'Usual spate of dips up the market. Always get that just before Christmas. There's some people who are sadly lacking in Good Will to All Men.'

'Nothing else?'

'Bit of looting and a few drunk and disorderlies. Biggest job's the warehouse break-in. Twenty crates gone missing. Whisky.'

'When was that?'

Jack knew from the flicker of surprise that passed over DC Bell's usually melancholic features that he'd sounded too eager. Trying to relax, he managed a half-smile and an admission that he was bored. 'It's driving me mad,' he said, half lifting the arthritic arm from its resting place inside his jacket and then wishing he hadn't.

'Lady wife swears by a massage with wintergreen, sir.' Ding-Dong flicked through a stack of paper until he found an incident report which only appeared to contain the briefest of details at present. 'It was last night. Well, evening rightly. But the dark makes it feel like night, doesn't it?'

'Anyone caught?'

'Only the night watchman. By someone's fist. Probably decorated with a knuckle-duster.'

'Is he badly hurt?'

'Mostly just pride, which in his case really did goeth before his fall. They put him in a bed down St Pancras Hospital but they weren't planning to keep him for long.' Scuffling amongst the debris on his desk, Ding-Dong produced a notebook. 'Want to read my report, sir?'

'Thanks.' Flicking it open one-handed, Jack scanned the DC's copperplate handwriting. The watchman had, according to his statement, *been taking a decko over the roof like to see if any incendiaries had lodged up there*. Since there had been no raids on London for eight days, Jack translated this as *having a quick nap*. The statement went on: *I heard this noise out back and went out to look and saw this bloke, bold as brass, loading*

*crates up into the lorry. Mindful of my duties to my employer I
immediately challenged him and invited him to put his fists up.
Instead of taking up my invitation, he scarpered down the alley.
I gave chase and apprehended him by the arm. My actions
caused him to run into the wall but I want it known that I never
intended him no harm and my only wish was to protect my
employer's property.*

'What's this about him catching one?'

'Grabbed him by the arm, sir,' Ding-Dong explained. 'Seems
the bloke spun round and slammed into the wall.'

Jack flipped through the rest of the report. 'There's no
description?'

' "A six footer with an expression of obvious criminal
intent",' Ding-Dong quoted. 'I didn't put it in on account of the
watchman being five eight in his socks.'

'And you didn't see him tackling a six-footer?'

'I reckon he'd have run a mile if anything with its ears higher
than five feet off the cobbles had yelled "Boo", sir.'

Maury O'Day was five foot four. With a heavy heart Jack
asked if the man thought he could recognise his assailant.

'No. It's pitch out back of the warehouse. And the second
one jumped him from behind. He was the one who laid him
out, by the sound of it.'

'Any leads at all?'

'Description of the van. And a hat one of them may have
dropped. It was lying in the gutter by the alley. 'Course, that's
not to say either of our gentlemen ever had their head inside
it.'

From behind his desk he produced a brown paper bag and
held the ends open so that Jack could see the stained trilby.

The DC gave his opinion that their best chance of solving
this one would be down to a tip-off. 'But frankly, sir, what with
it being ten days before Christmas, if anyone hears of bottles
of whisky for sale . . .'

'They'll probably start a queue rather than calling the
police,' Jack finished for him. He passed the notebook back
and told Ding-Dong to keep him informed before remembering
that he was on sick leave.

131

'Shall I tell the sergeant you was asking for her?' the DC asked.

For a moment Jack was flummoxed, then he recalled he'd ostensibly called at the station to speak to Sarah about those damn letters.

'No. I'll . . . er . . . catch up with her later.'

He stepped out into a morning that was cold with a tinge of raw dampness that promised a hard winter. His arm reacted by thumping with each pulse of blood along the arteries. For once he didn't notice. Instead he was conscious of a sickness in his stomach that had nothing to do with the fact he'd had no breakfast. If Maury had been involved in theft and assault there was no way he could overlook it in the way he'd turned a blind eye to the vaguely unspecified bits of petty pilfering and evasion of the rationing regulations. He would have to take official action, with all that that could imply for his relationship with Eileen, Pat and Sammy.

The air-raid alert started just as he huddled deeper inside his overcoat and turned his footsteps towards St Pancras Hospital. It seemed appropriate. There could indeed be explosions in the very near future.

Chapter 14

'Death' turned out not to be a skeletal messenger arrayed in Coty pancake and lipstick. Instead Sarah discovered that her fellow tenant was a traveller in cosmetics.

'It's pronounced "Dee-arth",' he explained, when she encountered him in Bridget O'Mara's basement kitchen.

'Oh, sorry,' Sarah apologised.

'There is no need. A common mistake. And it has its advantages.'

'Does it?' Sarah found it hard to imagine any.

'Yes indeed. If you were told a Mr Death wished to see you, would you not be tempted to take the tiniest peep to see whether I really looked as ridiculous as my name suggested?'

'I suppose I would.'

'There you are, you see.' He smiled, revealing twisted teeth in his long-jawed face. 'Already I am a step ahead of my rivals. I have made eye contact with my potential customer. I am on the first rung to that elusive order.'

'I wouldn't have thought you'd have to try very hard these days. You sell make-up, don't you? Aren't there shortages?' Sarah was aware that her question said a lot about her social life – or lack of it.

'Not as many as one might hope,' admitted Mr Death with a twinkle in his black eyes. 'And I must confess my employer's range is not . . . how shall I put it . . . the most sophisticated. Still, we are well known in our own small market. Ah, thank you, Bridget,' he added as Mrs O'Mara entered with a pile of freshly washed shirts that she'd just retrieved from the brick washhouse in the yard.

'Sure now, you're welcome, haven't I always said? I did

mention I'd be happy to do your laundry, didn't I, me dear?'

'Yes. You did. Thanks,' Sarah agreed.

'It's the least I can do for those who protect these shores,' Mrs O'Mara said placidly. 'And you'll find me charges are very reasonable. For the ironing too.' She looked pointedly at the shirts clasped to Mr Death's chest.

'Thank you. But I couldn't impose on your good nature any further, dear lady.' Turning away, Mr Death dropped Sarah a fractional wink and left.

Biting her cheek, Sarah asked for the pint of milk Mrs O'Mara had promised to put by for her.

It was duly produced from a pail of water under the sink. 'And if you want me to pick up any other little bits and pieces, me dear, you've only to ask. There's no sense you standing in queues when I can be doing it for you.'

Murmuring her thanks, Sarah backed from the room, aware that the icy bottle was staining her tunic jacket. She'd already formed the impression that Bridget O'Mara had a price for every 'little service' imaginable and would be more than happy to whip out a list of charges on request.

Making her way up the internal stairs and into the hall via the small door under the stairs, she emerged just as Nell De Groot opened the front door.

Sarah gave a friendly smile: 'Good morning. We didn't get a chance to meet properly yesterday. I'm Sarah McNeill.'

Evidently it wasn't friendly enough, since it merited the briefest of nods and a tight-lipped twitch that might – just conceivably – have been a smile.

She tried again. 'Have you been on night duty too?'

'Yes.' Nell put her hand on the staircase post. 'Excuse me.'

Had this been a normal social encounter, Sarah knew she'd have given up at that point. She could receive a 'get lost' message as well as the next woman. However, gritting her teeth in the line of duty, she followed on Nell's heels up the stairs. 'The shelters smell something dreadful,' she said chattily. 'I think I'll have a hot bath first and then try and get a few hours sleep. Oh.'

This last was for Mr Death, who was hovering on the landing

nattily arrayed in a chequered dressing gown and Turkish leather slippers. The sponge bag and towel signalled his intentions.

Nell surprised her by saying: 'Hello, Max.' Perhaps Nell reserved her cold shoulders for police officers.

'Good morning, Nell. A quiet night, I trust?'

'Yes. It was. I wish it hadn't been really. At least the time goes faster when we're called out. Is there any hot water?'

'Is the Pope Catholic?' A wide-eyed look of alarm flitted over Max Death's face, making it look even more absurd than usual. He turned anxious eyes on Sarah and hoped he hadn't offended her.

'Me? Good heavens, no. I'm not religious,' Sarah said cheerfully. 'I do Christmas and Easter but that's about it.'

'Very wise. Keep your name on the list but don't overstay your welcome.'

'Is the water off?' Sarah asked. It was a common phenomenon these days, when the frequent bombing raids were liable to disrupt water, gas and electricity supplies. But not so in this case. The water was gushing in a positive Niagara, as Max was happy to demonstrate by sending it crashing into the white enamel. Unfortunately it was gushing a temperature that would give an Eskimo chilblains.

Nell unexpectedly spoke up. 'She never heats the water unless she wants it herself. We ought to say something.'

'She'll fall back on the boiler again,' Max remarked. Crossing his hands over his chest, he wailed in a fair imitation of Bridget O'Mara's Irish brogue: 'Oh, sure now and isn't it me pipes? Me pipes is furred up worse than Temperance Club's beer pumps. And not a day-sant plumber to be had for love nor money.'

Nell laughed. Max relaxed and smiled in her direction. And Sarah made an interesting discovery. Mr Death was in love with Miss De Groot.

She announced her intention of getting some sleep and going down the public baths later. 'Good night . . . I mean, morning.'

'Good morning. I wonder . . .' Nell looked directly at her for the first time. 'The milk. I haven't got . . . could you spare a little?'

Delighted that she'd finally managed to establish some sort of contact with the woman, Sarah sacrificed half a jugful. 'Sorry about the room,' she said, belatedly noticing the haphazard tumble of possessions. 'I haven't had time to unpack.'

'I hadn't noticed,' Nell said with a coolness that suggested either good breeding or a worrying lack of eyesight in an auxiliary driver. Delving into her gas-mask case, she pulled out a change purse.

'Don't,' Sarah said quickly. 'I'd rather you put it on the slate.' The blank expression on her visitor's face indicated she might as well be speaking Chinese. Marvelling at the sheltered lives some people led, Sarah elaborated: 'On account. It's difficult sometimes, getting shopping in when you're working shifts. I'd like to know I can pop over the landing and borrow some milk if I'm stuck.' *And*, she added silently to herself, *take a look round your room*.

'Yes, of course you may,' Nell agreed. 'Although I'm on shifts myself.'

'Mrs O'Mara said,' Sarah replied, flopping on to the bare mattress and easing off her shoes. 'You're at Good Hope Station, aren't you?'

'Yes. Please excuse me, I'm rather tired.'

Nell drifted out with an almost ghost-like silence, and a second later Sarah heard the sound of water running into a container. Kettle, she decided, filling her own. Digging out a handful of coppers, she fed the gas meter, lit one of the cooking rings and turned on a bar of the gas fire. The stale smell of burning dust filled the room as the single bar glowed first blue then red. It didn't seem to have much effect on the chill air, but she worked herself warm unpacking. Her sheets and blankets gave off a slight aroma of damp and mould after their spell in her neighbour's basement down Mornington Crescent. Spreading them out round the inadequate gas fire whilst she put away pots, crockery and clothes and scrambled into her nightdress, she found herself wondering why Nell De Groot lived in this lodging house.

The two other tenants were, she suspected, motivated by

reasons of economy. Ruby Rawkins, 'the ground floor back' wore clothes that had been fashionable twenty years ago with a shabby limpness that suggested they'd not been off her back much in the two decades since. And whilst Max Death's dark three-piece suit was unfrayed and neatly pressed, it had plainly seen better days. And he'd said himself that he didn't sell top-class products.

But Nell was a different kettle of cold fish. She had those cool manners and rounded vowels that screamed a comfortable middle-class upbringing. Since she could afford to pay out eighteen bob from her two pounds a week wages for a room she only used occasionally, it rather suggested her family might be making her an allowance. So why hadn't they stumped up for something decent like a small hotel or flat?

Finishing her tea, Sarah made up the bed, turned out the fire, set her alarm clock and fell into bed.

It seemed to her that she'd scarcely closed her eyes before the alarm clock was clanging out its summons. Automatically she sat up, swung her legs out of bed immediately and flicked back a curtain. Any temptation to lie in was fatal she'd discovered, after losing several days of precious pay by being late on parade as a newly attested WPC.

The street below was quiet, with a few pedestrians strolling unhurriedly. On the steps of the house opposite two toddlers were playing, watched over by a girl who was scarcely a few years older than them. Twisting sideways and narrowing her eyes, Sarah examined as much of the sky as she could see from the sash window. There was no sign of any barrage balloons aloft, nor any telltale drifts of smoke from beyond the rooftops. The quiet morning she'd fallen asleep in had turned into a quiet afternoon.

Dressing in civilian clothes this time, she folded her towel into a hessian shopping bag, picked fluff off a bar of yellow soap that had ended up in the packing case with her pots, locked her door and walked across to Nell's.

She thought at first the other woman might have gone out, but after several repeated raps the key was turned and Nell opened the door a few inches. It was enough to afford Sarah a

137

glimpse of a table similar to her own, except that this one was covered with a lace cloth anchored by a blue and white cachepot containing a rather straggling geranium. But it was the other item on the table that jumped to Sarah's attention: an open writing pad.

'Yes?'

Blinking her eyes back to Nell's enquiring ones, Sarah quickly asked if she had an old tin she could spare.

'What kind of tin?'

'Just something small. To put this in.' Sarah displayed the soap bar. 'You know how it just slides all over the place in the baths if you don't have something to keep it in.'

'I'm not sure . . .'

Nell took her hand from the door, allowing it to fall open a few more inches. Sarah took the opportunity to move with it, more or less forcing Nell to let her into the room. 'Anything will do. Tobacco tins are best. Right size.'

'Do I look like I roll my own?'

'You can never tell these days. Mind you, you never could,' Sarah replied, edging her way a little nearer the table. 'When I was stationed at Leman Street a few years back, we had this Rolls-Royce with a flat tyre in the Whitechapel Road. The woman inside was a real . . .' She was about to say 'classy piece' but amended it to 'lady. Lovely full-length fur coat and one of those hats that's more net than hat, if you know what I mean?'

Nell nodded, interested in the story despite herself.

Drifting a little closer to the open pad, Sarah went on, 'Anyway, she got out and stood by the kerb while the chauffeur and the copper on point duty changed the wheel. Then all of a sudden she produces a packet of papers and a tin of ready-rubbed mixture from one pocket of this mink coat and a roller machine from the other. Stood there rolling up a fag, cool as you please. One-handed too. The locals were very impressed.'

Unexpectedly Nell smiled. It made a surprising difference to her pale oval face, emphasising as it did the high cheekbones and glittering pale-blue eyes under a fringe of long lashes. But it was her eyebrows that were the most striking feature; for rather than the silky blonde that might have been expected

138

with such silver fairness, they were nearly black.

'As a matter of fact,' she said, 'I rolled one once myself. My father showed me how to do it. It made me most dreadfully sick. I expect that's what he intended, because I never felt inclined to try it again. There's nothing like parental encouragement to make something forbidden suddenly seem dreadfully mundane, is there?'

Sarah, whose introduction to smoking had been a shared Weights fag on a stone tenement stair, at the slum in Litcham Street where she'd spent part of her childhood, agreed with a straight face.

'I have got a tin,' Nell admitted. 'I keep my hairpins in it. Just a moment.'

She crossed to the table, flicking the writing pad closed and scooping it up in one movement. Opening a drawer in a small bedside table which Sarah guessed hadn't been part of Mrs O'Mara's original fixtures and fittings, she pushed the pad inside and removed a flat tin. Tipping the pins on to a rose-coloured bedspread, Nell extended the empty container towards Sarah.

'Will that do?'

'Thanks.' She made a play of re-juggling the bar and fitting the lid. Nell watched, her face returned to its normal emotionless state.

'I'll tell you what,' Sarah said, as if the idea had just occurred to her. 'Why don't you come with me? It will be quicker than waiting for Mrs O'Mara to find a day-sant plumber.'

'I've never been to the public baths,' Nell said evenly. 'But then I daresay you've already guessed that.'

Something in her tone warned Sarah just in time that straightforwardness would be the best approach here. For all her middle-class sheltered upbringing, Nell De Groot was no fool and would recognise any attempt to patronise for what it was. 'Well it doesn't matter, does it?' she suggested. 'Everyone's doing things they never thought they would since the war started. Its OK down there, the Prince of Wales Baths, I mean. They're clean. Come and see. You don't have to go in if you don't fancy it when you get there.'

It was touch and go; she saw refusal and acceptance fighting across Nell's face. Acceptance won. 'Do I have to take a towel?'

'Up to you. You can hire one down there, but they're rough enough to sand down doorsteps.'

'I'll get mine.'

Her towel was fluffily white, her soap Lux and contained in a china box patterned with carmine roses and golden ribbons. As they left the house together, Sarah took a quick inventory of Nell's outfit too. The wide-legged trousers and pink twinset were the latest fashion. And the grey double-breasted coat Nell had belted over them had probably only seen a couple of winters. Definitely money somewhere in the family.

'Do you want to bus it?' she asked.

'I'd rather walk.'

'Fine.'

Coat collars turned up, they both set off briskly down Junction Road. Sarah was pleased to find the other woman was a good walker. She couldn't abide the dawdling stroll that a lot of her sex used. The wind was behind them, its raw blast sending wisps of hair dancing in front of their faces and bowling desiccated leaves along the pavements and gutters with a sound like pattering goblins.

'It gets dark so fast these days,' Sarah remarked, casting a wary eye at the sky, which had suddenly turned the dirty grey that often heralded sleet.

'It's the shortest day in less than a week,' Nell said.

By unspoken consent they'd both increased their pace to a fast stride. Others were doing the same. There was little incentive to linger now. The brightly lit Christmas window displays of pre-war days had been sacrificed to the blackout. Fortunately the baths were still doing brisk business. A pungent smell of chlorine, wet tiles and disinfectant hit their nostrils as soon as they stepped through the front doors.

'Numbers eight and nine,' the women's bathhouse attendant directed them. 'Need soap? Towels?'

Shaking her head, Sarah led the way down the cubicles and went into number eight. She heard the bolt shut next door and the sound of undressing. She'd got down to her own slip and suspenders when there was a tentative tap on the door. 'Yes?'

'Sarah?' Nell whispered.

Puzzled, Sarah opened the cubicle door. Nell was huddled inside her overcoat, her bare feet and legs indicating that she was stripped underneath it. 'Something the matter?'

'There's no knob on the tap,' Nell murmured. 'How do you let the water in?'

'You don't,' Sarah explained. Leaning out into the corridor she shouted in the voice she usually reserved for official duties, 'Oi, water in eight and nine, please.'

'Keep your 'air on, love, I only got one pair of 'ands.' The sound of flat shoes slapping on the floor was followed a moment later by the gush of water. A thin stream of steam rose from the cascade.

'Shout out if it's not right,' Sarah instructed.

'Yes. I see. Thanks.'

Nell returned to her own cubicle, leaving Sarah to sink back into the warm water and soap herself all over. The washing business was soon finished, leaving her time to relax in the warmth of the greyish suds for a moment. All around her gossiping voices exchanged news of husbands and boyfriends in the forces; plans for Christmas celebrations; and scandals involving neighbours – usually identified as ' 'er down the end with the blue curtains, well I won't say more, you know who I mean.' Occasionally the chat was interrupted by cries for 'more hot in number four'; 'more cold in number ten, me bum's burning off here'; or demands to 'hurry up in number twenty, you ain't rented it for the night, yer know'.

There wasn't a peep from Nell's cubicle, which came as no surprise, Sarah thought, reluctantly heaving herself upright and stepping out. She suspected Nell would rather have scalded herself to death than shout out in this crowd. Once she'd got her clothes back on, she knocked quietly on the cubicle partition and called, 'Ready?'

'Yes. I shan't be a moment.'

The steam had coaxed a pink flush into Nell's cheeks and curled further wisps of hair in a frame around her face when she joined Sarah at the desk a few minutes later. Their arrival into the Prince of Wales Road was heralded by a burst of 'O Little Town of Bethlehem' from the Salvation Army band who'd stationed themselves outside the baths. The coins that Nell dropped into their collecting tin were accepted with a joyful 'Merry Christmas to you both, my dears.'

'Some hopes,' Sarah said as they fell into step and headed back towards the high street.

'The lull might last,' Nell remarked. 'It's been eight days since the last raid on London. Most of the bombing activity has been concentrated further north, in the Midlands.'

Taking her cue, Sarah asked whether Nell had any family in that area.

'No, my parents live in St Albans. There have been some raids, but nothing like . . .' She made a vague circling gesture towards the east. Then, in an apparent change of subject, she said: 'I'm glad there were cubicles. I thought perhaps the baths would all be in the same room. Like in a hospital.'

'Are they?' Sarah had always been blessed with good health, but she'd sat on 'suicide watch' in several hospitals over the years and couldn't recall ever having seen one with communal bathrooms.

'They were in . . . the place where I was. The attendants used to stay and watch us bathing.' The icy blast that screamed round the street corners by the Palace cinema might have accounted for Nell's sudden convulsive shiver.

'We'll be walking into the wind going up the hill,' Sarah said quietly. 'Let's see if we can get a bus.'

Turning back to see if one was coming, she was met with a sharp whistle and 'Evening, Sarge, get that note I left you?'

'Evening, Ding-Dong. And yes, thanks.' She waited for the detective constable to dash across the road, holding his hat against the fiercely buffeting wind, before introducing Nell.

'A pleasure, miss.' Ding-Dong raised his hat. His words mingled with droplets of beer-perfumed breath.

Sarah lifted one eyebrow. 'On duty, Ding-Dong?'

'Intelligence.' He tapped one side of his nose. 'Nothing like a public bar for that.'

'Not the ones I've been in,' Sarah said with some asperity.

'Couldn't pass the School Certificate between them.'

'You know what I mean.' Ding-Dong huddled further into his overcoat. 'Couple of pints of wallop and I've got a lead on the van used in the whisky job.'

'I don't suppose the villains were obliging enough to have their names painted on the side?'

'Not quite that daft, these two,' Ding-Dong agreed. 'Mind, I've known those that were. This lot had a blue van . . .' He consulted a small notebook, anchoring the page with a nicotine-stained thumb. '. . . torn canvas cover,' he read on. 'And a dodgy tailboard; bolt on one side is working loose.'

'That sounds like . . .'

'Sounds like what, Sarge?' Ding-Dong returned his book to his pocket and waited.

'Is something wrong?' Nell asked when Sarah rejoined her a moment later. She'd tactfully moved away a few steps to read the cinema posters while the police discussed official business.

'Yes. No.' Sarah sighed. 'I think I've just done something . . .'

Something what? It was hardly stupid to tell Ding-Dong that the van sounded like the one owned by Maury O'Day's helpful mate. It didn't mean that Maury had been involved in the robbery. On the other hand, Sarah told herself, aware of the hole widening in the pit of her stomach, if she was a betting woman, she'd have laid money on the fact that Eileen's second youngest *was* mixed up in the theft somehow.

'I've done something . . . unfortunate,' she finished with a heavy heart.

Chapter 15

By the time Nell reported for duty on Monday night, Betty and Ruth were already manning the watchroom phones. After formally reporting her presence to the officers in charge, Nell checked the board behind the two women. It showed that all the appliances were in the station.

'No incidents?'

'Didn't hear no sirens, did you?' Ruth said.

'No. But there might have been a normal fire, mightn't there?'

'Well, there ain't been. So you can go put your feet up.'

'Thank you.'

As Nell turned to leave, Ruth called out sharply: 'Nell.'

'Yes?'

'Sorry if I sounded a bit fishwifey, like. It just gets a bit boring, sitting here with no calls. Don't it, Mrs Shaw? Mrs Shaw?'

'What?' Betty Shaw jumped. 'Sorry. I was miles away.'

'I was just saying to Nell. It's boring, sitting here all night, with the bells never going down once.'

'Oh, yes. It is a bit.'

'You all right? You've 'ad your 'ead in the clouds ever since you come in.'

'Yes. I'm fine . . . just thinking about Christmas. Wondering whether I'll get Christmas Day off.'

'Rotas ain't out for next week yet. Except you'll be hoping to go 'ome, Nell. Or are you going to spend the day with your boyfriend's folks?'

Nell murmured that she had no plans. She was drifting towards the door again, but Ruth persisted.

'Difficult these days, ain't it? I mean, it ain't like when blokes had regular jobs. If your bloke's in the air force, say, you wouldn't know when he was gonna show up.'

'I imagine not. But since I don't have a bloke, it hardly applies.'

'Then who . . . ?' The rest of Ruth's question was interrupted by the urgent buzz of the phone. Betty answered, scribbling on the pad in front of her with the other hand. Nell and Ruth stayed quiet; details had to be taken down accurately. An appliance sent to a wrong address could mean that few moments between rescue and death.

Betty finished writing and rang off. 'House fire, Carlton Street. DP only.'

'Why can't they take it themselves?' Ruth asked, leaping up and hitting a switch. Above their heads the bells clanged loudly on the floor. Furniture was thrust out of the way and heavy feet thundered across the bare floorboards.

'Their appliances are already out on another call. Here.' Betty shoved the scribbled sheet at her as Ruth ran to the foot of the stairs.

Taking a deep breath, Ruth bawled the details at the men thundering down from the recreation room. Those that weren't riding the dual purpose appliance that night turned back with groans and good-natured insults for the four-man crew, who continued down the stairs and rushed out to scramble into their boots and tunics.

The sub-officer in charge was still clutching a copy of the *St Pancras Chronicle*. He exchanged it for the slip of paper Ruth was holding out, with a 'Would you be so kind as to mind this for me?'

'Pleasure,' Ruth dimpled, resisting the inclination to mimic his Knightsbridge tones. When she'd first started at the station she'd had a habit of imitating her favourite film roles when answering the phones, until a woman officer had given her a stern dressing-down and informed her that callers did *not* expect to find themselves speaking to a Russian empress or a French trollop when they reported an incident.

Returning to the watchroom, she found Betty already

marking the DP's location on the vehicle movement board. Ruth reseated herself and turned to the back of the newspaper. 'I like reading the announcements, don't you?' she said, scanning the columns.

'Deaths?' Nell was surprised out of her usual icy reserve.

'Well, deaths is quite interesting. Dad likes the deaths. The place he works always checks to see which ones they ain't buried. Then they send someone round to ask if the family wants to join their funeral club. That way they get to bury the next one that goes. Dad says funerals is a very cut-throat business. But what I really like is the weddings.' She flicked to the relevant page and creased it into two. 'Let's have a look: Smith . . . Pinchpenny. Pinchpenny – Gawd! Fanshaw . . . Browne. Gideon . . . Butterman. Nope, don't know any of them. I always see if anyone I was at school with has got themselves wed. Don' you do the same back at . . . where is it you come from?'

'Hertfordshire.'

'Yeah, right. Er . . . do they have a lot of airfields in Hertfordshire?'

'A few.'

'I expect you get to meet a lot of pilots then, when you're back home?'

'Not really. Did you say Butterman?' Reaching over, Nell picked up the paper. 'Oh dear.'

'Someone you know?' Ruth pricked up her ears. Perhaps it was another pilot. Someone stationed with Paul. What an idiot she'd been not to ask the name of his airfield.

'He rents a room in the same house as me,' Nell replied, handing the *Chronicle* back. 'Or should I say he used to rent it. My landlady had . . . expectations. It looks like the Widow Gideon has beaten her to it. I'll be in the mess if you need me.'

She was gone before Ruth could think of any more delaying tactics. Mentally she kicked herself. If only she could find out where Paul was stationed. She might never know if he'd been heroically shot down in flames. The idea caused tears to start to her eyes. Hastily she brushed them away with the back of her hand and glanced at Betty, to see whether she'd noticed. But the blank, unseeing gaze with which Betty Shaw was minding her telephone tended to indicate she wouldn't have noticed if Ruth had ripped off her clothes, covered herself in ashes and rolled on the floor wailing and beating her breasts.

'Mrs Shaw? Mrs Shaw?' Ruth waved in front of the glassy stare. 'You OK?'

With a start, Betty refocused on the office again. 'Yes. I'm sorry, Ruth. I've got things on my mind . . . Why don't you call me Betty?'

'No one likes to. On account of you being the station officer's wife.'

'No. Right.' A worried V appeared between Betty's brown eyes. Abruptly she asked Ruth if she'd heard anything about anonymous letters people were getting.

'Sure. There was a copper up here yesterday asking about them. Reckoned Pat O'Day had set him on to us.'

'Fortyish, auburn-haired, something wrong with his arm?'

'That's him,' Ruth agreed. 'You know 'im?'

'Pat brought him up Good Hope the other day. Len ordered him out.'

It was Ruth's turn to look worried. 'I showed 'im round. He said he had permission.'

'He does. Now. Headquarters have authorised the investigation. It's something to do with national security.'

'Honestly?' Ruth breathed, her eyes sparkling.

'Yes. But . . . it's not general knowledge. Need-to-know only, according to Len. I probably shouldn't have told you, Ruth.'

Almost luminescent with excitement, Ruth swore she wouldn't say a word.

'Have you ever had one?' Betty asked.

'Me?' Ruth hesitated for a fraction of a second. 'No. Never. How about you?'

'I haven't either, but I think perhaps . . .'

'Yeah?'

'Nothing, it doesn't matter.'

'OK.' Ruth patted her pockets. Not finding what she wanted, she dragged open several drawers. 'Got any fags? I'm out.'

'Here.' Betty produced a packet of Players and a box of matches.

'Ta.'

Lighting one each, they both inhaled deeply and sent a steady stream of smoke up to the yellowing ceiling.

The pump returned an hour later, having dealt with the consequences of a chimney blaze. 'Would you kindly put it down as "chimney alarm",' the sub-officer asked, booking himself and his crew back in.

'An hour?' Betty said doubtfully. 'They'll guess it should be "chimney on fire".'

'But it's not as if we were wanted elsewhere, is it? And you'd not wish the poor woman to get a five-shilling fine from the pencil pushers at LCC for letting her chimney get that dirty? And her with three little mouths to feed.'

'Oh well. Go on then.'

With a wink, the sub-officer reclaimed his paper and tramped back upstairs.

Sighing loudly, Ruth rested her elbows on the table, linked her fingers and rested her chin on her hands. 'Wish something exciting would 'appen.'

'Ruth! We've just had an alarm. The less excitement the better, I should have thought.'

'Yeah. I didn't mean a raid . . . I meant . . .' She took an enormous breath and rushed out: 'Don't you ever feel like there's something else? Something heaps better than this, outside Camden and Kentish Town?'

'If you feel like that about it, why join the local fire service? You could have joined another service, got yourself a posting somewhere else.'

'Nearly did.' Ruth disengaged her fingers and cupped her cheeks instead. 'Me and my mate Lulu were gonna join the ATS. But Dad got the mumps, caught it off one of the mourners, he reckoned. The doctor said we'd be infectious so I wasn't to join up. Lulu went on her own. Which was lucky really.'

'Was it?'

'Yeah, 'cos it turned out the doctor was right. About me and Hatty getting the mumps. Horrible it was. Made me feel ever so queer. I was sick for weeks. Hatty too. She couldn't hardly cook the food Dad brought home.'

Betty wasn't aware that she'd shown her feelings at the breathtaking selfishness of this statement, but they must have shown somehow on her face because Ruth bristled suddenly, her eyes flashing.

'It ain't like it sounds. After me mum died I did try to do things, but Hatty didn't want me to help. She wanted to do the washing and cooking and things her way. She used to get rotten ratty if I did something wrong. And it's no good arguing with Hat. If she sets her mind to something she's that stubborn like you wouldn't believe. When she was nine she 'ad to 'ave all her hair cut off 'cos she had the scarlet fever. She was dead set on not going back to school until it was grown again. So she locked 'erself in our bedroom. Three days she was in there. In the end me dad 'ad to borrow a ladder and break the window. So if she says not to touch the 'ouse 'cos it's her job, it's best to do as she says.'

Betty was inclined to believe her. She'd known housewives who'd made a rod for their own backs in much the same way and then spent their lives moaning about their lot. At least Hatty seemed content with her humdrum home life. Steering the conversation back to less controversial paths, she asked why Ruth hadn't joined the ATS once she'd got over the mumps.

' 'Cos Lulu 'ad done her training by then and been sent to the middle of a field up Bedfordshire way.'

'A field? You mean she was in tents?'

'Only when she was doing her training. Said they were freezing. And the uniform was rotten itchy. And she had this real cow shouting at her about marching and saluting all the time and telling her 'ow stupid she was 'cos she was always doing it wrong.' Thrusting her seat back from the board and crossing her ankles, Ruth chatted on. 'She's a filing clerk cum telephonist for these officers. It's miles from town and the last bus goes before the picture palace finishes. Sometimes they take them in the back of a truck to dances. But there's no camps or nothing around, so Lulu has to dance with civilians. She says the blokes are ever so old or ever so young. Anyhow, that's why I joined the fire service, so's I could stop near the shops and cinemas.'

Trying hard not to show her amusement at this catalogue of misfortunes that poor Lulu was having to suffer, Betty remarked that she must have been pleased to see Ruth again so soon.

'What?'

'Last Sunday. Hatty said that's where you were going.'

'Oh? Yeah. That's right. The days all seem awful the same sometimes, now we've got used to the bombing. That's what I meant. About there being more than this. I mean, don't you sometimes screw up yer eyes,' Ruth demonstrated by squeezing her own tightly shut, 'and just *see* yerself in a few years' time?'

'And what do you see?' Betty asked.

'A big house,' Ruth said promptly. 'With one of them grand staircases that kind of bend down to the hall, like in the films. And I'd come gliding down . . .' She placed one hand elegantly on an imaginary banister '. . . in this long black dress, with a big white fur stole over one shoulder.' She slid her fingers down the imaginary ermine. 'Me hair would be piled up in curls like.' One finger described several twirls over her head. 'And Pau . . . a handsome RAF officer would be standing there at the bottom in his uniform, overcome wiv passion at the sight of me,' she finished triumphantly, suddenly flicking her eyes open on the final sentence.

Betty just managed to hide her grin in time. 'It sounds very . . .'

'Like a kid's dream . . .' Ruth finished for her, showing that sudden unexpected streak of shrewdness again. 'Well, I don't care what nobody else thinks. It's my dream and I'm gonna *make* it happen, so there.'

'Well, I hope you do. And I wish you the best of luck, Ruth. Everyone needs a dream.'

'Yeah.' Ruth's mulish expression was replaced by her normal sparkling smile. 'That's what I think too. Ain't you got one? I mean, don't you want a big posh house, or . . .' It occurred to Ruth that it would hardly be tactful to suggest Betty might prefer to find a handsome RAF officer at the bottom of *her* staircase. 'Or something else?'

'A baby...' Betty said softly. The words came out unconsciously. She'd never admitted that particular longing to anyone but Len before. Looking back now, it struck her that the reticence had been to protect his masculine pride. To avoid suggestions within the service that he somehow wasn't up to it. Just at present, however, she didn't particularly care about Len's pride. In fact, since yesterday's row, she wasn't entirely sure how much she cared about Len.

'Just a kid?' Ruth said incredulously. 'That all?'

'Isn't there a nursery in this dream house of yours?'

'Well, yeah, I suppose so. I expect we'll have a nursemaid to look after them. Upstairs,' Ruth added, dismissing her future offspring to the attics.

'Oh, I shouldn't want that.' Betty's fingers sought and found the gypsy's charm under her tunic jacket. 'I'd want to care for my own child.'

'That's all Hatty wants. To have a little house, and an ordinary bloke, and a couple of kids.'

Betty drew the charm out and slid it between her fingers. The cheap metal felt rough beneath her skin. 'It sounds like Hatty and I have a lot in common.'

'Yeah, you do. It's funny, that.' Ruth cocked her head on one side and regarded the older woman as if seeing her for the first time. 'You know something, Mrs Shaw? You even look like our Hatty. I don't mean you're fat...' she added hastily. 'It's just you're sort of the same colours and...'

The urgent buzz of the phone interrupted her. Betty beat her to the line again. 'Good Hope Stati... sorry, I mean auxiliary Fire Station 75X... yes...'

Ruth caught the glance in her direction. Her heart beat faster. *It's probably Dad phoning from Mottram's*, she told herself.

'It's for you, Ruth.'

Ruth announced in her most formal tones: 'Auxiliary Firewoman Miller speaking.'

'Would that be Hatty – short for Richmal Harriet?'

'You know it ain't, I mean isn't,' Ruth giggled. Her heart thudded with such intensity that it was threatening to jump into the back of her throat and prevent her speaking altogether.

151

Swallowing hard, she told him sternly that it was against regulations to take personal calls whilst on duty.

Laconically Paul informed her rules were meant to be broken. 'Listen, I think I may be able to get up to the Smoke Thursday. Are you still on for cocktails?'

'Oooh, yeah. I mean, that would be delightful, thank you.'

'Wizard. Shall I pick you up in the motor?'

'Yea . . . I er . . .'

Perhaps for the first time, Ruth saw her own home as an outsider would see it: a narrow terraced cottage overshadowed by the railway arches at the end of the street and drenched with the coal smuts of the constantly passing trains and the clouds of lime, cement and brick dust that arose periodically from the barges negotiating the canal on the far side of the bridge.

'No,' she said firmly. 'I'm not sure . . . what time . . . I'll meet you somewhere.'

'Café de Paris. Rendezvous twenty hundred hours. Got to go, popsie.'

'Yes. Goodbye . . .' The line was already dead. Looking up, she met Betty's eyes.

'The dream lover?'

Ruth's cheeks burnt brightly. 'He's, he's . . .' The intrusive switchboard interrupted her again. She was half terrified Paul might be ringing back to cancel their date, but a glance told her it was the link with the control office.

Anxiety flickered in Betty's chestnut eyes. Ruth tensed. She was on her feet before Betty rang off.

'Red alert,' Betty said briefly.

Ruth hit the alarm bells.

152

Chapter 16

The first bell had hardly started vibrating above their heads before the answering wail of the air-raid sirens sounded outside the station.

'What is it?' Ruth called across.

'Raiders sighted over Hackney Marshes, according to Control,' Betty said, scribbling details on her pad again. 'They're on course to pass directly over us.'

' 'Ow come they didn't spot 'em sooner then? We never even had a yellow alert.' Ruth dragged open the watchroom door. The noise of bells and sirens instantly increased a hundred times and was joined by the crashing feet of the watch pouring down from above again.

'Red alert,' Ruth called formally.

The news was passed back up the stairs by the first men down. This time there was no return to the recreation room. Running out to their assigned vehicles, they hurriedly took their places, dragging on boots and checking belts for axes, spanners and bobbin line pouches.

'No orders yet,' Ruth said, flicking a glance over her shoulder to where she could make out Betty on the switchboard. Betty shook her head, confirming Control hadn't asked them to mobilise their vehicles. Ruth stood for a moment in the quiet dimness of the corridor. It was surprising how you never noticed the sounds in the station until they were all gone. Without the click of dominoes, the good-natured arguing of the rec room philosopher and the off-key notes of the watch's mouth-organ player murdering 'Silent Night', Good Hope seemed eerily quiet. Almost like a ghost station.

Shivering at her own silly fancifulness, she looked back to

153

the reassuringly well-lit watchroom. Betty raised her shoulders and spread her hands. As yet there was nothing to do but sit and wait.

'Mrs Shaw,' Ruth called, lowering her own voice to match the quietness of the echoing corridor, 'I'll just nip outside for a tick. See if I can 'ear anything.'

'Don't be long.'

'I'll stop near the door,' Ruth whispered loudly. 'Yell if yer need us quick.'

Slipping out of the back door into the yard, she stood for a moment, letting her eyes adjust to the darkness. A muted whistle of enquiry from the nearest engine made her shake her head and scissor her hands across each other. Nothing yet.

The skies were silent. Low cloud obscured the stars and the moon was a dull gleam barely distinguishable behind the drifting banks of dirty greyness. It certainly wasn't a bomber's moon. The raw threat of the day was even more noticeable now. Shuddering, Ruth balled her hands and pushed them into her jacket pockets. Trying to keep her chattering teeth still, she strained to catch the first throaty raw of approaching planes. Someone shouted outside in the street and several pairs of feet walked past. *Going to the big shelter further up the street*, Ruth decided. Even so, there was no sense of urgency in their pace. Obviously they couldn't hear any bombers either.

Now that her eyes were adjusted, she looked out over the waiting vehicles. The paler discs above the uniform collars told her that most of the men were turned full-face in her direction, waiting for her to release them in a helter-skelter of bells and exhilarating excitement. She couldn't oblige. The skies remained stubbornly silent.

Smaller sounds became magnified. The clank of metal and muted voices from beyond the yard suggested that some of the track men were walking along the railway lines which stretched behind Good Hope. An indefinable humming sound solidified itself into a rendition of 'Wish Me Luck As You Wave Me Goodbye', being sung under their breath by the regular firemen on the turntable ladder. Good Hope's sub-officer bawled at them to shut up. After a further defiant chorus to demonstrate that as Red Riders they considered themselves above the orders of a mere auxiliary fireman, they duly did so.

'Ruth!' The urgent shout from within the station sent Ruth's heart into her mouth. She heard the intake of breath from the waiting crews as she spun round to fly back to the watchroom.

'False alarm,' Betty said, meeting her at the door. 'Control says to stand them down.'

'Plagues of locusts on 'em,' Ruth said, borrowing her father's vocabulary. 'What did they want to get us all fired up for?'

'Well, I can't help it,' Betty pointed out. 'Tell the sub.'

'Yeah, OK.'

Ruth wandered back outside, her casual approach to the pump signalling her news long before she formally reported the stand-down to the officer in charge. All around her crestfallen and disgruntled men climbed out of their vehicles. The expectation of action which had been coiling ever tighter inside them as they sat in the waiting vehicles now found expression in curses and grumbles.

From the farthest side of the yard, a louder 'bleedin' hell' was followed by the sound of something heavy thumping on to the cobbles. Shouted calls for an explanation brought another curse followed by a groan. Ruth followed most of the other men over to the turntable ladder. She found one of the crew sprawled on the cobbles, clutching his leg.

'What 'appened?'

'Stupid sod's tripped over his own feet jumping down from the cab.'

'Take more water with it,' someone shouted from behind.

'It ain't funny,' the aggrieved fireman moaned. 'I think I've broken my ankle.'

'Let's have a look, old man.' The sub-officer bent and ran both his hands over the twisted leg. 'Don't know about broken, but it's swelling up a treat. Best get that boot off before we have to cut it. Would you take a shoulder each there, lads.'

The all-clear sounded as a wailing accompaniment to the moans of the injured man as his leather boot was dragged from the rapidly ballooning ankle. Groaning and cursing, he was supported on either side as he hopped back to the station.

Perched on the stairs cradling the injured limb, the man asked if they weren't going to call an ambulance.

'Don't be daft, old man. They'll be needed for the sick people. You can go up the casualty post, get that strapped up.'

'How can I? I can't fuc . . . I can't stand on it.'

'One of you go up to the locker room. See if a good Samaritan from the off-duty watch will go with our wounded hero. Mrs Shaw, would you get the control office on the phone? Tell them the turntable's a man short.'

Betty nodded and duly relayed the information across the road. Since the turntable ladder was crewed by regular firemen, they'd have to supply a stand-in for the injured man. Or, more to the point, they'd *insist* on supplying him, since the gleaming red appliances were jealously guarded by the regulars.

By the time a sleepy auxiliary had been roused and sent off with the injured fireman, who was hopping erratically like a drunken Long John Silver, the station officer had made his way across to Good Hope with a leading fireman and a female auxiliary in tow.

The sub-officer greeted them jovially. 'Wouldn't you think all that training the Red Riders get, they'd have included a lesson climbing out of a cab without falling flat on your arse?' The auxiliaries who were still within earshot laughed.

Len Shaw scowled. 'Isn't it about time for a meal break?'

Having had his bit of fun at the regulars' expense, the sub-officer jerked his head in the direction of the mess. 'Go on, lads. Smells like Snakey's got supper on.'

'Right,' Len Shaw snapped. 'Where's the injured bloke? Adele here has had first-aid training.'

The sub-officer explained that the man had already limped away into the night. 'Shouldn't think we'll be seeing him back on duty for a while.'

'That's up to the doctors, isn't it?' Len said shortly. 'In the meantime, Leading Fireman O'Day will be standing in on the turntable.'

'Pleased to have you aboard, Pat. Aren't we, girls?'

Ruth flashed the come-hither smile that she switched on automatically in the presence of anything male and still with a discernible pulse. Betty gave him a perfunctory 'Hello' but her attention was plainly on her husband. He, in turn, was studying a yellowing map pinned to the wall and designated 'Targets for Tonight'.

'Right,' the sub said, becoming aware of the chill. 'Why don't you get your kit stowed in the turntable, Pat, and then be getting yourself down the mess before the crew scoff the lot.'

'Yes, sir.' Pat left with obvious relief.

Ruth wrinkled her nose. 'Phew. What's that stink?'

Glad of the diversion, the two men and Betty sniffed loudly and voraciously at the fug-filled air.

'It's you, Adele,' Ruth said accusingly. 'It smells like . . .' She snorted another breath. 'Disinfectant.'

'It's not, it's not me,' Adele wailed. Red-faced and close to tears, she hunched herself into her uniform and backed towards the door.

'Have you had casualties over the road?' Betty asked, wondering if Adele's first-aid skills had already been pressed into service.

'Not that I'm aware of,' her husband said, speaking to a spot somewhere over her shoulder. 'Good God, Adele, Ruth's right, it *is* you. What on earth have you been doing, girl, bathing in the stuff?'

Adele's mouth wobbled. Her face screwed up in an effort to control her tears. It didn't work. With a howl of despair she turned and fled from the room.

'*Len!*'

'Not my fault.' Len refused to meet his wife's eyes. 'What did I say?'

'It's probably women's problems,' the sub said complacently. 'Now isn't it time one of you girls had a meal break? Mrs Shaw, why don't you get yourself down to the mess and tell the first man you find with a clean plate that I said he's to come up here and relieve you for half an hour?'

Nodding, Betty left the watchroom. Muttering about returning to duty, Len followed her. As soon as they were in the dimly lit corridor, Len cast a wary look up the stairs to check for eavesdroppers, then hissed pleadingly: 'Betty.'

157

Betty turned. She was several yards away from him, her face in shadow, but her stiff-backed posture told him her mood hadn't improved since Sunday's row.

'How long you going to keep this up?'

'Until you tell me the truth.'

'I *am* telling you the truth.'

'You had a letter on Sunday, Len. And it wasn't for number fourteen like you said, because I asked them.'

'You'd no right to go checking up on me like that. I'm your husband. I deserve some respect.'

'And don't I deserve to be trusted?'

'I do trust you.'

'You lied to me.'

'For your own good. I told you. The letter was rubbish. Real filthy. Not the sort of thing I'd want my missus to see. I tore it up for your own good.'

'Then why not tell me?'

It was the same argument that they'd had for hours after his return from the pub on Sunday afternoon, until they'd both finally retreated into self-imposed and self-righteous silence.

'For heaven's sake, woman, will you shut up about the damn letter? It's none of your business.'

It was that 'woman' which convinced Betty more than anything else that something was seriously wrong. Never, in the whole of their marriage, had Len ever called her 'woman'. She felt suddenly cold and frightened.

'I have to go. Half an hour, the sub said,' she mumbled, turning away.

A few steps down the corridor towards the mess, she turned back, half hoping he'd come after her and tell her everything was all right. But the dim tunnel stretching to the back door was empty. A thick band of gold light sprung across it as the watchroom door was pulled open.

'Forgot your fags,' Ruth called. She flicked the packet underarm and Betty caught it one-handed with muttered thanks.

The mess was already thick with wreathing clouds of tobacco smoke swirling up into the ceiling. It was overlaid with the smells of sizzling lard and frying fish. In the galley

158

Snakey was shaking several hissing pans with professional assurance. Seeing Betty approaching, he whipped the tea-towel off his shoulder and used it to protect his hand as he picked up a plate from the rack over the burners, dipped a fish slice into the biggest pot and scooped a mound of chips on to a tin plate. A fast shovelling movement hooked a lump of fish covered in golden batter from the next.

'There you h'are, Mrs Shaw. Best grub you'll h'ever taste in this mess.'

Pools of glistening grease slid in globules over the metal plate's shiny surface. The tea-cloth was stained a dirty khaki. Betty suddenly felt very sick. Taking several quick, deep breaths, she swallowed the bile burning the back of her throat and accepted the plate with a tight-lipped smile.

She'd half hoped to have a word with Pat. Since he was obviously friendly with that Inspector Stamford who was investigating the anonymous letters, perhaps he could tell her what they said. And then maybe she'd know what it was that Len was so keen for her *not* to know. A search through the smoke showed her she was out of luck. Pat was seated at a table with three other regular men, engrossed in a conversation from which snippets such as 'offside', 'ref must have been blind', and 'dummied him to the left' floated across to her.

Nell was at a table alone. 'Do you mind?' Betty asked.

Shaking her head wordlessly, Nell bent back to her plate, slicing each piece of fish or chip with almost surgical precision.

Returning to the galley, Betty collected a mug of tea and cutlery. She half expected Nell to have gone by the time she turned back. The ice-blonde frequently did disappear at the first hint of a possible close encounter. Tonight, however, Nell stayed fixed to her seat.

'It's better than it looks, isn't it?' Betty said after a few mouthfuls of Snakey's cuisine had settled the worst of her queasiness.

'It's quite adequate,' Nell agreed, placing her knife and fork neatly together.

Adequate. Snakey would be pleased, Betty thought. 'Nell . . . ?'

'Yes?' The silence after the tentative use of her name caused Nell to finally raise her eyes from her plate and give Betty her full attention.

'I was wondering ... have you heard about these letters people are getting? The anonymous ones.'

'What are you asking me for?'

The sharpness of Nell's tone caught Betty by surprise. Why *shouldn't* she ask her? 'Well ... you know ... Ruth and I were speaking about them earlier. We were just saying we'd never had one. Have you?'

'No.'

'Strange that, isn't it? It seems to be the blokes who get them.'

'Does it?'

'Mmm.' Betty sought her charm and drew it out from beneath her jacket, massaging it between her fingertips in an unconscious nervous habit. 'Snakey had one accusing him of fiddling the mess rations.'

'How very unpleasant for him.'

'He didn't seem bothered. I imagine most people just tear them up, wouldn't you think?'

'I wouldn't know.'

It was, Betty reflected, rather stupid trying to draw information from the person who was least likely to be the recipient of anyone's gossip. Glancing round for a more promising source, she saw Ruth coming through the door.

'You're all right,' Ruth shouted, seeing Betty looking at her watch. 'One of the blokes is standing in for me too.' Accepting a plate and a mug from Snakey, she made her way across and sat herself down with a thump. 'I remembered something I meant to tell yer,' she hissed.

'Why are you whispering?' Betty enquired, instinctively lowering her own voice.

' 'Cos it's about that det ... that bloke who come up the station the other day. *You know*, the one we was nattering about earlier.'

Betty cast a warning look in Nell's direction. Ruth missed it totally. But Nell she was pretty certain, intercepted it. She gave

160

no sign, but the tips of her ears beneath the smooth sweep of silver hair suddenly glowed pink.

'Anyway,' Ruth continued in an exaggerated sibilant whisper, 'this . . . bloke . . . 'ad a couple of kids with him. One of 'em was Pat O'Day's brother.'

Relieved at the direction the conversation was taking, Betty said she'd met Sammy. 'Pat brought him up the station once to look at the engines. Nice little boy. He's lucky to have a big brother that takes an interest. Their mum's a widow.'

'He said. Anyhow, the other kid was a right cheeky little blighter. *And*,' Ruth paused for effect, '*he* reckoned Pat is gonna marry some teacher from Riley Street school. Do you think we'll get asked to the wedding?'

'Well, I suppose Len might. It's traditional. Getting your senior officer drunk at your expense is considered a good way of getting on in the fire service.'

'Not us?' Ruth pouted. 'I've got a smashing hat for a wedding. Bought it in Daniels last summer. It's navy with these big feather plumes up the front. You couldn't rightly wear it nowhere else 'cept a wedding, or maybe at Ascot.'

'Ascot?'

'At the races. Yer *know*. Like they have on the Pathé News, with all them toffs with Rolls-Royces and them big picnic baskets.'

'I shouldn't think they do now, Ruth,' Betty said, pushing away her plate and draining her tea mug.

'Yes they do,' Nell said unexpectedly. 'At least they live quite well, I believe. One of our neighbours is a great racing man. He has no trouble at all apparently in obtaining petrol coupons to attend the meetings.'

Ruth looked up from her own plate. 'Honest? Is he in the forces?'

Maybe that was it? If Paul wasn't Nell's bloke, perhaps he was a neighbour. On the other hand, if she could find out about his interests before their Thursday date, it would be quite handy. A few knowing remarks on form and handicap over the candlelit dinner table were bound to intrigue him.

'No. He's an archdeacon. Why did you think he might be in the forces?'

'Oh, you know.' Ruth found herself reluctant to tell Nell about meeting Paul – whatever her relationship to him might be – although she couldn't have said why. It was just a vague, superstitious uneasiness. As if the ice-blonde might somehow have the power to spoil her chances of stepping from the drabness of Camden Town into the brilliantly lit world of handsome officers and beautiful women that she'd watched so avidly on the screen of the Gaisford as she showed customers into the one and threepennies.

'I saw a fireman's wedding once. Down St Barnabas's it was,' she said, deliberately ignoring Nell and speaking to Betty again. 'It was smashing. They made an arch with their axes and the bride and groom walked under it. Have you seen her? Pat's girl? What's she like?'

'I don't think girl's the right word,' Betty said, checking her watch and standing up. 'She's a widow. Lost her husband at Dunkirk.'

'Really? Gawd, less than six months and she's found another one already. Doesn't rightly seem fair when some of us haven't even got down the aisle once yet. Maybe they should put blokes on ration too. What do you reckon, Nell?'

'Excuse me. I think I'll go and get some air.'

Raising mutely understanding eyebrows at each other, Betty and Ruth watched the slim auxiliary weave her way out of the smoky mess.

'Stuck-up cow,' Ruth said, without heat.

'It takes all sorts. I'll get back to the watchroom.' Betty glanced across at Pat. He was still talking animatedly to the other regulars. With any luck, if the raids held off, she'd get a chance to talk to him about the letters later.

Unfortunately, whilst the crews remained in the station for the rest of her shift, Pat always seemed to be in a crowd of other firemen.

The house was cold and unwelcoming as she let herself in the front door. *It doesn't feel like home any more*. The thought popped into her mind from nowhere. *Of course it does; you're getting fanciful in your old age, Betty Shaw*, she told herself sternly. Lighting the cooker, she set pans of water to boil. A

162

scrubbing brush and a session on her knees scouring the linoleum would soon get rid of any fancies. The house started to fill up with the smell of suds, vinegar and steam. Dust flew in clouds as she attacked bedding she hadn't touched for months. Thick wax polish released aromas of lavender as she ground it into wood with almost maniacal ferocity. It was as if she was possessed.

'For heaven's sake, *woman . . . woman . . . woman . . .*' Len's voice kept being in her head.

Don't think about it, she told herself. *He'll be home soon, you can talk then.*

The rattle of the door caught her by surprise. Aware of her clothes sticking to her sweaty body, she hastily tidied her hair and hurried through to the front hall. It was just the second post. Three envelopes lay on the mat. The first was covered with the spidery writing of the coal merchant's clerk; the other two looked identical. One for her and one for Len. *Christmas cards?* she wondered. Except who sent separate cards to husband and wife? And who wrote in pencil?

She slit the flap of her letter with her thumb and pulled out a single sheet of paper. The writing jumped from the page at her:

SPY. SPY. SPY.
YOU OUGHT TO BE IN PRISON WITH THE OTHER
SPIES.

It took a few moments for the words to make sense. Spy? It was a mistake, surely? She turned the crumpled envelope over and reread the name on the front. It wasn't a mistake; her own name was printed clearly in pencilled capitals: MRS BETTY SHAW.

Stunned, she groped for the stairpost and lowered herself down on to the bottom step. Shock gradually ebbed away, pushed back by a rising tide of anger. How dare they! How dare anyone imagine they had the right to . . . And then she became aware of the second letter, still clutched in her other hand. The flap of the envelope was slightly torn on one corner.

She worked her finger under it, easing it slightly. The cheap gum gave up its grip without a struggle. Inch by inch the triangular flap peeled back. Drawing out the letter, she started to read.

Chapter 17

Jack received the invitation to dinner at the O'Days' house with mixed feelings. On the one hand he was pleased to be called back from the exile into which he'd been plunged since the business of Maury's escapade on Sunday night. On the other he was worried as to where even a simple conversation with the O'Days might lead these days. He hadn't had to accept the situation, of course. Damn it all, his daughter lived with the O'Days most of the time. There were a thousand reasons why he should have taken those few steps across the road to ask after her. But he hadn't. For much the same reasons that prevented Eileen from facing him. Neither of them wanted to deal with the truth about Maury.

It would seem, since Eileen had been the first to capitulate, that she was braver than him. Or perhaps she'd discovered that she had less to fear than she first thought. The evidence that Maury had been involved in the warehouse robbery was circumstantial at best. Jack's own visit to the injured watchman had been warmly received as a token of police concern. But whilst he was flattered to get the personal attention of a chief inspector, the man had nothing to add to his original statement. Which just left Maury's hat and the description of the lorry. The hat was a non-starter; there was no way of proving it *was* Maury's. The lorry was the best bet. They'd no registration number, but the description was distinctive enough for it to be recognised.

'I got a lead on the motor,' Ding-Dong had said when Jack dropped into Agar Street Station in another abortive attempt to speak to Sarah about Nell De Groot. He'd missed her again, but gleaned enough information from the CID office to know that the current theory was that the whisky raid had been carried out by a pair of lucky local amateurs.

'Local because they seem to have known the watchman was Rip Van Winkle's twin brother,' Ding-Dong explained. 'And amateurs because they used a van that looked different even in the blackout.'

'Why lucky?' Jack queried.

'Crates had only arrived that morning. Even the owner didn't know they were coming. Reckons his number must have come up on the distillery's tombola, because he hadn't seen a delivery for weeks.'

'Inside job?'

'Doubt it, sir.' Ding-Dong sucked his teeth. 'Luck, I reckon. Someone saw 'em coming off the carrier's lorry. Better to be born lucky than rich, the lady wife always reckons.'

Jack found himself praying that if Maury *was* involved his luck would hold. Because if it didn't, his reception at the O'Days' tonight didn't bear thinking about.

So far it seemed it had. Pat opened the door to him that evening with the news that it would just be the five of them for dinner. 'You, me, Mum, and the kids, I mean. Maury's gone down his girlfriend's house for his tea.'

'Where's that then?' Jack asked, allowing himself to be ushered down the passage into the kitchen, where Sammy and Annaliese were busy making paper-chains on the wooden table.

'Cutter's Wharf. Pansy's family owns the builders' merchants on the canal.'

'Sounds like Maury's landed on his feet,' Jack remarked.

'He has.' Eileen straightened up from the cooker and closed the oven door carefully. 'There's money down there all right. And they've taken to our Maury, even if Pansy's too young to be thinking of courting seriously.'

Jack got the unspoken message: Maury had expectations, therefore he had no need to go out thieving. Unfortunately it didn't work like that, but he let the matter pass and bent over to kiss the top of Annaliese's head. The incautious movement jarred the pain in his arm from a dull throb to a searing poker-red blast.

166

'Jesus . . .' He bit back a gasp of shock.

Eileen reached up into a high cupboard, took down a near-empty bottle of brandy, and poured the last few drops into a teacup. 'Medicinal,' she said briefly. 'Bought and paid for too.'

'Thanks,' he said, gratefully allowing the burning liquid to explode into fire in his stomach. Part of his mind noted that she knew it was the whisky robbery that Maury was suspected of being implicated in. How? he wondered. Was it just the back-garden gossips in action, or had she and Pat got the truth out of Maury on Sunday night?

He knew with certainty that they'd never tell him because they'd expect him to behave like a policeman and put the truth before any demands of friendship. He wished he could be as sure. Would he really put the job before any ties of loyalty? Or, more to the point, before his own selfish need for the O'Days' practical assistance in his present crippled condition? Before this had happened he would have said yes unhesitatingly. Now he was discovering that his principles were as susceptible to selfishness as the next sufferer.

'Clear that lot off the table now, you two,' Eileen ordered briskly.

'Just a minute, Mum, we're nearly finished, see.' Sammy shook the chain of multicoloured paper links. Several of them snapped open.

'You *broke* it,' Annaliese said. The accusatory tone surprised Stamford. He was used to the quiet, shy whisper that the little girl had used ever since she'd returned to England six months ago. Was it possible she was finally coming out of her shell? Perhaps she might even start to talk about what had happened to her missing mother.

'Get out from under me feet, Sammy,' his mother ordered. 'Take that lot upstairs. You can do the rest in your 'oliday.'

'You gonna have decorations in your 'ouse, Mr Stamford?' Sammy asked, obediently gathering the sticky bundle to his chest.

'I don't suppose I'll bother,' Jack said.

'What, nothing? No tree?'

'He can share our tree,' Eileen said, briskly scrubbing dried paste from the tabletop. 'If they got any up the market. Now go on, get upstairs.'

'I'll give you a hand.' Pat scooped up the remaining chains, carrying them like a baby over his forearms.

After the children had gone the awkwardness of unspoken questions descended on the kitchen.

'There's a children's party at the police station . . .'

'Rabbit pie, one of Shane's mates brought 'em round . . .'

They both spoke at once and broke off in confusion.

'How are the rest of the boys?' Jack asked, breaking the silence first.

'Well enough, I think. At least Brendan and Shane are. They both sent Christmas cards. Haven't heard from Conn for a while. Pat says he'll be at sea. Says we'd have heard if anything had 'appened.'

'I'm sure that's right. No post boxes in the middle of the Atlantic.'

'That's what Pat said.' Eileen's hands laid cutlery into five place settings with the sureness of a stud poker dealer. 'I was 'oping maybe they'd get a bit of leave for Christmas.'

'I don't think I'd rely on that too much, Eileen. There's plenty with the same hopes this year.'

'Suppose so. And I daresay it's the officers who'll get the leave tickets. You and Annie will be eating your dinner here, won't you? I thought, seeing as how Pat's off Christmas Eve this year, we'd 'ave our special dinner then.'

Without waiting for an answer, Eileen rushed on, throwing words into the pot so that there was no room for that dangerous topic of conversation: her second youngest. 'I can't promise a bird. But I been saving our meat coupons best I can, and the butcher promised to try and put by something a bit special for us. I thought I'd ask Sarah to 'ave her dinner here. I don't suppose she'll 'ave got to know anyone much up her new lodgings. Unless . . . will she have to work Christmas at the police station?'

'Even if she does, she might get off part of the day.'

'Good. I can always keep her dinner hot on a low gas.' Adjusting a fork without looking at him, Eileen said briskly,

'I'd best get them spuds mashed before they burn through me saucepan.' Seizing the heavy pan, she marched into the scullery and a second later disappeared in a cloud of steam.

'Mr Stamford . . .'

The low voice from the doorway startled him. He hadn't heard Pat come back down the stairs.

'I've got one,' Pat said quietly. 'It came this . . .' The thundering crash of his youngest brother's boots on the stairs, followed by an even louder crack as Sammy leapt the last few steps, made him bite off whatever else he was going to say.

'Sit down. I can't dish up with you lot under my feet.'

With the ease of long practice, Eileen scooped potatoes and greens on to the plates and swiftly dissected the pie; a quarter each for the two men, with the remaining half shared between herself and the children. Pat fetched three glasses and poured beer for them.

' 'Ow about me?' Sammy said, surfacing from a mouthful of pie.

'Touch one drop and I'll lather you until you can't sit down for a month,' his mother warned.

'Like Maury,' Annaliese said, sucking the tines of her fork.

Only Sammy seemed unaware of the sudden chill in the atmosphere. 'I could 'ave ginger beer. Or cream soda. There's bottles in the parlour cupboard. There's biscuits and sweets and stuff too.'

'They're for Christmas,' his mother informed him. 'It's taken me months to get them together. Don't you touch a thing in there, understand?'

'Yeah, all right. What's for pudding?'

'Wait-and-see surprise,' Eileen said tartly, bending back to her plate.

Jack became aware that he was holding his breath and let it go in a rush. Once again the dangerous subject of Maury had been neatly side-stepped.

Once the meal was finished, Eileen ordered the children to fetch their nightclothes. 'I'll get them washed and changed while the kitchen's still warm,' she said in a plain note of dismissal to the men.

169

'Come outside for a smoke, Mr Stamford?' Pat suggested. His tone was casual, his waggling eyebrow anything but.

'Good idea.'

They stood for a moment at the back door, allowing their senses to become accustomed to the total blackness. The moon was hidden behind heavy scudding clouds and the stars had no effect on the impenetrable blanket of the blackout. Jack's hearing adjusted to the environment first. It picked out the uneasy fluttering and clucking of Eileen's hens, which was explained a moment later by a yowl and clatter as two foraging cats discovered a bin lid that hadn't been closed fully. Farther away, over the rooftops, the distant, rhythmic clank-clank of moving rolling stock from the railway lines provided a counterpoint to Pat's slightly too fast breathing. Jack caught the rustle of cardboard and something knocked his arm.

'Sorry,' Pat apologised in response to Jack's involuntary flinch. 'I keep forgetting.'

'I wish I could.' Guessing that the fist held an open cigarette box, he fumbled one free and clenched it between his teeth. Both heads dipped forward to insert wavering tips into the brief flare of flame that was shielded behind Pat's cupped hands.

'So what's the problem?' Jack asked. *Apart from Maury*, he nearly added.

'I got one,' Pat said. 'One of them letters.' His voice was low and tense. The orange tip of his cigarette bobbed out of Jack's sight, spraying an arc of tiny glinting tobacco flakes behind it. The movement betrayed his backward glance towards the house.

'Your mother doesn't know?'

'No. She was up the market with the kids when it come.'

As they talked they'd both been moving cautiously away from the house. The clods of earth under their feet released a sour smell, betraying the waterlogged nature of this area of London clay.

'Come down the Anderson, Mr Stamford, we can 'ave a light on down there.'

The shelter door shrieked in protest as Pat pushed against it.

At the far end of the garden, the inhabitants of the coop set up a token fluttering and squawking.

'Best leave it open,' Pat murmured, feeling his way inside the box. Jack prudently remained by the door until Pat had fumbled his way to the other end and lit the oil lamp. The yellow light flared then died as Pat adjusted the wick to its lowest setting and set it on the shelf.

Jack groped his way forward to join Pat on one of the bunks. He hated this shelter, and after one excruciatingly uncomfortable night inside it, he'd vowed to be bombed in his own home in the future. Shuffling on the duckboards that had been laid to deal with the water seeping from the buried tributaries beneath the earth, he eased carefully between the two double bunks that occupied the sides of the shelter and lowered himself on to the bare slats on the bottom of the home-made contraption.

Delving inside his trouser pocket Pat pulled out an envelope folded in two. 'Here.'

Jack went to use his teeth to extract the single sheet of paper.

'Let me.' Pat laid it on the shelf beneath the lamp. The light was so low that Jack had to bend within six inches of the paper to make out the block capitals.

WERE YOU CARRYING ON WITH THAT WIDOW BEFORE HER HUSBAND GOT KILLED? BET YOU WERE. BET SHE COULDN'T WAIT TO GET RID OF HIM. SOMEONE OUGHT TO TELL THE SCHOOL ABOUT HER.

Jack looked into Pat's tight-lipped face. 'It's the first one?'

'Yes.' The rest of the words exploded from him. 'The lousy bastard. If I ever get my 'ands on him he's gonna wish he'd never been born, so help me, Mr Stamford.'

'Don't do anything silly, Pat,' Jack warned. *There's no sense two of you getting a record*, he silently added.

He examined the envelope, feeling the feeble lamp flame hot on his cheek through the glass funnel. The letter had been posted locally early that morning. The paper and envelope were both cheap commercial stationery; the sort that could be purchased at any newsagent's. The writer had used pencil. Holding the thin sheet to the light, Jack checked for any hidden impressions. The back glare revealed virgin spaces between the words.

'Lead's too soft to come through, pity they didn't use a pen,' he muttered to himself.

'I tried not to touch it too much,' Pat said.

It hardly made any difference. The paper and envelope had probably been fingered in the shop, passed through the sorter's and postman's hands and smeared all over with Pat's prints. Even if Jack could get the prints isolated, he had nothing to compare them with. And suggesting a mass fingerprinting of both the main and Good Hope stations was hardly in keeping with his brief to be discreet.

'Good.' He smiled. 'It would help if you could get your hands on some other letters . . . sent to someone else, I mean.'

'I'll try,' Pat promised. 'But you see it ain't . . .'

He was interrupted by a soft voice from the doorway. 'Pat?' Ducking inside, Rose Goodwin came forward. Her slimmer, smaller size made it easier for her to move between the bunks much faster than either of the men. She'd slid on to the bunk opposite before either of them could react.

'Your mum said to come out. You haven't forgotten we're going to the Forum? Hello, Mr Stamford.'

'Good evening, Mrs Goodwin.'

'Can we still count on your support at the Nativity play tomorrow?'

'Yes, of course.' Jack tried to fold the letter one-handed. Gritting his teeth against the pain, he forced his injured arm forward and made his hand open the envelope. 'How's it going?'

'It's terrible,' Rose admitted. 'Most of the boys seem to be tone-deaf. The Virgin Mary's so bossy she ought have been cast as Pontius Pilate and the Angel of the Lord keeps forgetting his lines.'

'Sounds just like the one I was in when I was a kid,' Pat said. 'I was an ox.'

Jack could sense Pat's anxious effort not to look in his

direction as he chased the infuriatingly slippery envelope round the shelf.

'I know,' Rose laughed. 'I was in the same class, remember? You stood on my lamb's tail and I hit you.'

The injured arm stubbornly refused to send messages to his fingers. The folded letter flicked from Jack's grasp and dropped to the duckboards.

'I'll get it.'

Pat's dive wasn't fast enough. Rose stooped and took the sheet by one corner. The rest of the paper fell open. She glanced down, incuriously at first, then both men saw her knuckles whiten.

'It's rubbish,' Pat said quickly. 'Someone sick in the head, Rose. Everyone knows it ain't true. Everyone's been getting them. I told you.'

'You also told me there was some truth in the ones you'd heard about.' Refolding the sheet, she handed it back to Jack. 'Do you know who sent it?'

'No, of course I don't. If I did, I'd knock their block off. Mr Stamford's gonna find out.'

'Are you, Mr Stamford? That's very good of you. I mean, it's hardly a police matter, is it? Just a putting into words of what several of my neighbours have been saying.'

'Have they? You never said, Rose. Why didn't you tell me?' Pat demanded.

'There was no need.' With a sudden glimmer of a smile, Rose remarked that her own mother had sorted them out more thoroughly than Pat could ever have done. 'They don't say anything in my hearing any more. But of course that doesn't stop them gossiping behind the net curtains.'

'They don't know what a bast . . . how Peter treated you. If they did, they'd be on our side.' Leaning forward, Pat clasped her hands between his. Wordlessly, Rose twisted them free.

'Why are the police involved, Mr Stamford?'

'We aren't – officially. Pat just asked me to ask around while I'm . . .' He lifted the swollen elbow fractionally.

'I see.' Her voice conveyed her disbelief.

'I'll leave you two alone.' Jack stood up too fast and winced

173

as his head came into contact with the top bunk. Swinging his legs up, Pat let him past. They both stayed silent until he'd clambered back into the garden. As he reached the kitchen door, however, he heard the two voices drift up from the sunken shelter, Rose's sharp, Pat's pleading. Wishing Eileen and the children goodnight he made his way back to his own house, hoping that Pat's persuasive powers were enough to dispel the mischief done by their malicious correspondent.

Evidently they weren't. Jack was roused the following morning by a thunderous onslaught on his front door. Hurtling down the stairs, he dragged the lock open with difficulty and was nearly knocked off his feet by Pat barging into the hall.

'I'll kill him, you hear me, Mr Stamford. When you get your hands on that bastard, you just let me know and I'll . . .'

Jack's initial worry – that something had happened to Annaliese – was swiftly replaced by irritation at the rude awakening. It was compounded by a thumping headache from the additional brandy he'd swallowed at three o'clock this morning in a desperate attempt to knock himself out so that he could forget the arthritis which had risen to an indescribable pitch of agony as soon as he climbed into bed.

'For God's sake, Pat. Come into the kitchen. Have you had breakfast?' he asked, shaking the kettle. It was empty but he'd pretty well managed one-handed tap-turning and gas-ring-lighting by now.

'Hours ago,' Pat snapped, straddling a chair. 'She's called it off.'

'Sorry?'

'Rose. She's called it off. Us. Says we ought to wait a bit. June, she reckons. 'Ave a full year's mourning for Peter. It's bloody daft, Mr Stamford. She hated the bloke. He beat her up. What's she want to mourn him for? Glad to be shot of him I'd have thought.'

Opening the larder, Jack found the end of a loaf. It felt suspiciously hard. 'It's not that easy to forget a marriage, Pat. No matter how bad it was, the other person will always be part of you. They'll have seen a side of you that no one else ever will. You can't just switch all that off.'

'Well Peter has, ain't he?' Pat said, taking the crust and hacking off two slices for him. 'He's switched off for good in some army cemetery somewhere. I don't want her to forget him. I just want . . . I want her,' he finished simply. Delving into his uniform jacket, he pulled out a small red leather box and opened it. An engagement ring winked its ruby and diamond message at Jack. 'I was going to ask her at Christmas.'

'I'm sorry, Pat.'

'Yeah, well . . .' Pat stood up again abruptly. 'I got to go. I'm on duty. You find him, Mr Stamford. You find who's been sending these letters before me and the lads do. Otherwise we might just sort him out ourselves.'

'Pat, don't do anything stupid . . .' His warning was cut off by the slamming of the front door.

Chapter 18

The kitchen felt even colder and the bread staler now he was left to his own devices. Munching on the toast, he went back to the hall and opened the door to the coal store. The sudden cloud of dust made him sneeze, sending another jolt of pain through his arm. He ground his teeth in frustration. The pain was an enemy that he couldn't even fight, let alone defeat. He knew now how sufferers could cut off a diseased limb in order to rid themselves of the agony. It was a sort of victory in a way. A triumph over the pain, by separating it from the blood and oxygen it needed to survive.

He leant over, carefully put several small lumps of coal into a battered scuttle and carried them through into the front room. Unlike most of his neighbours, who reserved this room for 'best', he used it for everyday. Now he carefully swept out the grate one-handed, crumpled newspaper, added the virgin coal and applied his lighter.

After he'd relit the damn thing four times, he tried to hold a sheet of newspaper across the opening to encourage the blaze to draw. The paper rippled tantalisingly in the down-draught. Annoyed, he pinned it to one corner with his hand and, balancing precariously, clamped the other edge with one foot. It wasn't an easy posture to maintain. Feeling himself over-balancing, he hopped to maintain his equilibrium, crashed backwards and landed on the base of his spine. His elbow caught the scuttle and tipped its dust over the carpet, whilst one flying foot sent a chair over.

'Hell and blast and . . .' With a furious kick at the scuttle, which hurt him far more than it did the uncaring metal, he stormed out.

It took him a further two hours to complete dressing and shaving, leaving him panting with the effort and nursing the depressing knowledge that he'd spent an entire morning making breakfast and getting into his clothes.

The door knocker provided a welcome diversion. For a brief second his brain acknowledged that it knew the round-faced woman whose chestnut eyes regarded him from beneath the brim of a black felt hat, but his memory refused to provide a name.

'I hope you don't mind my coming to your home, Inspector,' she said, mistaking his expression for disapproval.

The sound of her voice jolted his recall into action. 'Mrs Shaw. Of course I don't mind.' He stood back. 'I didn't recognise you out of uniform. Go through.' He opened the living room door and was confronted by the mess he'd left after the abortive firelighting attempt. 'Er, the kitchen is warmer.'

Betty obediently preceded him down the short flight of steps. 'I went to Pat's house first. His mother told me where you lived. She said to tell you she'd be over at quarter to two and no excuses.'

'School Nativity play,' Jack explained, taking the seat opposite her and noting how her fingers plucked restlessly at the black leather gloves she'd removed. 'My daughter's an angel. Figuratively speaking.'

'How old is she?'

'Six.'

'That's a lovely age, isn't it?' The glove fingers were stretched and released with the rhythmic movements of a cow being milked as Betty Shaw looked round the room. Her attitude suggested an uncertainty that hadn't been evident on their previous meetings. Something, he concluded, had happened to knock the stuffing out of Mrs Betty Shaw.

'Why don't you just tell me?' he suggested, sensing that she was regretting her decision to come.

'It's about the letters. Len said . . . I mean, there shouldn't be secrets between husband and wife, should there, and anyway I won't say anything, I promise.'

'I gather Mr Shaw has told you this investigation is now . . .'

177

Is now *what*? Jack wondered. 'Is now quasi-official,' he finished, feeling rather pleased with himself for plucking that obscure word from his subconscious.

'Yes.' The glove fingers were now being well and truly throttled.

'And which bothers you? The fact or the knowing of it?'

'What?' Incomprehension spread over Betty's round face. 'Neither,' she said finally. 'It's just . . .' Snapping open the lock on her handbag, she drew out an envelope identical to the one Pat had received and passed it across the table to him.

Using his fingertips to hold the edge of the paper, he shook it free of the envelope, and used his teeth to open it out. Flattening it on the table, he silently read the message. It had been printed in block capitals in soft lead pencil, the same as Pat's. He'd need to compare them of course, but at a cursory glance he was pretty certain they'd both been written by the same person. The smudged postmark was local too. And the stationery identical to that used in Pat's letter.

Looking up, he met Betty's anxious eyes. 'This came yesterday morning?'

'Second post.'

'Have you ever had one before.'

'No. I'd have said, when you came to Good Hope station, if I had.'

Perhaps you would, Jack thought, holding the letter up to the poor light from the back window. *It rather depends how near the bull our mysterious writer's poisonous dart had landed, I suspect.* Evidently this one was so ridiculous that Mrs Shaw had no qualms about showing it to him. 'Have you any idea who sent it?'

'Me! No, of course not. How could I?'

'This . . . unpleasantness . . . seems to be centred on the fire stations. That rather suggests someone with an intimate knowledge of the various staff there.'

'Someone who works there, you mean?'

She seemed genuinely surprised, suggesting to Jack that if Nell De Groot was responsible for the outbreak, her colleagues had no cause to suspect her – yet.

'Not necessarily,' Jack temporised. 'It could be someone who's related to a fireman, perhaps. Someone who listens to the gossip. Have you any idea what's behind this particular piece of nastiness?' He tapped the sheet with his forefinger, rapping the word 'SPY'.

'I've been racking my brains and all I could think was this.' Unbuttoning the top of her coat, she fumbled beneath her blouse and pulled out something on a chain.

'A swastika.' Jack experienced a surge of revulsion and anger. Was she a Fascist supporter? You could never tell. Some of the most rabid blackshirts had hidden behind a façade of sweet reasonableness.

'A fylfot,' she corrected him. 'It used to be a symbol of good luck.'

'Well it's hardly that now. Frankly, Mrs Shaw, I think you'd be well advised to get rid of the thing immediately. It could land you in serious trouble.'

'That's what Len said.'

'Then I strongly suggest you listen to your husband.'

'Do you?' There was an edge to her question which was partially explained by her bitter comment that in order for her to do that, her husband would have to talk to her, wouldn't he?

Jack wasn't interested in the Shaws' marital problems. Fortunately Betty Shaw seemed as disinclined to talk about them as he was disinclined to listen. She changed the subject immediately, deflecting it back to the fylfot and firmly stating her intention to keep the charm.

'That's your prerogative of course, Mrs Shaw. Thank you for bringing me the letter.'

He half stood, expecting her to do the same. Instead she said: 'Why do you think they're doing this?'

'Malice, spite. Perhaps some form of mental disturbance.'

His explanation, rather than reassuring her, seemed to cause her more anxiety.

'I'm sure they're unlikely to progress to violence,' he said, wondering if perhaps the words 'mental disturbance' had ignited images of lunatics running wild.

'No.' She grasped her bottom lip with her top teeth and

gnawed it. 'But then why . . . well, Len didn't say *why* it was to do with national security.'

'Morale,' Jack said glibly. 'It's classed as interference with persons engaged in essential services. Defence Reg. 1A.'

'Oh . . . so . . .' Betty hesitated, then said more firmly, 'Why's it a secret? I mean, why haven't you asked the crews to save the letters and pass them on to the police? You haven't, have you? Not officially?'

'There are reasons for the procedures I'm following,' Jack said, introducing a note of *I'm the professional, please let me get on with my job* into his tone whilst silently cursing Special Branch and their obsession with not letting the right hand know the left even existed, let alone what it was doing.

'Why do you think people haven't been reporting them?'

'Frankly, Mrs Shaw, I suspect most recipients have put them where they deserve to be; on a hook in the lavatory.'

'Do you think any of them are true?'

'Statistically speaking, I suppose our malicious friend must hit the truth occasionally. Or at least a distorted view of it.'

She seized on the word. 'Distorted. Yes. Things can be distorted, can't they? I mean, things aren't always what they seem, are they?'

'Is there something else, Mrs Shaw?' Jack said directly. 'This isn't just about someone taking exception to your jewellery, is it?'

She'd been nursing her bag on her lap. Now she placed it on the table and opened the clasp again with obvious reluctance. Drawing out another envelope, she placed it on the wood surface next to its twin. 'It's for Len,' she said unnecessarily.

'So I see. Did this come with the other?'

'Yes. Len doesn't know. I . . . I hid it.'

Using a pen, he flattened out the sheet and read:

YOU'RE STILL CARRYING ON WITH HER AREN'T YOU? HOW LONG BEFORE MRS SHAW FINDS OUT? MAYBE I SHOULD WRITE HER? LET HER KNOW WHAT HER LOVING BLOKE GETS UP TO WHEN THE CAT'S AWAY?

* * *

Her eyes had grown huge. He read the question in them: did he think it was true? Did she? he asked.

'I . . . I don't know. I mean mine isn't, is it?'

'But . . . ?'

'Why didn't he tell me? It's not the first, you see. There was another, Sunday. He lied about that at first. Then he said it was to protect me.'

'Perhaps it was. I mean, in his job he must be particularly aware of the fact that people think there's no smoke without fire.'

It was a feeble joke, and she wasn't fooled. 'There isn't. There has to be a point of combustion smouldering somewhere. No matter how deeply hidden it is.' She stood up abruptly. 'I'll leave the letters with you then, Inspector.'

She was nearly at the front door before he caught up with her. 'May I ask what you intend to do, Mrs Shaw? About your husband?'

Pausing with her hand on the latch, Betty said, with a spark of her old spirit, that she hardly thought that was any of his business.

'It is if he intends to come round here and thump me for stirring things up,' Jack said with feeling.

'Oh, I doubt if he'd do that. Anyway, you've got two days' grace to get a police guard on the door. Len's on duty now until Saturday. Goodbye, Inspector.'

The afternoon produced all the opportunities for embarrassment that he'd been dreading. And threw up one that hadn't even occurred to him.

As Rose Goodwin had predicted, there were few men amongst the audience for the school Nativity play. In consideration for the limited size of the school hall, only the relatives of the budding thespians were invited. These were conducted to wooden seats ranged in three rows along the back of the room.

Jack lowered himself gingerly onto a seat designed to hold a child's posterior and prayed that the spindly legs would take his

181

weight. From the corner of his eye, he inspected the fifty-odd adults settling themselves around him. Mothers, grandmothers and those who stood in that position, like Eileen, were out in force. But there was only one other man present. Perched awkwardly in the front row like Jack, his legs spread and knees bent to accommodate the inadequate seating, he was massaging a tweed cap between his fingers with the intensity of a baker kneading dough. Catching Jack's eye, he exchanged a flicker of understanding as they shared a mutual moment of awkwardness. Then the rest of the classes trooped in and arranged themselves cross-legged on the floor between the visitors and stage.

Any restless fidgeting and whispering was stilled instantly by the arrival of the headmaster and staff. After a moment of total silence, during which Jack found himself holding his breath in anticipation, Rose played a scale on the piano and the makeshift curtains swept jerkily aside to reveal a group of shepherds seated around a papier-mâché fire. Backstage somewhere a chorus of childish voices rose in 'While Shepherds Watched Their Flocks By Night', demonstrating their musical abilities with enthusiasm but very little talent. When the final verse ground to a merciful conclusion, one of the shepherds raised an arm and pointed.

' 're, wha's that?'

The Angel of the Lord swooped on in white robe and gold wings and shouted: 'Be'old I am the Angel of the Lord and I bring yer ... er ... er ...'

'Tidings,' hissed a woman behind Jack. 'Yer bringing 'em tidings, Roger.'

'Tidings,' bawled the red-faced angel.

Jack was forced to bite the side of his mouth whilst the familiar story unfolded. After the Virgin Mary had duly lined up the stable animals to her satisfaction, Annaliese appeared in a cluster of cherubs and the tone-deaf chorus launched into 'Away In a Manger'. As Rose reached the final notes, several seconds behind the chorus, the three kings trooped on. Predictably enough, the audience was treated to a rendering of 'We Three Kings of Orient Are', before they knelt and bestowed their gifts on the infant.

'That's not our gold coins,' the Virgin Mary said loudly, examining the contents of one king's box. 'What *have* you done with them, Philip Wright?'

'Hush, Peggy,' Rose pleaded.

'Those aren't the chocolate coins off our tree, miss,' Peggy announced. 'I bet he's eaten them.'

' 'Ave not,' the accused whined, snatching the box back.

' 'Ave too,' yelled the Virgin Mary, clutching the infant Jesus by one ankle and using it as a flail.

'Peggy!' shouted Rose.

'We saved up for that chocolate. It was only lended, wasn't it, Mum?' She appealed to the seated audience. Before Mrs Abbott could respond to her daughter's question, Rose brought her hands down firmly on the piano keys. To a crashing musical accompaniment, the whole class shuffled on stage and quavered their way through 'Hark the Herald Angels Sing', whilst Peggy and the sweet-toothed king jostled and hissed insults at each other.

The story wound to its ragged close and ended in a final crashing chorus. There was a moment's silence; then the adult audience launched into enthusiastic applause. Handicapped by only having one hand free, Jack found himself grinning inanely instead.

'Wasn't she good?' Eileen shouted in his ear.

'Wonderful,' he agreed, beating his good hand against his knee.

'I'll go round, help her out of the costume. Will you wait?'

'At the gate.'

Eileen nodded. As they stood to shuffle out again, Jack glanced across the hall towards Rose Goodwin. He'd half wondered whether he should have a word with her about the anonymous letters, or whether that would only make the situation between her and Pat worse. Rose solved his problem by disappearing behind the stage curtains, leaving him to make his way to the school gates and wait for Eileen and his daughter.

Other pupils flowed out in an excited, chattering chorus. They were free for a whole three weeks and there was Christmas, with all its promise of presents and treats, to look forward to. The anticipation was as tangible as an electrical charge in the air.

' 'Lo, Mr Stamford,' Sammy O'Day beamed, tumbling out on to the pavement.

'Hello, Sammy. Your mum won't be a minute.'

'See 'er back 'ome,' Sammy shouted, skipping and hopping down the road in an excess of energy and joy.

His mother followed more slowly, the angel wings clutched in one hand and Annaliese holding the other. 'She wants to keep them,' Eileen said by way of explanation as they started home.

'Quite right. Never know when you might want to fly, do you, Annaliese? He smiled down at the red head bobbing at waist level. She stared back solemnly. And then took his hand.

Jack felt an almost absurd surge of pleasure. It was the first voluntary sign of affection his daughter had shown to him since her rescue from occupied Europe the previous summer. He could almost have skipped and hopped down the road like Sammy.

Except when they turned the corner to the square, it was a very different Sammy who ran to meet them.

'What's the matter?' his mother said sharply, taking in his wide-eyed, pale face. 'It ain't one of your brothers, is it? Oh God, we haven't had a telegram?'

'No, Mum . . . it's . . .'

They all saw them at the same time. Two uniformed constables standing awkwardly to attention outside the O'Days' house.

'What on earth . . . ?' Jack hurried forward.

Detective Constable Bell came down the front path. 'Good afternoon, sir,' he said, tipping his hat to Jack.

'Ding-Dong. What's going on? Do you want me?'

'No thank you, sir. Mrs Eileen O'Day?'

'Yes.' Eileen flashed a bewildered look in Jack's direction, and he remembered that she'd never met the DC.

'Detective Constable Bell. A colleague.'

'Pleased to meet you. Don't all stand outside me door like

that. You'll have people thinking you've come to arrest me. Come inside, I'll put the kettle on.'

She included the two uniformed men in her smile. One looked at his boots and the other seemed fascinated by the chimney pots on the roof opposite. A warning tingle shot up Jack's spine just before Ding-Dong reached into his raincoat and produced a folded paper.

'Mrs Eileen O'Day,' he said formally, 'this is a search warrant. I intend to search these premises which I have reason to believe may contain stolen property.'

Chapter 19

Jack drew the DC aside and demanded to know what was going on. Did Ding-Dong know what the hell he was doing?

'It's a properly executed warrant, sir,' he said. 'Issued on the basis of information provided to the magistrate.'

'Yes, of course it is.' He made a conscious effort to relax and apologised to the DC. 'Sorry, Ding-Dong. It's just a bit . . .' He raised an eyebrow in Eileen's direction.

She was standing by her front gate, the children on either side of her. Her eyes were fixed straight ahead, but he could tell by the set of her mouth and pink streaks of colour along her cheekbones that she was as aware as he was of the twitching curtains and drifts of spectators collecting at the corners of the square.

'I can see it would be, sir,' Ding-Dong agreed. 'However, without fear or favour, you know . . .'

'Quite. I just wish you'd favoured me with a bit of advance warning.'

'I thought that might add to your problems, sir.'

On balance Jack realised he was probably right. After all, if he'd known the warrant was going to be served, what could he have done? Warned Eileen and risked her trying to move evidence? Or taken himself off somewhere for the afternoon to a pretended urgent appointment?

'Let's get on with it, then.'

For a moment Eileen remained firmly rooted between the gateposts, arms folded and defying the constables to move her. None of them seemed inclined to try.

'Eileen,' Jack pleaded softly.

'Did you know about this?'

'No.'

She held his eyes for a second, then spun round on her heels, strode to her front door and flung it open. They'd expected her to stand aside but instead she swept in, catching the police off guard. With an impatient jerk of his head, Ding-Dong signalled to the two uniformed men to follow and knelt by the sideboard, carefully removing Eileen's precious stock of treats collected for Christmas and laying them out on the carpet.

'What's this about?' Jack asked the DC. Privately he had no doubt at all what lay behind the search. But not to ask would be to suggest a prior complicity with the O'Days.

'Warehouse robbery, sir. I'm on the trail of the whisky.'

'Here? It's twenty crates, for God's sake.'

'Plenty of room, sir.' He craned his mournful face upwards, peering at the ceiling as if he could somehow see through the whitewash and joists to the floors above. 'Big house this for just the one family. And sons away fighting for King and Country, if I'm not mistaken?'

'Three.'

'Be a spare room, then?'

'Not for stolen property. Not in Eileen's house.'

'I'm not saying as how she'd *know* it was here, sir. But mothers has a remarkable capacity for not seeing how things really stand when it comes to their own. The lady wife is just the same.'

This was the first intimation Jack had ever had that Ding-Dong had any children. But rather than following this less treacherous conversational path, he plunged straight down the one marked 'Danger – Minefield'.

'Maury, I take it?'

'That's the ticket, sir,' Ding-Dong agreed. He explained he'd traced the van used in the robbery to one 'Eddie Hooper – villain of this parish. Does a bit of fetching and carrying, sir. Anything needs shifting, our Eddie will shift it. Unfortunately there's times when he gets so carried away with the call of his profession, he forgets to tell the lawful owners he's doing the shifting. He's got previous, sir. Burglary and housebreaking.'

'And now he's moved into the commercial sector?'

'The war's brought opportunities to a lot of folk,' Ding-Dong said without a trace of irony.

The uniformed constable had finished his search of the front room. He was directed to do the kitchen and then move the coal in the hall cupboard. His expression suggested he'd have argued with that one if Jack hadn't been there.

'Have you searched this Hooper's place?' Jack murmured.

'First thing this morning. The gent was still in bed with his wife. Leastways that's who she claimed to be. Funny that, because I could have sworn the lady was the betrothed of a coster up Queen's Market. Still, no doubt Mr Hooper knows his beloved best.'

'I take it you didn't find any sign of stolen whisky?'

'Not a tot, sir. Not that I really expected to. Hooper's fly enough not to stash the stuff under his bed. He keeps the lorry in a lock-up under the arches at King's Cross. Nothing there either.'

They watched silently as the constable slouched from the kitchen, shook his head mutely at Ding-Dong and pulled open the coal cupboard with a reluctant grimace.

'Don't you mess up my floor,' Eileen snapped. 'I've just put the mop over it.'

'Got any newspaper then, Ma?'

'Don't you ma me. Sammy, salvage pile.'

Sammy sped through to the back and came back with a pile of damp papers clasped to his chest. 'Shall I 'elp 'im, Mum?'

'Don't you dare!' A crash of falling furniture from above sent her flying up the stairs two at a time. Sammy and Annaliese scrambled up after her. Now they'd got over the initial shock, they were beginning to view this new experience as free entertainment.

'Are you certain that Maury's involved?'

'Known associate, sir. Had several sightings of young Mr O'Day in our Eddie's company over the past few weeks.'

'Is that all?'

'Well, there's the hat as well, sir. The one found in the vicinity just after the watchman got his lights put out. I daresay you recall me showing it to you when you came up the station the other day?'

'Brown trilby.'

'That's the one. Seems young Maury wears the self-same titfer. Lots of witnesses noticed it, sir.' *So how did a chief inspector come to miss it?* The unspoken question filled the air between them as they concentrated on the growing pyramid of coal lumps on the spread sheets of the *Daily Mirror*.

The search revealed nothing more than a cloud of grit and dust at the bottom of the cupboard. 'Put it back and we'll take a look out back,' Ding-Dong instructed. 'There's an Anderson.'

Allowing a loud stream of breath to flow over his teeth in noisy disapproval, the constable jumbled the lumps back inside, adding another layer of dust to his already filthy hands and face.

'Why are you doing this, Ding-Dong?'

'I explained the evidence, sir . . .'

'No. I meant, why are *you* handling it? Shouldn't DS Agnew be in charge?'

'He's sick, sir.'

'*Again!* What is it this time, for heaven's sake?'

'Some disease with one of them fancy Latin names. Can't get my tongue round it myself. The lady wife reckons her Gran's Mustapha had it.'

'Your wife has Arabic connections?'

'No, sir. Mustapha was the cat.'

Ding-Dong led the way through to the back garden. In the fast-descending dusk the narrow rows of freshly turned beds stretched down the sides of the Anderson and provided a bright strip of clay-yellow carpet in front of the hen house. He waited until sounds of collisions and cursing indicated the constable's painful progress around the cramped shelter before saying: 'CID's still under-staffed, sir. I mean, we have been for months, sir. You know that . . . I was wondering whether you'd be returning, sir?'

It was something that had been occupying Jack's mind a lot too since his enforced sick leave. His original appointment to Agar Street had been on a purely temporary basis, and his desk

189

at the Yard was still vacant. On the other hand . . . he touched exploratory fingers to the swollen elbow. It had been mercifully quiet for hours, but the hard, knobbly distortion beneath his suit jacket told him it was still an unexploded grenade waiting to erupt into mind-numbing agony at any second.

'I don't know,' he admitted. 'At present I seem destined to be pensioned off.'

'I'm sure they wouldn't do that, sir. There's reservists around now probably wrote up the notes on Jack the Ripper.'

'I am not *old*.'

'Never thought to suggest you were, sir. Just saying there's a place for everyone to do his bit these days. Personally I hopes we will be having the pleasure of your company back at Agar Street.'

The constable scrambled from his tin burrow, replacing his helmet. 'Nothing down there.'

'Check under the duckboards?'

As proof, the man held up his hands. The coal dust had been washed off by dirty water, which had seeped up to stain his armlets, turning the white stripes brown and the dark blue ones a sooty black. Ding-Dong advised him to get his uniform changed before the station sergeant clapped eyes on him, then told him to search the chicken coop.

The chickens weren't keen on this plan. Having settled themselves on their perches in the warm shed for the night, they violently objected to being rooted out into a chilly pen. A pen which was surrounded by a threatening darkness which an atavistic race memory told them could hide predators. Clucking like a worried knitting circle, they paced in wary procession round the dirt floor. Every few seconds an imaginary threat would send them scuttling in a display of sheer cowardice as each fought to be the one in the farthest corner from the supposed danger.

'Have you seen anything of Sar . . . Sergeant McNeill recently?' Jack asked. 'Eileen had to put her up for a couple of nights recently. Just as well she found herself new digs before you started rooting under her bed.'

'Not much, sir, her being mostly on nights the last week and me having the day shift. Though I did happen to run into her a few days ago. She was in the company of another young lady. Had a foreign-sounding name.'

Nell De Groot, Jack decided, pleased that at least part of his officially unofficial – or was it unofficially official – investigation into the anonymous letters was going to plan.

'Where did . . . ?'

He got no further. An angry shout from the house was followed by a shriek from Eileen and the sound of running feet. They both turned as the back door crashed back on its hinges. Maury appeared in the gap. Seeing the two men staring at him, he froze on the balls of his feet. Since there was no back way into the gardens, presumably his intention had been to vault the fence and escape through the houses opposite. Now he was trapped.

'Hello, Maury,' Jack said mildly.

Maury squared his shoulders. Thrusting his hands into the pockets of his trousers, he sauntered forward. ' 'Lo, Mr Stamford. What's going on?'

'You tell us, son,' Ding-Dong invited.

'Wouldn't know, would I? All I know is, I just set foot in me own front door and some copper comes charging down the stairs and tries to throttle me. I had to defend myself.'

As proof of his statement, the other uniformed man appeared in the scullery door holding a gore-stained tea-cloth to his nose. 'The little sod 'it me when I tried to nick him.'

'Who told you to arrest him?' Ding-Dong asked.

'Well, ain't that what we're here for?'

'We're here to search for stolen property, like it says on the warrant. Unless Mr O'Day would like to tell us where he's hidden it and spoil the fun?'

Maury leant against the wall of the lavatory. Hands still in pockets, he raised indifferent shoulders. 'Dunno what you're talking about, do I? Nothing stolen here. Ain't even got anything on tick. Cash on the nail or you do without, that's the way it is with us O'Days. Tell your bloke 'ow it is, Mr Stamford. You know Mum wouldn't allow nothing like that in 'er house. Don't yer?'

It was a challenge to Jack to declare his colours. But he was spared the necessity by a shrill whistle from the coop. Maury stiffened, pushing himself away from the wall with one foot. The Rhode Island Reds muttered and fluttered amongst themselves and then rushed to one corner like a delegation of outraged temperance spinsters as the constable emerged from the shed into their compound, clutching two bottles of golden liquid. His teeth gleamed whitely in his soot-smeared face as he raised them by their necks like a couple of juggler's clubs.

They took Maury back to the station in the police car, sandwiched on the back seat between Eileen and the constable who was still sniffing pink froth into the tea-towel. The dirty looks he was shooting sideways at the prisoner suggested he'd very much like to meet him in a quiet alley in the blackout.

Ding-Dong had originally instructed the injured man to walk back, since the car would only hold five adults. 'You'll be wanting to sit in on the interview, sir?' he'd asked Jack.

Did he? It was irregular but . . .

'Just as an observer. It's your investigation.' He'd declined the lift. 'I'll walk round.'

Eileen was pulling on her hat and coat whilst she issued instructions to Sammy and Annaliese to go next door if a raid started. 'Should I get him a solicitor?' she asked Jack.

'I don't need no solicitor,' Maury snapped. 'I ain't done nothing. No law against having bottles of whisky, is there? If they're saying I've stolen it, let's see the bluebottles prove it.'

His attitude didn't improve once they got him to the police interview room.

Ding-Dong placed the two bottles square in the centre of the table. 'Where'd you get them, son?'

'Bought them, didn't I . . . *Dad*.'

Ding-Dong duly wrote this statement in his notebook in a laboriously neat hand. Maury watched him from beneath half-closed eyelids, then pushed his chair back from the wooden table and crossed his ankles in an attitude of casual relaxation. But from where he was sitting, Jack could see the pulse beating behind his jaw line. Maury was scared. Which was fortunate. Perhaps he was scared enough to be deflected from the path to easy money which he'd been sauntering down since he was nine years old.

'Where?' Ding-Dong licked the stub of his pencil and waited with it poised over the lined pad.

'Can't exactly remember. It was this off-licence. Limehouse way, I think. See, this mate of mine give me a lift. At night it was. Well, you can't see nothing in the blackout, can you?'

'This mate got a name?'

'Yeah.'

Ding-Dong waited. Maury grinned.

Putting down his pencil, the DC linked his fingers on the table and leant forward. 'Let me give you some advice, son. At the moment I'm thinking of charging you with receiving stolen property. We'll overlook the little matter of assaulting PC Dixman in deference to the seasonal spirit of goodwill to all men – even villains who are still wet behind the ears. Now once I've made this . . .' he jabbed at the bottles, 'formal, I'm going to go on looking for evidence to charge you with the robbery as well. But . . .' He let the word hang in the air between them.

Maury broke the silence first. 'But . . . ?'

'But if you were to assist us in our enquiries . . . well, when are you seventeen, son?'

'Ninth January. Why, you want to send me a card?'

'Not long to start seeing sense then. Seventeen and it's an adult court. Adult prison too.'

'If I done anything wrong. Which I ain't. I bought them bottles. They're presents for me mum and me brother. Hid 'em in the chicken shed in case they found 'em before Christmas.'

'Got a receipt?'

'Lost it.'

'Pity, that. I mean, when I bring you up before the juvenile court for receiving and they hear how you've been consorting with a habitual criminal, they're bound to feel you're in need of proper supervision. Expect it will be approved school. They can keep you there until you're nineteen, you know. Pity to waste a couple of years in one of them places.'

193

'*Nineteen?* They can't do that . . . not for two measly bottles . . .' Maury broke off abruptly.

'They can be terrible scrupulous some of these beaks, son. See it as being for your own good, you see. Put you on the path to righteousness. Now if we could show them you'd already seen the light . . .'

'And how we going to do that?'

'By telling them about the voluntary statement you made; all about how you was led astray and persuaded to go on that warehouse robbery by those older, but not a lot wiser, than you.'

'Turn King's evidence?'

'Mean a fine or probation at worst, wouldn't you say, sir?' Ding-Dong appealed to the silent Stamford.

'Probably,' he agreed. 'First offence.' *Well, the first one you've ever been caught out on*, he added to himself.

Maury appeared to consider. Then he grinned. 'Pity I don't know nothing then, ain't it? Shame not to be able to oblige all them public-spirited beaks, but like I said, I bought the bottles. And I don't know nothing about no robberies.'

Ding-Dong sighed and shut his notebook. 'Have it your own way, son. No one can say I didn't give you a chance.'

'What's happening?' Eileen asked, starting up when they reappeared from the back of the station thirty minutes later. 'Is Maury going to court?'

'We're bailing your son while I carry out further enquiries, Mrs O'Day,' the DC explained. 'He's to report back here in three weeks' time. Unless we come for him sooner.'

'What's that mean?' Eileen looked from her son to Jack in bewilderment as Ding-Dong disappeared back into the cell area.

'It means,' Jack said grimly, 'that he's going to be looking for evidence to charge Maury with the warehouse robbery.'

The uniformed policeman who'd come into painful contact with Maury's forehead during the house search was passing through the corridor with an elderly reservist. In a voice loud enough to carry to the listeners, he remarked that Ding-Dong had an easy job there then. 'Any stupid little chuff who lives with a copper and thinks we ain't gonna find out he's up to his greasy little barnet in villainy ain't got the brains to wipe up his mess after him.'

Eileen stopped abruptly, drawing in her breath in a sharp, short gasp. Jack tensed, assuming she was about to give the man a piece of her mind. Instead she rounded on him. 'It was you!'

'What?'

'And to think I believed you when you said you didn't know they was going to come tramping through my house. Turning all me things over and looking into places they had no business to be. And you hadn't even the backbone to admit it to my face, Jack.'

'Eileen . . . I didn't . . .'

'What did you do? Tell them to come round when I was up the play?'

'Eileen, I honestly had no idea . . .'

'Don't give me that, Jack. That job's always been what matters to you. It's the reason your missus walked out. Job, job, job . . . and her alone in that house night after night with Annie screaming her head off with her teething and her croup. I'm not surprised she 'ad enough. Well, I tell you this, Jack . . .' She drew another gasp of air. 'You're not 'aving Maury. He ain't going inside. And you stop away from us. I don't want no informers in my house.'

'Eileen!'

She was gone, dragging Maury from the station in frantic haste. At the door Maury resisted long enough to flick a glance over his shoulder. A self-satisfied smirk glinted in his eyes as they met Jack's.

195

Chapter 20

Jack found himself wandering the streets, reluctant to return to the square and yet having nowhere else he wanted to go.

Once again he was struck by the unwelcoming coldness of the windowless houses. Behind the curtains and shutters they were no doubt cosily lit and brightly decorated with paper-chains and holly. He'd noticed as a uniformed constable on the beat that even the poorest rooms usually managed to improvise some sort of Christmas decoration, even if it was only a few bunches of illegally cut holly and mistletoe from the public parks and heaths. But that sort of celebration was for families. There was no sense in decorating a house that only you were going to see. And no point in buying and cooking special foods if you were destined to eat them alone. Even assuming, he thought ruefully as the arm objected with a throbbing ache to its lengthy exposure to the penetrating December cold, he could cook the damn meal.

At the thought of food, he considered finding a café to eat in. His head told him he should be hungry. But his stomach was churning with a sick misery. It was only now that he'd come to realise how much he'd been relying on Eileen. It wasn't just the practical assistance, it was the sense of support. The O'Days had become a safety net since his wife had walked out. Whilst he had them, he hadn't had to face the truth: that he was very much alone in the world.

He half considered making his way up to Vorley Road to see how Sarah was getting on with the De Groot woman, but knew it was just an excuse. He couldn't expect Sarah to act as an emotional pit prop to his rapidly collapsing self-confidence.

Drawing his hat down further against the wind, he used his

good hand to roll his coat collar up and bent his steps down Kentish Town Road. He was vaguely aware of other feet doing as he was, using the white lines painted along kerbs and around hydrants and fire alarms to negotiate the pavements safely. With his eyes downwards and the hat partially obscuring his line of vision ahead, he didn't see the boots until it was too late. He stepped sideways as they loomed up in his path. The boots did the same.

'Sorry.'

They both swayed the other way.

'Just one more dance, sir, and you'll 'ave to excuse me. I'm taken for the foxtrot.'

Glancing up, Jack found himself looking into the face of PC Dave Wilkins.

The young constable flashed Jack his usual cheeky grin. 'Evening, sir.'

'Good evening.' Jack found himself unconsciously tensing, waiting for some comment on his recent visit to the station with the O'Days.

'Reckon all the brass monkeys are tucked up safe in the shelters tonight, don't you, sir?' Dave remarked, slapping his hands together.

'More than likely,' Jack laughed.

Lightly hurrying footsteps had been approaching from behind him whilst they spoke, but he hadn't realised how close she was until he stepped backwards and she ran full tilt into his bad arm.

'Oi! Watch it!'

Jack saw her wobble on the kerb, arms flailing as she tried to regain her balance, but was unable to help. Dave was quicker. A striped armlet shot forward.

'Steady, miss.'

'Oh, 'ello, Dave.'

'Watcha, Ruthie. 'Ow you doing?'

'OK, ta,' Ruth Miller said. She was feeling with both hands over the scarf covering her head, her fingers lightly flicking the paisley material back. 'Is me hair all right, Dave? I just been up the hairdresser's. He ain't knocked no bits out the pins, has he?'

'It's pitch out 'ere. Couldn't see if you was bald as a boiled egg.'

'Well, put yer torch on.'

'Ain't exactly an emergency, is it, Ruth?'

'It is to me. I got a very important h'engagement tonight. Cocktails ecktually.'

'I know they do. Me mum keeps bantams. Lovely tails them cocks has got.'

'You're so sharp, Dave Wilkins, it's a wonder you ain't cut your own tongue off. Go on, see me hair's all right. If it's not, I'll run back to the shop, get her to put it up again.'

'I don't think a quick glance would be a major breach of the blackout regulations,' Jack said, guessing that it was his presence that was preventing Dave from obliging the girl.

She seemed to recognise his voice. 'Oh, it's you. You come up Good Hope with a couple of kids. You was asking about . . . Oh Lord, I ain't supposed to say, am I? Well?' This last question was directed at Dave, who was allowing the shaded light of his torch to play over the curled and pinned hair.

'Looks smashing to me, Ruthie. What do you reckon, sir?'

'Very attractive.'

'Yeah? Thank heavens.' She flicked the scarf back. 'I got to run. See ya, Dave.' She was gone before he could switch the torch off; rushing down the hill with an awkward sideward flicking of her legs.

'Me Cousin Stan's sweet on her,' David said, restoring his torch to the coat. ' 'As been for years. Too soft-headed to see he's at the back of a very long queue.'

'You don't think he's "cocktails ecktually" then?'

'Shouldn't think so, sir. Pint of wallop's more our Stan's line. Night, sir.'

'Goodnight.'

Ruth flew on down Kentish Town Road. She'd never meant to be this late, but the hair stylist had only been able to give her the last appointment and then the stupid woman hadn't been able to copy the picture of Bette Davis's hairstyle that she'd torn out of her film magazine.

She mustn't be late. He might think she wasn't coming. He'd drive away and she'd never see him again because she'd been too stupid to ask for the name of his airfield. She *had* to get to the Café de Paris on time. Her heels clicked out the name as she shot down the nearly empty road. *Café – de – Paris. Café – de – Paris. Café – de – Paris.*

A whiff of Four Square baccy met her nose as she dived through the front door. 'Evening, Dad, you're early.'

Duggie emerged from the back in his shirt, with his braces dangling round his hips. 'Not many customers today. It's funny that, but nearer it gets to the Lord's birthday the more they hang on. Don't matter what's wrong with 'em. They stop around long enough to pull their cracker and eat their pudding. Then they knock St Peter up Boxing Day.'

Duggie Miller found himself talking to a pair of feet which were rapidly disappearing up the stair treads. 'Where's the fire?' he shouted.

'I've got a date.'

'Stupid to ask really.'

She'd hung her best dress on the door of the wardrobe. It was a calf-length royal-blue chiffon, with a swath of beads coming from the shoulders and crossing under the breast. It had been much admired at the town hall dances. Taking her fancy underwear from its tissue paper, she buried her face in the rich material and inhaled the scent of lily of the valley from the cologne-soaked hanky she'd folded inside it. It was only rayon but it looked like real silk, and the stockings she hooked on to the suspender belt *were* silk.

The blue dress slid on over her head with ease. Bending over at the waist, she dabbed pancake over her flushed skin, letting the escaping grains drift in a cloud to the carpet. Rouge, eyebrow pencil, a deep ruby lipstick and a diamanté hair slide completed her preparations.

They had no full-length mirror. Just the small one that stood on her dressing table. By standing well back and twirling on tiptoe, she was able to examine the finished effect in twelve-inch oval segments. Her lips curved in a small, triumphant smile. It was the best she'd ever looked. Paul couldn't fail to adore her. There was just one more thing.

Opening the wardrobe, she stooped down and took out the box. Sitting on the bed, she inserted first one then the other foot into the high insteps of the precious black velvet shoes with her diamanté heels.

'Five guineas,' she breathed, standing up. The undersoles felt slippery. She'd never worn them anywhere but on this rug, and the leather was unscratched. Experimentally she walked forward a few steps, swaying her hips. It was incredible, the heels were only four inches, but she suddenly felt a good foot taller. She caught a glimpse of her sparkling eyes in the mirror. 'This is it,' she told the reflected Ruth. 'No more pretending.'

She didn't have to; it was all happening just like she'd always dreamt it would.

'Ruthie!' The sharp rap on the door jerked her off her pink cloud.

Swaying with increasing confidence on her heels, she sashayed over the room and turned the handle.

'He's here,' Duggie said.

'*Here?* But . . .' A train clanked past on the viaduct, rattling the bottles on her dressing table. What on earth would he think? This house was horrible; a dingy, poky dump that smelt of boiled cabbage water. 'How did he know where I lived?'

'Know where . . . ?' Duggie paused in his fight to extract his collar studs. 'You done daft, Ruthie? He's never off the step.'

'Who?'

'Stan, of course.'

'Stan? What's he doing here?'

Duggie stepped inside the room and took a good look at her. 'You feeling all right, Ruthie? Ain't sickening for something, are you?'

He tried to feel her forehead, but she knocked his hand down. 'Mind me hair, Dad, I 'ad it done special for me date.'

'Well that's what I just said, isn't it? He's here.'

'But I'm not going with *Stan*.'

' 'Course you are, Ruthie. I was there when he asked you. Thursday evening, pictures.'

Those final seconds before she'd dashed out of the house last Sunday came back to Ruth. 'But I can't go with Stan,' she wailed. 'I've got a date with Paul.'

'Who's he?'

'He's . . . he's . . .' Ruth had a fair idea her father wouldn't be too happy to hear she was going out with a bloke she didn't know. 'He's a friend of one of the other girls up Good Hope,' she said, reasoning that this was almost the truth. 'Nell. She introduced us. You'll 'ave to tell Stan I'm sick.'

'Why'd you say you'd go with him if you'd already fixed to go out with this Paul?'

' 'Cos I hadn't, not then.'

She knew as soon as she saw the tightening lips that she'd said the wrong thing. 'So Stan was first, was he?'

'Yes, but . . .'

'Then you'll go with him, Ruthie. It's only fair, he's a good lad and I'll not see you messing him about.'

'But Paul . . . he'll be waiting.'

'Then you'll 'ave to get word to him. Where you meeting him?'

'In . . . in a café.'

'Well there you are then. Get Stan to walk you past the phone box. You can give this café a ring.'

'I can't . . . it's not . . . I mean . . .' A spark of anger ignited and sent flames of resentment through Ruth. What did it have to do with him? She was grown up, weren't she? Earning her own money. 'I'll go out with who I like. I ain't a kid any more.' She tossed her head, then remembered the curls and settled for hands on hips and a defiant lift of her chin.

'Not while you're living in my house you won't, my girl. You'll do as I say, when I say. Honour your father, Ruthie. Or stop here.' He took the key from the door before she realised what he was going to do and inserted it in the outside lock.

'Dad! You can't!'

'And who's going to stop me, I'd like to know?'

'Stan!'

'Wha'?' The stairs creaked as he came up the first few treads. 'Should I come up?'

201

'I, er...' Ruth stared at her father. He rocked the key between his middle and forefinger and raised enquiring eyebrows. 'No,' she shouted back. 'I'm coming down.'

'Good girl.' Duggie pocketed the key.

Stan's eyes widened as she trod carefully down, clutching the banister. 'Blimey, Ruth ... you look like a film star.'

Ruth paused. It was so exactly like her dream: the staircase, the outfit, the man in uniform lost in admiration staring up at her. But it was the wrong man!

Digging her fingers into the banister, she wobbled the last few steps and handed him her coat. 'Well 'old it out for me, then.'

'What? Oh yeah, sorry.' He held it awkwardly and caught her hair with his jacket buttons.

'For 'eaven's sake, you clumsy idiot.' Ruth jerked herself free.

'Sorry.'

Ruth tucked the wisps tickling the nape of her neck into a pin and told him to get a move on.

'OK. 'Night, Mr Miller.'

' 'Night, son. 'Ave a good time.'

Still off balance, she took his arm as soon as they stepped outside. He covered her fingers with his other hand, mistaking her gesture for affection. 'Thought we'd go up the Doric. They got a double bill: *Zanzibar* and *Danger on Wheels*.'

'No we flaming won't, Stanley Wilkins. I ain't had me hair done special to sit in the back row of the Doric. I want to go up west.'

'Up west?' He let go her hand and she caught the rattle of coins in his pocket.

'I got the bus fair,' she said, unconsciously cuddling closer as the wind whipped round her silk-clad legs.

'No. No girl goes out with me pays her own bus fare,' Stan said grandly. 'We'll go wherever you like, Ruth.'

They had to run for the bus, which carried them through Camden and Euston and down Tottenham Court Road. At its junction with New Oxford Street, Ruth stood up and told Stan to shift out of the way.

'We getting off here then?' Stan said. 'I paid through to Marble Arch.' He held up two punched tickets as proof but led the way to the back platform anyway.

'I got to *go*,' Ruth hissed as soon as they'd alighted on to the pavement.

'Go where? Oh . . . yeah, right.' Stan tried to take her arm again. She dug her fingers into her pockets.

'Let's get up the cinema then.' He took out a handful of silver and copper and sorted the coins in the palm of his hand. 'Or we could go to the Paramount if you want to dance?'

'There'll be queues,' Ruth said, jigging on one foot. 'Didn't you see 'em from the bus? I can't wait. I got to find a lav now.'

He hadn't much choice but to follow her. It was busy in this area. There were plenty of people taking advantage of another raid-free night to have a good time whilst they could. Stan tried to put a proprietorial arm round Ruth's waist as a group of army uniforms jostled and laughed noisily towards them.

'There's one. Stop here.'

Ruth clattered down the flights of steps and into the underground lavatory. It was empty apart from herself. For a moment she stood quietly, breathing in the urine and disinfectant smell. It had, as she'd hoped, two entrances. Stepping delicately over the tiled floor, she crept up the opposite stairs until her head was at pavement level and peered across to the wrought-iron barrier where she'd left Stan. His back was to her as he chatted to the soldiers they'd just passed. A loud burst of laughter gave her her chance. Pulling off the precious five-guinea shoes and holding them in one hand, she fled on stockinged feet across St Giles Circus and into Charing Cross Road.

Chapter 21

She hailed the taxi and sank inside with a casual '*Café de Paris, please*,' as if she was in the habit of riding in cabs every day. He took her along Shaftesbury Avenue and around Piccadilly Circus with its darkened advertising hoardings and shrouded figure of Eros, before drawing up outside the Rialto Cinema.

'I want the Café de Paris.'

'It's under here, ducks.' He pointed out the doorway she'd missed.

'Oh. Thank you.' Scrabbling in her bag, she handed over the fare on the meter and added an extra sixpence with an airy: 'You may keep the change.'

'Ta, duchess.'

He drove off before she could think of a suitable retort.

Paul wasn't here. Had he meant he'd meet her inside? What should she do if he wasn't there? Would they let her in by herself? She looked round, suddenly unsure of herself.

'Ruth!' The loud hail was accompanied by a blast of car hooter. Relieved, she looked back the way she'd just come. Leaning over, he flicked open the passenger door invitingly and shouted: 'Room for one co-pilot.'

A hard knot of disappointment formed in Ruth's chest. 'Aren't we going to the Café de Paris?'

'Lord, no. Stuffy place. Polly's is more fun.'

At a reckless speed, Paul slung the car round corners and bumped over hastily repaired roads in a way that made her teeth rattle and her knuckles turn white as she hung on desperately. The wind was ripping and shredding her carefully curled and pinned hair but she didn't dare let go to push it back into place. She had no idea where she was, although they seemed to be heading north again.

Polly's turned out to be a basement club that was reached down a flight of steep steps. There was a jumble of unlit neon tubes above the door which, as she passed underneath, she could see formed the shape of a roosting parrot. The room was already thick with tobacco smoke. Through the dim lighting and swirling fug she could make out a tiny dance floor surrounded by small tables. All of them seemed to be taken by RAF officers and their partners. The low-roofed room caught and trapped the noise of chattering and laughter mingled with the efforts of the five-piece band. Feeling slightly disorientated, Ruth took Paul's arm.

He seemed to be well known. Other men called and shouted across as they wove their way through the crush.

'Good show last week, Skip.'

'Hear about Foxy's prang? Doesn't he know the tax-payer paid for that Spitfire?'

'Who's the new popsie, Skip?'

The voices were light-hearted and slightly mocking, but the underlying tone was warm and affectionate. He was obviously well liked and admired by his colleagues. Ruth felt a small swell of pride. He was hers. He could have had any woman he wanted, but he'd asked her, Ruth Miller.

'Over here, Skip.' A series of cat-calls and whistles to her left caused Paul to steer her in that direction. There were four other airmen and three women crushed round a table. The surface was already crowded with dirty glasses and overflowing ash-trays.

'Whose round is it?' Paul asked, dragging two chairs over.

'Mac's.'

The men ordered whiskies. Ruth asked for a martini. 'With an olive, please.' She knew that was right because she'd seen it in loads of films. The others seemed to find it funny.

'Who's the popsie, Skip?'

'This is Ruth, which is not short for anything . . . unlike her cousin, who is called Hatty, which is short for Richmal Harriet. The latter apparently being too posh for the likes of Kentish

Town and therefore not to be spoken north of King's Cross.'

Ruth felt pleased that he'd remembered this detail about Hatty. At least it showed he must have been thinking about her. Although she didn't much care for the way he seemed to be laughing at Hat.

A chorus of introductions followed. The men were called Rocky, Hedge, Mac and Jumper. The women were Eunice, Darlene and Sally.

'How'd the meeting go, Skip?' one of the men – Hedge, she thought – called over the music.

'Waste of time as usual. These desk johnnies wouldn't recognise a Heinkel if it shoved its guns up their bloody arse.'

The conversation degenerated into a shouted slanging match against desk johnnies, office wallahs and stupid bastard civil servants until Sally stood up, wriggled down her dress and told them to shut up being so boring and come dance.

'Anything to oblige a lady,' Rocky said, standing up. 'Or even you, Sally darling.'

'I'm out of ciggies,' Darlene said, opening her case. 'Get me some, Paul sweetie.'

Ruth stiffened. What the hell did she mean asking *her* bloke to buy her fags? But Paul didn't seem to mind. Clicking his fingers in the air, he summoned the cigarette girl. 'What do you want?'

'Passing Cloud.'

'Eunice?'

Eunice languidly waved one of the strange brown cheroots she'd been chain-smoking since they arrived.

'Ruth?'

She smoked Weights, but there weren't any in the girl's tray, so she picked out a box of Passing Cloud as well.

More drinks came. She was beginning to feel a bit queasy and her throat was raw from the smoke, but she lit up anyway to stop her stomach from rumbling. She'd eaten hardly anything all day in anticipation of her cosy dinner at the Café de Paris with Paul. Perhaps they'd get some supper later. If she'd been out with Stan he'd have bought her a bag of chips and they'd have walked home licking the hot grease and vinegar off their fingers.

What on earth was she thinking of Stan for at a time like this? She looked quickly at Paul to recapture her dream. He caught her eye and gave her a lazy wink. Reassured by this gesture of intimacy, she said: 'Aren't we going to dance?'

'Of course.'

He held her close on the floor, his arms wrapped round her, one hand on her back, the other on her seat. If any bloke at the Camden Hall dances had dared to hold her like that she'd have slapped his face and given him a piece of her mind. But here it seemed stupid to protest when everyone else was doing the same.

Burying her face in his jacket, she let herself sway in tempo with his body.

'You're really something special, Ruth,' he murmured into her hair.

'Am I?' She raised her head and his lips found hers. They circled slowly. She could taste the whisky on his tongue as it probed her mouth.

'Really special,' he murmured.

They shuffled in the same six inches of space. Other couples circled them. Ruth was suddenly struck by how young the men were. In the dim lighting their uniforms seemed to melt into the ether, leaving their hands and faces disembodied in the darkness. Their skin gleamed with an odd greyish-white tinge. *Like the dead bodies in Dad's chapel*, Ruth thought. She felt odd, as if she were floating in another world. Panic gripped her, she was dancing in a vault of dead men. With a violent shiver, she clung harder to Paul.

'Steady on, old thing. Plenty of time for that later.'

'I was just . . .' She struggled to explain about her premonition. 'Everyone's so young. I mean, they don't look older than me. Are they all pilots?'

'Most of them. It's a young man's job, Ruth.'

'You mean they have to be fit?'

'I mean most of them don't get to grow old. My squadron's lost eight since August.'

'I'm sorry.' She wanted to sympathise, but the closest experience she had to offer was: 'My mum died when I was

207

eleven. I remember I was ever so cross with 'er for going off like that. Do you get angry with the ones who die? Like they shouldn't 'ave done it?' She was frightened that her question sounded silly, but he seemed to take her seriously.

'I get angry at the ones who needn't have died. The stupid sods who were showing off, or who forgot their training at that one vital second they needed it most.'

Ruth looked anxiously into his face. His blue eyes were gloriously close. 'You won't do that, will you?'

'Not if I can help it, old thing.' The band struck up a faster rhythm and he swung her into it. She was beginning to feel distinctly odd, as if the top of her head was floating away from the rest of her body. From a long way off she heard herself telling Paul about Mottram and Cropper's.

'My dad's a partner,' she said grandly, embroidering the truth with ease. At least that's what she meant to say. But her tongue had trouble forming the words.

'Whoops, don't pass out on me yet, old girl. Better sit down.'

Gratefully she let him steer her back to the table.

'Jumper bailed out already?'

'He and Darlene have . . .' Rocky pointed to the ceiling.

Paul flung himself in a chair and signalled the waiter. 'Hedge too? How very perverted.'

'Hedge is spewing up,' Rocky drawled.

'What a waste. Same again?'

'I think . . .' Ruth stood up with great care, 'I'm just going to the toilet.'

'Toi . . . oh, the lavs. That way . . .'

He'd indicated the area beside the bar. It looked like a solid wall, but as she got closer, she saw the slit which led to a narrow corridor. There were two doors. She opened the first and found a flight of stairs. The second was the powder room. Groping her way to the far cubicle, she bolted herself in and sank down on the toilet seat. Everything seemed to be wavering up and down and her skin was burning. If only she could get some air, she was sure she'd feel much better.

There was a tiny window next to the cistern, papered over in a permanent blackout. Stepping with care on the wooden seat, she pulled herself up by the pipe, and forced the catch open. A wonderful draught of cool air played over her cheeks. Perching on the seat with her legs drawn up and her arms wrapped around them, she rested her head on her knees and waited for the nausea to pass.

The outside door of the powder room swung open and Sally's voice assaulted her ears. It was funny how she hadn't noticed before how shrill it was.

'What do you think of Paul's new sweetie?'

Eunice's drawl answered her. 'Hold on, darling.'

Ruth heard her moving along the cubicles. She guessed Eunice was looking under the doors and sat hardly breathing.

'All clear, darling.' Water splashed into the hand basin. 'She's the same as the rest really, isn't she? He always goes for that type; fresh out of ankle socks.'

'And common as muck.'

'God, *yes*. Darling, did you see the *shoes*?'

'I know. She looks like a five-bob tart. Finished?'

The water ceased and the door banged again. Ruth sat frozen to the seat, heedless of the hot tears flowing down her cheeks.

It was the cat that brought her to her senses again. A spitting yell above her head made her jump from the seat with heart thumping. The narrow tabby head was thrust through the partially open window, its eyes regarding her with a cunningly feral stare. She moved again, and the cat jerked back out of sight.

Standing unsteadily, she made her way shakily out to the washbasin. Using the back of her fingers, she dabbed cold water over her cheeks, then dried them off on the hem of her dress. Repairing the damage as best she could with pancake, she took a deep breath, repeated: 'Stuck-up cows, stuck-up cows, stuck-up cows' several times through gritted teeth, and marched back to the table.

Eunice had moved to the chair next to Paul. With one elegantly manicured talon resting on his shoulder, she was whispering in his ear, her thickly lipsticked mouth almost touching the receptive lobe.

'There you are.' Paul grinned, pulling Ruth down on to his

lap. He slid an arm round her waist, holding her so that she faced away from him, and nuzzled at her bare neck. Catching the look on Eunice's face, Ruth squirmed back against him with an appreciative murmur. That would teach the cat to keep her claws to herself.

'Come on.' Paul stood, decanting her on to her feet again. The rush of adrenaline fuelled by her anger had worn off and she was grateful for the support of his hand gripping her elbow as they wove across the floor. He took her back down the passage and opened the door to the stairs.

'What's up here?'

'Paradise, sweetie.'

'Lay up for yourselves treasures in heaven,' Ruth giggled.

'Couldn't have put it better myself. In here.' There were two doors on the landing. One open, the other shut. He guided her through the open one, and back-heeled it shut behind him.

Ruth looked round. Everything in the room was pink: heavy rose-coloured floor-length drapes; thick carpet the colour of strawberry blancmange; a bedspread that had the look of quilted raspberry jam; frilly bedside lampshades with the delicate pinkness of sugar mice. She tried to compare them with something else, but it was no good. That particular combination of sickly foods insisted on swirling round her head. Swallowing quickly, she tottered across the room and sank gratefully on to the foot of the bed.

'I don't feel very well.'

'Don't worry. I've got something that will make you feel a lot better.'

He switched on the bedside lights. Blearily Ruth saw that they were copper statues of naked women. Paul took off his jacket and came to sit beside her. Putting his arm round her, he searched greedily for her mouth. He was making the bed bounce up and down. It increased her feeling of nausea.

'Paul,' she wailed. 'I feel awfully funny . . .'

He'd got both his arms round her now, his fingers fumbling with the fastenings of her dress.

'What are you doing? You stop that!'

She wriggled. He grabbed a handful of her skirt and pulled it up to her waist.

'Stop it. I ain't that sort of girl.' Angrily she got her arm free of his grip and slapped his face. It wasn't a hard blow, but it would have been enough to have any boy in Camden Town backing off mumbling his apologies and promising he wouldn't try it on again if she'd stop with him for the rest of the evening.

Paul laughed. 'Oh, like it rough, do you? OK.' He threw her back on to the bed, grabbing at her pants and dragging them down.

She screamed. Kicking out, she caught him a glancing blow in the stomach.

'Yow! Watch it.'

He started to undo his trousers. Ruth's sex education had consisted of vague warnings from her dad and fumblings in the back row of the cinema; she had no exact idea of what Paul was going to do, but she was pretty damn certain she wasn't going to like it. His face was twisted in a funny expression and she didn't like the violent way he was pinning her to the bed.

'Let me up. I want to go home.' He'd got one of her wrists pinned. Twisting sideways she managed to bite his hand.

'Pack it in, you silly bitch. That hurt.'

'Let me go.' His weight was crushing her. She was, she realised, completely helpless. Struggling to pull in a lungful of air, she screamed.

'For heaven's sake!'

His grip slackened and his weight shifted off her. With a sob of relief, she sat up. He'd crawled to the head of the bed, stripping back the counterpane, and grabbing a pillow.

'What are you . . . ?'

It was as far as she got. He pushed the pillow over her face. And then he raped her.

She was lost. The blacked-out streets all looked the same. The nameplates high on the walls were unreadable. Blankly she wandered across another road. She didn't know how long she'd been drifting around like this. It seemed hours since she'd run from Polly's.

'Stop making such a fuss,' he'd drawled when she'd finally sat up, shaking with shock. 'For heaven's sake, what did you think I brought you up here for? There's no need for this little miss innocent act. There's a war on, it's all right for nice girls to enjoy it these days.'

'I'm not . . . I didn't . . .'

'First time, was it?' Rolling over, Paul had taken his cigarette case from the jacket he'd hung over one of the naked lamps, and clamped a cigarette between his teeth. 'Well, you'll know what to do next time.' Cradling his forearm behind his head, he leant back against the bedhead and blew smoke rings at the ceiling whilst she struggled to dress.

'I think . . . I want to go home, Paul.'

'Please yourself, sweetie. But the night's still young.'

His calmness frightened her more than his earlier violence. It was as if he didn't think he'd done anything wrong. Well perhaps he didn't. Like he said, she'd gone up to the bedroom with him, hadn't she? Maybe he really thought that was what she wanted.

'I'm not . . . I didn't . . . I *hate* you!' With a gasp, she fled downstairs, pushed her way through the dancing couples and stumbled past the doorman.

Fright and shock had carried her several streets before the cold penetrated and she remembered she'd left her jacket behind at Polly's. Even if she'd been able to go back and face all those knowing faces, she couldn't have done. She didn't know where the club was and couldn't remember which way she'd come. There were still people around, but they burst out of the darkness in groups, chattering in low voices, the scents of alcohol and tobacco trailing in their wake, and she couldn't bring herself to break in and plead for their help.

She was sure she was going round in circles. Sometimes she seemed to recognise buildings. She'd passed a sign reading 'First-Aid Post' several times. Its painted arrow sign pointed downwards to a sandbagged door. Once she'd hesitated by it, but a Red Cross nurse had come to the door. The idea of telling this grim-faced, crisply starched female what had happened had overwhelmed Ruth. She'd trudged wearily away.

It was cold. She really wanted to lie down somewhere and curl into a ball and never wake up again.

Aware only of the cold and the pain in her abdomen, she limped on. She had to get home. Her dad would kill her if he knew what she'd done. Maybe he'd kill Paul too. But that didn't matter. She just wanted to be safe at home. She wanted a bath. Her whole body cried out to be clean again.

Her nose was running. Rubbing the back of her hand heedlessly under it, she nearly fell as her heel caught in a grating. Wrenching herself free, she took off the shoes and stared at them. There was a hole in the road ahead, the danger protected by sawhorses and ropes until the council repair team could get round to filling it in. With great deliberation she sent the left shoe spinning in an arc into the gap. For a moment the diamonds glistened in the hazy moonlight; then they disappeared in a quiet splash. Taking the right shoe's heel, she flicked it with a vicious strength. This time it hit the water with a loud 'whoosh'.

Grit cut into the bottom of her feet as she wavered uncertainly forward again. There was a gap in the buildings ahead. It led to a wider street which seemed familiar. Straining against the darkness, she made out a large department store on the opposite side of the road. There was another one next to it. Oxford Street. She recognised it with a gasp of relief.

The buses had stopped running. The tubes too. And she'd no money left for taxis. Hugging her arms around her body, to shut out the cold and the hurt, she turned right and started limping towards Tottenham Court Road.

'Good night, Stan?' someone called down the barrack hut.

'Yeah, great.'

He'd waited twenty minutes by the entrance to the public lavatory before he'd become alarmed and asked a couple of passing girls to go down and check Ruth hadn't been taken ill. Even when they'd come back with embarrassed smiles to tell him the cubicles were empty, he still hadn't believed she'd dumped him. She'd just come up the wrong entrance and got confused, that was it. It had taken another two hours of scouring the neighbouring streets, returning to the iron-railed entrance to the Ladies after every circuit before he'd finally acknowledged the truth.

'Has tha' heard t'news?' someone else called as he dragged off his uniform.

'What?'

'They reckon we're shipping out. Abroad.'

It was the news he'd been wanting for weeks. Now he couldn't have cared less. What was the point in fighting to make your girl proud if the girl didn't want you?

'When?'

'Don't know. Soon, I reckon. Any'ow, all leave's been cancelled. So I 'ope thee showed tha' lass a reet good time, 'cos that was they last chance. No more leave passes for Private "*I'm reet chummy with the adjutant*" Wilkins. We're all confined t'barracks until further notice.'

'Oh.' Stan flung himself on his bed. Something crackled beneath him.

'Oh, thy 'ad a letter,' his chatty barrack mate said belatedly.

Puzzled, Stan stared at the envelope. The writing was familiar, but it took him a while to recognise it as his mum's. What on earth did she want to write to him for? He saw her practically every week! Turning his back on the rest of the room, who were scrabbling to get themselves sorted before 'lights-out', he slit open the cheap envelope and read:

Dear son,

Dad and me thinks you ought to be told about our Lulu. She got took bad last Saturday with her appendix and they took her into the hospital and operated. Her officer wrote us and said she was doing well and we wasn't to worry. Maybe they'll let her have a bit of sick leave and come home for Christmas. See if you can get a pass too, son. It would be real nice if we could all be together. I got a lovely piece of pork put by special for our dinner.

An alarm sounded in Stan's head. Last Saturday, his mum had said. But when he'd called round the Millers' house on Sunday,

Ruth had just got back from a visit to Lulu. Why hadn't she said anything about his sister being rushed to hospital?

There was only one explanation. Because she hadn't been to Bedford to see Lulu at all. In which case, where the hell *had* she been?

Chapter 22

Any hope that Eileen had changed her mind and decided to believe that Jack hadn't laid information against Maury was dispelled by Sammy's arrival on Saturday morning and his mumbled 'Mum says to ask about kids' Christmas party up the police station. You taking Annie?' He wouldn't meet Jack's eye. Instead he stood in the hall, hands thrust into his pockets, the heel of his boot grinding into the linoleum.

Jack was torn between compassion for Sammy's obvious embarrassment and a stubborn mulishness brought on by yet another sleepless night. 'When is it?'

'This afternoon, Mr Stamford.' He hunched his shoulders, digging his hands even deeper into his pockets. 'There's games and stuff, with prizes. And cakes and lemonade. One of the kids in my class, his dad's a copper and he reckons it's whizzer.'

The heel ground into the lino with even more ferocity. Jack guessed what was coming next, and it did.

'Me and Nafnel was finking maybe I could come? I mean, I know you ain't my dad, but it's sort of like my mum's Annie's mum too, ain't it? So that sort of makes her my sister.'

'I don't think it works like that, Sammy. Anyway, I doubt if your mother would allow you to come. She doesn't see me as a fit person to associate with.' He was sorry as soon as he'd said it. It was ridiculous to drag an eight-year-old into the argument between himself and Eileen.

'I could ask 'er.'

'Best not, Sammy.'

Sammy sighed. 'Yeah, OK.'

'Does Annaliese want to go?'

He'd expected a 'no'. Since her return from Holland to

Kentish Town six months previously, his daughter had been clinging, shy and unnaturally wary of men – even her father. But surprisingly Sammy nodded vigorously. 'Yeah, she does. Me and Nafnel showed her how to play all the games.' A happy thought occurred to him. 'You could take Naf. You ain't 'ad a fight with his mum.'

'I don't think so, Sammy. It's policemen's children only.' Ushering the little boy out, he continued his one-handed assault on life's obstacle course.

He'd pretty well mastered washing and shaving by now. Shoe-polishing was achieved by anchoring them under the leg of a chair before brushing and buffing, and ironing had been mastered by the simple expedient of ignoring it. Cooking was the biggest problem. There was little food in the house. He'd grown used to relying on police canteens and Eileen, eating only the sketchiest meals at home. So he'd resorted to using the local cafés and restaurants. In what he knew to be a futile gesture of defiance to demonstrate to himself that he really didn't *need* the O'Days, he'd eaten breakfast, lunch *and* dinner in three different cafés yesterday. He'd had no appetite for any of it. Lack of activity, pain and misery had all combined to make every mouthful taste like cardboard. Only guilt over wasting food that was becoming scarce made him force it down.

Now he had to do it all over again. It was too late for breakfast, he decided with some relief. He could just make a cup of tea now, and then have an early lunch. Except the tea caddy was empty. And he couldn't buy any because Eileen had his ration book. And he couldn't go and ask for it because it would look like capitulation . . . not that there was anything to capitulate about . . .

Frustration with life, the pain and his own damn helplessness exploded. He hurled the caddy into the wall cupboard. It bounced back, spewing tea dust over the floor.

The force medical officer was sympathetic, but held out little hope: 'It's like I said, dear boy,' his loud and – to Jack's heightened senses – rudely healthy voice crackled down the telephone receiver. 'Arthritis is a damned tricky one. Comes out of the blue and can go the same way. Or it just keeps spreading. There's not much we can do for it. Lots of quack cures around: sea bathing, blood purifying tonics, beds aligned to magnetic north, but basically . . .'

'They don't work . . . ?'

'That's about the ticket, dear boy. Tell you what . . . if it's really bad . . .'

'It's bloody agony . . .'

'I can let you have some painkillers. I'll ring your GP to square it with him. Then I'll see what I can do.'

It took two hours, and just when Jack had given up, a police messenger drew up on a motorcycle and formally handed over a sealed envelope with a smart salute. Four white tablets were contained in a slip of paper with the caution: *Morphine, take one as necessary. Do not take more than two in any eight hours*.

He had the sticky dregs of a bottle of Camp coffee in the cupboard. Wrenching the cap off with his teeth, he added boiling water and a defiant slug of brandy and washed the first tablet down with the bitter chicory- and cognac-flavoured draught, not caring that it was scalding his tongue and throat. Then, sinking back into a chair in the chilly front room, he crossed his ankles, switched on the radio, closed his eyes and waited for the dose to take effect. The news wasn't encouraging. London might still be blessedly quiet but Liverpool had suffered a major raid the previous night.

He must have dozed. He woke with a start, his neck stiff, and stood warily. The combination of alcohol and morphine had left him slightly light-headed, but he found he could – mercifully – walk normally without each step on a hard surface sending a jarring shaft of pain along his arm. With his wrist held in an improvised sling made from an old tie, he threw back his shoulder and strode out.

The streets were thronged with shoppers taking advantage of the last Saturday before Christmas. He told himself he was relieved not to be involved in all that frantic madness. He could always eat his Christmas dinner at Agar Street canteen. Some sort of improvised catering arrangements would be made for the officers on duty over Christmas and Boxing Day. And as for presents – he had no one to think about except Annaliese and Sammy.

He'd already bought a second-hand doll's pram which he'd left upstairs in his daughter's bedroom – unhidden because he knew she wouldn't use the room. On impulse he turned back and made his way to Woolworths. Half of Kentish Town seemed to have had the same idea. Cradling the injured arm as if it were made of eggshells, he joined crowds jostling at the counters.

It said something for the effectiveness of the morphine that when he fought his way out half an hour later, the pain still hadn't returned. Clutching a board game and an imitation steel helmet to his chest, he made his way down Great College Street. The council in their collective wisdom had recently chosen to remove the 'Great' and substitute 'Royal' but he saw no reason to adjust his thoughts accordingly.

The window of the café where he'd had his breakfast the previous morning was covered in condensation. Pushing open the door, he found the interior was already packed. A harassed waitress squeezed through the tables. 'I'm afraid we're full, sir. Unless you wouldn't mind sharing?'

He wasn't feeling very sociable, but an edge of unreality had started to creep into his perception. Her voice seemed to be coming from the end of a long tunnel. The stupidity of drugs and alcohol on an empty stomach was about to send him head-first into the café's 'welcome' mat unless he ate something fast.

'I don't mind at all.'

She bustled across the room and leant over a table occupied by two plump middle-aged women. He couldn't hear above the babble of noise, but he saw the look being sent in his direction. Evidently he passed muster, because the waitress waved him over and drew out a chair.

'Ladies.' Putting the toys on the checked tablecloth, he removed his hat. They acknowledged the greeting with brief smiles, but happily seemed intent on a shopping list spread on the table. It was hard to imagine what else they could possibly have to buy, given the bulging bags leaning against the table

219

legs, but evidently they were catering for a small siege.

'Sir?'

The waitress had reappeared, pencil poised expectantly over her pad. The writing on the menu was wavering in and out of focus. He caught sight of the word 'Special' chalked on a board by the cash desk and ordered that.

'Soup and meat course, or meat and sweet? I'm only allowed to serve you two courses.'

He chose meat and the sweet. It proved to be roast beef with potatoes and carrots, and treacle pudding to follow. Except he couldn't cut the meat.

Seeing his efforts, one of the women reached over, picked up the knife and fork and diced the meal into squares with fast, efficient chopping movements.

'One of my sons lost his arm at Dunkirk,' she said matter-of-factly. 'But at least I've got him safe home. My sister lost both her boys.' She replaced the cutlery neatly on the plate and turned back to sharing out the queuing with her friend.

Aware that he ought to feel desperately ashamed of his recent self-pitying tantrums after that conversation, and feeling even more ashamed because his own problems were still more important to him than the deaths of two unknown soldiers, Jack concentrated on his plate. Gradually his ears became attuned to the various sounds around him. Individual voices sorted themselves out into separate skeins of chatter. One voice was familiar.

'Don't spoil things, love. I thought you'd like being treated to a nice meal out.'

'No you don't. You thought I wouldn't be able to make a fuss in public.'

Jack risked a quick glance round. They were behind him, at a table against the far wall. Len Shaw was still in his fire officer's uniform. He'd have come off duty this morning like Pat, Jack assumed. The man's face was flushed with the effects of heat, food and – possibly – anger, judging by the taut lines between his nose and mouth.

Betty Shaw's face was partially obscured by the black felt hat she'd worn when she'd called at his house with the

220

anonymous letters, but the low, vibrating anger in the words he'd just overheard suggested she'd been brooding on the accusations of her husband's infidelity ever since.

God damn the letter writer: did she – or he – know the trouble they were causing? Jack cursed to himself, stabbing circles of carrot and trying not to listen. But it was impossible. The low voices, pitched to go under the general chatter, had the effect of making them conspicuous. It was like a dripping tap; now he knew they were there, his ears returned to them however hard he tried to concentrate on other conversations.

'For the last time, there's nothing in what the letters are saying.'

'Then why didn't you show me them when they started?'

'Because I knew you'd carry on like this.'

'No you didn't. I've always trusted you, Len.'

'Then trust me now, love, please.'

'I can't. You won't talk to me.'

'I've done nothing but talk to you. You won't let it go. You're like an ache, nagging away at the same tooth day and night. I never thought you'd turn into a nag, Betty.'

'I'm not nagging, I just want the truth, Len. Please.'

The sudden silence made Jack risk another glance. He was half-afraid that Len Shaw was considering telling the truth, the whole truth and nothing but the truth. It was with some relief that he saw the interruption had been caused by the arrival of the waitress with two cups of coffee. It was a short-lived lull in the storm. As soon as the woman left, the voices started again:

'I can't believe you, Len. I just can't.'

'Well don't then. I've said all I'm going to say on the subject. It's probably your age.'

'What's my age got to do with it?'

'Women go funny at a certain age. It's well known. My mum used to get up in the middle of the night to wash herself down under the outside pump. Reckoned she was boiling even when the water pipe was iced solid.'

'I'm not that old, Len. There's years before . . . all that business.'

'Well, there's something wrong with you.'

221

'Yes, there is. I'm married to a man who's carrying on and hasn't got the backbone to admit it. Do you want a divorce?'

'No.'

'Why not? If you've told the poor girl you love her . . . ?'

'I never told . . .'

Without looking round, Jack could picture the defeat on Len Shaw's square face. She'd tripped him up. The belligerence had gone when he spoke again.

'It meant nothing, honestly, love. It was just . . . I got carried away . . . it's got nothing to do with you and me.'

'*Did* you tell her you loved her?'

'No. Of course I didn't.'

'What's she like? Is she prettier than me?'

'No, she couldn't hold a candle to you.'

'Then why do it? She must have something that I don't have. What did she give you that I couldn't, Len?'

'Look, just leave it. I've admitted it and I've said I'm sorry. It will never happen again, I promise, love. Now we won't talk about it again. OK?'

'How many times?'

'For heaven's *sake*, Betty. I told you to leave it.'

'Where did you do it?'

'Betty!'

'Did she know she was just a bit of fun, Len? Or did you tell her she was the only girl who you'd ever really loved?'

'No! I never tell . . .'

'You never tell them that. Is it *them*, Len?'

'No. Jesus, woman, where'd you get these crazy ideas?'

'Same place I got the crazy idea that you love me, I suppose.'

'Don't start crying. People are looking. What happened, it just did. It's nothing to do with you and me.'

'No?'

'No.'

'So if I go with another bloke it'll be nothing to do with you and me, eh, Len?'

'Don't be daft. It's . . . it's different for a bloke. We got, you know . . . needs.'

'Which I didn't satisfy?'

222

' 'Course you did. The others . . .'

'Others? How many have there been? Three? Four? Ten? Twenty?'

He knew without looking up from his treacle pudding that the blast of air that buffeted him was from Betty's rush past the tables. The door bell jangled violently.

'Betty! Wait!'

'Your bill, sir!'

They'd both disappeared by the time Jack paid his own bill and left the café. No doubt hostilities would recommence when they reached home. Dismayed to find the weather had turned even colder, he turned up his coat collar and hurried home to prepare himself for the social whirl at Agar Street police station.

Chapter 23

Pat delivered Annie at three o'clock. 'Mum says party starts at half past,' he said.

'Fine.'

They were much of the same height and for a moment they held each other's gaze.

'It wasn't me who told DC Bell about Maury, you know.'

'Maybe not, Mr Stamford. But you would 'ave done if you'd have known about the whisky in the chicken shed, wouldn't you?'

'I don't know. Yes, yes, I probably would have. I can't keep one law for friends and another for everyone else, Pat, you must see that?'

'Yeah. 'Spect I do. 'Spect Mum does too really. Only the thing is, see, Maury's family. And we got to do whatever we can to keep him out of clink. Once a bloke's been inside, well, that's it, ain't it? He never really gets rid of the smell.'

'Then for heaven's sake tell him to be sensible, Pat. Helping the police would be taken into consideration. He'd probably get probation.'

'I tried telling him, Mr Stamford. Thing is . . . he won't grass.' Pat thrust his fingers through his light-brown hair in a gesture of exasperation. 'I'd like to knock some sense into the little . . .'

Belatedly they both became aware of Annaliese standing wide-eyed between them.

'We'd better go. I'm glad we're still on speaking terms, Pat.'

'Yeah. Em . . . I wanted to give you these. Letters.' He handed Jack a brown paper bag. 'I 'ad a word with Adele. She's one of the girls from the control room.'

'I remember her,' Jack said, recalling a shelter dance he'd attended a couple of months previously where the AFS had supplied the band. 'She plays the violin.'

'That's 'er. Used to be a professional musician. She's been acting so odd recently I was sure she'd had some. I 'ad to pretend I was going to look for the writer meself, Mr Stamford. She wouldn't let a stranger see them.'

'OK. Thanks, Pat.'

'I hope you catch the bas . . .'

Jack coughed warningly and took his daughter's mittened hand. She twisted it out of his grip.

'Let's go see Father Christmas then, shall we?'

As children's parties went, the Agar Street police station event was generally considered a riotous success. Demonstrating the truth of Ding-Dong's earlier remark that policemen bred vandals in order to keep themselves in employment, thirty children flung themselves into the games with a single-minded determination to get one of the coveted parcels under the gaily decorated Christmas tree.

'Well, Annie seems to be enjoying herself, doesn't she, sir?' Sarah laughed, wandering over to join Jack, who'd prudently taken up a position in the quietest corner of the canteen.

'She certainly does,' Jack agreed.

In honour of the party, Eileen had brushed the little girl's auburn hair until it shone like copper and tied it into plaits with new green silk bows. They spun out now like propellers as she hurtled round in an energetic game of musical chairs.

'I thought . . .' Jack said hesitantly, 'I didn't think she'd want to come. She's always so withdrawn with me. I'd assumed she was like that with everyone . . .'

'I think you can thank Sammy and Nafnel for the transformation, sir. They were rehearsing her when I stayed at Eileen's.'

The game had been reduced to a single chair and the last two children: Annaliese and a chunky boy a couple of years older.

'You could say,' Sarah explained, 'that she's their forward raiding party. Sort of plunder by proxy.'

WPC Crimmond, who'd been banging out 'Jingle Bells' on the piano, took her fingers from the keys. The boy flung himself at the chair, a self-satisfied smirk on his face as part of his grey-trousered bottom touched it. With an audible gasp, Annaliese leapt into the air and hurled herself sideways into the soft body. The chubby grey bottom skidded off the polished wood and hit the floorboards three feet away. The chair rocked dangerously, but with grim determination Annaliese gripped the sides of the seat, wrapped her white socks and black patent shoes behind the crossbar and defied anyone to move her.

'Blimey, sir, you got a right 'andful there,' a uniformed constable murmured as the snivelling second place was helped to his feet. There was a touch of admiration in his tone.

She was presented with a knobbly package which proved to be full of chocolate logs and aniseed balls. Jack was entrusted with them whilst she joined the rest of the children, who were arranging themselves cross-legged on the floor for 'Uncle Sebastian and his Magic Show'.

'Sebastian, good heavens,' Jack muttered as DC Bell swept on in a purple cape decorated with silver stars, and a pointed hat. The children watched with delight as the normally morose DC pulled pennies from their ears, showered lemon bon-bons and liquorice all-sorts from empty jars, drew coloured scarves and paper flowers from his mouth and made playing cards and half-crowns disappear into thin air.

Tea was served next. The canteen cook had worked miracles and the decorated table was loaded with sandwiches, biscuits, cakes, jelly and a Christmas cake decorated with real marzipan reindeer. It took at least thirty minutes for the guests to eat themselves silly. After which they were told they could take whatever was left over home with them. Hauling up her pleated skirt Annaliese took a neatly folded brown paper bag from the pocket of her navy knickers and presented it to WPC Crimmond for filling.

'Well, if the war lasts long enough, one of those two is definitely destined for a career in tactics and forward planning,' Jack said.

'Nafnel, I expect.' Sarah smiled, helping to usher the guests into line for Father Christmas's visit. 'I mean, Sammy's a nice little boy, but the other one's . . .'

'Smarter,' Jack finished for her, remembering Nafnel's own modest assessment of his capabilities. 'Yes, his foster mum agrees with you.'

'Foster? Oh, Mrs Goodwin. I still think of her as his teacher. Is there any news on that front?'

'News?'

'Her and Pat O'Day. I mean, I rather got the impression . . . but it's probably none of my business.'

'There's no news at all. Our anonymous letter-writer has suggested their relationship was immoral in the light of Mrs Goodwin's fairly recent widowhood. A load of tommy-rot of course, but unfortunately Rose has taken it to heart. I suspect it rather reflects what she's been thinking herself. Society seems to think even rotten marriages deserve a decent period of mourning. How are you getting on with the letter business? Have you made any progress with Nell De Groot?'

'Not a lot. It's not easy to keep bumping into her when we both work shifts. But we had a bath together on Monday.'

'Isn't that taking fuel economy to ridiculous lengths?'

'Not literally, sir.' She told him about the tight-pursed Bridget O'Mara and then went on to describe Ruby Rawkins, 'the ground floor back', and Max Death. 'He's some kind of commercial traveller in cosmetics, he claims.'

'Claims?'

'He's a bit vague on the details. I did wonder whether he might be selling something slightly less glamorous. I mean, a traveller in drain-cleaners or rat poison is not every girl's knight in shining armour, is it? He's in love with Nell.'

'Reciprocated?'

Sarah hesitated, then said truthfully, 'She keeps her feelings hidden. But I'd say not. He's very pleasant, but he's an ugly bastard. And there's an RAF officer hovering around who looks like a film star who's been hired to *play* an RAF officer, he's so damn perfect.'

'Not many of us mere males measure up to your exacting standards, do they, Sergeant?'

She gave him an odd look, but any answer she was about to offer was interrupted by the arrival of the divisional superintendent, swathed in cushions, red robing and cotton-wool whiskers. Clanging the brass school bell he'd borrowed for the occasion, he self-consciously intoned, 'Ho-ho-ho, who's first for Santa's sack?'

Under cover of the children's noisy shrieks, Sarah murmured: 'If Nell's writing the letters, there's no evidence in her room. At least there wasn't when I searched it yesterday.' In response to an enquiring flick of Stamford's eyebrows, she said, 'The landlady has spare keys for all the rooms.'

'How did you square that one with her?'

'I didn't. Ding-Dong's not the only one who can make things disappear. And unless Nell De Groot shares our abilities, there's no cheap lined paper in that room. Her stuff is the expensive quality type. Sort of thing you'd expect her to use.'

'Do you like her.'

Sarah showed no surprise at the abrupt change of subject. 'Yes. I don't think we're ever going to be sisters under the skin, but yes, she's all right. I certainly don't like to think we're easing her into the loony bin, sir.'

Any further discussion was halted by Annaliese flying back in triumph with her present.

'Aren't you going to open it, then?' Sarah asked.

The barley-twist plaits flicked in alternate flying ropes of green silk. 'Auntie Eileen says I've got to bring it back and put it under the tree. You have to open them on Christmas Day.'

The party was breaking up and Sarah was pressed into sorting out coats, scarves and woollen mittens.

'Thank heavens that's over for another year,' she said with feeling as the last of the children was dispatched into the raw December evening. 'Give me a decent pub riot any day. Allow me,' she added, rescuing the chocolate logs as Jack attempted to scoop up all Annaliese's prizes in one hand and succeeded in dropping most of them on the floor. 'You take the present, Annie,' she instructed, 'and I'll carry these.'

'I can manage,' Jack said shortly.

'No you can't, sir. Come on.'

She led Annaliese out by the hand, which left Stamford to trail behind them, noting with some annoyance that his daughter had made no attempt to prevent Sarah holding on to her. The pain that had been mercifully absent since he'd taken the morphine that morning had started to creep back again. By the time they reached the house, the cold weather and the walk had stirred it into a fierce internal blaze again.

Two figures erupted from the O'Days' step, where they'd plainly been on watch. 'What d'ya get, Annie?'

With outstretched arms Annaliese indicated that she wanted to reclaim her booty. Sarah duly relinquished it and it was carried over in triumph for inspection. The children disappeared into the darkened front door and Sarah would have followed them. Jack turned away.

'Sir . . . ?'

He looked back. Sarah had paused in the centre of the road. The tilt of her head asked the question.

'I'm *persona non grata* over there at the moment. But I'm sure Eileen would be pleased to see you.'

She came over to him instead. 'Can I help?'

He knew that she meant with the situation between him and Eileen, but he chose to ignore that and asked her to open the front door instead. 'The key sticks.'

'Of course.'

He'd expected her to return the key and step away, but instead she went into the house. 'Blackout up?'

'In the front room.'

'It's freezing,' she remarked, flicking the lights on. 'Haven't you got any coal?'

'Yes, I just can't light the damn thing.'

Sarah had turned to face him. Her eyes, blue in some lights and grey in others, narrowed. 'You look worse than a dead cod on the fishmonger's slab. What's the matter?'

Jack collapsed on to the sofa. 'This damned arm. There's some morphine tablets in my breast pocket, can you . . . ?'

She displayed her usual cool efficiency in finding the tablets, fetching a cup of water and applying a match to the fire he'd laid but disastrously failed to light the previous day.

229

'Thanks.' Leaning back, he closed his eyes as the waves of pain bit deeper, telling himself it wouldn't be long before the morphine kicked in. When he opened them again he found Sarah had remained standing. 'Don't look so concerned. And for heaven's sake sit down, you're giving me a crick in my neck.'

She perched on the edge of a chair and asked if the doctors couldn't do more.

'Apparently not. It's a question of wait and see. Either I get better, or I don't. Judging by the number of Job's comforters I've met recently, most people don't.'

'What will you do?'

'If it's no better by the new year, I shall apply to be pensioned off.'

The flicker of surprise that passed over Sarah's long-jawed face mirrored exactly his own feelings. Until now he hadn't put it into words, but now it was out in the open he knew he'd been nurturing the idea ever since the arthritis had started.

'What will you do, sir?'

'I don't know. I daresay even an old crock like me can find an office job of some kind in the present circumstances.'

'You could do that in the force, surely?'

'Yes . . .'

He could, of course, they'd find a niche for him at the Yard. He'd seen them there over the years: grey men who came in each day clutching their Thermos flasks and packets of sandwiches and lurked in dark offices filling in forms in meticulous copperplate. Most of the time you had no idea what they did or why they did it. In fact there was an apocryphal story that one had been employed by an insurance company near the Yard. For twenty years he'd come into the wrong building, and no one had noticed.

'. . . but I'd like to make a clean break,' he said.

'Oh? I'm sorry.'

He gave her a bleak smile. 'Perhaps it won't come to that.' The pain was easing sufficiently for him to remember his duties as host and offer her something to drink. 'I'm out of tea. And coffee. But there's some brandy in the kitchen.'

'Thanks.'

She returned with the bottle and another glass, poured herself a measure and lifted the bottle enquiringly. Reasoning that he could fall on his own doormat this time, Jack extended his water glass.

This time Sarah sat on the hearth rug, slipping off her uniform jacket and folding it neatly on the chair she'd just vacated. Delving into her pocket she produced a brown paper bag similar to Annaliese's. 'Sandwich, sir?'

'What are they?'

'Sardine or . . .' she sniffed, 'Marmite and celery.'

'I'll pass, thanks.'

Sarah calmly took a child-sized square from the squashed mass in the bag and started chewing.

'You must have a stomach like a dustbin . . .'

'We just ate anything that came to hand when we were kids, sir. Before someone else did.'

'Your mother wasn't much of a cook, then?'

'Not much. Why did you quarrel with Eileen?'

He accepted her right to change the subject, but unfortunately she'd chosen one he didn't want to talk about. So he switched it to yet another track. 'Pat brought some more letters round. They belong to another one of the AFS women.'

There were six of them. All similar to the ones he'd already seen, with their cheap paper and pencilled messages in capital letters. Sarah peered at the smudged postmarks. 'All local, about one a fortnight since September.'

'Mmm . . .' He used a pencil to spread the sheets out, aware once again of the futility of the exercise unless he could take prints from the crews at the fire stations for comparison.

'Do you think you could get me a set of Nell De Groot's prints, for elimination?'

'I should think so. Although I imagine she's probably got enough nous to wear gloves if she's doing it.'

'Do you think she is?'

Sarah hesitated, then said: 'I don't know. I don't want it to be her. But . . . I just don't know her well enough to say.'

The letters to Adele were all on a similar theme:

YOU STINK. WHY DON'T YOU WASH PROPERLY?

SOAP'S NOT ON RATION YOU KNOW. WHY DON'T
YOU BUY SOME, SMELLY?

HAVEN'T YOU SEEN PEOPLE LEAVING THE ROOM
WHEN YOU COME IN?

TO MISS STINK-BOMB OF 1940 – FIRST PRIZE FOR
SMELLING LIKE ROTTEN EGGS.

WHY DON'T YOU SEE THE DOCTOR? ANYONE
WHO SMELLS THAT BAD MUST BE DEAD AND
ROTTING.

YOU'RE MAKING PEOPLE SICK. CAN'T YOU
SMELL THE CRUD?

'Number three suggests it is someone from the fire station,'
Sarah remarked.

'Well that was a pretty sure bet, wasn't it?' He'd snapped
without meaning to because the morphine hadn't worked as
effectively this time. 'But what the hell I'm supposed to do if
I can't even fingerprint them . . .' Frustrated, he screwed up
one of the letters and sent the paper ball into the hearth.

Retrieving it, Sarah placed it back with the other sheets.
'Do you think you should be destroying evidence, sir?'

'Evidence of what, for heaven's sake? There's no threats, no
demands for money. There never are.' Briefly he gave her a
resumé of the letters to the Shaws and Pat. 'I've sent them over
to the lab to be checked for prints, but heaven knows why.
What the hell would *you* charge the writer with?'

'Nothing at all. But that's not the object of the exercise, is
it? We're ensuring Dr De Groot can have total peace of mind to
concentrate on brewing up nasties in his test tubes.'

'Mmm . . .' The pain was blessedly subsiding. He closed his

eyes and let the agony ooze out of the end of his fingers and drift away.

Opening them again, he found Sarah's anxious eyes fixed on him. 'Shall I cook you something, sir?'

'Can you? Cook, I mean.'

'Not really.'

'Just as well there's no food in the house then. Anyway, I had something earlier. But thanks for offering.'

The brandy and morphine were finally inducing a warm euphoria. He felt good and at peace with the world. He stood up, intending to fetch his cigarette case from the mantelpiece. The world suddenly swung in alarming fashion. Sarah scrambled from the rug. He was vaguely aware of the disc of her pale face opposite his, before he found his good arm was round her waist and they were collapsing back towards the sofa. His weight pulled her down with him and pinned one of her arms between him and the sofa back.

'Sorry.' He tried to sit up. The movement pulled Sarah harder against his chest. He was vaguely aware of the faintly perfumed smell of her skin: it had a sharp edge to it, as if it came from soap rather than cologne.

'It's all right . . . can you just . . .' Sarah tried to wriggle free. He could feel her ribs sliding beneath the cotton blouse. She felt good; warm and soft. Pulling her closer her sought for her mouth and pressed his lips against it. She responded, sliding her hand round the nape of his neck and caressing the fine downy hairs there as her tongue tentatively flicked between his teeth.

It was the damned arm that jerked them both back to common sense. An incautious movement leant Sarah's weight full on the elbow joint. It responded by turning every nerve end into a razor-pointed needle. Jack sat up with an involuntary gasp. Sarah was pushed away. For a moment they remained frozen, staring into each other's eyes. A dispassionate corner of Jack's mind saw that the brown hair she'd twisted up was escaping from its pins, allowing the blonder ends to sparkle like gold in the firelight. He noted the pulse flickering as if it wanted to escape from the pale flesh in the soft hollow at the base of her throat, and the stain of pink on her cheeks. Then the cool mask descended again.

'I think I should go now, sir.'

'No . . . wait . . . I'm sorry. . . That was stupid . . . I didn't mean . . .'

'Goodnight.'

She scooped the jacket from the chair and walked quickly into the hall. By the time he'd managed to stand, there was only a cool draught and the slight scent of her soap lingering in the unlit passageway.

Chapter 24

For once she was grateful for the blackout. Safe in the concealment of waning moonlight largely obscured by scudding clouds, Sarah hurried towards the high street. By the time she reached the shops, she'd managed to rebutton her jacket, tuck her hair back and compose a glib reply about the cold snap raising chilblains on her cheeks for the benefit of any beat copper she happened to run into. Chances were, she reflected bitterly, she'd run into the whole complement of Agar Station between here and Vorley Road.

As it happened, however, she was in luck. Glancing down the hill as she turned the corner of Prince of Wales Road, she made out the bulky shape of a bus, the faint glow of its destination board announcing that its route would take it up the Archway. There was only one other passenger at the top. Another woman, shorter and plumper than Sarah herself. As the bus drew up she stooped and lifted a suitcase on to the rear platform. The conductor heaved it effortlessly into the luggage space beneath the stairs.

'Put that under here for yer, missus. Going far?'

'Just up to the Archway, please.'

'Penny then.'

The ticket was punched off and the woman took one of the bench seats just inside the door. Sitting opposite her, Sarah handed over her own penny. It was too dark inside the bus to make out the other woman's features clearly, but the way she strained forward from the waist, her head leant towards the open back platform, suggested she was looking for someone or something outside on the pavement. As the bus moved away and picked up speed, her tense pose relaxed. She flopped back

235

against the seat in an attitude that could have been relief – or resignation.

Laying her cheek against the side barrier, Sarah let the cold glass draw out the last of the hot colour from her face as she recalled how she'd nearly climbed down Jack Stamford's throat. At the same time a tingle spread down her stomach and thighs as she imagined how much further things might have gone. Who was she kidding? Not *might* have, *would* have, if he hadn't flung her off like that.

And then what, Sarah? she asked herself fiercely. *He can hardly make an honest woman of you, can he? He's already got a wife in Holland.*

The moral dilemma didn't bother her; she wasn't a virgin, that had gone in an enthusiastic tussle one hot summer in a back shed in Litcham Street when she was sixteen. It wasn't even the gossip and knowing looks; she could have ridden those out easily if Stamford hadn't been a policeman. But he was; and if they were found to be having an affair, then they'd both get black marks on their records and one of them would be transferred to another station. Probably her. How would she ever convince another senior officer that she was suitable to be transferred to CID permanently if she carried a reputation for causing trouble? And she had no doubt at all, the blame would all be laid at her door.

She found herself hoping that Stamford's arthritis *would* get worse. At least if he was invalided out that would solve her problem. But in the meantime, how on earth was she going to face him if he came into Agar Street Station?

Her moody reflections were brought to an abrupt halt by the conductor's shout of 'Archway, Archway.' Stepping around the woman who was dragging the case clear, Sarah jumped off.

'Excuse me! Hello.'

Belatedly realising the shout was being directed at her, Sarah swung round. Her fellow passenger was weaving an uncertain course towards her, her lopsided walk weighed down by the suitcase. Thirties, Sarah guessed. Darkish hair under a dark hat as far as she could make out. Medium height and build.

The woman came within a foot of Sarah and dumped the

case with obvious relief. 'Sorry, I didn't mean to yell like that. It's just that everything looks so different in the dark and I didn't want to lose you before I asked directions.'

'Are you lost?'

'I'm afraid so. Vorley Road, is it up or down the hill from here?'

'Follow me, I'm going there myself.'

They walked in silence, with just the sound of their footsteps for company and a distant chorus of 'O Little Town of Bethlehem' sung in childish trebles from the Sally Army chapel.

'This is Vorley,' Sarah said, turning the corner. 'And this is me.' She indicated the steps to Mrs O'Mara's. Her companion had stopped too. Assuming that she couldn't see the door numbers in the dark, Sarah asked which one she wanted.

'I'm not sure. I mean . . . there's an auxiliary firewoman lodges in this street. She's in her twenties, very fair . . .'

'Nell De Groot?'

'Yes. Do you know which house . . . ?'

'This one.'

'Oh. Right.'

She was hesitating, her head beneath the rimmed hat tipped backwards to take in the three storeys. Sarah sensed that this was a crossroads. The house was one route; taking the bus back down the hill would be another.

The woman took an audible breath, hefted her case into a more comfortable position and started up the steps.

Intrigued, Sarah followed. From all she'd heard and seen, Nell De Groot had no friends except for the inhabitants of this house. She used her own key to let them both into the front hall, sliding quickly into the dimly lit space before the light spilt into the street.

'Nell's room is at the top. But she's probably on duty.'

'No. She's off tonight.'

Curiouser and curiouser, Sarah decided, taking a better look at this woman who knew Nell's duty movements but not her full address. The dark hair proved to be chestnut. And the face was pleasantly round without being spectacularly pretty. Apart from the black felt hat, she was dressed in a black belted coat, black high heels and plain leather gloves. Trying not to stare, Sarah quickly took in the red-rimmed eyes inadequately concealed beneath thick face powder.

'Shall I give Nell a call, or do you want to go up? I'm Sarah McNeill, by the way. Top floor front.'

'No. Thanks. That is . . . I don't want to see Nell. I really wanted to see the woman who runs the house.'

'Mrs O'Mara?'

'I heard she had a spare room now.'

Sarah supposed she was right. She'd never seen the elusive ground floor front, and now the Widow Gideon had snatched him from under Bridget's nose, she didn't imagine the poor man would ever get over the doormat again. Unless, of course, he had a death wish.

'Bridget lives in the basement. Hang on.'

Her exploratory shout flushed out not only Bridget, but also Nell, who followed her out of the under-stairs door holding two uniform blouses on hangers.

'Sure now, I was just finishing Miss Nell's bit of ironing before I popped up the Bush. It's not a proper Saturday night, is it, me dear, unless you have a bit of a knees-up.'

In preparation for gracing the Hampstead social scene, Mrs O'Mara had encased herself in a tight purple two-piece, liberally embellished with assorted brooches, rings and chains, and topped off by a short fur jacket with dangling rabbit fibbets. It was one of these she was adjusting as she spoke. Consequently she failed to see her visitor hovering in the gloom by the front door.

Nell's eyes widened in enquiry. 'Hello, Mrs Shaw. Did you want me? Am I to come on duty?'

So this was Station Officer Shaw's wife, was it? Sarah thought with interest. The letters had accused her of being a spy and her husband of adultery. One of them had obviously hit the target, judging by the suitcase. And she'd rather have expected a spy to head for the nearest port. So Mr Shaw had been caught out, had he? Her train of thought promptly carried her back to DCI Stamford's front room and the remembrance that she'd been about to happily collude in a spot of extramarital sex herself. By the time she came back to the present, Bridget was already blessing the luck that caused her to have a fine room free just when the lady happened to be wanting one.

'I'll have to be charging you a bit more, it being a ground-floor room and . . .'

Bridget's voice faded behind the closed door as she led Betty inside, leaving the watchers in the hall to stare at each other.

'Oh dear,' Nell said finally. 'That was the station officer's wife. Not Good Hope, the regular station over the road.'

There was no point Sarah pretending she hadn't noticed Mrs Shaw's suitcase. 'Probably something and nothing,' she said, moving up the stairs. *But rather more something*, she added silently to herself. As Betty Shaw had stooped to pick up the suitcase and follow Bridget into the room, the sleeve of her coat had risen up. There were weals on her wrist; deep red and purple marks like fingerprints. By the looks of it, someone had imprisoned Betty by the arms and hung on until they'd left virulent bruises that would mark her for weeks.

The front door opened as they reached the first landing. Both turned back and peered unashamedly over the banisters. Had Betty changed her mind? The dim lamp bulb reflected on a bald spot the size of a two-shilling piece.

'Good evening, Max. Good day?'

Sarah was under no illusions as to which of them had lit the spark of pleasure that ignited Max Death's ugly features.

Touching his homburg to his chest, Max gave a slightly old-fashioned bow. 'Good evening, Nell. Miss McNeill. Yes, thank you. I have obtained several moderately gratifying orders and, even better . . .' He sprang lightly up the stairs and rested the small attaché case he always carried on the banister rail. He'd positioned it so that the raised lid blocked their view of the contents. Rather in the manner of DC Bell's magic show, he drew out a carton with a flourish. 'Freshly laid eggs.' He held the half-dozen out to Nell. 'For you, if you'd care for them?'

'Oh, I couldn't.' Nell's hands dropped. She stepped away.

'Just a small Christmas gift.'

She put her hands behind her back. The gesture caused her breasts to thrust against the soft pink wool of her jumper, emphasising their full roundness. Apparently she became aware of the provocativeness of this pose and hastily clutched at her hair instead. For once it wasn't in a smooth pleat, but hung in a long heavy plait over one shoulder. Twisting the ragged end of this rope, she murmured that she couldn't possibly accept. 'Really. It wouldn't be fair, six to myself.'

Max's face fell. He looked towards Sarah. She saw the opportunity for a bit of chumming up. 'Perhaps we should all share them?'

The suggestion was seized on by Nell with surprising enthusiasm. 'I could scramble them. And I've got some bread. If the pressure is high enough, you can make toast on the gas fire.'

Max predictably enough, was all for it. In fact he offered his butter ration and a little ham he had put by. 'And I have a little treat. I'll fetch it up with me. Would half an hour be convenient?'

'Perfectly. Would you bring your own cutlery and plates, please.'

When the party reconvened in Nell's room in thirty minutes, Max's hair gleamed with Brylcreem and his chin had the soft pinkness of new shaving. His skin exuded a faint smell of dampness and Lifebuoy. Mentally Sarah saluted him for taking a bath in the freezing-cold water that had gushed from her own taps.

'The butter and ham,' he said, almost shyly tendering two small greaseproof packets. 'And . . .'

And was a bottle of gin.

Sarah was placed in charge of the toasting fork. Holding it to the hissing gas bars, she watched as Nell neatly chopped the ham and stirred it into the creamy yellow mixture she was simmering on one of the gas rings. Max busied himself pouring three measures of gin into cups and apologising for not being able to offer them anything with it. 'I tried to obtain some lime or orange cordial, but there doesn't seem to be any to be had.'

'It's Christmas,' Nell said, flicking the heavy plait behind her shoulder. 'People will have bought whatever they can. Especially if it's something that children might care for.'

'Yes, of course. Having no family to celebrate the joyous season with, one tends to, well . . .'

'Be not so joyous?' Sarah suggested, burning her fingers as she levered the toast free and put it on a plate by the fire.

'Detached, certainly. I generally catch up with paperwork over Christmas. And you, Miss McNeill . . . shall you be on duty?'

'Sarah, please. And no. Not this year. Unless there's an emergency, of course.'

As she'd worked every Christmas Day since she'd been stationed at Agar Street, they hadn't really been able to argue with her request to book this one off. She'd been looking forward to spending it with Eileen and the rest of the O'Days. But now . . . ! She had no idea what Jack and Eileen had argued about, but she anticipated a Christmas truce, given that Annie would almost certainly be spending Christmas with the O'Days . . . The idea of facing Stamford across the roast potatoes and brussels sprouts made her glad that she could blame her high colour on the hissing gas bars.

She returned her attention to the toast. As she speared the next slice, she caught a glimpse of Max's rapt face. His whole attention was fixed on Nell as she carefully drew the creamy mixture from the pan side. There was no mistaking the hunger and longing in his eyes. At that second he looked away and caught Sarah's eyes. The corner of his mouth lifted in a small, resigned smile, acknowledging that she'd caught him out but making no attempt to hide his feelings.

Feeling embarrassed that she'd intruded into a very personal pain, Sarah said quickly, 'What about you, Nell? Are you on duty over Christmas?'

'No.' Nell scraped at the eggs with unnecessary vigour. 'I should have been. It's not my day off, but something dreadfully embarrassing has happened: my mother telephoned the divisional office and asked if I might have leave to go home.'

Max's features fell. 'And they have agreed?'

Like a shot, I'll bet, Sarah thought, given the efforts the fire brigade were making to rid themselves of Firewoman De Groot as discreetly and permanently as possible.

241

'Yes. I had to work some off-duty days during the raids, so they do owe me the time. But I could have died when the sub-officer called me and told me I was booked off for the twenty-fourth and twenty-fifth. I think this is ready.' She stirred the mass doubtfully. 'There's rather a lot. I shouldn't have put all six eggs in, should I? I'm so sorry, I wasn't thinking. Should we perhaps see if any of the others would like to share?'

Sarah had a pretty shrewd idea that Max thought there was one person too many in this room already, but he rallied and pointed out that he'd heard Bridget go out. 'And Ruby will be working. Saturday is one of their busiest nights.'

'She works in a box office at the Bedford Cinema in Camden Town,' Nell explained in answer to Sarah's look of enquiry. 'She used to be dresser when it was a theatre.'

'She has seen some of the finest in their corsets,' Max said. He and Nell exchanged a brief laugh. Evidently this was a house joke.

'Well, that just leaves Mrs Shaw.' It was Sarah's turn to explain their new tenant to Max.

'Well, yes, we must make her feel welcome. However, make sure she brings a cup. There don't appear to be any spare.'

'I only have one,' Nell said. 'You two . . . I mean . . . it's the first time anyone else has ever been in my room. Except Bridget.'

And the boyfriend, Sarah added mentally.

Nell seemed to have an uncanny knack sometimes of reading her mind. The pointed chin went up and she looked Sarah straight in the eye as she added: 'And my brother.'

Sarah kept her expression blank whilst her mind whirled. She was damn sure she hadn't mistaken the purpose behind that scuffle on the landing the day she'd moved in. Was there a brother she'd never seen? Or was Nell trying to pass off the seriously gorgeous RAF officer as a relative in order to overcome Mrs O'Mara's rules about male visitors in the rooms?

'Would you ask Mrs Shaw whilst I serve?' Nell said coolly, her tone daring Sarah to probe further on the subject of the RAF.

Determined that she *would* probe when she was good and

ready, Sarah abandoned the toasting fork and ran lightly downstairs.

The soft sobbing carried across the small hall. Creeping closer to the door, Sarah listened quietly for a moment and then slipped away. She reported back to her fellow diners that Mrs Shaw wasn't in the mood for a party.

Dinner was served on the bed, with the plates balanced on their knees. Max got the only chair and the luxury of using the table. Gin was dispensed with pleasing liberality.

'No raids again,' Nell said as she scraped up the last morsels with a piece of toast. 'Do you think perhaps we'll be lucky over Christmas?'

'If we are, I fear someone else will suffer in our place,' Max replied. The toast and ham had left a greasy film around his mouth. Removing a spotless handkerchief, he swabbed the offending area. 'Liverpool is, I understand, quite devastated.'

'One of the women I trained with at Peel House moved to Liverpool,' Sarah remarked, draining her cup. 'She married a bloke who worked on the ferries. She normally sends me a Christmas card.'

Her post was sparse enough for Kitty's card to be missed. For the first time she guiltily wondered if her old room-mate was safe and well.

'I expect it's gone to my old address down Mornington,' she said, thinking aloud as Max dispensed the last of the delicious clear liquid. 'It's con . . . con . . . condemned,' she finished, suddenly aware that the room was beginning to feel rather too warm.

'All my cards will have been sent to my home address,' Nell confided. Her normally pale face had become flushed and her eyes were unnaturally bright. 'Mummy didn't tell anyone my new one. She thinks the auxiliaries are undignified. She wants me to be a WAAF. But I won't be. A WAAF is the very last thing in the whole wide world I shall ever be.' This last statement was delivered with a hint of belligerence, as if she was afraid they might try to talk her into joining the air force.

'Fine,' Sarah said, taking the cup from the other woman's

hand and passing it to Max. He, at least, still appeared to be relatively sober.

'Can I ask you both something?' Nell said. The question finished on a violent hiccup. 'Sorry,' she apologised, slapping one hand to her mouth. 'I was wondering if you'd care to spend Christmas at my home.' Before either of them could respond, she took a deep breath, regained control of her speech and said more clearly: 'Unless of course you have made other plans, Sarah?'

She had. But now she desperately needed a valid excuse to get out of them. And what better than working on an undercover job? Who knows? she thought, Nell's home might be stuffed with evidence of her scribbling activities.

'Thanks,' she said. 'I don't finish until at least two on Christmas Eve. Maybe later. Will that be all right?'

'I very much fear . . .' Max looked crestfallen. 'I very much fear I have made appointments for the twenty-fourth. Out of town. I'm so sorry . . . I shan't be back until the early evening.'

'It doesn't matter,' Nell said. 'There's a train to St Albans at seven. I have some shopping to do during the day. We could all go together. And I'm sure Daddy will give us a lift back after Christmas lunch.'

The invitation was accepted and the last of the gin raised in a toast to the delights to come.

And God bless us every one, Sarah thought ironically, helping Nell to wash up after Max had been diplomatically shooed from the room. *Or more likely God help us*.

Setting a kettle on to boil, she jumbled plates and cutlery into the small washbasin and suddenly became aware of the silence behind her. Assuming Nell hadn't been able to hold her gin, she swung round, half expecting to see the blonde fast asleep on the bed. Nell was standing less than a foot away. Her eyes were wide and strange in a way that Sarah had never experienced with drunks before. Almost involuntarily Sarah found herself staring at what was clutched in Nell's hand.

Nell extended it slowly. 'It's a letter,' she said, as if Sarah couldn't see the cheap envelope and letters written in pencilled block capitals.

'Yes?' Was this going to be a confession?

'It came yesterday. Read it.'

Sarah eased the single sheet out with the handle of a spoon and spread it over the table. Nell didn't seem to find the behaviour odd. But Sarah knew from experience that seen through the haze of alcohol, an awful lot of things seemed perfectly rational. Once her own father had had a skinful, he'd never questioned even the most bizarre actions by her mother. The day she'd eventually set fire to his bed, he'd actually lain there giggling insanely as the flames spread to his legs.

The letter was as simple and to the point as the rest she'd seen:

THAT DON'T TOUCH ACT ISN'T FOOLING ME. YOU KNOW WHAT YOU ARE UNDERNEATH, DON'T YOU? WONDER WHAT THE BLOKES AT THE STATION WOULD SAY IF THEY KNEW WHAT YOU ARE REALLY LIKE.

'This came yesterday?'

Nell nodded.

'So why are you showing it to me?'

Tears welled in the ice-blue eyes. 'Because I'm so scared. And I don't have anyone else to talk to. I can't show it to Max, he'd wonder . . . I mean, the things it says . . .'

'What are you scared of?'

Nell's mouth twisted. The tears spilled and welled in glittering drops down her cheeks. 'That I'm going mad again. That they'll send me back to *that place*.' Seizing Sarah's hand, she gripped it with a strength that was at odds with her fragile appearance.

'You see, I'm terribly afraid that I wrote the letter and sent it to myself.'

Chapter 25

Hatty was frightened. Her safe, cosy world was sliding inexorably away.

Christmas had always been her favourite time of year. She'd start her preparations months before, making weekly payments to the butcher's Christmas club for a chicken and ham and adding a little extra bit to her weekly shopping until she'd collected enough to make the cake and puddings. In October their tiny house would be full of the delicious scents of spices and dried fruits as they stirred up the toffee-brown mixtures, made their wishes, and dropped in the silver threepenny bit that Grannie Miller had used in *her* pudding when Uncle Duggie and her dad were kids.

On Christmas Eve she'd join the crowds at the markets, pushing amongst the brightly lit stalls, jostling for the best bargains among the vegetables and fruit. At midnight, just before they went to mass, she'd cut vegetables into pans of cold water and polish the Cox's apples and the oranges, placing each one in a neat pyramid in the wooden fruit bowl that was only used once a year. Finally she'd make up a stocking for each of them and hang them from the mantel.

She'd always imagined her life would follow the same pattern until she was old. She'd seen herself on future Christmas days, seated at her own table, with her husband and children gathered round, and Ruth and *her* husband and kids, and Uncle Duggie of course. She'd even made her uncle promise to let her take the special threepenny bit with her so she could pass it on to her own daughter.

And once Len Shaw had taken an interest in her, the picture had become even stronger; the hazy husband who'd sat at the head of her imaginary future Christmas table now had a face. Big, strong Len; the rock who'd protect her and her children in all the years to come.

Only everything had gone wrong. Len was avoiding her. It was no good pretending to herself he was busy any more. He'd come over to Good Hope Station several times in the last week whilst she was there, and even though she'd made a point of lingering in the corridors and equipment yard to give him a chance to talk to her, he'd walked quickly past with his head down, refusing to meet her eye.

At first she'd been hurt, but over the past couple of days a small knot of anger had taken root and blossomed in her chest. He *had* said he loved her, Hatty thought, slapping slices of bread into the sizzling dripping for the men's breakfasts. And he'd said that what they'd done together was something only married people should do. So now he ought to marry her.

She desperately wanted to talk to someone about her problems, but there wasn't anyone to confide in except Ruth. And Ruth was acting oddly as well. She hadn't been her usual self since Friday. Hatty recalled how she'd woken in the small hours of that morning with a pressing need to visit the privvy. Easing herself off the creaky mattress, she'd pulled her coat on and thrust feet into her shoes. The air was cold, they never had fires in the bedroom. It would be even worse out in the yard.

It was only then that it had struck her something was wrong. Her mind had registered the lack of soft breathing in the room as her eyes accustomed themselves to the dense gloom and showed the flat, taut blanket stretched across Ruth's bed.

Her first concern had been Uncle Duggie's reaction. He'd been angry enough when they'd gone to bed at midnight and Stan still hadn't brought Ruth home. Heaven knows what he'd do if he woke up now and found her bed empty. It wasn't as if there'd been a raid and Ruthie could claim to have gone down a shelter. Making her way out to the back privvy, Hatty had done her business as quickly as she could and scuttled back to the relative warmth of the kitchen.

The back yard latch had lifted as she made to shut the door again.

'Ruth,' she'd whispered with relief. 'You'd best get upstairs quick before Uncle Duggie sees yer.'

The slight figure hadn't answered her. Instead she'd come slowly towards the house with a limping, uneven gait.

'Ruth? What's 'appened?'

'Nothing. Gives us an 'and, Hat, me feet 'urt something rotten.'

She hadn't let Hatty turn the light on. 'Fill us a bowl of water, Hat. I wanna wash.'

'Do it in the morning, case Uncle Duggie comes down.'

'No.'

There had been the sound of slithering and cloth hitting the floor. Hatty had guessed she was undressing, but since the blackout was still down, there was no light to see by until she struck a match and set it to the gas, intending to heat a kettle.

'Ruth!'

She was perched naked on the discarded pile of clothing, examining her feet. The flesh was ripped and bruised and bleeding from dozens of small cuts.

'Lost me shoes. 'Ad to walk miles,' she'd said matter-of-factly. 'There's bomb damage all over the place up west.'

She'd refused to say any more. Hatty had been forced to creep round the dark house, collecting soap, towel, nightdress and disinfectant and ripping one of the pillowcases into strips to make bandages for her cousin's torn feet.

Ruth had washed herself with such vigour that Hatty had been half-afraid she'd scour her skin off. And all the time she hadn't uttered a word except, 'Don't say nothing to me dad, Hat. Spit and swear.'

Obediently Hatty had spat on her hand, placed it over her heart and sworn. Afterwards she'd scrubbed the kitchen floor by the light of a candle stub, swabbing away Ruth's bloody footprints and carefully pouring the pink soapy liquid away down the outside drain whilst her ears strained for any sound from Uncle Duggie's room.

Since then Ruth hadn't been Ruth any more. She'd become a pale, drawn copy of someone who looked like Ruth, but wasn't.

An angry hiss and crack as a fat bubble exploded jerked Hatty back to the present, and the cooking ranges of Good Hope Station. The smells of frying had drifted upwards and drawn the men down from the sleeping room into the mess. 'Like h'a bunch h'of rats h'as scents the rubbish tip,' as Snakey was fond of describing the stampede at mealtimes.

He was second in the queue this morning, behind 'Doing-Her-Bit', who'd manned the watchroom phones last night.

'Got them Christmas puds safe, my lovely?' he enquired, watching Hatty adding the mess manager's 'perk' of an extra rasher to his plate.

'Locked in the store cupboard,' Hatty said listlessly. The puddings were currently in their separate ingredients. The recipe had said not to mix up until needed, the mixture didn't keep. There had been no stir-up and wishing this October, just like there would be no brightly lit Christmas Eve market to bring her senses to the pitch of anticipation. She and Ruth were working Christmas Day anyway. They'd have to eat here in the mess with the rest of the watch.

'What's the matter with that lovely cousin h'of yours? She's got white roses in her cheeks like I h'aint seen since me ma was taken h'off to the consumption ward. H'aint sickening from something, h'is she?'

'No. I think she's 'ad a row with her boyfriend, Snakey.' Hatty couldn't really believe that Stan Wilkins would have left Ruth in that state, but the explanation seemed to satisfy Snakey.

After she'd finished serving the men, Hatty filled a plate for herself. Normally she enjoyed tucking in, but this morning she had no appetite. In the end she tipped the fry-up into the bin, guiltily aware that she was breaking the law by wasting food. But then what else could you do with it? Some of the men had talked about starting a pig club and setting up sties in the equipment yard, but nothing had ever come of it.

Still oppressed by the weights that suddenly seemed to be attached to her arms and legs, she boiled water, added soda and started to scrub: cutlery, plates, mugs, pots and pans were dunked through the greasy tide that soon floated on the surface of the sink. The bells went down twice whilst she cleaned, but they were only minor domestic alarms and the crews were soon back. It was almost getting to be like before the Blitz, when you could get a regular night's sleep and know the world would look exactly the same when you went out on to the streets again.

Other areas were suffering in their place, though. They'd got a radio upstairs now, and on his frequent trips up and down to 'check the stores', Snakey informed her that Manchester had had 'h'a right bucketful last night. Burning worse than the 'oly fires of 'ell.'

'God protect them,' Hatty said automatically.

'H'I reckon they'd prefer h'a couple of dozen ack-acks and h'a squadron of Spitfires to do that job. No disrespect to the h'almighty intended. Where's the sugar?'

'Back of the cupboard.' Hatty stooped, shuffling tins out of the way, to retrieve the blue package she'd hidden at the back. 'It's gone!'

The suspicious look she flashed at Snakey was countered with an indignant denial. 'Not from me h'own, my lovely. Not from me h'own.' Marching to the bottom of the stairs, he bawled up to the recreation room, demanding to know, 'Which of you buggers has 'alf inched the sugar?'

A cut-glass accent informed him that the cook from the regular station had availed herself of a loan last night.

'Cheek!' Hatty said. 'Without even asking!' Rolling down her sleeves she buttoned her cuffs and marched across the road.

'It's her day off,' the regular brewing up informed her laconically.

'She's taken our sugar. Helped herself from my kitchen without even a please.'

'Galley,' the regular reproved, continuing to stir the enamel pot. 'Houses have kitchens. Cafés have kitchens. Fire stations have galleys, my dear. And I'm sure we'll be happy to return your sugar. Providing you can prove it's yours. Don't know how I could myself. Can't rightly tell one packet from the t'other. Tea's up, mateys.' The last remark was directed at the clatter of feet behind her. Hefting the pot up two-handed, he started to swing it over the mugs lined up on the counter.

Despite her size, Hatty found herself jostled forward by the crush. She caught a glimpse of glazed blue paper on the shelf beneath the counter, reached over, tucked the packet of sugar into her tunic blouse and glared at the temporary tea boy. 'That one was ours.'

'If you say so, gorgeous.'

'Gorgeous,' echoed an amused voice. 'Blimey, Marty, you're getting to be as silver-tongued as the guv'nor. 'Ere, is it right? His missus 'as seen the light and told him to sling his hook?'

'Couldn't say, matey.'

Hatty backed away, still clutching the awkward shape beneath her blouse. Around her the good-natured banter swirled. Someone had seen Betty Shaw with a suitcase last night. Another reckoned the guv'nor had had scratches down his face. 'Said he'd cut himself shaving. Darndest razor cuts I ever saw.'

Her heart was beating harder. She could feel the glazed packet bumping with the rhythm. Betty Shaw had left! Deserted her husband.

The door to his office was locked. Her sharp rap raised no response.

'Gone to Division,' Adele in the control room informed her. 'Big flap on. Important, was it?'

Suddenly aware how unlikely it was that an auxiliary cook could have anything to discuss with a station officer, Hatty flushed, mumbled she 'spected it could wait and fled back to Good Hope.

The rumours followed her. Sly whispers and nudges that were hastily choked off whenever Betty Shaw appeared from the watchroom. Not that she did a lot there. Whenever Hatty looked in, both Betty and Ruth were staring blankly into space, their white, hollow-eyed faces practically mirrors of each other.

'Sure now, and how much do you beauties charge to haunt a house?' one of the firemen had asked flippantly. His strident tone had penetrated Betty's private nightmare for a moment. The look of anguish she'd turned on him had been enough to send the man out of the room with an embarrassed apology. Witnessing the scene, Hatty had had to have some stern words with her own conscience. After all, Betty hadn't been a proper wife for years. What sort of woman went out to work instead of stopping home and having babies once she'd got wed. Betty couldn't even be bothered to starch his shirts. Len would be much happier with her, Hatty.

As she cooked the men's evening meal, she made bargains with herself. If he didn't send for her by Tuesday morning when his trip ended, she'd find some way to go round his house.

Christmas Eve! Her hands trembled as she slid mashed potato on to the plates. Maybe they'd even go to midnight mass together. Her day-dreams of her and Len walking arm in arm to the Christmas church service were so vivid that for a moment she didn't register the reality standing before her.

'Len!'

Casting a quick look over his shoulder, he told her, through gritted teeth, to call him Mr Shaw at work.

'But it doesn't matter now, does it? I mean, now Mrs Shaw's gone and left you there's no reason you and me can't get wed – praise the Lord.'

A dark-red flush spread over Len Shaw's handsome face. 'Who said Betty had gone?'

Hatty looked at him in surprise. 'Everybody, Len.'

'I told you. It's Mr Shaw on the station.'

'But why? Mrs Shaw calls you Len at work. And now I'm gonna be your wife, seems to me I ought to be allowed too.'

'You aren't . . . I mean, I never . . . Look, keep your voice down, will you, woman. The crew's coming down.'

The shuffling two-steps of shoes left unlaced so they could be kicked off if the alarm sounded announced that the first men were coming down from the locker and recreation rooms.

Hatty didn't bother to lower her voice as she demanded: 'You are going to marry me, Len, aren't you?'

Len stared at her face, turned red by the heat of the kitchen. She had a streak of mashed potato across one cheek and a film of sweat collecting in beads along her upper lip. The whole unattractive package wore an expression which he had never seen on her before, but which Ruth or Duggie Miller would instantly have recognised as Hatty's 'stubborn as a whole herd of mules' mood.

'Look, give it a few weeks, there's a good girl. No sense rocking the boat right off. Might look bad for me at Brigade.'

'No.'

'What?'

'No, I won't wait no more, Len. Why should I? I'll pack me stuff and come round your house Tuesday when your trip ends. Uncle Duggie will be all right if I tell him we're getting wed, you'll see.'

Len didn't want to see. At the moment the only thing he could see was himself walking down the street with this great lump on his arm. Everything about her irritated him, from her rolls of flesh to her habit of uttering religious platitudes in the midst of conversation. How on earth had he ever fancied her? Casting his mind back, he decided it was those big brown eyes that had sunk him.

He'd taken the female auxiliaries for drill and fire hydrant practice a few times last spring. Not that they were expected to fight fires, but a basic knowledge on how to hook up to a hydrant and run out the hose was considered necessary just in case they had to tackle an incident at the station whilst the men were out.

All the time he'd been conscious of Hatty's shining eyes watching his every move. A man would have to have been made of granite not to respond to her obvious admiration. And when it hadn't been bent over a red hot stove, her face could actually be fairly attractive.

It was her size that had been his downfall. It made her look far more mature than she was. He'd assumed that she under-stood the game like all the other women in his married past. A few drinks and a couple of tumbles to spice up a hundrum life until one or other got bored, then it was *goodbye*, with no hard feelings.

When he'd run into Hatty that day on Parliament Hill Fields and she'd told him her uncle and cousin were away for the night, he'd thought she was tipping him the wink that they'd have the house to themselves.

It wasn't until later that it had dawned on him that Hatty wasn't just shy but also very naive; almost childlike in some ways. The loving words he'd trotted out because that was how most of them liked to play it, had been taken seriously. Alarmed and feeling ashamed of himself, he'd tried to deal with the situation by ignoring it and hoping she'd go away. But she hadn't. Hatty was still expecting to play happy families.

He felt guilty every time he looked at her now. But he just couldn't see any way out. He could tell her straight out to get lost, of course. Uncle Duggie didn't bother him; no undertaker's spook was going to frighten him. And he didn't seriously imagine the brigade was going to discipline an experienced station officer for a bit of slap and tickle off duty. But he did have enough imagination to realise how Betty would react if she found out his latest piece was a woman she'd been working with every day.

The crews entered the mess room. Boisterous voices cut off suddenly when they saw Len. Shuffling round to collect their plates, one or two wished 'G'evening' to a point somewhere over his right ear.

'Evening,' Len said gruffly. 'Pat,' he added, raising his voice as the crew of the turntable ladder trooped in, noisily debating the army's big push in Libya.

'Sir?'

A nod indicated that Pat should join him in the corridor. Whatever he had to say took only a few seconds. Judging by the pale set of Pat's usually good-natured face when he returned, it hadn't been a happy interview.

Hatty waited for Len to return too. He didn't. The anger smouldered into life inside her chest again. He wasn't coming. He'd sneaked away again. It wasn't fair. Dropping the serving ladle with a clatter which brought several heads round in surprise, she made for the corridor, intending to follow him across to the main station if necessary.

When she got outside, however, she found she'd been unfair to him. His leather boots were descending the stairs from above. Even though he was only visible from the ankles, she knew it was him. Standing in the gloom, amidst the smells of cooking, sweat, polish and tobacco smoke, she felt her heart grow and swell with love as each inch of his muscular body came into view. He'd keep her safe for ever, her Len.

He didn't see her until he turned to walk back into the mess room. 'Oh. You're out here. Good.'

Hatty smiled. She wanted to throw herself into his arms and press kisses on his face, but she sensed he wouldn't like that. So she contented herself with imagining herself in bed with him, curled safe and snug against his back, with their first child sleeping peacefully in his cot a few feet from the bed. She was sure it would be a son. She'd have a daughter second; someone to inherit the Christmas pudding silver threepenny. Lost in her day-dream, it took a while for what Len was saying to penetrate.

'You do understand, don't you, Hatty? It wouldn't be fair giving you special privileges. Anyhow you wouldn't want people saying you're not doing your bit, would you?'

'No. No, 'course not, Len. But what ... I don't understand ...'

Even in the dim lighting, she saw the exasperation tightening the corners of his mouth. 'Haven't you listened to a word I've been saying?'

'The canteen van,' she said, dragging some vaguely heard words from the recesses of her memory.

'Yeah. Right. The canteen van. You've manned it before.'

A hand took her arm. But what she thought at first was affection was simply Len trying to move her out of the way so Pat O'Day could get past.

'Is your oppo here?' Len called.

'Just come across, sir,' Pat shouted back, hurrying towards the front door.

'O-five-hundred hours on the dot, understand?'

'Sir.' Pat's voice floated back hollowly.

Hatty said in surprise. 'Is the watch changing over?'

'No. I've given Pat leave to go home and get a few clean bits and pieces. You'd best do the same soon as you've cleared up here.'

'But *why?*

'For Pete's sake, woman . . . go up to your sub-officer, he'll give you your orders.'

The orders were brief and to the point. At six o'clock on the morning of the twenty-third of December, Hatty found herself sitting in the passenger seat of Good Hope's canteen van, staring blankly into the cold, grim dampness of the approaching dawn. Far up ahead she thought she could make out the humped bulk of Pat O'Day's turntable lorry.

'Here we go,' whispered the Euston Street auxiliary firewoman who'd been assigned to drive. Slipping off her brake, she eased the van forward. Swaying and jolting, they joined the tail of the convoy of over fifty London pumps, lorries and vans that had been dispatched northwards in response to an urgent message from Manchester that the local brigades were in danger of being completely overwhelmed by the inferno.

'Do you think we'll be back for Christmas?' Hatty asked.

'Shouldn't think so,' the other girl said, offering the cigarette she'd been smoking in noisy gasps. 'Do you?'

Hatty shook her head. She swallowed the large lump that was aching in her throat and blinked back hot tears. 'No. No. I don't think so, either.'

Chapter 26

'Magistrates should be strung up with holly from the nearest flaming Christmas tree.' With this heartfelt announcement, Sarah McNeill collapsed on her bed and levered off her shoes by scuffing her toes down their backs and flicking them into the air. They soared in arcs through the chill air and landed with a satisfying thump on the floorboards.

Resting the back of one leg on the knee of the other, she wriggled her toes in their regulation black stockings. Her feet ached, her back hurt and her stomach was still smarting from where somebody's little treasure had kicked her. She'd spent twenty hours yesterday and another ten today rushing between juvenile courts, police stations and remand homes and now she was finally, blissfully on leave until Boxing Day. Unless, of course, there was some kind of situation requiring a female officer. Given the chronic shortage of female police officers in London, they'd send a car for her . . .

Abandoning the idea of soaking her feet in a bowl of hot water, she scrambled out of her uniform and into civvies. At least if she was out they'd go on to the next station with a WPC in its contingent. Duty and patriotism were all very well, but there were times when a bit of looking after number one was called for.

She still had at least three hours to kill before she was due to join Nell and Max on their Christmas jaunt to St Albans. Time enough to slip round to Eileen O'Day's with the presents she'd bought for the children and then go on down to her old rooms and see if any post had been left there.

In the event her visit to Eileen's proved abortive. There was no answer at the O'Days' and when, after a short tussle with herself, she crossed the road and rapped sharply on Jack Stamford's knocker, that house also remained silent. Leaving the wrapped presents on Eileen's back step, she made her way back to the high street, intending to catch a bus down to Mornington Crescent.

Despite the blackout and early closing, the streets were still full of shoppers, carol singers and a few pedestrians who were so full of the seasonal spirit that striking a match anywhere near them would probably constitute an explosive hazard. In fact the only thing that was suddenly in short supply was buses. Squinting through eyes accustomed to dealing with the unlit streets, she made her way south, casting hopeful glances over her shoulder every few minutes. She'd reached the railway arch before a soft shout echoed up into the metal bridge which had started to vibrate with the approach of a train: 'Sarah. Wait.'

Nell De Groot flew over the road to join her. 'I thought it was you. You've not changed your mind, have you? I telephoned Mummy. She said she'd be delighted.'

Sarah explained about her former home. 'The postman might have left something with the neighbours. They've not got my new address yet. I won't be long. Max wasn't back when I left.'

'No. I know.'

The note of regret in Nell's voice surprised Sarah. Perhaps Max had more chance in that quarter than she'd previously thought.

'No one was in when I got back,' Nell said, huddling deeper into her thick coat.

Sarah, whose own coat was several guineas less warm, shifted in the icy blast that was gathering strength as it bowled down the road. 'I'll see you a bit later,' she shouted, raising her voice over the crashing rumble of the train's overhead rush.

'I'll walk with you if you don't mind. I was just buying a few last-minute presents.'

'I'll be glad of the company,' Sarah said, wondering if Nell was very selective, very unlucky or just plain lying. There was certainly no sign of any parcels on the slim blonde. Perhaps she was about to be treated to more confessions from Nell's past.

When Nell had handed over the anonymous letter following their supper party on Sunday night, she'd haltingly told Sarah as much of her previous history as Sarah already knew. Feeling like a snake in the grass, Sarah had kept a straight face, produced all the appropriate responses and promised to undertake a discreet investigation of the matter. After which she'd bundled up Nell's anonymous letter with a brief explanatory note to Stamford, sealed the package securely, marked it for the DCI's personal attention and dropped it into Agar Street's CID office – squaring her conscience with the happy thought that someone would take it round to his house if he didn't call into the station soon.

Her thoughts seemed to have communicated themselves to Nell, who said abruptly: 'Have you done anything with it yet?'

It would have been pointless to pretend she didn't know what 'it' was. 'I left it with . . . a friend . . . He can see about checking for prints. Comparing handwriting, that sort of thing.'

'Oh. Good.'

Sarah glanced sideways. There wasn't much to be seen except the glinting sweep of silver hair which had once again been tied in a single plait. Nonetheless she caught the hesitation in the response. Nell, she reckoned, was beginning to have second thoughts about her impulse to do the right thing and hand the letter over. Given the few details she'd let slip about the horrors of treatment in the mental hospital, Sarah couldn't say she really blamed her. If analysis proved that Nell had written it herself, she doubted the young woman would voluntarily place herself back under treatment. In which case, what other course of action was open to her?

'Can you really not remember writing the other letters?' she said abruptly.

'No. I know it sounds unlikely, but I truly can't. Even when they showed them to me in hospital, I honestly had no recollection of them. I was convinced it was a dreadful mistake for months.'

'So how'd the doctors convince you in the end?'

They'd reached the busier streets of Camden by now and were forced to separate by a large bassinet loaded with what at first glance appeared to be stones. An acrid whiff of dust as it wobbled between them revealed that they were actually large chunks of coal. Sarah's nose twitched suspiciously. Being surrounded by so many railway depots, the area had always been fair game for a bit of private enterprise in the combustibles line.

A throaty roar overhead distracted her for a moment. Along with most of the street, she stopped dead and peered into the winter sky, trying to locate the approaching planes. The ripple of tension was tangible, jumping from shopper to shopper. Was the lull over? Were the bombers coming back for Christmas?

'They're ours, Mum,' a treble voice piped up.

'Yep,' another eight-year-old confirmed. 'Three Lancasters. Let's go 'ome, Mum. I want me tea.'

A collective breath of relief was released along the street.

'I convinced myself,' Nell said.

'What?' Sarah glanced back. The woman with the pramload of coal had already disappeared in the pitch black. There was just the vaguest squeak of an unoiled wheel somewhere in the distance.

'I convinced myself,' Nell repeated. 'About the letters. It was . . . weird I suppose is the only way to describe it. I was just standing there one day in my . . . well, room, they called it . . . and I saw myself. Not in the mirror or anything. I mean, I was literally standing in one corner of the room watching myself sitting at a table. And I was writing; all this dreadful filth was pouring over the page.'

'Who were you writing to?'

'My mother. I . . . I wrote a lot of the letters to my mother.'

'Do you know why you picked on her?'

'N . . . no.'

The fractional hesitation was enough to alert Sarah to the fact that this was one of those times when 'no' meant 'yes'. Still, 'why' wasn't her problem. Hers was to find definite proof of the 'who' for Dr De Groot's benefit. One thought had occurred to her, and she put it to Nell now: 'The envelopes and paper are cheap stuff. Do you have any of that brand?'

She certainly hadn't when Sarah had searched her room

earlier, and it seemed she didn't now. 'But Bridget does,' Nell said discouragingly. 'She has lots in the kitchen drawer. She bought loads in case they brought in paper rationing. She's a big family in Ireland to write to.'

And all the tenants wandered in and out of Bridget's flat whenever they pleased. Oh, great!

They finished the rest of the walk to Mornington Crescent in silence, each lost in her own thoughts.

Sarah's former neighbour produced two letters in answer to her enquiry and apologised for not dropping them off at the police station. 'I meant to, lovey, but I've been run off me feet what with Christmas and doing me bit on the refreshments down the shelters.'

'It's OK,' Sarah assured her, noting with relief the Liverpool postmark on one. At least her old room-mate had been safe and sound when she posted this three days ago. 'It's still standing, then . . .' She indicated her one-time home.

The woman sniffed. 'Council stuck a notice on the door saying it was condemned, but that's all they 'ave done. Wish they'd either pull it down or stick it back together. Well, I wish you Merry Christmas, lovey.'

Taking the hint, Sarah moved off the doorstep and rejoined Nell on the pavement. Experiencing a brief pang of nostalgia, she walked a few more steps down the street, intending to bid a silent goodbye to her old rooms. It was then that she saw the lorry.

After they'd demolished what was left of the end house following its encounter with the airborne double-decker bus, the council had shored up the exposed wall with two huge wooden struts. A canvas-covered lorry had been pulled off the road and inserted under these two beams. In the dense blackout, it was virtually invisible. It was, however, vaguely familiar. Edging round the side of it, Sarah double-checked by locating the loose catch of the tailgate.

'Is there something wrong?' Nell had followed her on to the small patch of waste ground and was now watching with a puzzled expression.

'This is the van that moved my things when I got evicted.'

'Oh?'

She could appreciate that Nell might not see the significance of this fact. But Sarah could. Eddie Hooper – suspected whisky thief and accomplice of Maury O'Day – had known that this building was going to be empty over Christmas. And what better place to store a few crates until they could be disposed of safely than a condemned building?

A slight sound caught her ears. It might be rats, of course. They often moved into bombed-out and deserted buildings. On the other hand . . . if this particular rat had two legs . . . ? She grabbed Nell's arm and pulled her back on to the pavement.

'Listen, can you find a police box and tell them I've got a suspected burglar here. With stolen property. Get them to send someone to this address, quick.'

To her relief Nell didn't ask for any further explanations, but hurried away.

Sarah hovered. A silence had descended on the street. It was so intense she could hear the rumble of a passing train along the underground far below the pavement. There was no further movement from the house. Supposing she'd got it wrong. Maybe Eddie Hooper always left his van here? There was no law against daft parking.

Placing her feet cautiously to avoid overbalancing on the rubble, she made her way round to the back of the house. There was no outside access to the basement, but there was a small barred window back here at ground level. And through its grimy and miraculously intact glass, she thought she caught a glimpse of light that flashed briefly and then swiftly disappeared. Shaded torch, she decided, crouched to one side of the window.

The back door opened smoothly and silently when she tried the handle. Stepping through, she ran an exploratory finger over the hinges. It came away wet and – she sniffed – smelling of oil.

The rat below moved again.

Sarah eased towards the internal door. The room was empty, the furniture having been carted off by the tenants or sent for storage in the council repository. Its very emptiness magnified every sound she made, sending each floorboard

262

squeak on a victory roll round the plaster ceiling.

Something brushed against her cheek. With a suppressed gasp of alarm she jerked away. The thing whispered at her again; harder this time. Wood, she decided. She grabbed it as it swung in for the third time. A creak of protest from the tackle above her head confirmed her guess; it was a drying cradle someone had left hanging at head height as they'd grabbed washing before being bundled out of the house, by the terpsichorean borough surveyor. Holding it still until it lost its momentum and hung straight again, she slipped round it and eased open the door to the passage.

Her eyes had become sufficiently adjusted by now to the more intense internal darkness to let her see that the door to the basement steps was standing open. Moreover, it was being held in that position by what appeared to be two wooden crates. She hesitated. She ought to wait. Nell would have found a police box by now and rung through to the station.

Eddie Hooper solved the dilemma for her. A heavy footfall on the stairs, accompanied by strenuous breathing, told her he was nearly at the door. She froze. Perhaps if she stayed still he'd miss her in the dark. There was a bolt on the cellar door; if she could just get to it when he made his next trip down to the basement . . .

It might have worked. He deposited the crate on top of the others with a grunt and turned away. She gathered herself, ready to drag the boxes aside quickly and slam the door shut. The movement dislodged something on the floor, sending it rolling down the linoleum with a noisy 'bump-bump-bump'.

'Wha' the . . .'

Eddie Hooper could move faster than his size suggested. He was half a head shorter than her, but he made up for his lack of height with a broad chest and powerful arms. In the unlit passage, Sarah saw him crouch, his square head thrust forward on a short powerful neck.

'Police!' she called, putting as much authority and force behind the word as she could. 'Stand still, Hooper, we've got the place surrounded.'

'Oh yeah, darlin'. And I'm Empoora of bleedin' China.'

His first rush carried her backwards and sent her sprawling against the wainscoting. She was still floundering when he seized her arm above the elbow and hauled with such violence that she thought it was about to be wrenched out of its socket. Allowing herself to be dragged backwards on her bottom was the only way to ease the pain in her shoulder.

'Now who are yer, yer nosy cow?'

'I told you, you dolt, I'm a police officer.'

With another grunt, Hooper hauled her nearer the cellar steps. 'Oh yeah. And since when do they send women coppers in? Scotland Yard think there was a bunch of kids down here scrumping apples, did they, darlin'?'

'My colleagues are on their way,' Sarah said through gritted teeth. She braced her heels and free arm against the linoleum, ignoring the protest from her other shoulder.

Her shoes skidded on the greasy surface but her hand closed on something cool and metallic. It felt smooth and curved to the touch. The empty shell case the ground-floor tenants had used as a doorstop had been overlooked in the hasty move and left to betray her to Eddie Hooper. She scrabbled for some kind of fingerhold on it. If she could just swing it into his knee – or even further up his anatomy . . .

Her resistance annoyed him. He gave her another socket-wrenching jolt. Taking a deep breath, Sarah prepared to play dead. It could only be a short time before help came.

'I say. You do know you are trespassing, I presume?' The indignant shout from the kitchen caught them both by surprise. Hooper relaxed his grip sufficiently for Sarah to get her arm free.

A third figure appeared in the passage. Back-lit by the faint starlight behind him, he paused, one foot at nine o'clock and the other at three. Sarah groaned silently as she recognised the ballet-loving borough surveyor.

'This building is condemned.' Tobias Goole flung his arms out. 'Condemned. An official notice has been posted. You are lucky I noticed your vehicle. There could have been a most unfortunate accident . . .'

Tobias's unfortunate accident met him head on with flailing

264

fists and sent him flying back into the kitchen. It gave Sarah time to scramble to her feet and stagger after them.

'Hooper!'

In response to her shout, Eddie sprang round and received the swinging drying cradle straight across his nose. It was sufficient to knock him off balance, and tripping over the groaning borough surveyor's body completed his crash to the floor. Before he could recover, Sarah brought the empty shell case down on his forehead with both hands.

The car that arrived in response to Nell's phone call ended up having to transport the casualties to St Pancras hospital. Eddie Hooper – safely handcuffed to a burly constable – was treated for concussion and a split forehead, whilst loudly telling everyone that the ponced-up bloke had landed a lucky punch in the dark. From beneath an ice-pack, his glare challenged Sarah to say different. She decided to let him keep his dignity, and the confused Tobias Goole found himself being congratulated as a civic hero. She hoped it would make up for the broken nose that was rapidly spreading across his bruised face.

Once the doctors had finished, the problem of what to do with Hooper had to be sorted out. Normally a cache of stolen whisky and a known villain caught red-handed would be a welcome 'collar'. But who wanted to be stuck with writing up statements and preparing court papers on Christmas Eve? Eddie was about as welcome as a live grenade as far as the arresting officers from Mornington Crescent were concerned.

In the end Agar Street was persuaded to offer Eddie bed and board in the cells over Christmas and Boxing Day, on the grounds that he represented 'on-going enquiries'.

'Now I'll 'ave to stick someone on duty down the cells,' the station sergeant resentfully informed Ding-Dong. 'And the lads were looking forward to a nice quiet card school in the canteen. Perks of the season.'

'Don't suppose Eddie's going far,' Ding-Dong remarked.

'It ain't him that needs watching . . .' He kicked the whisky crates. 'It's this lot.'

'You'll put him up in court on Friday?' Sarah asked as she

and Ding-Dong made their way back from the cells to the front desk, where she'd left Nell waiting.

'I shall give them the pleasure of his company soon as they reopen for business,' Ding-Dong agreed. Something that might almost have been a smile flitted across his usually doleful mouth. 'Caught red-handed with the goods, and three counts of assault on top. I'd say Eddie will be enjoying His Majesty's hospitality for quite a while. Now, if you'll excuse me, Sarge, I must go and find a bottle of ginger wine. The lady wife is particularly partial to a tipple after the Christmas pud.'

'Ding-Dong.'

They'd reached the entrance to the CID office. The DC was reaching in to extract his coat and hat from the stand just inside the door. At Sarah's quiet call he turned back.

She raised her eyebrows and nodded slightly. 'A word inside?'

With a heavy sigh, Ding-Dong allowed her to precede him inside the dingy office with its odours of mouldy paper and stale tobacco. 'Mr Stamford?'

'Someone should tell him. I mean, given the way things are between him and the O'Days. If Maury's going to be pulled in . . . I would go round, but . . . there's Nell, you see. I just can't seem to get rid of her,' she pleaded. 'And I don't think Mr Stamford will be too pleased if I turn up on his doorstep with a member of the public.' *Particularly this member of the public*, she added to herself.

'Telephone him,' Ding-Dong suggested.

They both stared at the receiver. The DC cracked first. Jiggling the bar, he asked the operator to get him Stamford's home.

She knew by the short looks shot in her direction that she was the subject of several of the monosyllabic replies: 'Yes'; 'No'; 'Doctor said not'; 'Yes, sir, she looks in good health.'

When it came to Hooper, Ding-Dong became more animated. At least it was animation for him, although it would probably have passed as incipient rigor mortis in a lot of people. For the next two days, Eddie could enjoy the finest hospitality that Agar Street cells could provide, as far as he was concerned.

He'd have a word on Friday morning. And if Eddie wished to volunteer information so that his co-operation could be brought to the court's attention, that was entirely Eddie's privilege.

'Yes, well I'd say so, sir,' he said in response to a crackle from the earpiece. 'Not got much to trade, has he, except the name of his accomplice in the warehouse job.'

A further burst of crackles culminated in Ding-Dong solemnly agreeing that his superior officer should of course do whatever was best in his judgement. 'And may I wish you the compliments of the season, sir, from myself and the lady wife.' Replacing the receiver, the DC stood up, pulled on his hat and held the door open for Sarah.

Sarah took the hint and preceded him into the corridor.

'He'll have a word if it seems appropriate.'

'Poor Eileen,' Sarah sighed, pushing her way through the swing doors into the front reception area. 'What a Christmas. Let's hope she and Pat can talk Maury out of doing anything daft – like trying to skip bail.'

'From what I've seen of young Mr O'Day, it will take more than talking. A left hook would do more good, I'd say. A Merry Christmas to you, miss.'

He raised the hat courteously to Nell, who'd been reading police notices whilst she waited, and swept out to track down his lady wife's desired tipple.

'Were you talking about Pat O'Day's brother?' Nell asked diffidently.

'Yes. Do you know him?'

'Oh no. But I hear Pat talking about them sometimes. At work. He'll miss them over Christmas, I expect.'

'He'll get one day off, won't he?'

'It won't do him much good in Manchester if he does, will it?'

'Manchester!' Sarah stopped dead on the station steps and stared blankly.

'They've drawn off fifty vehicles from all round London to reinforce the Manchester brigades. They sent Pat's turntable lorry from the main station and the canteen van from Good Hope auxiliary. I . . . I did volunteer to go on the canteen, but

267

they sent Hatty Miller instead. Pat could be gone for weeks.'

Forgetting her pretensions to correct speech, Sarah summed up her feelings in three succinct words: 'Oh soddin' hell.'

Chapter 27

The train they'd planned to catch was cancelled. The next one rumbled through Kentish Town Station without stopping. Finally they managed to scramble aboard an express that had been brought to a halt by a red light by ignoring the station master's warning that 'This 'ere train don't stop 'ere.'

Sarah found herself jammed between a group of sailors, complete with bulging kitbags, and a woman perched on a large suitcase which jolted against her ankle every time the train went over points. Further down she could see Max sandwiched between the door and several girls in some kind of uniform which she couldn't identify. Beyond him Nell was holding a wriggling toddler whilst its mother attended to another child, who was insisting that it had to go *now*.

The train gathered speed, causing the corridor passengers to sway like a field of corn. Occasionally when a blind rattled away from the window, they caught a glimpse of unlit stations whose nameplates had been removed.

It occurred to Sarah that it might have been a good idea to check that 'this 'ere train' actually stopped at St Albans. She was just beginning to have visions of spending Christmas Day on Crewe station when the rapid *tiddly-dum* of the wheels started to change rhythm. The slower *dum-dum-dum* was eventually counterpointed by a reedy voice shouting 'S'norbans, S'norbans' over the throaty, belching rush of steam from the engine and a sudden application of the brakes.

Several blinds were let up, doors slammed and crashed along the length of the train and shouted voices called 'hello's and 'goodbyes'. Sarah saw Nell being propelled out of the end door like a cork and Max dragging their luggage to freedom. Using

269

her elbows, she managed to get to the nearest door, only to find the wretched thing wouldn't budge.

'Stand clear!' A warning whistle was accompanied by a more determined blast of steam from the engine.

'Oi! Hang on!' Banging the window down, Sarah threw her case on to the platform and turned to the sailors. 'Give us a hand.'

'Sure will, ma'am.'

Linking their hands into a cat's cradle, they swept her up and sent her through the window feet first just as the engine started to pull away. She landed more or less upright, bending her knees to absorb the shock. Straightening up shakily with one hand clamped firmly over her hat, she found herself gazing into a set of deep-blue eyes that were dancing with laughter.

'Bravo. Wizard landing.' He clapped briefly. 'Make the introductions then, Nellie.'

'Sarah McNeill, Max Death . . . my brother Paul.'

So it hadn't been a ploy to get round Bridget's rules on gentlemen callers. But if the bloke really *was* her brother, what had that tussle on the landing been about? From what she'd seen, Sarah reflected, the De Groots had a pretty weird idea of filial affection.

'Sarah's a policewoman.'

'I remember.' He took her hand in a firm grip. Despite the uneasiness she'd felt on their first brief encounter on the lodging house stairs, Sarah found herself being sucked into the easy aura of charm Paul De Groot exuded. So did most of the other female passengers, judging by the envious looks she was getting.

'How do you do, Squadron Leader,' she said, hoping she'd read the insignia on his uniform correctly.

'For goodness' sake, Paul. Please. And I'll call you Sarah, if I may? And . . . Max . . . was it?' He included Max in his welcoming smile and offered another handshake. 'Car's out front. Shall we go?'

'Your car?' Nell asked.

'The old man's. Couldn't fit you all in the Chain Gang, could I? Unless Sarah wants to sit on my lap. And that's

270

probably against some traffic regulation, isn't it, Sarah?'

'Road Traffic Act 1930, Section 11,' Sarah replied promptly, and then wondered why she was working so hard to hold on to her earlier dislike of this man.

'Where's Daddy?' Nell asked. 'He said he'd meet us.'

'Closeted in the study working on another report. The old fruit's furious. He was supposed to be dispensing sherry and mince pies to the neighbours. Still, she got to show me off instead, which she seemed to think was a fair swap. Jump in.'

Rather than let her guests choose, Nell promptly got into the back seat of the Wolseley. Sarah slipped in beside her, leaving the front seat for Max.

'Right. Chocks away, then.'

Somehow Sarah had created a mental picture of the De Groots living in a mock-Tudor detached house, surrounded by neat flowerbeds that had been patriotically sown with rows of vegetables. So the winding street of terraced houses came as a surprise. She got a further shock when she got out of the car and discovered the pavement was at waist height.

'Up you come.' Reaching down, Paul slid his hands under her armpits and hauled her up from the road as the door behind them opened.

'Paul darling, I was becoming quite worried. Charles, they're here.'

'You're showing a light, old fruit.'

'Oh dear, am I? Come in quickly. Hello, Nell.'

'Hello, Mummy.'

Margot De Groot was another lesson in not jumping to conclusions, Sarah discovered. The refined, slim, middle-aged female she'd imagined turned out to be sturdy and above average height, with hair of a somewhat unlikely gold shade primped into sculptured waves. Her apology that her husband hadn't been able to pick them 'oop' betrayed a northern origin that was now almost buried under Home Counties refinement. It was a relief to find out the doctor actually looked like most people's idea of an absent-minded academic. Grey-haired, slightly distracted and half a head smaller than his wife, Charles

De Groot shook hands with his guests and embraced his daughter in a fierce hug.

'It's good to have you home, chicken.'

'Thanks, Daddy.' Nell buried her face in her father's shoulder.

Margot was fussily organising the dispatch of cases to bedrooms. It gave Sarah the chance to take a quick look round. The house was bigger than she'd assumed from her brief glimpse from the street. Rooms seemed to lead off in higgledy-piggledy fashion in all directions. Most of the floors and walls had the uneven kilter of a very old house. The room in which they were standing was blessed with exposed oak beams and an open fireplace that could have roasted a whole pig if one happened to stray in. In daylight the heavy wooden furniture probably made it dark and gloomy, but tonight a combination of a decorated Christmas tree, holly wreaths and soft candle-light were combining to give the place a cosy feel that put the war a thousand miles away.

'Mummy, you can't put Max in the attic.' Nell's protest reclaimed Sarah's wandering thoughts.

'I'm sure Mr . . . er . . . Death will be perfectly comfortable in Gladys's room, Nell.'

'I expect you're right. If Gladys doesn't object.'

Margot permitted herself a tight-lipped smile and informed Max that Gladys had given notice a month ago and there didn't seem to be a maid to be had for love or money. 'Fortunately I still have daily help. We have laid out supper in the dining room. I thought we'd eat before we go to midnight mass. I don't think we'll bother to change, Miss McNeill.'

Trying to look as though she was in the habit of slipping into her cocktail frock before she ate her saveloy and mash every evening, Sarah murmured that that was OK with her.

'Why can't Max have the guest room? Sarah can share with me.'

It was on the tip of Sarah's tongue to say she'd be happy with Gladys's room if they liked. She didn't imagine the attic was anywhere near as bad as some of the places she'd slept. As a child she'd frequently been bundled up and told to keep quiet as the family did a moon-light flit from one set of grimy rooms to the next. But a sudden flash of pleading in Nell's eyes made her agree to the shared room instead.

'Oh well, I suppose . . .' Margot plainly didn't care for having her plans upset. On the other hand, guests were guests, even if they wanted to play musical rooms.

The luggage having been duly rearranged, they all trooped in to supper. Sarah found herself seated opposite Paul.

'Are you stationed locally, Paul?' she asked.

Before he could reply, Margot jumped in: 'The squadron leader is based in Kent, unfortunately.'

Lifting the lid from a large china tureen and examining the contents, her son added: 'But I'm on temporary attachment in Whitehall for a couple of weeks. That's how I managed to wangle this visit. What's this?'

'Cold pheasant.'

Paul prodded the lumps of meat with a fork. 'If there's any left over save it for me. My flying boots need resoling.'

'Oh I know, darling. It hasn't been hung long enough. But I didn't like to refuse. It came from the Deanery. Did I tell you we're invited to drinks on Boxing Day?'

'You did. At least six times.'

'Are you sure you can't stay? They'd be so thrilled to see you.'

'Absolutely certain. I'll be shooting off after lunch, unless you want me on a charge for desertion.'

'They wouldn't do that, would they?'

'Rip my wings off and march me to the glasshouse if I'm not back at my desk by eighteen hundred hours.' Across the table, Paul caught Sarah's eye and dropped his own in a slight wink. Despite herself she couldn't help responding to the man's charm with a small smile. Oblivious to the teasing, Margot remarked that she was so glad they'd given the squadron leader an office job. 'I do worry so when you're flying. Such dangerous things, planes.'

'I think you might have guessed I'd have to climb into the odd aircraft, old fruit, when I won the scholarship to Cranwell.'

'Well of course, darling. But that was before the war. I mean, it's all right being in the armed forces when there's no war. The squadron leader passed out top of his year,' she informed Max and Sarah. 'But now with all these horrid bombs and Messerschmitts and things . . .'

It would have been tempting to laugh at her, but her very genuine concern for her only son shone through her silly chatter.

Her husband, who'd previously been applying himself to a plate of cold ham and pickles, said: 'We're neglecting you, Mr Death. I believe Nell said you were in cosmetics, do I have that right? Are you involved with their manufacture?'

Max, who Sarah sensed was even more ill at ease than herself, admitted he was only a traveller. Then unexpectedly he added: 'But I should like to produce my own ranges one day. After the war, of course. I do have some training in chemistry. I had a position with a manufacturing company but I was forced to leave when my father became ill and needed me at home. And after he died . . . well, a job is a job . . .'

'Indeed?' The mention of a scientific background seemed to light a spark inside the doctor. Bending forward eagerly, he asked where Max had trained. Within two minutes they were lost in a world of resins, cohesive properties and soluble waxes.

'Oh Lord, he'll not surface for a month,' Paul groaned. 'More wine, Sarah?'

She didn't like wine much, but she hadn't the nerve to ask whether they had any beer. Sipping decorously, she tried to respond to Paul's attempts at light-hearted flirting in a similar vein. It proved to be something of a struggle at first. Her own naturally straightforward nature didn't lend itself to the innuendo and half-spoken messages that were part of the verbal game. By the time they'd reached the preserved plums, however, she found she was beginning to enjoy herself. Which, the cynic in her decided, was further proof – if it was needed – of Squadron Leader De Groot's experience in this particular game.

Whilst she flirted with the son and listened to the mother listing the squadron leader's achievements since he'd taken his first toddling steps ('quite six weeks before anyone expected'), a detached part of Sarah's mind noted that Nell, rather than blossoming in the warmth of a family celebration, was slipping further and further into her icy, touch-me-not reserve. By the time they'd muffled up to make their way to midnight mass, Nell's conversation had been reduced to monosyllabic replies if anyone addressed her directly. Her father reached over and squeezed her hand gently.

'What's the matter, chicken? Aren't you feeling well?'

'I'm fine, thank you, Daddy.'

From the darkness, where she'd been fussing with a fur wrap, Margot said loudly, 'Oh dear, I do hope you're not about to have another funny turn, Nell. I said that job was a mistake. I really don't want to visit that horrid hospital place again.'

Her breathtaking tactlessness drew an angry: 'Margot!' from her husband.

'What?'

'I think we should leave. *Now*.'

'Oh yes, all right, I'm coming.'

Sarah had assumed that they'd go to the Cathedral for the service. But apparently the De Groots remained loyal to their previous parish church which lay on the outskirts of St Albans near an earlier house that had been owned by the family. This led to a round of musical cars. When everyone had finished politely passing up places, Sarah found herself in the passenger seat of Paul's car.

'Do you want the hood up?' he asked as they crawled up the narrow street after his father's shaded brake lights.

'Heavens, no! No one would see I'm riding with a real live air ace then, would they?'

She caught a glimpse of his white face beneath the cap as he turned towards her. Then he gave a shout of laughter. 'You mean you think *I* want them to notice.'

'Don't you?'

He accelerated away from a junction before saying: 'Of course I do. Everyone wants a bit of admiration, don't they? But a chap's got to play the modest hero.'

'And leave it to his mother to blow his trumpet?'

'Yes, the old fruit does go on a bit, doesn't she?'

'She's obviously very fond of you.'

'Dotes on me,' he agreed calmly, sending the car swooping past his father's with a warning toot of the horn.

'Even before you were a squadron leader?' Sarah couldn't resist shouting against the rush of icy wind that was whipping her scarf into streamers around her cheeks.

'Even when I was a mere sprog with a wooden plane in the nursery,' he laughed.

'She doesn't seem quite so fond of Nell.'

They'd sped up another hill and rounded a low wall. Sarah had a quick glimpse of a square tower topped by a squat steeple before Paul pulled into a gateway and bumped to a halt beneath a dense row of overhanging trees.

'Nell was always Daddy's girl. That's the way it is in most families, isn't it?'

Not from personal experience it wasn't, Sarah thought, climbing out into rustling drifts of dead leaves beneath the trees. But it did tie up with what she'd already been told about Nell. It was the doctor who was going to have to be convinced if they wanted to ease his daughter into a secure 'rest home'. And now that Nell had admitted she wasn't sure herself if she was writing the current batch of letters, how very easy it would be to tell her that she had done. All they had to do was fake up some evidence to prove to her she was responsible for the copy she'd handed over. She'd probably even confess to her father. And then what . . . ?

'It's worse than prison,' Nell had said that night in her room when her tongue had been loosened by Max's generous measures of gin. 'At least in prison you know the length of your sentence. But in the hospital . . . you don't *know*, you see. The doctors smile and nod and pretend to be on your side. And then they take you back to the room and say we'll talk again tomorrow my dear . . . and you realise they haven't believed a word. Some of the women, they'd been locked in there for years. Everyone had forgotten them. If I hadn't known Daddy would get me out, I think perhaps . . .'

'Shall we?'

Mentally dragging herself back from the fuggy boarding

house in Vorley Road to the cold country churchyard, Sarah took Paul's proffered arm and joined the crowd walking towards the porch. Smiles, nods and Christmas greetings came at them from all directions. It was obvious that a lot of the congregation shared Margot De Groot's opinion of her beloved son.

The service was conducted by candlelight, shielded to comply with the blackout regulations. In the flickering lights and monstrously dancing shadows, the congregation listened to the old familiar story.

In the general shuffle along the pews, Sarah had somehow become separated from Paul. She found herself now at the far end of the row, with Max on her left and Nell on her right next to the narrow side aisle. From what she could see in the distorted lighting, Nell appeared to be moving through the whole process in the same state of detached disinterest she'd shown since dinner. The only time she showed any signs of life came when the vicar invited them to pray for the safety of 'those brave soldiers, sailors and airmen who are protecting our shores'.

Above the general indistinguishable mumble, Nell's voice rose in an intense, desperate whisper: 'Please, please, God, don't let Paul die.'

Sarah flicked a glance to her left. The doctor and Max both wore expressions of solemn reverence. Margot De Groot's smile of approval was predictable. But it was Paul's reaction that interested her most. Just for a second, a look of pure triumph passed over his face.

Getting out of the church was nearly as much fun as extracting themselves from the train. The entire congregation were caught in a bottle-neck at the front door as they shuffled forward to shake hands with the vicar. All except Nell. Glancing behind her as she approached the head of the queue, Sarah found that the other woman had made her way forward to the small crib beside the altar. With muttered apologies Sarah slipped down to the front of the church. Nell acknowledged her presence with a tilt of her head.

'I was looking at the statues. They're all beautiful, aren't they?'

In the draught from the door, the yellow light danced over the tiny figures' glossy robes and pink painted flesh. Sarah agreed they were cleverly done. 'Not that I'm much of an expert on art.'

'No. I didn't mean it like that.' Nell rebelted her coat and turned up the collar. 'I mean, the artist has made them look perfect. They always are. No one ever produces shepherds with big noses, or wise men with harelips, or gives Joseph a squint. Why do you think that is?'

'Perhaps the artist was afraid people would think he was just a lousy painter.'

'Perhaps.' Nell replaced her service sheet and turned to leave. 'Or perhaps it's because people associate evil with ugliness. And they assume the beautiful must be good.'

A sudden shout of laughter from the church door drew both their heads round. Paul was holding the hands of a grey-haired woman in a flowered hat whilst she giggled and chatted animatedly.

'The vicar's wife,' Nell said abruptly. 'She's always adored my brother. But then most people do.'

She pushed her way past Sarah and thrust herself into the straggling line with an uncharacteristic rudeness. Ignoring her mother's attempts to catch her sleeve and draw her into the admiring group around Paul and the vicar, she hurried out into the dark. By the time Sarah extricated herself, Nell was hovering halfway down the drive to the gate, exuding waves of her 'leave-me-alone' attitude.

Deciding she'd had enough of all this middle-class tiptoeing round the subject, Sarah marched across the gravel and took Nell firmly by the elbow. 'I think it's time you and I had a chat. This way.'

She'd managed to take Nell by surprise, and they were into the heavy blackness of the small graveyard before it even occurred to her to put up a token resistance. 'I don't think I wish to . . .'

'Yes you do. Why invite me otherwise? It's not as if we're particular friends.'

The gravestones were hard to find in the dark, and the surest way was to walk into them. She managed to locate the slab covering the last resting place of some long-departed alderman by the simple expedient of barking both her shins against it. Biting back an impulse to swear loudly, she drew Nell down beside her on the moss-covered stone.

'Now . . . would you like to tell me what Max and I are doing here? You don't like either of us that much.'

'I do like Max.'

'But not me.'

'I did.'

'Did?'

'I . . . I . . .' Nell had seated herself so she was half turned away, quite literally presenting a cold shoulder. Now she wriggled round, placing her pale face with its startling dark eyebrows only inches from Sarah. 'You're just like all the others. One smile from Mr Perfect and you're all over him. I thought you were different.'

'We're talking about Paul here, are we?'

'Well of course we are. Do you think he's going to swear undying love? Are you fantasising about waltzing down the aisle under an arch of RAF swords?'

'Best not. At my height they'd probably slice me veil off.'

'It's not *funny* . . .' A sob burst from Nell.

'No. All right.' The arm she tried to put round Nell's shoulders was angrily shrugged off. Undeterred, Sarah grabbed both arms and forced her round so that they were face to face again. 'Talk to me, Nell. I can't help you unless you tell me what's up.'

'Nobody can help me.'

'So what is it? Bit of the green-eyed cat?'

'I beg your pardon?'

'Are you jealous?' Sarah translated. 'Do you want to keep brother Paul all to yourself?'

'Keep him?' There was a second's silence, then Nell gave a shrill, hysterical laugh. '*Keep him.* Oh my God, I wish I never had to see him again. *I hate him. I hate him. I hate him.*' She took an enormous shuddering breath, pushed Sarah's grip away and sat up straight. 'Do you want to know? Do you want to know what my brother did to me?'

Chapter 28

She kept her voice low, although the only other living souls wandering around the stone memorials at that time on Christmas morning were a couple of cats who were celebrating the season by making life unpleasant for anything small, furry and slow on its paws.

'You must understand that when we were children, I adored my brother. It never occurred to me that anything he did could be wrong. I'd have jumped into the kitchen range if he'd asked me to.'

'Did he?'

'No . . . he . . .' Nell broke off with a gasp as the grass rustled behind a stone angel whose face and wings had been weathered into ugly deformity.

'Cats,' Sarah said succinctly. 'Go on . . . what did Paul ask you to do?'

'He . . . em . . . you see, Mummy had never spoken about that sort of thing. I mean, I hadn't even started my periods . . .'

'So brother Paul decided to give you a few practical lessons?' She'd come across it before – with a father or elder brother deciding it was his job to 'break in' any female approaching puberty.

'Yes. He said it was a special way to be happy. A grown-up way.'

'How old were you?'

'Eleven. The first time.'

'And Paul?'

'He's three years older than me.' She paused, took an audible breath and admitted: 'He made me promise never to tell. Said it was our special secret. I was quite proud . . . that he'd trust me like that. It never occurred to me it was wrong . . . it wasn't until ages later that I started to wonder . . . I suppose you must think I'm incredibly naïve.'

'Not really. You'd be amazed at the number of runaways we pick up from the streets who hadn't a clue they could get pregnant from "obliging the gents". Did you ever . . . ?'

'No. Never,' Nell said quickly. 'Paul's too astute for that.'

'How long did this go on for?'

'It . . . Sometimes he still wants me to . . .'

'Do you enjoy it?'

'Of course I don't. I hate him. Oh God, I *hate* him.'

'Then why don't you tell him to get lost?' Unconsciously she'd slipped into her official voice, directing her questions with a professionally crisp briskness.

'I just . . . He doesn't listen when I say no. I mean, it's like he doesn't think I really mean it. And I know I ought to be firmer, only he just laughs if I try to push him off. And I don't know what to do.'

'Yell; scream; kick him in the family jewels.'

'But don't you see. No one would *believe* me. He'd tell them I was hallucinating. You've seen what he's like. Everyone thinks Paul is just wonderful. And I'm the little sister who's crazy. Nutty Nellie, that's what the children used to shout after me.'

'You do realise he's relying on you keeping your mouth shut?'

'Well of course I do,' Nell snapped. 'I'm not stupid. I just . . . Everything keeps going round and round in my head until I think it will explode. And I just can't see any way out . . . and then . . .'

'And then you write letters saying all those things that you'd like to say to their stupid faces?'

'Yes. I suppose I do.' She half rose and was only driven back down by a sudden burst of song from beyond the church. Since church bells were now banned, the vicar had organised carol singers to welcome in Christmas Day. More car doors slammed and the gravel drive scrunched under tyres.

'They'll be looking for us in a minute. Tell me the rest,' Sarah urged.

'I'll deny it all,' Nell hissed. 'You can't prove anything.'

'I'm not trying to, am I?' Sarah said irritably. What she'd learnt so far explained a lot about Nell. Her decision to live in a crowded lodging house rather than a solitary flat, and her sudden desire for company during her visits to the family house. Anything to lessen the chances of her ending up alone with brother Paul, in fact.

'Paul was sent away to boarding school,' Nell said. 'I used to write to him. All the time. I missed him so much when he went, you see. At first . . . before I knew it was wrong . . . I wrote about . . . about things we did.'

'In detail?'

'Yes. He asked me to. He said he liked to read about them.'

'And he's still got the letters?'

'Oh yes, he's got them.' She shivered. The sound of cars had stopped and the carol singers were coming to the last verse of 'O Little Town of Bethlehem'. 'He keeps them at the base. They're all sealed up and addressed. His last letters to his loved ones. At least that's what the officers who post them will think.'

'Who are they addressed to?'

'Some are for Mummy and Daddy. I know there's one for the vicar's wife. I'm not sure about the others.'

Sarah slid along the stone slab and took one of the other woman's cold hands in hers. 'Surely he must realise that if he exposes you, he exposes himself as well? What you . . . he . . . is doing . . . is against the law. He could go to jail.'

'Not if he's dead. Weren't you listening – they're for his chums to post after their hero has crashed in flames or whatever. The brave squadron leader who gave his life for his country and left a few comforting words behind for his family . . . *stiff upper lips, old things, and remember me in happier times* sort of thing.'

'But your parents . . . your mother . . . doesn't he know what effect this would have on them?'

'Paul despises our parents. Particularly Mummy . . .' Nell's own voice took on a tinge of contempt. 'The more people fawn on him, the more he despises them. Oh, he smiles and charms and flatters . . . but deep down inside he finds them quite pathetic. It would amuse him, sitting in hell, watching them all opening those letters and realising what total fools they were to ever admire him.'

'Does he know you'd be arrested?'

'He wouldn't care. He despises me too, you see. I despise myself,' she added softly. 'I feel so . . . dirty.'

'You mustn't . . . you're not to blame.'

'That doesn't matter, does it? Illegitimate children aren't to blame, but there's plenty around still call them dirty bastards. It's always there, you see. At the back of my mind. I mean, when people try to be friends, I think of their faces if they found out . . . so there's no point. Because when they know . . . they'd be sick to their stomachs.'

'*I* know,' Sarah pointed out. 'And my stomach is suffering from nothing worse than the dinner wine.'

'Yes. But you're different. Harder. I expect it comes with the job.'

This calm assumption that she wouldn't mind being called hard upset Sarah more than she would have expected – or admitted.

'Anyway,' Nell said, returning to an earlier question, 'I doubt that I'd be arrested. I don't think my parents are likely to go rushing to the police, do you?'

'What about the others?'

'No. They'd probably totter around clutching Bible tracts and smelling salts, full of assurances that they wouldn't breathe a word and agog for a little vicarious sin. After all, we don't get the travelling freak show round any more.'

Making a mental note to look up 'vicarious' when she got home, Sarah said: 'I thought you didn't know who the rest of the letters were going to?'

'No . . . I don't. Not exactly.'

'But you can guess.'

'Yes.'

'And that's why you got in first with your own dodgy correspondence?'

'Dodgy?'

'Strange. Peculiar.'

'Oh. Yes. I suppose so. I didn't consciously pick them out . . . but yes, you're right. All the people they say I wrote to, they're all big fans of Paul's. All stupid, gullible, vain middle-aged women who'd never believe he could do anything that wasn't honest, upright and decent. God, if only they knew what he really thought about them.'

'Can't you find some way of getting the letters back?'

'Of course I can't! Don't you think I haven't *thought* and *thought* and *thought*? They're on an RAF station, for heaven's sake. If you're so clever, you tell me . . .' She broke off with a gasp and stood up quickly.

'Well, target sighted at last. What are you lurking out here for?' Paul extended a hand to help them up. They both pretended not to see it.

In single silent file they made their way back to the front of the church. It was virtually deserted apart from the vicar and the choir, who were fluttering in their white surplices like ghostly bats.

'Here they are. Nell, wherever did you get to? The vicar is waiting to lock up.'

'Sorry. Sarah wanted to see the churchyard.'

'In the middle of the night?'

'I wasn't sure you'd be coming back tomorrow . . . I mean today . . .' Sarah said blandly.

'Oh no,' Margot said loudly. 'Midnight mass does for both days. There's really no need to attend the morning service as well.'

'Absolutely. Don't want to bring too much religion into Christmas, do we, old fruit?'

'Paul, darling. Don't be so outrageous. The vicar . . .' Margot gave an almost flirtatious giggle. 'Now where's Mr Death got to? Oh, there he is . . .'

Max came striding round the opposite side of the church. 'I'm afraid I couldn't locate . . . Oh, you're back.'

'I'm sorry, Max. Were you looking for us?'

'Your mother was concerned.'

'Can't think why.' Disentangling himself from his mother's grasp, Paul offered an arm to Sarah. 'Not when we've got our very own police escort. Shall we, Sarah?'

Not in a million years, you perverted creep, Sarah thought rebelliously.

Max ran his hands reverently over the Chain Gang's bonnet and down the front mudguards and wheels: 'It really is the most magnificent machine, isn't it? Quite splendid. I suppose there's no chance of a short spin . . . perhaps before breakfast?'

'Go now,' Sarah said promptly, heading for the De Groots' Wolseley. 'Paul won't mind, will you?'

You couldn't fault his manners, Sarah admitted to herself. He leapt into the driving seat and flicked the passenger door open for Max without a glimmer of disappointment or annoyance. 'See you back at base,' he yelled, accelerating away in a swish of flying gravel.

Doctor De Groot's style of driving was a good deal less flashy than his son's, but nonetheless they arrived back before Paul and Max. Margot peered up and down the winding street. 'Oh dear. Do you think they've had an accident?'

'If they had, my dear, we'd have passed the wreckage on the way.'

'He's just showing off the car to Max, Mummy. Come inside. I think it's going to freeze.'

The bleakness in Nell's voice mirrored the icy winds which were increasing in strength as they found the cracks between the tightly packed houses. Sarah understood. One more friend had turned traitor and succumbed to her charismatic brother's charm. She found herself suddenly sick of the whole business. She wanted to be home, in London, sharing Christmas with Eileen O'Day and the children, not stuck here with this polite, refined, unhappy family with whom she had nothing in common.

'If you'll excuse me,' she said as soon as they'd checked the blackout curtaining and lit the candles, 'I'm rather tired. I think I'll turn in.'

'Oh, but you can't,' Margot protested. 'We haven't had the mulled wine yet. It's a little family tradition when we get back from mass. I left it heating on the stove.'

More wine. Sarah's stomach cringed. When it smelt the sickly aromas rising in clouds from the pan Margot carried into the sitting room, it started waving a white flag.

'Home-made elderberry. Come in, boys,' she trilled in response to a closing door and an icy blast of air round their ankles. 'I'm just about to . . . Paul, darling!' The pan hit the carpet.

The sight of the elderberry concoction fountaining out in all directions was nearly as satisfactory to Sarah as the bloody graze that was rapidly swelling down one side of the squadron leader's handsome face.

Behind him Max was mutilating his hat brim as he spun it round his long, bony fingers. 'I'm so sorry. I can't apologise enough.'

'Oh, good heavens. Nell, get some hot water. And there's antiseptic under the sink.'

'Don't *fuss*, Mother, for heaven's sake.'

'I'm not, darling. But you don't want blood poisoning, do you? Am I to understand you are responsible for this, Mr Death?'

Shame and anxiety added to the general unattractive arrangement of Max's features as he stammered out an explanation. They'd taken a jaunt down some back roads, realised the front tyre was flat and stopped to change it. 'I'm not entirely conversant with technical matters, but I was attempting to assist by holding the torch and I'm afraid I inadvertently knocked the jack.'

'Damn mudguard came straight down my face. Inch or so nearer and it would have taken my brains out. Is there much damage?' Paul peered into a wall mirror, twisting his face this way and that as he examined the marks.

It was his father who replied. Settling a pair of reading glasses on his nose, he peered closely at the scraped face and gave the opinion that his son and heir would live. 'Don't fuss the boy, Margot.'

'I'm *not* . . . Not those rags, Nell. We need a clean cloth.'

'They're for the wine,' Nell said, dropping the greying rags on to the floor.

Belatedly Margot became aware of the wine-sodden carpet. 'Oh dear . . . I ought . . .'

Leaving his female relatives to dab at the bruising, the squadron leader's unconcerned father drifted out, muttering something about an urgent report. Sarah dropped to her knees and started pushing dish-rags into the elderberry puddle. Without speaking, Max disappeared, returned with a bucket of cold water and knelt to help her.

Lost in her own thoughts, Sarah was only conscious of the soft grunting of his breathing for a while. Leaning over to wring out her rag, she realised this rhythm had changed, and flicked a quick look in his direction. He was taking a rest; sitting back on his heels, watching the trio by the fire. The embarrassed guilt that had been plastered all over his face when he'd been describing the accident had gone. Instead the eyes that were fixed on the injured RAF officer were cold, angry and contemptuous.

She must have moved slightly. The action brought Max's attention round to her. They sat on their heels, caught in the flickering firelight, locked together in a mutual moment of understanding. Max knew. At some point the scraggy hunting cat prowling the graveyard had been replaced by a shabby, unattractive cosmetic salesman.

She had a sudden mental picture of Max running his hands over the car's front tyres in the churchyard. A flat, they'd said. An appreciative smile twisted the corners of her mouth. It was only a small gesture, but she was glad Nell had found herself a champion. Not that it would do her much good, she thought, as the moment was broken and the rags wrung out again. Nell was right: there was no way to reclaim her letters. They would sit there, in Paul De Groot's desk, like small, deadly unexploded bombs. Until the day that a better flyer or a lucky gunner sent Paul into oblivion and detonated the hatred he'd left behind him.

Chapter 29

Sarah woke quickly and with the vague conviction that something had disturbed her. Her first thought was for Nell. But twisting over, she made out the darkened hump under the blankets of the other bed and located the light, rhythmic breathing.

Gently lifting down the bedside lamp, she shielded the light and fished out a few wrapped packages from her bag. The first one was from Eileen and contained a purple and blue patterned scarf. She'd plainly taken the children shopping with her, because Sammy's tiny package proved to be a white metal scarf ring with a large bright-blue stone stuck in the centre. Annaliese's present was a cardboard photo frame which she'd decorated by embroidering scraps of wool in a pattern round the outside. The small collection brought a lump to Sarah's throat. Once again she found herself passionately wishing she was spending Christmas in Kentish Town with her family.

Only they're not your family, she reminded herself, carefully putting the gifts into her bag. *Any more than this lot are*.

But the O'Days felt like family. Or, rather, they'd made *her* feel like family since she'd first become involved with them last spring during her participation on that first CID case with Jack Stamford. She'd known them by sight, of course, before that, thanks to her beat duties around the district, but it was only when she'd had to visit Stamford's house during the investigation that she'd been introduced to his cleaner and those members of Eileen's family who weren't away serving King and Country. They'd absorbed her into their lives with an easy-going friendliness for which she was grateful, but it was only now she was away from them like this that she started to realise just how much she'd come to depend on them to take the place of her own long-scattered family.

A scream, hastily shushed, sounded outside. Standing quietly, she switched off the lamp, groped her way to the window and twitched up a corner of curtain. It was still dark; it could have been almost any time. But her internal clock told her it was early morning.

A squeal drifted up to her. 'I found another one, Matty. Look!'

Pushing her nose against the cold glass, Sarah craned sideways. Two very faint light beams were bobbing up the neighbour's lawn, about a foot from the ground. Intrigued, she quietly laced on her shoes, tucked up her nightdress and pulled her coat on over the top. The twisting stairs creaked and protested as she stole silently down, but there were no curious calls from the other rooms as she made her way to the back door and slid back the bolts. The chill struck her across her face and flowed round her bare legs like cold water. She stood still for a moment, letting herself adjust to the dark.

'There's another one, Derek. Up on top the Anderson.'

Moving cautiously, Sarah made her way across the lawn to the wall. It was low enough for her to lean over and see two small figures walking in zigzag patterns, their heads lowered and shaded torches playing over the ground.

'Hello.'

Two faces, framed in knitted balaclavas, looked up.

'Merry Christmas,' she whispered, remembering most of the street was still asleep.

'Mer' Christmas,' they both piped.

'I'm Sarah. Who are you?'

The larger child took charge. 'I'm Matilda Brown – Matty and he's Derek.'

'Pleased to meet you. What are you doing?'

'Looking for reindeer footprints. We found some, see.' The light beam slid up the earth-packed side of the Anderson shelter and hovered by the wilted remnants of some kind of plant. There were indeed several large hoof-prints in the soft soil.

'That's wonderful,' Sarah whispered. 'Did he leave you presents?'

' 'Course,' Matty said scornfully. 'He always leave us presents. We makes lists. Do you live here now?'

'No, I'm just visiting.'

'Oh.' Matty trod carefully in the soft earth of the dug-over patch until she reached the wall. 'Have you got any boys or girls we can play with?'

'I'm afraid not.'

'Why not?' Matty demanded.

Why not indeed? Sarah found herself thinking. Most women of her age had three or four. She ought to be helping with present lists and fretting about what to fill their stockings with. Not being the spare part in a strange house. She informed Matty she just hadn't got around to it yet. It seemed to satisfy her.

'We have to go now,' the little girl said with sudden grown-up formality. 'It was very nice to meet you.'

'It was nice to meet you too. Goodbye.'

' 'Bye.'

Leaving the amateur naturalists to it, Sarah crept back to the kitchen. The sudden burst of light that shot out as she opened the door took her by surprise.

An apparition appeared from the walk-in larder. 'Oh, good morning, Sarah, and a Merry Christmas. I didn't think anyone else would be up yet.' Margot De Groot didn't seem at all embarrassed at being discovered in her dressing gown with her hair bristling with dozens of small metal curlers. 'Breakfast will be a while, but I can offer you a cup of tea?'

'Thanks. Shall I make it?'

'If you would. I'll get this bird stuffed.' She hauled a plucked goose from the larder, and proceeded to thrust handfuls of mixture from a covered bowl into the cavity.

Sarah made the tea and then sat with her elbows on the kitchen table, watching this operation, wondering how the De Groots' meat ration had stretched to such a large bird and deciding it would hardly be tactful to ask. Particularly if she wanted any dinner today.

'There.' Margot pushed the last morsel of stuffing into place

291

and started to truss the bird. 'Always have a goose at Christmas. My mother wouldn't have a turkey. Foreign rubbish she called them.' She finished with a pant and slapped a satisfied hand on the plump breast before heaving the bird into a roasting tin. 'I'll get the breakfast now. It's only porridge. I spent all the coupons on lunch. I wanted to make it a bit special . . . it might be a while before the whole family's together again at Christmas.'

'Can I help?'

'No. You're a guest. Nell will help me. My woman can't come today; she's her own lot to do for. That's a London accent you've got there, isn't it, Sarah?'

'Born and bred.'

'I'm surprised you didn't want to be with your own family.'

Sarah took the gentle probing in good part and informed Margot that her family were fairly scattered at present.

'War's done that,' Margot said, ladling oatmeal into a large saucepan. 'There's no telling where we'll end up these days. Mind, I never thought Nell would go to a fire station in Gospel Oak. She could have had a posting in the WAAF, you know? Shorthand typist at the Air Ministry, probably. She used to type in the bishop's office before . . .' She stopped abruptly, aware that she'd been about to say too much.

'Nell told me about the hospital.'

'Did she? Well, that's good, I suppose. The doctors said she'd have to talk before she could get better. Would you lay the table before you go up to dress? There's cutlery and plates in that dresser.'

Recognising her cue to shut up, Sarah obediently made her way to the dining room. She was used to eating breakfast in kitchens. Were tablecloths *de rigueur* for breakfast, or did one only use them for dinner?

There was a bureau that looked hopeful. She pulled open drawers stuffed with linens, casually glancing over the collection of framed photos clustered on the polished top. There were a few of a younger Nell, one of a grim-faced woman in Edwardian dress who bore a vague resemblance to Margot, and a formal wedding portrait of the De Groots. But by far the largest group were of Paul. From wide-eyed baby to smiling air force officer, you had to admit he'd been first in the queue when the gorgeous looks fairy had been handing out the old magic dust.

She found a cloth and spread it over the table, adding place mats, spoons and a cruet set.

Outside it was growing lighter, the inky blackness giving way to a pigeon grey. She flicked the curtains open and was struck once again by the sheer quietness of the country. Presumably this did count as country, even if it was listed as a town. Anywhere you could see proper fields rather than fenced-off parks or heaths was the country as far as she was concerned.

Making her way back to the stairs, she ran into Charles De Groot. He gave a guilty start and then looked relieved. 'I thought you were my wife,' he admittedly candidly. 'I promised her I shouldn't work today.'

'But you're going to?'

'Unavoidable, I'm afraid.' He pushed open a door she'd assumed was a cupboard. She had a glimpse of another lopsided room, its walls lined with book-crammed shelves. 'The deadline cannot be moved.' Wishing her a Merry Christmas, he disappeared inside.

By the time the remaining five of them had negotiated for bathroom space and hot water, morning had well and truly arrived. 'We shall have to start the lunch immediately, Nell,' her mother said briskly, collecting up teacups. 'Since everyone has to leave so soon.'

Once again Sarah's offer of help was rejected. As was Max's. But he at least was claimed by Charles, who wanted to discuss chemistry again in his study.

'Why not go for a walk, Sarah?' Margot suggested, clattering together crockery. 'There's a lovely park.'

'Good idea,' Paul said promptly. 'Shall we get out from under their feet, Sarah?'

It was a sensible suggestion when they were both at a loose end until lunch. And she couldn't think of a reasonable excuse not to. Come to think of it, she couldn't even think of an unreasonable one. 'I'll get my coat.'

He was waiting for her in the hall when she came down; a wrapped parcel under one arm. For a terrible moment she thought he was about to present it to her. But instead he just opened the door and let her out with the laconic instruction: 'Right wheel.'

The park proved to be just beyond the back gardens of the opposite row of houses. It was indeed lovely, with rolling greens, a meandering stream and a large lake with a tree-clad island in the centre. The only drawback was the lack of water.

'What the devil's happened?' Paul exclaimed, staring at the vast muddy expanse, where flocks of geese, coots, moorhens and ducks were moodily probing the odd puddles that were left in the lake bed.

'Perhaps they've had to pump it for water supplies,' Sarah suggested. 'The fire brigades run relays from several parks in London.'

'There's been no Blitz here. The odd house maybe . . . but nothing that justifies this. Excuse me . . .' He hailed an elderly couple. 'We were wondering about the lake? Why is it dry?'

'They reckon the German bombers were using the reflection as a landmark, sir.' As he spoke the elderly man had been stretching his spine and straightening his shoulders. 'I was in the last lot, you know. Served on the Somme. Lost most of my friends there.'

Paul touched the man's shoulder lightly. 'It wasn't for nothing, even if it seems like that right now. We won't let you down this time, I promise. We'll try to match up to you lads.'

The man flushed with pleasure. His shoulders moved back a fraction further.

'Come on, Harry, we'll be late for the service. Merry Christmas, my dear.' His wife took his arm and bestowed a warm smile on Sarah. She sensed that the good wishes were mainly based on her choice of escort.

It was the same all the way round the park. The smiles, nods and warm seasonal greetings were mostly directed at Paul. At present squadron leaders had knocked cleanliness off its perch next to God. He knew a lot of people anyway, and she found herself listening to plenty of local gossip, as well as to Paul inventing explanations of how he'd come by the injuries on his face. With each telling the stories became more fantastical and had his audience in fits of laughter. And each time he'd draw her forward into the group with a light touch and make sure she never felt the outsider. It was probably just polished manners, but Sarah began to fight against feeling relaxed and comfortable in his company.

They walked up the hill to admire the impressive bulk of the cathedral and gatehouse, and then back down again to take another turn round the dry lake. The paths were slippery with goose droppings and the last of the leaves that were dropping from the winter-dead trees. She nearly slid at one point and he steadied her, tucking the hand he'd seized into the crook of his arm. It took more of an effort than she liked to admit to pull it free again and thrust it into her coat pocket. Despite her determination to dislike the man, and her knowledge of what lurked behind all that charm, she couldn't help being aware that he was very good-looking.

'Let's sit a minute, unless you're cold?' he suggested.

'No, I'm fine.'

They perched on a bench by the pond. A hopeful gaggle of water birds waddled over; their mud-coated beaks looking as though they'd been dipped in chocolate. Paul unwrapped his package, took out a seed cake and started crumbling it around their feet. They watched the undignified scramble for titbits in silence for a moment.

'Are you married?'

The directness of the question took Sarah by surprise for a moment. 'No,' she said finally. 'If I was, I wouldn't be in the police. Women resign on marriage. Why do you ask?'

She was half expecting some polished patter about wanting to know who his rival was, but he just gave a small smile, shrugged and admitted: 'Curiosity, that's all. Why did you join the police force?'

'As a gesture against my family. They never had much time for the police. They wouldn't have been shocked if I'd been arrested, they'd have just shrugged it off as a sort of natural disaster. So I became one of the arresters instead.'

'Sort of a black sheep in reverse?'

'Something like that.' She hadn't meant to tell him so much, but he had this knack of looking directly at you, as if you were the most important person in the world. Breaking the eye contact, she asked why he'd joined the air force.

'I never considered doing anything else. It's all I've ever wanted. To be up there ... free and alone ... it's the most incredible feeling, Sarah.'

'It's not the uniform then?' She tried to sound light-hearted. 'Every woman in this park has been admiring you.'

'Except you. You don't admire me, do you, Sarah?' He crumbled more cake into the squabbling flocks that had surrounded the bench. 'Nell's been talking about me, hasn't she?'

'Naturally. You're her brother. She would do, wouldn't she?'

'Don't dissemble. It doesn't really suit you.' He twisted slightly. His thigh was pressed against hers. 'What am I accused of this time? Spreading lies about her? Hitting her? Abusing her?'

'Have you?'

'Yes. At least,' he added before she could react to this startling confession, 'I have in her mind. Nell is ... not like other people, Sarah.'

'She told me about the breakdown. But that doesn't mean she's crazy.'

'I never said she was. But she does get muddled. Reality becomes a dream, and things that she's imagined are very real to her.'

'She doesn't strike me as a liar.'

'She's not. She truly believes everything she's saying.'

He took her hand, and this time she didn't pull away. 'Nell and I have always been close. She was a funny little thing. Always following me around. She never seemed to want to make her own friends. She just wanted me. It hit her very hard when our gran paid for me to go away to boarding school. She started to make things up, stories about me. It was her way of punishing me for going, I suppose. Although I didn't really have much choice in the matter myself. It was the same when I got into

296

Cranwell. I suppose she saw it as some kind of desertion. I do love my sister, Sarah. I could never hurt her. Please believe me.'

His face was very close to hers now. He really was bloody good-looking. The bench they'd chosen was half-hidden by overhanging branches. Even though they were bare of leaves they still provided some degree of privacy. The path was quiet for a moment.

The loneliness of this morning's realisation that she had no real family who wanted to spend Christmas with her hit her again. Paul seemed to sense her mood. He bent his face fractionally closer to hers, inviting her to take the initiative and move their relationship on to a more intimate footing.

Who knows, her mind reasoned, *maybe Nell did make up the story about him blackmailing her with incriminating letters.* After all, she only had Nell's word for their existence. Nell had already spent one spell in an asylum for letters she claimed not to remember writing.

Something flashed into her line of sight and hit Paul in the ear.

'What the devil . . . ?'

The ducks scattered as a toy Spitfire dropped amongst them, and then regrouped to see if it was edible.

'They're *eatin*' it, Grandaddy!'

Sarah recognised the reindeer hunters from this morning. Derek flapped frantic hands, turning the mittens that were sewn to his coat into whirling propellers. A curious goose, nearly as tall as him, extended its neck, and he retreated with a shriek behind his sister.

Paul laughed, bent down, picked up the plane and restored it to the little boy. 'Hello, Robert. On duty?'

A middle-aged man in an ARP uniform came up. 'Just manned the post for a couple of hours this morning. Keeps these two out of the women's way.'

Once again there were introductions all round, scorned by Matty, who announced that this was the lady from next door who didn't have any little boys or girls.

'Did you find the reindeer?' Sarah asked as they all started to move towards the park gate.

'No. He'd gone. Father Christmas has a lot to do, you know.'

'Still got the old wooden foot, Robert?' Paul said out of the side of his mouth.

Robert gave him a conspiratorial wink. 'It's good to have you home again, son. Your mum will be pleased.'

'Yes. She is. Want to feed the ducks, kids?'

He dished out lumps of seed cake to the two children. Matty happily started drizzling out a string of crumbs behind her. Derek ate his.

'Have you heard anything from their dad?'

'Letter came this morning. His wound's cleared up. He sounds well enough. Even started a football team. They've moved him to another camp. Oflag 1XA. It's in Germany.'

'Well at least you know he's OK.'

'Yes.' The ARP man gave a heavy sigh. 'But I hope this lot's over soon. He shouldn't miss too many of their Christmases. You can never get memories like these back, see?' He nodded to where Derek was flying his plane with loud 'vroom-vrooms' and 'yeee-ows'.

Paul swooped on the little boy and lifted him up. 'That's a pretty fine plane you've got there, Derek. I fly one just like that. It goes right up like this . . .' he lifted the boy high over his head, '. . . and then we swoop down like this . . .' He swung the child in an arc. Derek gave a shriek of pleasure. 'And then we land like this.' He stood the child back on this boots. 'Fancy flying in my squadron, Derek?'

Wide-eyed, the little boy nodded.

'OK. Get in formation, then.' He stretched his arms out sideways like plane wings. Derek did the same. 'Engines on. Chocks away.'

Much to the amusement of the rest of the strollers, he ran off across the grass making loud aircraft noises. Shouting with delight, Derek did the same. Sarah and the children's grandfather stood for a second, watching them.

'He's a knack with them,' Robert said. 'Ought to have some of his own.'

She caught the speculative look. 'I'm a friend of his sister, not Paul.'

'Grandad!' Matty bawled. 'I haven't got any more cake. Can we go home and get some?'

'Later, Matty. After dinner. Come on now.'

Paul and Derek returned in a sparkling flurry of bright eyes and misty breath.

'I want to do it *now*!' Matty stayed stubbornly, refusing to move.

'Chocks away!' her brother screamed, hurtling towards the gate out of the park.

'Derek. Stop! Wait.' Their grandfather stood in a dither of indecision, not sure which child to abandon.

'It's OK. I'll get her,' Paul said, taking the last remnants of cake and wrapper from his overcoat pocket.

Relieved, the man hurried after the boy. Sarah hesitated, then started walking slowly to the gate, glancing back occasionally to check on the other two. Matty was offering crumbs on her outstretched hand to the eager birds. Crouching down, Paul joined her. They made a charming picture together, the handsome RAF officer and the pretty blonde child in her fur-trimmed bonnet. There was an ill-natured jostling as more birds arrived, landing in a flurry of wings and webbed feet. A small teal duck in the front flew up and seemed to bounce off Paul's face. He swore loudly and sat down, his hand clamped to his cheek. Redness oozed through his fingers. Sarah guessed that the bird had reopened one of the wounds from last night's encounter with his car. Frightened by the blood and noise, Matty ran towards Sarah.

'Are you all right?'

In response to her shout, Paul raised a reassuring hand and waved them on.

'Come on, let's catch your grandad up.' She took the child's willing hand and they hurried down towards the gate. Paul overtook them as they crossed the road to walk back up the narrow street.

'Damn bird,' he said, dabbing at the blood with a blotched handkerchief.

Smoke was drifting in ragged columns from most of the chimneys now, and the smells of cooking tantalised from each crack and crevice. Her fright forgotten, Matty joined her brother in jumping off and on the sandbags stacked against the basement windows, until their grandfather ordered them to stop.

'Well, I'll wish you a Merry Christmas,' he said, stopping outside the De Groots' door. 'And a Happy New Year if I don't see you again.'

Wishing him the same, Sarah and Paul went inside, where the combination of delicious smells was even stronger. Margot and Nell appeared from the back of the house. Both had dressed in identical long-sleeved belted frocks in some kind of shiny fabric; Margot's green and Nell's a deep blue.

'Oh, here they are. Darling, your face!'

'It's nothing. Cold opened it up again. Don't fuss.'

'I never fuss. Thank you for the necklace.' She touched a gold chain with a pearl pendant. 'And look how well Nell's earrings suit her.'

Nell's thanks for her pearl drops were politely formal.

'Did you have a good walk? You've been an age.'

'Very good, thanks, old fruit. I think Sarah enjoyed it, didn't you, Sarah?'

He reached to help her out of her coat. Twisting away, she said: 'It passed the time.' Her words were casual, but the look she gave him would have turned salt water to ice.

He stepped back, confused. Nell gave her a half-smile of gratitude for what she plainly perceived as moral support. Sarah let her. It made her feel better about how close she'd come to making a fool of herself. She knew now that the first impression of pure evil that she'd sensed on that landing in Vorley Road had been right. All the rest was just sham and play-acting.

At the park gate she'd paused and looked back to see if he was catching them up. He was still in the same spot, scattering the final crumbs to the birds. As the little teal duck that had flown into him stretched out to scoop up a morsel, he'd calmly and deliberately lifted his boot and crushed the life out of its gleaming chestnut skull.

Chapter 30

'Happy Christmas, Eileen.'

'And to you, Jack.'

It was a forlorn hope, and they both knew it. But an unspoken desire to try and regain some of their former easy-going relationship made them clink their beer glasses over the Christmas table. Sammy and Annaliese raised their tumblers of lemonade and murmured a subdued 'Merr' Chris'mas' before gulping down the clear liquid.

Stretching out his legs beneath the table, Maury leant back in his chair, took a deliberate slow swig of his own beer and replaced the glass on his mother's best linen cloth. He seemed absorbed in watching the lacy pattern of froth sliding down inside the glass. Eileen opened her mouth; then shut it again with a snap, and they all went back to the activity that was least likely to cause any conflict: eating.

Eileen had given up her idea of cooking Christmas dinner on Christmas Eve. 'It was supposed to be so Pat could share it. But now they gone and sent him to Manchester, we might as well have it same as usual,' she explained when she'd come over to Jack's to invite him in 'for Annaliese's sake'. 'Come early and you can watch them opening their presents.'

So he'd duly wheeled the doll's pram across the road as soon as he'd eaten breakfast, and watched as Sammy and Annaliese had dived into their stockings before falling on the wrapped packages below the Christmas tree. Their initial excitement had become more and more subdued as the uneasy undercurrents between the adults had penetrated their self-absorption. For once Sammy had raised no protest when his mother told him to go and get dressed.

'OK, Mum. C'mon, Annie.'

They'd shuffled out, socks half off and pyjamas trailing cords. The void they left had been filled by Eileen noisily opening her own presents: chocolates from Brendan, soap from Shane, a brooch from Pat, some violently hued perfume from Sammy and Annaliese.

'Conn sent a card,' she said, as if she felt she ought to excuse his apparent neglect. Climbing stiffly from her knees, she fetched the small cardboard picture of a robin. 'It came first post this morning. So at least his ship's docked, thank God.'

'What did Maury . . . ?' Too late Jack remembered the two bottles of Scotch sitting in the CID safe at Agar Street; one of which was allegedly a gift for his mother.

'I bought him a proper gent's hairbrush up the market,' Eileen replied, choosing to misunderstand.

She'd accepted his own uninspired gift of lace-edged handkerchiefs with polite thanks and then extended three large white linen ones for him. 'From Annie,' she'd said quickly before he could refuse. 'We put your initial on.' She pointed to the 'J' worked in shaky red cross-stitch.

'Thank you.'

There was nothing left to say . . . nothing that wouldn't lead to more recriminations and things that were best left unsaid. They weren't in the habit of going to church on Christmas morning, so they had no excuse to go out. And he could hardly plead work today. In the end Eileen hid in the kitchen, concealed amongst clouds of steam, using a flurry of activity and muttered instructions to 'Stay out from under my feet' to keep everyone else at bay. Jack took the younger children for a desultory walk, allowing Sammy to shoot passing dogs with his new cap gun and Annie to show off her new pram. Maury had made himself scarce until, inevitably, they'd had to meet over the dinner table.

Given that Eileen had produced a miracle of chicken, sausages, bread sauce, roast potatoes, brussels sprouts and braised celery, it was a pity no one seemed to have much appetite. Only Maury ate with defiant enthusiasm, cutting and chewing with a noisy enjoyment that eventually earned him an

302

angry instruction of 'Leave off. I've heard monkeys up the zoo eat quieter.'

Sammy's giggle was suppressed by a scowl and an order from Maury to shut his mouth.

'Will not. Yer wouldn' try an' boss me around if Pat were here.'

'Well he's not, is he? So shut it.'

'Leave him alone, Maury. If there's any telling to be done around here, I'll do it.'

'Don't see why. I'm the eldest now Pat's away.'

'Pat's grown up,' Sammy said defiantly. 'I don't mind Pat telling me. Or Brendan, or Shane, or Conn. But I ain't doing what you say. You're a crook. Piggy's mum says you'll be eating bread and water this time next year.'

'That's enough!' Eileen's palm hit the table with enough force to make the cutlery and glasses jump into the air. She pointed her knife at her youngest and told him that one more word and he could go sit in the Anderson shelter for the rest of Christmas. 'Understand?'

'Yeah.' With a shrug, he bent over his plate and started cutting what was left into extravagantly small squares.

'And you can tell Piggy's mum to keep her nose out of our business,' his mother snapped at the top of his head.

Sammy sniffed. A few moments later he asked: 'Can I go round Nafnel's after me dinner and show him me presents?'

'No.'

'Why not?'

'Because I said.'

Things got worse with the pudding. The rich dark-brown mound looked and smelt delicious. Eileen produced a medicine bottle with a quarter-inch of brandy swilling in the bottom. 'I got them to sell me a tot down the Mother Shipton. It's terrible the price they're charging now.'

'You should have asked me, Mum,' Maury said. 'I could have got you a bottle. Wholesale.'

Jack declined to raise to the bait. Using his lighter, he ignited the eerie blue flames and sent them flowing and flickering over the oily surface.

303

Eileen sliced the dessert into five portions with an almost vicious energy. 'Mind out for the sixpence,' she warned. They all duly chopped at their slices before adding any custard. There was no sign of the silver coin.

'Perhaps Maury nicked it,' Sammy suggested, then shot into the air and yelled with pain. 'Yer kicked me, yer rotten . . .' Flinging himself across the table, he brought the back of his spoon down hard on his brother's nose.

Jack, who was sitting next to the younger boy, grabbed the seat of his trousers and pulled him back into his chair.

'That's enough. Get down that Anderson . . .'

'It's not *fair*. Maury started it. Send him down the lousy shelter . . .'

Maury took a bite of his mince pie and remarked that the pastry was hard.

'I couldn't get enough cooking fats. And don't bother to tell me you can get me no Stork wholesale. Just go eat somewhere else if you don't like them.'

'No need to talk like that, Mum. I didn't mean nothing. What have I done?'

'What have you . . . you *know* what you've done! Don't you come Mr Butter-wouldn'-Melt with me, young man! I just wish your dad were here now . . .'

'Don't see me dad could help much.' Maury attempted a casual pose. 'But *he* could. After all the skivvying you done for him, seems to me he ought to be glad to tell them I didn't nick those bottles of whisky. Anyhow,' he added, deliberately removing a small cigar from his inside pocket in defiance of his mother's ban on smoking in the parlour. 'Anyhow,' he repeated, striking a match, 'the coppers can't prove I stole them. Just their word against mine.'

'And Eddie Hooper's,' Jack said grimly.

'What's Eddie got to do with it? That plainclothes flattie of yours never found anything round his place.'

Jack hesitated. After Ding-Dong's phone call yesterday afternoon, he'd made a deliberate decision not to tell Eileen about Hooper's arrest. She'd already extended the holly branch of peace by asking him to dinner, and he'd decided it would be kinder not to spoil her Christmas. A small voice in his head had told him he was a twenty-four carat coward and what he was really worried about was his own comfort. Now he was on the spot – and feeling anything but comfortable.

'There's something you better know...' The smug self-assurance ebbed from Maury's face as he told them about the discovery of the stolen whisky in Mornington Crescent.

'But that's nothing to do with Maury,' Eileen said sharply. 'He's not to know this Eddie'd hidden stuff down Sarah's old place, is he?'

'Yeah, how'd I know what Eddie gets up to?' Maury agreed, trying to draw on his cigar. The match was shaking and he couldn't quite touch it to the tip.

'It's more a question of Eddie knowing what you get up to, isn't it, Maury?'

Maury finally managed to connect cigar and match.

'What do you mean, Jack?' Eileen asked sharply.

'I mean ... Hooper has a record. He'll go down. If he has any brains at all he'll give the police something in exchange for a shorter sentence. Like the name of his accomplice on the robbery. Unless, of course, the accomplice has the sense to do unto Eddie before Eddie does unto him.'

'If this here accomplice,' Eileen said, 'were to confess, does that mean he wouldn't go to prison?'

'No. I couldn't guarantee that. But if he were still a juvenile, say, and this was a first offence ... well, it could be probation if someone was to put in a good word with the judge ...'

There was a moment of silence. Maury sat up. He put his elbows on the table and leant forward confidentially. 'The thing is, Mr Stamford ...'

'Yes?'

'Well, the thing is ... Eddie hasn't *got* any brains.'

Jack waited for more. Around him he was conscious that the other three were holding their breath. Maury sat back and busied himself with the cigar.

'Maury! You tell Jack what he wants to know right this minute. Or get out of my house.'

Shrugging, Maury stood up. 'See you then.' Sauntering into

the hall, he took a hat from the peg and snapped the brim into a jaunty position. It was identical to the one that had been recovered from the scene of the whisky robbery. Seeing Jack's pointed glance, Maury flicked his thumb and forefinger against the new headgear with a cheeky grin, clamped his cigar between his teeth and drew back the blackout curtain over the front door.

'Maury.'

'Yes.'

'I think you'll find that cigar draws better if you cut the end off.'

With a scowl, Maury thrust the soggy-ended tube back into his breast pocket and banged the front door shut. Ashamed of himself for enjoying such a petty victory, Jack turned back to the front parlour.

'You can get out too, Jack.'

'Eileen . . . !'

'I mean it. I don't want you here.'

'All right.' What was the point of arguing? There was nothing he could do to help her. He shrugged on his overcoat and buttoned it, noting how easily he was managing the one-handed task now. Who knows, he thought, perhaps in a few more weeks he'd hardly notice he was a cripple. He gave a final glance back into the parlour, intending to leave on a dignified 'goodbye'.

Eileen was crying silently, the tears sliding down her face and dropping on to the artificial green silk dress that she only wore for special occasions. White-faced and scared, but conscious of his position now as the man of the house, Sammy slid out of his chair. Skirting the table, he put his arm round his mother's shoulders and said firmly: 'It's OK, Mum. I'll take care of you.'

Jack stepped through the front door and pulled it quietly closed behind him.

He took the upper route, sauntering through Litcham Street where the beat constables went in threesomes, and deliberately walking on down Agar Street. The uniformed constable rocking back and forth on his heels by the sandbagged entrance whilst he scanned the quiet skies touched his helmet and wished Jack 'A very Merry Christmas, sir.'

Jack paused. He was half tempted to go in and have a word with Hooper. Get it over with once and for all. Send someone down to arrest Maury and finish the game. He knew he shouldn't interfere in Ding-Dong's case, but he didn't suppose the phlegmatic DC would complain.

The constable was looking at him expectantly. Jack nodded: 'And a Happy New Year to you, Constable.'

He walked on without any clear idea of where he was going. The weather was turning colder, but his arm was behaving itself. Perhaps he'd go up to Hampstead and talk a walk across the heath. It wasn't as if he had anything else to do. With a deep sigh he looked around at the deserted streets and silent railway lines and suddenly felt as if he were the only living soul in London.

Well, the only living soul bar one, he amended his self-misery to read. Betty Shaw suddenly appeared ahead of him. With her hands buried in the pockets of her regulation AFS trousers and her face half-hidden by her cap, she hurried past, ignoring his 'Merry Christmas'. He supposed he couldn't blame her. It was his digging into those wretched letters that had broken up her marriage. You could hardly expect her to hope his Christmas was merry, much less that his New Year was going to be happy.

Turning his coat collar up, he headed for his lonely stroll across the heath.

Betty hadn't ignored the Christmas greeting out of spite; quite simply, she hadn't heard it. Her mind was a whirl trying to decide what she was going to do with the rest of her life. She'd walked out on Len in a blaze of self-righteous anger, without really thinking about the future beyond hanging on to her self-respect.

But once the initial rush of fury had subsided, the practical aspects of what she'd done had started to intrude. She'd got her job, of course, so she'd have a little money coming in each week. But she'd left with only a hastily packed suitcase, leaving behind the sheets, towels, pots, pans and bits of ornaments she'd collected over the years. Well, she was blowed if Len's fancy piece was going to get her hands on them.

She'd asked for – and received – permission to take her meal break off the station. 'There's been no sign of a raid for days,' she'd argued. 'And if the siren goes I can be back in ten minutes from Patshull Street.' Regrets had been expressed that she hadn't chosen to accept the men's invitation to join their Christmas party in the recreation room – but she had sensed they were prompted more by politeness than anything else.

The house was still and silent when she let herself in. She'd been half expecting to come face to face with Len's woman and now felt an almost physical let-down. For the first time, she became conscious of how tensed her muscles were. She'd been keyed up to let fly, both physically and verbally, at the floozie, and now there was nowhere to put the anger.

Slowly she moved through the whole house, opening each door half-afraid of what she'd find, and then releasing a deep sigh as the cold rooms proved to be unchanged. Only the kitchen and their bedroom showed any sign of occupancy. Unwashed dishes in the sink and a tangle of unmade sheets and blankets on the bed were souvenirs of Len's twenty-four hours off yesterday. Her hand seemed to take on a life of its own. It peeled back the eiderdown to reveal the crumpled bottom sheet. She found her eyes straining for signs of intimacy.

With an impatient gesture of disgust at her own thoughts, she flung the bedclothes down and opened the wardrobe. Apart from the clothes she'd left behind, there were only Len's two suits and his overcoat swinging from the hangers. So he hadn't moved *her* in yet. Well, that was up to him. What did she care any more? Banging the doors closed, she dragged the big suitcase from the top of the wardrobe and started opening the chest of drawers.

The case was nearly full when she found the black tissue package tucked away at the back of the bottom drawer. Slowly she drew it out and sat down on the bed. Holding it tenderly on her knees, she gently unfolded the dry, crinkly paper. The white cotton of the baby robe was unyellowed, its smocking and blue

308

ribbonwork still as fresh as the month she'd lovingly stitched them. It was so long ago now. The first year of her marriage, when the future had seemed full of golden days.

Sliding her forearm under the tiny puffed sleeves, she gently stroked out the long skirts, smoothing them down as if there was a living baby inside them. She should have given it away years ago, of course. One of her nephews would have looked lovely in it. But she'd hung on to it stubbornly, as she'd clung to the swastika-shaped charm the fortune-teller had given her. They were tangible statements of her conviction that one day she and Len would have a child.

And now . . . She didn't even know she was crying until the hot drops splashed over the delicate material, spattering an irregular pattern of crinkly circles.

'Betty?'

She drew her breath in a gasp of fright and half rose before she recognised the shape in the doorway.

'Len? How . . . ? I mean, I thought you were on duty.'

'I am.'

Someone from Good Hope must have rung across to the main station as soon as she left. No doubt some ambitious AFS with his eye on transferring to the red riders and collecting the extra five shillings a week had seen a chance to ingratiate himself with the station officer.

He moved a few steps nearer. 'Have you come back?'

'Only to get the rest of my things.'

'Things . . . ?' He saw the open suitcase. 'Oh.'

She was trying to squeeze the tears back behind her eyelids, but they continued to stream, soaking her cheeks and running into the soft hollow of her throat.

'Betty, love. Don't.' He dropped to his knees in front of her and fumbled for a handkerchief. When his pockets proved to be empty, he reached round her and pulled something from the top of the suitcase.

'That's new,' she protested as he patted her face with a folded pillowcase.

'I'll get you another one. I'll get you a whole set. Sheets, pillowcases, bedspread. Whatever you want to fix the room up.

309

Might even find some wallpaper if I ask around. A fresh start, eh? That's what we need.'

She pushed his hand away. 'It would take more than a few yards of cotton and a bit of paste to do that, Len.' With a determined gulp, she choked back the rest of the tears and took a grip of herself. 'You'd best get back to work. You'll be on a charge if they find you absent.'

'Damn the bloody job. I want you, Betty.'

'But not only me.'

'They meant nothing. I told you, love.'

'Yes, you did. And do you know, Len, in a way that makes it almost worse.' He was still on his knees in front of her. In an unconscious gesture she ran her fingertips around his jaw line and noted he hadn't shaved properly this morning. 'If you'd fallen in love I might have been able to understand it. But just . . .' She gestured, unable to put her disgust into words.

He grabbed her wrists. She flinched, recalling his violent attempts to keep her prisoner when she'd originally walked out. The sight of the purple bracelets of bruising round her wrists seemed to remind him too. 'Sorry,' he muttered, dropping her arms again. 'I mean it, Betty. I'd do anything to get you back. Just tell me what it'll take.'

'Give me back the past eighteen years, Len.'

'Now you're being daft.'

'I know.' She stood up and he scrambled after her. 'You see, Len, everything's changed – inside my head, I mean. When I thought about you when we weren't together, it used to give me a warm, safe feeling. I thought I knew you. I thought I knew everything about you. And now it seems like I didn't know the half of it. I keep turning things round and round in my head; trying to work out *when*. When were you really where you said you were? And when were you off with one of your fancy pieces? Which ones were the lies, Len, and which were the truths?'

'Well, I don't know. Look, this is daft, love. Getting yourself in a state over a few girls who were . . . well, a bit of fun.'

'*A bit of fun!* Like a game of darts or kick-around with a football, you mean?' She could hear her voice rising. She'd

310

meant to stay calm and hang on to her dignity. But the casual way he was dismissing the destruction of years of her memories was working its way under her skin like a festering splinter.

Taking off his cap and thrusting his fingers through his hair in a gesture of exasperation, Len protested: 'There's no need to get clever. I'm just trying to say it wasn't anything like it is with you.'

'Why – aren't I fun?'

'For God's sake, if you're not even going to talk sensible . . .'

'There's nothing left to say, Len.' Swinging round, she banged the suitcase lid shut and clicked the locks down.

'Here.' Len scooped up the baby robe from the floor. 'You forgot this.'

She hesitated, her hand hovering over the delicate material. All those years wasted. And at her age, how could she even hope to start again with someone else?

'*No!*' She thrust the robe violently into his chest, sending him staggering back. 'You keep it. You and the latest fancy piece. And God help her, Len.' Dragging the case off the bed, she fled downstairs, scarcely noticing the crippling weight as it crashed and banged against each tread.

'*Betty! Betty!*'

Panting, she staggered round in the front hall and shouted back: 'I hope whoever she is, she is having a *hellish* Christmas!' And with a satisfying and thoroughly undignified crash of the front door, she stormed out.

If she'd only known it, the Christmas fairy had granted Betty Shaw's wish. Hatty *was* having a hellish Christmas.

She hated Manchester. Apart from her early years in Wales, the furthest she'd ever travelled from London had been on a holiday to Herne Bay with her aunt and uncle. She'd been totally unprepared for the biting coldness of the north and the physical pain of homesickness.

None of the other women on the canteen vans seemed to be affected. The Euston driver had even remarked how smashing it was to put three hundred miles between herself and her mum. So Hatty had rolled herself in the rough blankets they'd been

311

issued with and quietly cried herself to sleep on the floor of the school where they'd been billeted.

The days were even worse. From the van you could see the dreadful smashed wreckage of factories and houses all blasted into piles of rubble, joists and twisted metal girders. Over the top of them a pall of dirty smoke sat on the top of the shells of the tallest buildings and held in the smells of sewage, leaking gas and – occasionally – roasting flesh as something once living was incinerated before it could be recovered by the rescue services.

She'd tried to be brave. To dish out the doorstep sandwiches of corned beef and cheese with mugs of tea and exchange a cheery joke with the exhausted fire crews. She'd told herself sternly, again and again, that this was her duty and there was plenty worse off than her. You could see them everywhere; grey-faced, exhausted Mancunians who'd lost everything, queuing with buckets and saucepans to get water from standpipes. And clustered round temporary ovens waiting for the WVS to serve up a plate of stew for their Christmas dinner because the gas and electricity had been off for days.

You're lucky, Hatty, she told herself again and again. *It's only for a little while. At least you can go 'ome.*

But thinking of home brought back memories of Ruth and Uncle Duggie. And Len. Oh, she wanted so much to be with Len. Warm and safe in her own home with her man. The familiar lump swelled in her throat and she struggled to hold back the tears of homesickness again.

'Lathie. Oi, lathie. Can I have one o' them barm cathes?'

Hatty hastily blinked and focused on the crumpled figure in front of the hatch counter. 'Pardon?'

'Barm cathes,' he repeated, pointing to the pile of sand-wiches. 'Bit of cornbeef, lathie.'

He looked about eighty. A wrinkled walnut of a face crowned with tufted wisps of white baby hair.

'I'm only supposed to give them to the firemen, mister. Sorry. You can go over to the WVS.'

The man looked over to where the black iron chimneys were belching smoke over the women as they heaved boiling pans on to hot plates. 'Ith no good. I can't chew the lumpth in the meat, see. I loth me teeth.' In proof he opened his mouth wide to display a gummy cavern. 'Gith us something softh, eh, lathie? I've not had a bite for two dayth.'

Hatty hesitated. She would have handed over the soft bread and meat sandwich, but one of the regular fire officers shouted over to her to keep the supplies for the uniformed men.

'Sorry, mister,' she said.

He looked at her through rheumy eyes and sighed. 'Ith not your fault, lath.' The sticky gaze took in the grey people amongst the blasted remains of their homes, and he delivered his verdict on the season of goodwill to all men: 'Thou knowth, lath. I reckon is the worth bluidy booger of a Chrithmath thereth ever been!'

Chapter 31

Jack kept his eyes on Maury's face as the chairman of the magistrates intoned his verdict on those who 'transgress against society's laws and allow the tides of anarchy to lap round the shores of decent homes'. Given that this particular magistrate's father was the biggest villain in the district, Maury probably wasn't the only one choking back a disbelieving laugh as John Bowler droned on, enchanted by the sound of his own voice.

Since Maury was seated on the chair nearest the court doors, Jack guessed he wasn't quite as certain of Eddie's loyalty as he'd pretended to be.

A pointed cough from the clerk of the court finally brought Bowler down from the delicious realms of verbosity where he'd been drifting quite happily for the last five minutes. Reluctantly he refocused on the dock.

'I trust the prisoner is aware of the serious nature of the charges against him . . .'

The prisoner arranged his features into an expression that conveyed grave contemplation.

'. . . and the distress that such actions must cause to the unfortunate victims.'

The prisoner in the dock looked suitably distressed.

'We therefore have no option but to commit you for trial at the next quarter sessions . . .'

The prisoner squared his shoulders manfully, ready to accept whatever the King's court might throw at him, whilst his solicitor climbed to his feet.

'My client wishes to apply for bail, Your Honours. He has business interests that will suffer greatly from his absence.'

The prisoner rearranged his features into the worried frown

of a man who could see his commercial empire crumbling before his eyes.

Ding-Dong rose to his feet and formally opposed bail. 'The police are undertaking ongoing enquiries, Your Honours, which may be affected if the prisoner were to be given his liberty.'

A loud whisper behind Jack asked what the copper's mouthful meant.

' 'E sez Eddie'll duff up the witnesses if 'e gets out,' an answering whisper explained in an even louder tone.

The spectators' giggles were hushed by a stern glare from John Bowler. Having regained his audience, Bowler bobbed to the retired bank manager on his right and the factory owner on his left. He then delivered their collective verdict. 'The prisoner will be remanded in custody until he may be brought before the appropriate court.'

'Ya lousy rotten bastards,' bawled Eddie Hooper, diving for the edge of the dock. The two policemen on court duty dragged him back and down into the cells, still bawling promises of revenge and descriptions of the magistrates' parentage which – in Bowler's case – could well be ninety per cent accurate. Maury got up and sauntered out with a smirk in Ding-Dong's direction.

'You didn't get anything out of Hooper then?' Jack asked, joining the DC by the door.

'Not yet, sir. But I've had a word with his solicitor. Let him know that if there was anything his client should wish to discuss, my ears are open and the tram fare to Pentonville is always in my pocket.'

'Do you think he'll talk?'

'I think young Mr O'Day thinks he might.'

'Yes. You could be right.'

'I trust you had a pleasant Christmas, sir?'

'Er . . . yes . . . thank you.' Had anyone ever admitted to having a miserable Christmas? Jack wondered. Remembering his manners, he hoped the DC had too.

'The lady wife and I enjoyed an extremely pleasant celebration, thank you, sir.'

'And your family?' From the back of his mind Jack dredged

315

a remark Ding-Dong had made about parenthood. 'You've got children, haven't you? Grown-up now, I imagine?'

'It was a very pleasant day,' the DC repeated. 'If you'll excuse me, sir, I have some enquiries to make. Oh, by the way . . .' He drew a taped brown envelope from his inside pocket. 'This was in the CID office. I thought I might run into you in court today.'

'Thanks.' Wondering why Ding-Dong's children were a taboo subject, Jack ripped open the package, which was marked 'DCI J. STAMFORD – CONFIDENTIAL'. Nell De Groot's anonymous letter together with Sarah's explanatory note fell into his hands. There was also another envelope tucked inside the first. The contents felt hard. On the front Sarah had printed 'KNIFE – SHOULD HAVE TWO SETS OF PRINTS ON IT. MINE (ON RECORD) AND NDG'S.'

It took him a few seconds to assimilate what he was looking at. His expression, when he glanced up again, made Ding-Dong wish he'd left the packet where he found it, safely sinking into oblivion beneath a pile of papers in the office 'in'-tray.

'How long has this been at Agar Street?'

The DC was of the opinion it had probably been there since Christmas Eve. 'Might have been a bit before that, sir.'

Jack opened his mouth to ask didn't he check the post, damn it? Then the unfairness of this attitude struck him. Sarah, after all, could easily have brought the letter round to his house if she'd wanted to. And the most likely reason she hadn't wanted to was his own behaviour when she'd last called. He contented himself with asking if Sergeant McNeill was on duty today.

'Far as I know, sir.'

He couldn't go on avoiding her for ever. The best way, he decided, was to jump straight in, apologise for his drunken pass and try to put the whole depressing mistake behind him. It was a reasonable plan. Unfortunately it required two participants.

'Not seen her today, sir.' The station sergeant shrugged. He checked the duty rosters and admitted that Sergeant McNeill *ought* to be on duty. 'But she ain't,' he said firmly, washing his hands of any responsibility for missing females.

Fired with a determination to set things right with Sarah, Jack was reluctant to be deflected at the first hurdle. He'd walk up to Vorley Road and see if she was at home.

Struggling up Junction Road against the gusting north wind whistling down it, he tried to work out his next move as far as Nell De Groot was concerned. There had been no fingerprint report back yet from the Metropolitan Police laboratories on the other letters he'd sent in. Presumably Christmas was slowing things down there, as everywhere else. He could send Nell's letter in for comparison. Alternatively . . . the same thought that had crossed Sarah's mind now filtered into Stamford's.

Why not just tell the woman there was evidence she'd written the anonymous letters? Suggest that professional help was called for and get Daddy to book her ticket for the quiet, discreet nut-house with country views and room service? It would earn him a few merit marks from Special Branch, and who'd be any the wiser?

He entertained the idea for several hundred yards; then booted it firmly over the doorstep. What the hell was he thinking about? The more involved he became with these wretched anonymous letters, the more disgusted he was with his own conduct. He should have told Dunn at the beginning that if he wanted to put Nell De Groot in an asylum he could damn well make the whole business official, appoint an investigating officer and give the woman the chance to defend herself. But he hadn't, had he? And why not? Because he wanted to prove he was still of some use, that was why. That he wasn't on the scrap-heap because he was middle-aged and crippled by arthritis.

Well, enough was enough. It was time to stop kidding himself. He'd go on until the end of the year and then start the new one as he meant to go on; with a request to be pensioned off on medical grounds and a suggestion as to what Special Branch could do with their investigation into Nell De Groot.

Fuelled by the tiny burst of adrenaline that had been generated by coming to a firm decision, he marched confidently up the steps to Bridget O'Mara's house and tried the front door. His shouted 'Hello?' echoed up into the far reaches of the silent house.

The top floor, she'd said. He started up the stairs. The thundering crash of a water cistern coupled with a protesting groan from air-locked pipes announced that someone was home. What he'd taken to be a cupboard opened and he found himself sharing the first-floor landing with a bloke who looked as though he could have made a reasonable living modelling for church gargoyles.

Jack jerked a thumb at the second flight of stairs. 'Good afternoon. Straight up for Sarah McNeill?'

'Yes. But I fear there is no one else but me in at present. May I pass on a message?'

'No. Thank you. You don't happen to know where Sarah is, Mr . . . em . . . ?'

'Death.'

So this was the so-called cosmetic salesman who was in love with Nell De Groot, was it? Jack studied him with more interest.

He found his scrutiny being returned with interest. 'I believe Miss McNeill has gone to work,' Max offered. 'Are you by any chance another policeman?'

'Do I look like one?'

'Yes. You do rather. At least the way you are examining me – and Mrs O'Mara's somewhat dusty landing – does seem rather official.'

'Sorry.' Jack grinned ruefully. 'It's habit. I don't know I'm doing it.'

Max acknowledged the apology with a nod and moved towards another door on the landing. 'Work can dominate one's life, don't you find? I myself must put my nose to the grindstone or – to be more accurate – my bottom on the slow train to Oswestry.'

Jack caught a glimpse of a suitcase standing open on the bed and a smaller sample case on the floor.

'You've a big area to cover . . .'

Max turned back, holding the door knob behind him. 'You've heard of me then . . . Sergeant, is it . . . ?'

There seemed no way out of it. Jack introduced himself. 'Sarah was giving me a run-down on her new digs the other

318

day. She mentioned a cosmetic traveller. I assume that's you?'

'You assume correctly. Chief Inspector.'

Jack became conscious of an undercurrent of hostility. But why?

'Did you enjoy Christmas in St Albans? You were going with Sarah and Miss De Groot, weren't you?'

'It was most . . . interesting. No doubt Miss McNeill has given you all the details?'

'Sarah? No, I haven't seen her since before Christmas.'

'But you need to see her now?'

He was probing. Not very expertly, but nonetheless Jack sensed that the fact he was looking for Sarah was making Max uneasy. Had something happened over Christmas that Max would prefer the police not to find out about? Surely if something significant had occurred, Sarah would have reported it? Only Sarah should have been on duty today, according to the duty rosters. And nobody knew where she was. It wasn't like her to be absent herself from duty without informing Agar Street. He suddenly felt a chill.

'I think I'll go up anyway. She might have come back without you hearing her.'

'I doubt that . . . but as you wish. Perhaps you'd be kind enough to put the lock down on the front door as you leave.'

Standing on the second landing, confronted by two identical doors, Stamford tried to recall whether Sarah had ever mentioned whether she faced front or back. He leant over the banister, intending to shout down to Max Death, and then thought better of it. Choosing a door at random, he rapped sharply, waited a few moments, and then rapped again. He kept the sequence up until he heard Max leave the house, then he felt inside his breast pocket and drew out a key ring containing six metal bars with oddly shaped ends.

It was a long time since he'd been called on to pick a lock. And kneeling on the hard floorboards, cursing softly as the tumblers slid away from the probing picks, he began to think he'd lost the knack. Finally, just when the good elbow was becoming as cramped and painful as the crippled, he heard a distinctive 'click' and the handle responded to his push. He'd guessed right. It was Sarah's room. He recognised the clothes. A quick check revealed that her uniform jacket and helmet were missing. She'd plainly dressed with the intention of going on duty. So why hadn't she?

Now he'd got the hang of it, relocking the door proved relatively simple. He was finished just in time. Descending back to the hall, he pulled the front door open just as a tiny female in an unlikely collection of out-of-date clothes smelling of mothballs and lavender water tried to insert her key.

'Oh ... oh ... thank you. So kind ...' She trilled as Jack stood back for her to enter. A couple of battered feathers perched on what appeared to be a bird's nest of grey wire wool wobbled beneath his nose as she tripped inside with an arch smile.

Miss Rawkins regretted she couldn't help him since she hadn't seen dear Miss McNeill for some time. 'Indeed, I don't believe I've set eyes on her since ... before Christmas ... now I think about it. A bit like the Disappearing Lady ... one of the Great Giovanni's most spectacular tricks ... perhaps you saw him ... it was nineteen-thirty, I think ...'

Gently interrupting Ruby's reminiscences of the great days at the Bedford Music Hall, Jack disengaged himself and set out for Agar Street Station with considerably more speed than he'd left it.

A fast check amongst the on-duty men revealed that no one had actually seen Sergeant McNeill since Christmas Eve.

'Well, didn't anyone notice she was missing, for heaven's sake?' Jack snapped.

The station sergeant, to whom he'd addressed this angry query, pointed out that since the women's branch was separate, it was harder to keep a watch on them. 'And your Sergeant McNeill isn't one for rules and regulations, sir.'

'She's not *my* Sergeant McNeill.'

'If you say so, sir.'

'I do.' The arm, which had been stiff but pain-free for the past few days, suddenly started to throb warningly. 'Look,' he said, taking deep, even breaths to keep the pain under control. 'Start asking around. Question all the men as they come off their beats. Somebody must know where she is. Ring me at home as soon as you get an answer.'

It was brighter than usual when he stepped outside. The new moon was scarcely a pencil-stroke width, but the stars were twinkling with a clarity he hadn't seen for some time. Nursing the elbow against the pavement's hardness, he wondered whether he should join in the search. But where would he start? Once again he realised how very little he knew about Sergeant Sarah McNeill's private life. She let hints and glimpses slip occasionally, but most of her past – and the people in it – was a closed book. In fact, he could think of only one person she might have called on.

Sammy answered the door to him. 'Oh. 'Ello, Mr Stamford.'

'Who is it?'

'Mr Stamford, Mum. Can I let 'im in?'

Raising his own voice slightly, Jack called into the darkened passage: 'I'm looking for Sarah, Eileen.'

'You best come through then.'

She came to the kitchen door, pushing damp tendrils of hair off her flushed face. Clouds of steam escaped round her thin figure as she surveyed Jack with hands on hips. 'Have you seen Maury, Jack?'

'In court, this afternoon.'

'Court!' Eileen's hand went to her throat. 'You haven't . . . he's not been arrested?'

'No. He was listening to Eddie Hooper's hearing.'

'Thank heavens.' Eileen let her breath out in an explosive sigh.

'Haven't *you* seen him?' Jack demanded.

Eileen shook her head. 'Not since he walked out Christmas Day.' She pushed the damp hair from her sweaty face in a two-handed gesture of defeat. 'I wish to God Pat were here. You'd best come through, I suppose.'

She stood aside, and the reason for the steam became obvious. Kettles and pans were bubbling noisily on the stove, ready to replenish the tin bath which had been placed in front of the fire grate. Annaliese, her skin pink and gleaming, was playing with a paper boat that was bobbing on the sudsy

321

surface. But it was the person rubbing a soapy flannel over the little girl's back that drew Jack's attention.

'Where the hell have you been?'

'For the past hour, sir,' Sarah said coolly, continuing to soap in circular movements, 'I've been here, helping with the children's baths. Before that I was at Paddington.'

'Do you realise the whole station is looking for you? No one's seen you for days.'

'Paddington's seen me. In fact they've seen me almost non-stop since I was told to go over on Boxing Day. They've had a lot of juvenile cases and no female officers available.'

'Didn't you think to *tell* anyone? Good heavens, Sarah, I thought something had *happened* to you.'

She sat back on her heels, wiping soapy hands on the flowered overall she'd pulled on over her uniform blouse and skirt.

'My own inspector knows where I am. She was the one who sent me over to Paddington. And I did let the station sergeant at Agar Street know. But it was the one on the early turn, so he plainly hasn't passed it on. I really don't see there's any need for anyone to get in a flap. I can look after myself.'

'Like you did with Eddie Hooper?'

Sarah's chin went up. 'Nabbed him, didn't I?'

'Only because that chap from the council turned up.'

'Well, that's all you know . . . *sir*.'

Scrambling up, she half filled a large jug with cold water, topped it up from the kettle and ordered: 'Deep breath, Annie.'

Taking a huge gasp, Annaliese squeezed her eyes shut and blew out her cheeks. Tipping the cascade over her head, Sarah rubbed the soap bar into the tangled tresses and massaged vigorously. The act somehow shut Jack out. Piqued, he dragged over a kitchen chair and sat close to the bath. He was rewarded by a shower of rinsing water splashing up over his trousers. Annaliese giggled, tipping her head right back to laugh up into Sarah's face. Sarah bent forward and dropped a kiss on the child's upturned nose. Straightening up again, she looked Stamford full in the face. For a moment their eyes locked and he knew she was remembering their last encounter and that stupid drunken slobber. You could hardly call it a kiss.

'Look . . . em . . .' he began tentatively. 'I'm glad you're OK. Maybe I did overreact. It's just, when you're stuck at home all day, your perspective becomes a lot narrower. Stupid things get blown out of proportion . . .'

'Yes . . .' she said softly. 'Things that can seem really important when you're at home can be not worth a tinker's cuss when you get back out into the world, don't you think, sir?'

'Hardly worth the tinker drawing breath,' Jack agreed. 'Much less working himself up for a spot of profanity.'

'Oh. Good. I'm glad . . . I mean . . . best to put him behind us then . . . the tinker . . . don't you think, sir?'

'Couldn't agree more.'

'Fine. That's that sorted then. Up you come, Annie . . .' She pulled a towel from the drying rack by the fire and enveloped the little girl's pink and slippery body.

'How was your Christmas, Sergeant?'

'Ghastly. And yours, sir?'

'Pretty much the same.' He threw a quick glance to check that Eileen wasn't in earshot and then murmured, 'I suppose you've heard about M . . . A . . . U . . . R . . . Y.'

'I can spell Maury,' Annaliese announced, pushing her head through a gap in the towel. 'He's gone away. Auntie Eileen's sad, but Sammy's pleased 'cos he's got a whole bed to himself.'

Sarah laughed and hastily turned it into a cough as Eileen appeared, towing a sulky-faced Sammy.

'Go on, get in that water before it turns cold.'

'It is cold. Why do I always 'ave to go second?'

Watching Sarah brushing out Annaliese's wet tresses, Jack said: 'I met Death up at your lodgings.'

'Dee-arth,' Sarah corrected.

'He looked at me like he wished he was the Grim Reaper's messenger. I definitely got the impression that if he'd had a bit of plague and pestilence handy it would have come my way.'

'Max? He's a sweetie. Well . . .' Sarah temporised, 'he is normally. What did you do to upset him?'

'Me? Nothing. Except ask directions to your room. He's not switched his affections to you, has he?'

'No. It's still Nell. Very much so, in fact.'

'I had the impression he thought you might have told me about something that had occurred during the St Albans jaunt. I assume it was something a policeman shouldn't know about? In an official capacity?'

'I . . . em . . .' The dilemma fought a transparent battle across Sarah's face. Whatever knowledge she and Max Death shared, she obviously didn't want to tell him. He saw the problem resolve itself just before she spoke. 'No,' she said firmly. 'There was nothing I can think of . . . it must have been your imagination . . . sir.'

'I see . . .' *Only too well*, Jack might have added. It wasn't the first time he'd had to have words with Sarah over her somewhat individual interpretation of what constituted valid evidence. 'Now look here . . .' The scream of the air-raid siren cut straight through his words and reverberated round the steamy walls.

For a moment no one reacted. After nearly three weeks of quiet nights, it was almost a physical blow. How dare they bother London again? Hadn't they taken enough during the past four months?

'Maybe they'll go over,' Eileen said. 'I know it ain't very Christian to wish them on somewhere else. But they'll just have to do their own wishing and push 'em on a bit further.'

Flicking off the lights, Jack opened the back door. They could see the crisscross of silver searchlight beams probing the sky to the south. They were too far away to hear the howling scream of the descending bombs, but the rumbles of explosions carried clearly. An answering bark of ack-ack fire spat from several directions at once.

The rolling thunder came closer. When the guns in Regent's Park opened up, they moved as one, grabbing children, food and matches and stumbling out into the Anderson shelter. At the last second Eileen took a letter from her pocket and propped it against the teapot on the kitchen table.

'For Pat,' she explained briefly, her voice low so it wouldn't carry to the children. 'In case the house makes it and . . .'

Jack nodded. She didn't need to finish. Even Anderson shelters got hit sometimes.

Chapter 32

'Ruthie, that you? I've deceased to gather in . . . hospital morgue . . .'

His nose pointed towards the hall ceiling, Duggie Miller struggled to insert collar studs whilst his Adam's apple bobbed beneath his probing fingers. A final convulsive heave locked the sharp linen band into position and allowed Duggie to drop his gaze to the figure in the open front door.

'Hatty! You're back. Safe and sound. Praise the Lord!'

'Amen,' Hatty murmured. Her eyes closed and she leant wearily against the wall.

'You look awful, girl. Smell it too,' Duggie added, stepping closer and catching a full blast of the odours emanating from the uniform and sweating body.

Hatty opened her eyes and stared at him for a second. Then her plump mouth twisted, her throat gave a convulsive heave and she burst into noisy sobs.

'Hey, now, now. Don't take on so. I didn't mean . . .' Horrified at the reaction he'd triggered in his normally placid niece, Duggie steered her into the kitchen and picked up the kettle. 'Cup of tea, eh? Soon make you feel more yourself. I wouldn't worry about the smell. I daresay I just caught a whiff from the canal out back.'

'No you didn't. It's me . . .' Hatty hiccuped miserably. 'But there wasn't no hot water in the places they billeted us. And no soap. Just fleas and mice . . . And the girl driving the van smoked all the time.'

'Everyone smokes, Hatty.'

'Not like her. Woodbine Winnie they called her. She was picking dog-ends up out the rubble when she couldn't cadge fags off anyone. The whole van stinks of her. I had to scrub it clean before they let me come off duty. And I'm so *tired*.'

'Yes. Well, you would be. Stands to reason. Labouring in the Lord's vineyards, so to speak . . .'

'It wasn't a vineyard, it was a bomb site. It was hundreds of bomb sites.'

'Aye I know, Hatty love. Tough, was it?' He came to sit opposite her and took her plump hands in his slim ones.

'Yes. No. I mean it was *awful*, Uncle Duggie. There was people who'd lost everything. I mean, their houses and their families and just every blessed thing, Uncle Duggie.' She gave a convulsive gulp which set the rolls of fat down her neck rippling into the tunic of her uniform.

Duggie squeezed the fingers resting in his own. 'That's the way it is, Hatty. There's no sense getting yourself in a state. Just thank the Lord that we've been spared.'

'It's not that.' Hatty raised a guilty face. 'It's . . . it's that I didn't feel sorry enough for them, Uncle Duggie.'

For eighteen hours a day she'd handed out sandwiches, buns and biscuits, and lugged buckets of water from standpipes to refill the urns. At night she'd wrapped herself in blankets that smelt of damp and mice and tried to sleep on the floor of the abandoned school where they'd been billeted.

'And all I could think about, Uncle Duggie,' she confessed, 'was how rotten I was feeling. Every time I thought about Camden Town I just got this great big lump in me chest, and I cried – all the time.'

'That's nothing to get yourself in a state about, Hat. You were homesick, that's all. Happens to the best of us. Happened to me and your dad when we got sent to Froggie Land in the Great War.'

'You don't think I was being wicked, then?'

'You're the least wicked person I know, Hat.' With another reassuring squeeze Duggie picked up the whistling kettle and discovered they were out of tea. They were, however, he realised, well blessed at the moment with dirty pots, greasy plates and grubby towels and shirts. 'We've missed you, Hat,' he said with real sincerity. When there was no response, he turned back from the food cupboard and found her sound asleep at the kitchen table.

'Hat . . . ?' He had to shake her awake. She raised a drawn face framed by a curtain of greasy rat-tails. 'You'd best get yourself up to bed, my girl. Unless you want to open your presents first?'

'What presents?'

'Why, your Christmas presents, of course. Thanks for the baccy pouch, love. And Ruthie was real taken with her scarf. Proper silk, wasn't it?'

'It was a remnant. I sewed it up myself. You couldn't tell, could you?'

'Shouldn't think so. You know how particular Ruth is. Everything's got to be just right . . . Mind you, just lately she hasn't . . .'

Duggie stopped on a frown, leaving Hatty to guess that her cousin was still behaving strangely. Not that she really cared at the moment. Every part of her body seemed to ache. She longed for her bed. But before she could get to it, her uncle insisted on escorting her into the parlour and pointing out the knitted stocking they'd left hanging from the mantel-piece.

'Just like always, eh, Hat? Don't suppose you got much of a Christmas dinner, did you?'

'Corned beef sandwich and a bit of chocolate.'

'Well, there you are, then . . . there's an orange in the bottom . . . just like always. Go on, love, open it.'

Hatty found tears streaming down her face again. Turning, she flung her arms round her uncle and snuggled on to his shoulder. 'We'll always have Christmas together, won't we, Uncle Duggie?'

'God willing, love.' He patted her back reassuringly whilst discreetly trying to loosen her grip.

'When I'm married, you and Ruth will come to me for Christmas Day, won't you? Promise.'

' 'Course I promise, Hatty.'

For the first time it occurred to Duggie Miller how unlikely it was that Hatty would ever marry. He loved her like a daughter, saw all her good points and overlooked the faults. But suddenly, for a brief flash, he saw her as another man might see her: lumpish, shy and awkward. What chance would his poor Hatty have if this war killed off the young blokes with the ferocity that the last Great War had?

'Plenty of time for that, Hat. You don't want to be leaving your old uncle yet, do you?'

'No. No. But I wouldn't really be leaving, Uncle Duggie. I mean, I'll come round and do your washing and shopping. And you could have your dinner round our house whenever you want.'

'Our house?'

Hatty blushed and smiled shyly.

Duggie experienced a mixture of surprise and regret. So she'd got a bloke already, and pipped Ruthie to the altar. 'Well you're a quiet one, Hat. Why haven't you brought him round for his tea?'

'Oh, I *will*, Uncle Duggie. I went over the station soon as I got back to say he ought to come meet you, now it's sort of official. Only the crews are all out damping down.'

'Big raid last night, Hat.'

'A thousand fires over London, the control room said. But all under control by dawn.' Hatty delivered the news with the pride of a fireman's intended.

Duggie suppressed his regrets and concentrated on her pleasure. 'So does our Ruthie know she'll be tripping up the aisle as a bridesmaid yet?'

'No. I . . . we . . . haven't told no one yet, Uncle Duggie. Len didn't want me to say anything before . . . but we ought to start making plans now, oughtn't we?'

'Len who?'

They were still standing face to face. Hatty dropped her gaze and started fiddling with the buttons on his mourning waistcoat, as she stumbled through the whole story.

'I know it wasn't exactly right, Len being married. But Mrs Shaw never looked after him properly. And she's left him now. And it's me he loves.'

'He told you that, did he?'

Hatty raised her eyes. She'd never heard that tone in her uncle's voice before. 'Yes. God's honour, he did.'

'And he wants to wed you?'

'Oh yes.' Hatty nodded vigorously.

'Right. He's not up the station now, you say?'

'No. I told you. All the crews are marked out.'

'When's he due off duty?'

'I'm not sure.' Hatty tried to visualise the chalked notes she'd seen in the control room. 'The watch's trip ends eleven o'clock Monday morning, I think.'

The blare of a motor horn announced the arrival of Mottram and Cropper's hearse outside the house.

'I've got to go collect the deceased, Hat. You get yourself to bed. You and me will have another talk when I get home about this here wedding. And then, Monday morning, we'll go pay a call on this Len of yours.'

'I'll be at work, Uncle Duggie.'

'No you won't, Hat. You tell them it's a family emergency and meet me outside the station eleven sharp.' The hearse's horn blared impatiently, reminding Duggie that the dead in this case wouldn't wait. Pulling on his black frock coat, he asked if anyone else knew about this engagement of hers.

'No. Except Len, of course.'

'Not our Ruthie?'

Hatty shook her head.

'Right, now you listen to me, Hat. Don't you go telling *anyone*, understand? Best place for dirty linen is in your own washing copper – not hung out for all to gawp at.'

'Len's not dirty linen, he's the man I'm going to marry. And I will marry him, Uncle Duggie, no matter what anyone says. He's what I want.' Her lips compressed into a determinedly stubborn line that warned Duggie it was pointless to argue. Not that he had any intention of doing so.

'Oh yes, Hat, he'll marry you. Don't you fret about that. I'll see he does right by you. And if he don't, I'll be straight down Lambeth for a quiet word with a higher authority.'

'The archbishop?'

'The fire brigade headquarters,' Duggie said grimly. 'Now

330

you get to your bed and we'll talk after I've coffined the lately departed.'

Chapter 33

'Blimey, what a pong!'

The bottom section of the sash window crashed upwards. Hatty sat up with a gasp of fright. For a moment the nets streaming in the breeze and the rumbling of the goods wagons gathering speed over the railway arches at the bottom of the garden all mingled together. She was back in Manchester and a bombed building was falling on the canteen van, the tattered remnants of the curtains billowing towards her as the wall slowly toppled.

Then she saw Ruth perched on the edge of her own bed, pulling her uniform off.

'What time is it?'

'Nineish.'

'At night?'

'Sunday morning.'

Blearily Hat tried to assimilate the fact that she'd slept through a whole day.

Ruth stepped into a skirt and fastened it. 'They said at the station you come back yesterday. You didn't say hello.'

'You were asleep down in the basement.'

'Big raid Friday night. We was on the phones and movements boards the 'ole time. All the appliances were out, right across the whole division.' Shaking free her hair, Ruth gave thanks that this was her day off.

Pulling a blanket round herself, Hatty swung her legs over the side of the bed. 'Have you seen Uncle Duggie?'

'He's gone out. He's got funerals all day.'

'Sunday?'

Ruth raised her shoulders. That careless indifference to

the workings of the rest of the world that Hatty had noticed before she left was still there. Something had died in Ruth. The spark that had attracted others to her had somehow gone out. Tentatively Hatty asked if she'd seen Stan over Christmas.

'Stan?' Ruth stared blankly. 'No. Ain't heard a word from him. Why?'

'Just wondered. I mean, you want to be with people you love at Christmas, don't you?' Swimming happily in the warm certainty of her own love, Hatty wanted everyone else to jump in the water.

'Love? I don't love flamin' Stan. I don't love *anybody*,' Ruth declared vehemently. 'And I'm not going to. I'm finished with blokes.'

'You don't mean that, Ruth.'

'How'd you know what I mean?' Ruth rounded on her cousin, her eyes flashing dangerously. 'What you know about it anyway? You've never had a bloke look at you twice. Most of 'em don't look once.'

'Well, that's all you know . . . I'm going to be married . . .' Belatedly Hatty remembered she'd promised her uncle she wouldn't talk about the wedding until he'd spoken to Len. 'One day,' she finished lamely.

'Hell will freeze over first. In fact, it'll probably 'ave polar bears . . .'

'Why are you being like this? What have I done, Ruth?' Hatty stood up, clasping the blanket tighter. For a moment she was tempted to burst into tears. Then anger grabbed her tongue instead. 'Anyhow, I've got more chance than you. Blokes don't want to marry a wriggling bottom and a mouthful of sticky lipstick. They want someone who can cook proper and keep the house nice.'

Ruth gave a forced laugh. 'Since when did you get to be such an expert on men, Richmal Harriet Miller?'

'Longer ago than you think.' Banging open the wardrobe door, Hatty started rummaging through hangers. Only her feet and ankles were visible. Ruth watched them stepping into brown socks.

' 'Adn't you better have a wash first? Or does this bloke of yours 'ave a thing about pigs?'

Hatty emerged in her spare white uniform shirt, plain brown skirt and brown jacket. She was pushing a towel and her soap into a shopping bag. 'I'm on duty. I'll go in the Prince of Wales Baths on the way. And I think you're real mean, Ruth. I was so looking forward to coming home and now you've gone and spoilt *everything*.' She kicked her uniform, which was lying on the floor. 'And you can wash this if you don't like the stink. In fact, you can clean the whole house. Why should I have to do everything?'

Since she'd always jealously guarded her right to be chief cook and charwoman, the sheer unfairness of this remark kept Ruth open-mouthed until she heard the front door slam. Then she sat down heavily on her bed again, and sobbed herself breathless.

She hadn't meant to be nasty to poor Hatty. In fact, she'd been missing her more than she'd have believed possible. But that was how things were lately. One minute she didn't seem to care about anything; and the next the stupidest things got her so mad she'd start lashing around, saying all sorts of awful things she didn't mean. Sometimes it got so bad she just didn't recognise the voice coming out her mouth as her own. It was all Paul's fault. Everything had been all right before he'd . . .

That night in the club came back, filling up her mind with its sights and smells. Thick tobacco smoke; the young pilots who'd looked dead as they danced under the artificial lights; the knowing smirks and glances in her direction; her head whirling and the sickness in her stomach; the sweet, perfumy scent of the pillow as Paul had pressed it over her face, and the dreadful pain inside her as he . . . She gave an involuntary moan. The sound jerked her back into the present.

Hatty's uniform was still lying on the floor. 'Wash it,' she'd said; as though she thought Ruth wasn't pulling her weight. Bundling it up, Ruth fled downstairs to the scullery and flung the trousers and overalls in the sink.

There was no hot water, since there'd been no one home to light the back boiler; but she boiled up saucepans and tipped the steaming liquid over the navy material. She added cold, then looked round for the soap. The thick yellow bar was nearly as big as a housebrick – and twice as hard. Fetching the carving knife, Ruth forced thin slivers off the waxy lump and swished them into the water.

The weight of the uniform took her by surprise. She could scarcely lift it to rub the material together. Fetching the wooden scrubbing board, she rested it in the sink and started to work the overalls up and down the ridged board. The scullery shook as a train passed, setting a ripple of vibrations across the sudsy water. Looking upwards, Ruth followed the slow progress of the goods wagon passing across the brick arches. *Not even first-class coaches*, she thought to herself. *Just rotten dirty coal trucks*. She let her eyes move from the arches, that stretched above roof height, to the cramped yard with its outside lavatory and back again to the soot-smeared scullery window.

Even though Paul had never been to her home, she'd bet he'd guessed exactly what it would be like. It was the sort of place where people who didn't need to be taken seriously lived. Just working-class nobodies that no one would listen to if they complained about some posh RAF officer with a fancy accent.

'Well I ain't always going to be living here, Squadron Leader Bloody Smarty-Pants,' she promised the silent yard. 'I've got plans. I'm going to have a posh house and a posh car too. Then you'll see. You had no right . . . no right . . .' With each sentence, she angrily thrust the cloth over the scrubbing board. Her breath came in short pants. Globules of soapy froth flew up, sticking to her hair and splattering over the scullery floor. Her knuckles scraped over the board. Tributaries of blood sent pale-pink streams into the water. The heavy material blocked the plug hole and tidal waves of cold rinsing water splashed over on to her feet. She didn't care. She hardly noticed.

She had to get rid of Paul. Drown the awful memory of him.

A neighbour seeing her attempting to lift the soaked uniform over the washing line called across that it would never dry in this weather. 'You want to take it up the drying rooms in the public laundry tomorrow.'

Ruth ignored her. She felt a little better. She'd got rid of a bit of Paul. Now if she could just wash the rest of him away, perhaps she'd stop feeling dirty.

There was plenty of washing. She collected up sheets, towels, shirts and collars. She opened drawers and took out all her own underwear, then added Hatty's and her father's. Heaping it all in the centre of the scullery floor, she set all the pans she could find to boil on the gas stove. Deciding she'd need even more hot water, she lit the fire, poking up the coals with the brass poker until they glowed bright red.

She lost track of time as she scrubbed, plunged and wrung out. The hot water ran out and the icy cold opened cracks in her fingers, but she hardly noticed. There wasn't enough room for all of the washing out on the lines. She had to leave a great pile in the tin bath whilst the other half slapped protestingly in the cold December wind. Her shoulders and back ached from the unaccustomed exercise and her front and legs were wet through, but she didn't care. She felt oddly exhilarated.

A sharp rap on the front door brought her back to reality. It was late; the early-afternoon dusk was already falling outside and the hall was dark and unlit. Her caller was framed against the paler grey of the exterior light, and it took a second for her eyes to adjust. Long enough for him to step across the door mat, flick something over the stair banister, hang his hat on the newel post, and take the door handle from her.

'Hello, sweetie. Pleased to see me?'

He'd got an arm round her waist and was pulling her against him. She wanted to scream and kick, but none of her limbs would obey her brain. It was as if this was happening to someone else.

The taste of his lips on hers brought her back to life.

'Let go! Get out!'

He couldn't be here. He couldn't. She'd got rid of him; washed him away. She struggled against the uniform jacket, trying to push free, whilst her toes hacked at his shins with futile desperation.

'Whoa. Still lively, I see.'

She tried to claw at his face. That at least worked. He

dropped her and grabbed her wrists instead, holding her away effortlessly.

'Get out! Get out!'

'Oh come on, Ruth. You're not still in a miff, are you? It's pitch in here. Where's the light switch?'

'How did you find me? I never said where I lived.'

He picked up an article he'd draped over the banister. 'Left your jacket behind at Polly's.' He fished in the pocket and drew out a small beige card between two fingers. 'Identity card.'

She hadn't even missed it.

He flicked the blackout curtain across. The hall light illuminated her bedraggled hair and damp, creased clothes.

'Good heavens, sweetie, whatever have you been doing to yourself?' He flicked a tendril from her cheek. She flinched.

'Get away from me or I'll scream.'

'Whatever for?' He seemed genuinely amused.

'You . . . you *raped* me!' It was the first time she'd actually put it into words. Somehow hearing it out loud like that was almost as bad as the physical violation. She'd been raped.

'Raped?' Paul repeated incredulously. 'Oh come on, Ruth. All right, so I had to persuade you a bit. But you enjoyed it as much as I did once you got going. You know you did. There's no need for the missish act.'

'I ain't. I didn't.' Tears squeezed from her lids and rolled down her cheeks.

He took her chin between his thumb and forefinger and raised it. She wanted to run, scream. But she was frozen here at the end of the hall, with the scullery door handle pressed into the small of her back.

'Look, sweetie, if I raped you, why aren't I under arrest?'

'I . . . I . . .'

'Didn't report it?'

He read the answer in her eyes. 'And why not? Because it didn't happen, right? I didn't exactly have to throw you over my shoulder and carry you up to that bedroom, did I?'

Mutely Ruth shook her head.

'And a little cutie like you must know what a bed's for.' He kissed her lightly. 'Now come on, admit you enjoyed it really.

337

You don't need to pretend with me. I've got the car outside. Get yourself tidied up and I'll take you up west. Here, I've got you a little present. Merry Christmas.'

He pushed a slim box into her hands. It was gold and glossy, with '*Lucille*' flowing across it in black script. Ruth stared blankly at it.

'Well? Aren't you going to open it?'

She saw her hands moving without being conscious of telling them to do so. A silver powder compact fell into her palm.

'Like it?'

She looked up into his handsome face. For the first time she noticed the streak of purpling bruising stretching from forehead to jaw.

Taking her by the forearms, he lifted her up for another kiss. 'There's a matching lipstick case. Maybe I'll buy it for you next time.'

It was that 'next time' that galvanised her into action. She heard Eunice's amused drawl making fun of her shoes; calling her 'a five-bob tart'.

'Next time? You stuck-up *pig*. How dare you! D'ya think I can be bought with some cheap present? Here . . .'

She threw the compact into his face. More by luck than accurate aiming, it hit the healing bruise and cut the skin open before bouncing off and skittering away along the hall.

'You little . . .'

Drawing back his hand, Paul hit her across the cheek. The blow rattled her head against the scullery door. Her hand dropped on the handle and she half fell backwards through the opening door.

He tried to grab her. Whimpering with fright, she turned and sped towards the back door. Paul caught her round the waist and pulled her back. 'Whoops. No we don't, sweetie.'

They were by the sink. The thick yellow soap was still on the draining board, the carving knife thrust into its waxy crust. Snatching it up, she drew the blade across the hand pressed into her waist.

'Ouch. God! You little *bitch*!'

Panting, Ruth swung round, the blade held threateningly in front of her. 'Stay away from me!'

He was trying to fold a handkerchief round the cut hand. Blood was oozing from a long, thin cut. 'It'll be a pleasure, sweetie, believe me. Should I wait for an introduction to your next caller?'

He indicated the washing-strewn yard behind her. Ruth glanced out. A hand locked round the wrist holding the knife and twisted cruelly.

'Oh, sorry, my mistake. Must have been a trick of the light.' Paul stooped to retrieve the knife from the floor and placed it out of reach. 'Looks like it's just you and me, Ruth.'

He was still holding her wrist. He used it now to pull her towards him whilst his other hand fumbled with the fastening of her skirt. It dropped to the floor and he massaged her bottom appreciatively.

'Hmm . . . very nice.'

She drew in a huge breath, ready to scream her head off. He frustrated her by clamping his mouth over hers again. Deliberately she forced herself to relax, curving her body into his and running her free hand up the nape of his neck.

'Hmm . . . that's more like it.'

Ruth giggled. His grip slackened slightly. She snapped her teeth shut over his probing tongue and twisted free.

The poker was still leaning by the grate. She grabbed, spun and hit out in one movement. The metal caught him across the forehead and his feet skidded on the wet soapy tiles as he tried to regain his balance. Grasping the handle with both hands, Ruth lashed out again. This time he fell. She heard the crack as his head hit the corner of the stone sink and saw the surprise in his eyes turn to a fixed stare. Two-handed, she brought the poker down again.

She didn't know how many times she hit him. When she finally came to her senses, she was sitting in a corner of the scullery, hugging her knees, staring across at the slumped figure lying beneath the sink. She crawled across and touched the cold hand. It wasn't a nightmare; it was real. She'd killed a man. An RAF squadron leader. A hero with medals from the

339

Battle of Britain. No one would believe it was self-defence. They'd hang her as a murderess.

Whimpering quietly, she knelt up, using the sink edge for support. Leaning against the stone, she vomited into the basin.

It was completely dark outside now, the rows of washing cracking noisily in a ghostly semaphore across the yard. What on earth had she been thinking about? Nothing would ever dry in this weather. She gave a hysterical giggle. Fancy worrying whether Dad's combinations were dry when in a few weeks they'd be putting a rope round her neck and . . .

A movement in the sheets caught her eye. Not a gentle waving, but a definite ripple approaching the house. Someone was coming, pushing the washing out of the way as they made their way towards the door. Straining her eyes in the blackness, she tried to see whether she'd put the bolt across.

The latch clicked up and down. Ruth held her breath. Then her heart started to hammer in her throat as the door slowly swung open.

Chapter 34

Slowly – very slowly – the door opened wider. She could make out a hazy silhouette against the paler wall. A man.

He reached up and drew his hat off, squeezing it flat between his fingers. Seen like that, with the outline of the close-cropped hair, the curve of the cheek and the pug nose, she suddenly knew who it was.

'Stan!'

He swung round towards the direction of her voice. 'Oh, yer 'ere. I thought there weren't nobody in the kitchen . . .'

His voice died away. She saw his head tilt downwards and for a moment thought he'd seen the body. Then she followed the direction of his gaze and saw her own legs gleaming palely. She'd forgotten she wasn't wearing a skirt. It was still on the floor somewhere by the table, where Paul had dragged it off.

'Where is he?'

'Who? Wh . . . what?' Ruth stuttered.

' 'Im. Don't give me no whoppers, Ruth. I seen his motor parked out front. It's that flying johnny, ain't it? Well, if that's the sort of toffee-nosed useless . . .'

Indignation and hurt were carrying him towards her in a rush; his eyes on her face rather than the pitch-dark floor. One boot caught beneath Paul's ribs and he was forced to grab at the sink to stop himself tipping over.

'What the hell . . . ?'

His first wild thought – that Ruth had actually been doing it with the bloke on the kitchen floor – was dismissed almost as soon as it entered his mind. His brain chalked up the total lack of reaction to a pair of size twelves in the ribs, whilst his subconscious registered no sound of breathing. Anger changed to alarm.

'Ruth?'

'Oh Stan . . .' Ruth burst into noisy tears. Deep, shuddering breaths shook her entire body.

'What's 'appened?' He groped over the inert body, his hands confirming what his brain had already told him. The bloke was a goner. 'Did 'e 'ave an accident? Ruth, shut up will yer and tell us what's up.' Grabbing her shoulder, he tried to shake her quiet. It had the opposite effect and sent her into hysterics.

Burnt feathers or cold water, his mum had always said. Well, he weren't finding no flaming chicken, so . . . spinning the cold water tap, Stan grabbed Ruth's neck and pushed her under the stream.

It worked. She gave one final shriek then lapsed into quiet weeping. Satisfied, Stan let her up and clumsily dried her face with his handkerchief.

'I'll stick the light on. Get the blackout across.'

He could hear her hiccuping quietly as he felt his way across the room to the light switch. A deepening of the blackness told him she'd pulled the blind into position. He clicked the switch down, turned back, and saw Paul De Groot's face clearly.

'Gawd, Ruth! His head!'

The hiccups became stronger. 'I don't care, Stan . . . he deserved it . . . the rotten pig . . . he . . . he *raped* me, Stan.'

'He what!'

Stan crossed the scullery in two strides. The toe of his boot connected with Paul's ribs with considerably more force than the last time. Drawing it back, he lashed out again. The inert body jerked with each blow.

'Stop it! Stop it!' Ruth flung herself forward into his arms. 'Oh Stan, help me, please.'

'Yeah, 'course I will.' Awkwardly Stan patted her shoulder. This was his dream. He had Ruth half-naked in his arms. But instead of being a dream, it had turned into a nightmare. 'You stop here, Ruth. I'll go fetch a copper.'

'No!' She grabbed his uniform and shook him. 'No,' she repeated. 'They'll hang me, Stan.'

' 'Course they won't. I mean, if he really . . . done what you said . . . then they'll see you was just defending yourself.'

'They won't. He's an officer, Stan. A squadron leader. He was in the Battle of Britain. He's a *hero*. Nobody's gonna believe me. It's like he said . . . I went upstairs with him at the club . . .'

'What club?'

Pushing her wet hair off her face, Ruth retrieved her skirt from the floor, stepped into it and sat down at the table. Placing her hands flat on the scrubbed wood, she stumbled through an account of the night at Polly's.

Stan listened with a growing sense of unreality. Whatever he'd expected from his visit to Ruth it certainly hadn't been this.

Ever since they'd been confined to barracks the week before Christmas he'd been racking his brains to find some way to get out and demand an explanation from her as to why she'd been lying about her visits to his sister Lulu. Not to mention what the hell she thought she'd been playing at leaving him standing outside the ladies' lav on their last date.

Leave was out of the question. Only dispatch riders and officers were getting past the main gate. For days he'd kicked his heels in barracks, wondering whether he dare risk skipping camp. But how could he? Ready to leave at an hour's notice, those were the orders according to mess hut rumours. He'd be charged with desertion if he wasn't there when they got their movement orders.

Then, just when he'd run out of bargains to offer God, the Devil and anyone else who might be interested, fate had decided it was his turn for the luck. Which basically meant that his mate Charlie on the motorcycle had to get the hex. In this case a dog hurtling across his path as he approached the front sentry post. They'd heard the crack of Charlie's leg breaking clear across the parade ground.

Stan had been one of the first there. Hot on the heels of the adjutant.

'Blast it, man,' the officer had barked at the groaning rider whilst the bike was lifted off him. 'Those returns are due at the

War Office by four. Now I'll get it in the neck. They don't give a damn how many of you useless oiks I lose. But paperwork . . .'

Stan leapt in to offer his services. 'Drove a bus all over London,' he exaggerated. 'Be there and back before you can say "Be back by twenty-three-hundred-o-fifty-nine, Wilkins".'

'You'd better be back long before that, Wilkins . . .'

'Yessir!!' Grinning, he'd dragged off Charlie's gloves and dispatch pouches, to muttered curses and descriptions of his parentage from his groaning mate.

All the way down to Whitehall and back up to Camden Town, he'd been trying to imagine what his meeting with Ruth would be like.

He'd recognised the motor parked outside immediately as the one that had nearly knocked him over outside the auxiliary fire station the other week. He'd never doubted the driver had called on Ruth. Who else in this little street would interest an RAF officer with an expensive car like that? But some perverse belief that Ruthie was still *his* girl had made him slip round the back. He'd even had some wild idea about inviting the man outside to settle the matter with a bunch of fives. He'd been pretty confident he could smash some soft-living officer's face in. Never in his wildest dreams had he imagined that Ruth would have already done just that.

'Please, *please* help me, Stan, and I'll love you for ever. I swear.'

He knew that going straight round to the police was the sensible choice. Let the rozzers sort the mess out. If they caught him trying to hide an officer's body . . .

Ruth's blue eyes pleaded from across the table. Reaching across, she took both his hands. 'Please, Stan.'

The rising wail of the air-raid alert brought him another brief respite. A moment later they heard the guns barking in response to the first wave of planes.

'Stan?'

He made up his mind. 'Where's yer dad? And Hatty?'

'Work. They'll stop there until the all-clear now.'

'Right.' Stan stood up. Taking towels from the washing pile, he knelt and wrapped them round Paul's bloody head. 'That'll stop him leaking more. You get the rest of the mess wiped up. I'm going to fetch the bike.'

Grabbing up the floor cloth, Ruth mopped and rinsed with a will. Stan returned a few minutes later, heaving the motorbike into the kitchen.

'I can't risk nobody nicking it from the yard while we're shifting johnny.'

'Paul. His name's Paul.'

'I don't bleedin' care, do I?' He glared down at her where she was crouched rubbing blood spots from the bottom of the sink.

'Sorry, Stan,' Ruth sniffed.

'No, don't start snivelling again. Here.' He gave her his damp handkerchief.

'Ta. What we going to do, Stan? Maybe we could throw him in the canal?'

'And have him bobbing up a couple of days later? And his motor's still parked outside.'

Ruth raised trusting eyes to him. She was expecting him to come up with an answer. Outside, the distant roar and rumble of explosions to the south suggested that the Luftwaffe's efforts were being concentrated on the City and docks again.

'Where's yer uniform, Ruth?'

'Upstairs.'

'Go put it on.'

'But . . . why?'

'I ain't got time to explain. Go on, scarper.'

Ruth fled. Her damp clothes stuck to her skin. She fumbled with a tin of carnation-scented talcum powder that Hatty had bought her for her birthday. The lid came off, spilling the contents over her bed. Half sobbing with frustration, she patted handfuls over herself, dragged on her AFS tunic and trousers, scooped up the tin helmet and gas mask case and ran downstairs again.

Bursting into the scullery, she froze with shock. There was another RAF officer in the kitchen. His back was to her as he bent over Paul's body. She looked round wildly for Stan. But he'd gone. Made a run for it presumably when he saw the other officer coming.

He hadn't seen her yet. Maybe she still had a chance if she could reach the front door. Holding her breath, she backed away and collided with the resting motorbike.

'Watch it! We've really 'ad it if you go an' break yer leg too.'

The 'officer' grabbed the falling bike and righted it again.

'Stan! What are yer playing at?' Beyond him now she could see Paul had been stripped to his underpants and vest.

'Car,' Stan said succinctly. ' 'Ow many privates you think could afford a motor like that? Get pulled over by the first copper who sees us, we would. Anyhow, someone might have seen 'im drive up. And now they're gonna see an RAF officer drive off again, right? So it don't matter if he turns up as a stiff later, 'cos he was OK when he left here, get it?'

Ruth did. Her eyes shone with admiration for his cleverness. It was everything he'd ever wanted from her. But now – like a lot of people before him – Stan discovered that wanting something was often better than getting it.

'Is there any more of his stuff around here? Where's his hat?'

Ruth fetched it from the banister. The silver compact was lying by the door, where it had skidded after she'd thrown it at him.

'It was a present. I chucked it at him.'

Stan thrust it into a pocket without comment. 'I'll bring the car round the back. Does anyone shelter under the railway arches?'

'Some that use the lock-ups. But they'll not be working Sundays.'

'Go take a look.'

Mesmerised by this new, self-confident Stan, Ruth fought her way through the wildly blowing washing, peeked out the back gate, and came back to report that the doors across the lock-ups were all closed.

'Right.' Stan bundled up his own uniform and picked up the bloodied and bent poker. 'Get this light out and find a blanket or something to hide him under. Be ready to move soon as I come back, OK?'

Ruth nodded. She pulled the blanket from her own bed, sending clouds of highly scented powder into the air, and hurried back to the dark scullery. As she waited, she heard the throaty roar of the car burst into life and purr away. Somewhere farther away, she caught the clang of fire bells. Peeking under the blackout curtain, she thought she could detect the faint glow of orange on the undersides of the clouds to the south.

The gentle idling of an engine beyond the back wall announced Stan's arrival. She had the back door open before he reached it.

'Grab his legs,' Stan ordered, inserting his own hands under the armpits.

Between them they fought their way through the washing lines once more and out to the back alley.

'You'd better pray none of your neighbours was looking out their bedroom windows,' Stan grunted, swinging the body into the front. He'd already put the hood up, and by heaving and pushing they managed to thrust Paul over the seats into the small gap at the back and throw the blanket over him. 'Get in. And listen, if we get stopped, you're going on duty and I'm giving yer a lift there.'

'Where are we going?'

He didn't answer until they were moving swiftly down towards King's Cross. Then he pointed forwards. 'Into that, Ruth, that's where we're going. Into the raid. 'Cos that's where they're gonna find all the poor dead B's tomorrow.'

Ruth stared upwards. AA shells were bursting overhead, and she could hear, though not see, the whining engine of a plane straining to get clear of the guns. Her head was jerked suddenly sideways as Stan pulled over to let a fire convoy rush past, its bells clanging wildly in the near-deserted streets.

Ruth counted: six pumps; two escapes; four dual-purpose. 'It must be massive, Stan. Look, there's another lot going in!' She pointed to a convoy of red appliances turning into Pentonville Road ahead of them.

'Lucky for us. Plenty of places to put johnny. Wow, this is a terrific car, Ruth. I'll have one like this one day, see if I don't.'

Startled, Ruth glanced sideways and saw that Stan's eyes

were dancing beneath the RAF cap. She opened her mouth to snap at him that this wasn't supposed to be fun. Then shut it again. He was saving her life. And risking his own to do it. If he got to enjoy an expensive car for a little while, it seemed only fair.

The convoy went down City Road. Stan tagged on to the end of it.

'Follow a fire engine to find a fire, eh?'

'I don't think we need 'elp, Stan. Look.'

To the south the whole skyline was ablaze. Thick black smoke lay like pie crust over a glowing dish of flames.

The convoy had come to a halt opposite the lunatic asylum. Men were pouring out, connecting up hoses to hydrants and hauling pumps over to the temporary dam. A London Fire Brigade officer dressed in full uniform, including unbelievably white gloves and a brass helmet with a nodding coxcomb of black feathers, was strutting around, waving his arms and presumably shouting orders. It was becoming impossible to hear over the roar of flames and crashing buildings.

They caught the warning whistle just in time and ducked as another Molotov breadbasket of incendiaries burst in the road ahead. Shrapnel and glass rained down on the car's bonnet and splattered on the canopy.

'Stan!'

He'd already released the brake and was bumping slowly over the crisscross of hoses snaking across the road. The officer stepped forward with the intention of preventing them from moving into the danger area, but he was distracted by the appearance of two firemen stumbling out of a blazing building.

'Stan, one of them was on fire . . .'

Ruth strained to look back, but Stan had turned the car right, cutting off her restricted view. He tried to go down another alley and was halted by the appearance of a policeman.

'Not 'ere, sir. Get yourself down a shelter.'

Putting on a high-class accent, Stan explained that the lady had to get to work. 'Fire Control, you know. Absolutely essential in the circumstances, old boy.'

'Oh. I see.' A shaded torch was played over Ruth's uniform. 'Where d'you work, miss?'

The name of a city fire station popped into Ruth's head: 'Whitecross Street.'

'It's right in the middle of this lot. Best turn back.'

'I can't. I'll report in at another station if I 'ave to.'

'You've got a plucky one there, sir.' Saluting, the policeman stepped back, and then was forced to fling himself flat as another burst of high explosives blasted out the windows in the building behind him. With a loud 'whoosh', flames burst out through the shattered frames.

Forgetting the upper-class accent, Stan shouted out: 'Are you all right, mate?'

Still face-down, the policeman raised a thumb.

Slamming his foot down, Stan shot away. He took corners and turns at random. Contrary to what he'd told the adjutant, his bus-driving career had all been spent in north London, and he didn't know the rest of the city well. He needed to find a quiet spot that the raiders had already partially flattened; but it seemed as though everywhere he chose was ablaze and chock-full of firemen and their appliances.

The heat and smoke was becoming unbearable. The interior of the car was full of the smell of scorching from the hood. Where it had holed, warm, sticky sprays of water dribbled in from the jets rebounding from the burning walls. The din outside was beginning to batter against his skull, making it hard to think clearly. In addition to the collapsing buildings and roaring flames, there seemed to be a pump every hundred yards, all thumping and revving as they strained to drag water into the hoses. Several times he'd seen officers step forward to stop them, only to wave them forward when they saw Ruth's uniform.

Stan chose another corner, crashing and bumping over tangled hose lines and strewn rubble. He spotted a small alleyway that seemed abandoned. It was barely wide enough to take the car, but he'd manoeuvred it into the turn before he saw the orange flames dancing in a gutter at the far end. The gentle blaze erupted into a roaring tornado and swept along the rooftops faster than he could put the car into reverse.

'Stan!' Ruth screamed as a lump of blazing timber stabbed through the car roof and hung spitting sparks on to the blanket covering Paul.

'Get rid of it!' Stan shouted, backing up at full speed. Just in time he glimpsed the grey bulk of the auxiliary pump out of the corner of his eye, and swerved to avoid the collision.

Ruth had snatched off her tin helmet and was leaning over the back, frantically beating the smouldering spear loose. The fumes from it were making Stan's eyes water. It seemed darker to the right. Reasoning that this meant no flames, he spun the wheel again and found himself in a narrow street. The right-hand side seemed to be intact, but several parts of the left had already collapsed in on themselves, blocking most of the road with piles of brick, glass and timber. Running the wheels up on the pavement, he pulled in as close to the right-hand buildings as he could and switched the engine off.

Outside the car, the heat was even worse. 'Hurry up,' Stan hissed, folding the hood back. 'Before we get caught in this lot.'

Ruth didn't need to be told twice. The roads at both ends of this narrow street were already ablaze. She'd assumed they were going to throw the body into the doorway and drive away again, but Stan headed towards the bombed buildings.

'What you doing? Let's get outa 'ere!'

He was backing over the rubble, forcing her to follow. Her hands were slippery with sweat from the heat and she couldn't keep her grip on Paul's legs. Panting and gasping, she wobbled over the shifting piles of bricks.

'Down.'

Ruth's relief when she lowered her burden behind the half-shattered wall Stan had indicated changed to terror as he told her to stay put.

'What? Why?'

'Just stop here, Ruth. And take them towels off his 'ead.'

He disappeared the way they'd come, leaving her crouched alone with Paul. Gingerly she peeled the swaddling from round his head. The blood had mostly dried by the time Stan had wrapped him up, and the towels came away easily. Pulling the last one free, she jerked his head in her direction. His sightless eyes stared directly into hers. She gave a low moan and sat back abruptly. The hand she'd put out to steady herself fell on something warm and furry. The moan turned to a scream as a large rat twisted free and scampered under the debris.

'What's up?'

Stan clambered back down beside her and dumped the uniform and poker he'd just retrieved from the car.

'It was a *rat*.' She hit his chest. 'You left me here with a *rat*.'

'A ra . . . Are you mad, Ruth? There's you due for the drop if they catch us, and me for ten years inside . . . That is, if we don't get crisped up worse than the Sunday roast. And you're fretting about a bloody rat. Here, start dressing johnny.' Stripping off the RAF jacket and shirt, he pushed them into her hands.

'What! No, I can't. Let's just leave him.'

Pulling off Paul's blue trousers and hauling his own shapeless khaki ones up, Stan told her roundly that that wasn't on. 'He's got to look normal. Just some poor B who caught a packet. And he ain't likely to be driving round in his underpants is he? Now get a move on, Ruthie.'

Whimpering, Ruth tried to force the unresponsive arms into the shirt. Her fingers slid and skidded over the buttons, and in the end Stan had to redress him. Flinging the cap down beside the shattered head, he kicked and dragged at the rubble until a sizeable amount had buried the top half of Paul's body, just leaving the sprawled legs visible.

'That's it.'

'Stan . . .'

'What?'

'You sure he's dead? He still feels awful 'ot.'

'It's a bit late to check now, ain't it?' He gave the sprawled legs a parting kick and tugged at Ruth.

She found herself strangely reluctant to leave. 'I don't know his name.'

'Thought you said it was Paul.'

'His surname. I never heard his surname.'

351

' 'Oo cares? 'E ain't got no more use for it. We'd best get clear, Ruth. And pray.'

They climbed cautiously back over the rubble until they came to an incendiary smouldering amongst the bricks. Balling the bloodstained towels, Stan threw them on to the red heat. With a damp fizzle they ignited. The bent poker went down a drain. Then, checking there was no one to see them, they held hands and ran.

They spent the next couple of hours huddled in an air-raid shelter, and emerged at the all-clear to a world that was burning in every direction they looked. There were no trams or buses running. Nor any way they could have got through the fire-blasted streets if they had been. Police directed them on foot out of the danger area, and in the end they managed to hitch a ride with the driver of a bulk water carrier who'd discharged his load and was heading back to Finchley.

Clambering down into the quiet, blacked-out streets of Camden, the silence was so eerie that for a second Ruth managed to convince herself the whole thing had been a terrible nightmare. Then she looked back.

'Let's go,' Stan said, touching her arm lightly. She followed him automatically, her eyes still mesmerised by the billowing black smoke and orange glow that lit the whole horizon to the south-east.

They were greeted by an angry demand from Duggie Miller as to what the devil she thought she'd been doing. 'Have you taken leave of your senses, Ruthie?'

For a moment she thought he knew about Paul, then he pointed out that cleanliness might be next to godliness, but did she realise there wasn't a dry shirt nor towel in the house? Before Ruth could think of an answer, Duggie added, 'What on earth have the pair of you been doing? You look like a couple of chimney sweeps. Smell like it too.'

Stan jumped in to explain he'd taken Ruth for a drink down a pub he knew in the City and they'd got caught in the raid. 'We only just made it to the shelter, Mr Miller. And then we had to walk out a bit before we got a lift back. There's smoke and ash all over the place.'

352

'I can see that from here, Stan Wilkins. You'd best put your head under the tap before you go back. Can't go reporting in looking like that. And shift this motorbike. What's it doing in the kitchen anyway?'

'Sorry, Mr Miller. Didn't want any one stealing it,' Stan gasped, emerging spluttering and shaking drops of water from his hair. He stepped back from the sink, but left the tap running for Ruth. She shook her head, rubbing the back of her hands over her smoke-blackened face. 'I'll . . . I'll boil up the kettle later.'

'Best be going, then. 'Bye, Mr Miller. Might not see you for a while. We're shipping out. Africa, some of the lads reckon.'

'Oh. I see. Well, good luck, son. And I hope the Lord walks with you.'

'I hope he walks in front of me,' Stan said frankly. ' 'Bye.'

'I'll see you to the gate, Stan.'

She held the ice-cold soaking sheets up out of his way as he threaded the bike back through the yard.

' 'Bye, Stan.'

' 'Bye Ruth.'

'And thanks. You were . . . you were wonderful, Stan. Better than all them blokes in the pictures.' Taking hold of his jacket, she stood on tiptoe and pressed a kiss to his lips. 'I'll write you. If you want.'

Six hours ago, he'd have cheerfully sold his soul to the Devil, or even the company sergeant major – although regimental rumour had it they were one and the same – to hear her say that. But now . . . He'd saved her from a hanging, but as for the future . . . He tried to see himself coming back from work; sitting down to his tea across the table from her; maybe kissing the nippers before they went to bed. The picture wouldn't form. Instead, the battered body they'd left on that bomb site was there between them.

'Well, you know, Ruth, it might be a bit tricky. I mean, letters get lost, what with the war and ships being sunk and everything . . . And I'd have to write to me mum first.'

She understood. What they'd just done would always be a bond between them in one way – and a barrier in another. 'Yeah.

353

OK. I'll ask your mum 'ow you are if I see her up the shops then, shall I?'

'Might be best. 'Bye, Ruth.' He kicked the bike into action and roared away without looking back.

It wasn't until he was halfway back to camp that it suddenly occurred to him he never had got around to asking Ruth where she'd really been when she claimed to be visiting their Lulu.

Chapter 35

Despite the row with Ruth, and being ticked off by the sub-officer for reporting in without her uniform, Hatty spent most of Sunday drifting in a bubble of happiness.

After a Saturday of relieving the crews who'd fought the Friday raids, the men were all back on duty in the station, scrubbing, polishing, making up equipment and drying off. The joy of being amongst familiar faces, doing what she did best, was enough to send Hatty singing round the mess room. She even managed to exchange a few shy jokes with some of the men.

'You're h'in a good mood today, my lovely,' Snakey said approvingly. 'Found h'another love bird to share your nest, h'I'll be bound.'

Hatty was tempted to confide in him. But she'd promised Uncle Duggie not to say anything until he'd spoken to Len on Monday, so she simply smiled and continued to mash the potatoes.

'H'I knew it! Well, you trust me to see you right for the reception. If I'd been ten years younger, I'd have popped the question meself.'

A yellow alert had sounded as she dished up the dinners. With an eye and an ear cocked towards the watchroom, the men had shovelled down the food quickly before they were ordered out.

The bells went down to the accompaniment of Betty Shaw shouting out a string of instructions: 'Numbers One and Two report to Fire Control Westminster. Pat, turntable ladder to go to Redcross Street. No, wait. It's Cannon Street, not Redcross. Number Three appliance – Cheap . . . No, wait . . .'

Doing-Her-Bit rushed across with a sheet of paper from the teleprinter. Betty snatched it and scanned it quickly. 'They've closed off roads . . .'

Then they were gone. Within ten minutes the station was deserted, apart from the watchroom staff, Hatty and Nell De Groot. Hatty – who'd been avoiding Betty Shaw all afternoon – made herself go into the watchroom and ask after the main station.

'Adele said it was chaos over there,' Betty called from the board, where she was chalking up her vehicle assignments. 'All the appliances have been sent down to the City. Substations are empty too. There's only one pump left on stand-by in Hampstead to cover the whole area. Heaven help us if they start on us. We've nothing left to fight it.'

The telephone rang again, and after another quick conversation and a scribbled message, Betty said: 'Where's Nell?'

She was, as usual, reading quietly in a corner of the mess room. She received her orders to take the hose lorry to Whitefriars Street with her usual lack of emotion, and strolled out as if she'd just been told to take it to tea at the Ritz instead of into the centre of a major air-raid.

'My, she's so composed, isn't she?' Doing-Her-Bit said. 'Anyone would think she wasn't bothered about being killed.'

'Perhaps she's not.'

The bitterness in Betty's voice caused Doing-Her-Bit to raise her thin eyebrows and ask if the season of goodwill hadn't perhaps worked its usual magic.

'If you mean are Len and I back together – no, we're not. And not likely to be either.'

Doing-Her-Bit murmured regrets and apologies and was roundly told by Betty to change the subject.

Neither noticed the suppressed smile on Hatty's face as she slipped back to the galley to get on with her washing-up. She knew she ought to feel dreadfully guilty about Mrs Shaw, but she couldn't. Len was hers, hers, hers.

'When you wish upon a star . . .' Hatty hummed cheerfully, splashing through the washing-up and putting a mop over the floor. 'It's a hap-hap-happy day . . .' she informed the mop, quickstepping it round the tables. A final twirl sent the room spinning. Off-balance, she sat down quickly on a bench and rested her head on her hands.

'Hatty?' A hand touched her shoulder. 'Are you all right?'

'Yes, ta, Mrs Shaw. I just felt a bit dizzy.'

'I wish you'd call me Betty. Adele's just rung across. Division have asked if our canteen van's ready. I said it was. That's right, isn't it?'

'Of course it is. I washed out soon as we got back from Manchester. You could eat your dinner off the floor. Leastways, you could if I had anything to cook in it.'

'They're sending some supplies over. And a driver. You're to stand by to go out with it. But if you're not feeling well . . .'

'I'm fine.' Pushing down with the flats of her hand, Hatty levered herself up.

An hour later a small van drew up and the solitary female occupant started to bundle tins of cocoa and corned beef out the back. 'OK sugar?'

'I . . . er . . .' Hatty's attention was riveted to the south-east. Cocooned inside the centre of Good Hope Station, she'd not bothered to look outside until now.

'Oh yeah . . . terrible, isn't it? Worse than September, I reckon,' the driver said casually. 'OK butter? OK bread?'

She took Hatty's failure to respond as a 'no' and dumped the relevant supplies on the cobbles.

'OK chocolate? That's your lot then. Sign here.'

She grabbed the initialled delivery note back through the window and flung it on the passenger seat.

'Wait! What about me driver?'

'Sorry. If it's not edible, I haven't got it. 'Night.'

Hauling the supplies back inside, Hatty reported the oversight to the watchroom and started making up sandwiches in the mess room.

Betty Shaw came back just as the last round was cut and stacked in its box to announce that Euston couldn't send a driver. 'So I'm going with you.'

'But the watchroom . . . I mean, the phones . . .'

'Doing-Her-Bit can watch them. We've nothing to send out

357

if there's a fire anyway. Shall I help carry those out to the van?'

It was the last thing Hatty wanted, but what else could she do but direct Betty to carry out buckets of water and start filling the urns?

The all-clear sounded, and still they hadn't been given any order to move. 'Maybe they don't want us after all,' Hatty suggested hopefully. How on earth could she spend hours serving from the same hatch as Len's wife? Supposing he came to the van?

'Perhaps.' Betty yawned. 'I'm going to lie down, why don't you do the same? Once we're out we could be working all night.'

Hatty didn't want to share a bedroom with Betty any more than she wanted to share a canteen van, but she did feel suddenly very tired. They both crawled into the tiny female locker room, lay down and pulled the rough blankets over themselves.

'Mrs Shaw?' Hatty whispered after a few moments of listening to the other woman's light breathing. 'There's something I gotta tell you. I promised Uncle Duggie I wouldn't but I don't expect it counts with you . . . Mrs Shaw?'

Betty Shaw continued to breathe in a light, continuous rhythm. Hatty's last thought was *How can she sleep when half London's on fire and Len's right in the middle of it, maybe getting burnt?*

The next thing she knew, Doing-Her-Bit was shaking her awake.

They were assigned a site near Bunhill Row, with the warning to use their own judgement and move the van to a safer spot if the fires came too close.

'How can we find a safer bit, Mrs Shaw?' Hatty asked, staring at the devastation outside the cab. 'It's worse than September.' Everywhere she looked, buildings were collapsing in on themselves, forming giant chimneys that sent sparks soaring into the night sky. You could see the streams of water from the firemen's hoses turning into steam as they hit the flames. It was as if the fire was feeding on the water rather than retreating before it.

'I suppose we can always drive up to Hampstead,' Betty suggested.

Hatty started to protest – and then realised it was a joke. Which was good. It showed Mrs Shaw was getting over Len. Didn't it? She decided to try to explain again. It seemed fair really, no matter what Uncle Duggie said.

'Mrs Shaw, you know you and Mr Shaw are – yer know . . .' It wasn't as easy as she'd imagined. Somehow the words 'getting divorced' wouldn't come out.

Betty climbed into the body of the van. 'I'll get the hatch open.'

'No. Best get the urns on the boil first, or we'll 'ave nothing to give them,' Hatty said with the authority of her experiences in Manchester behind her.

As soon as they lowered the hatch, the men started materialising before the counter. Faces and hands black with smoke, they grabbed sandwiches and handfuls of biscuits greedily and sat around on steps and in doorways. Some talked in low, hoarse voices but most just slumped wearily.

The heat in the van was almost unbearable. Before long the floor and surfaces were covered with a layer of fine white ash. After a while they stopped trying to brush it away.

'Got a light, love?' one wag enquired after picking up his mug of cocoa.

Hatty shook her head mutely. The continual billows of oily smoke that kept rolling over the van were making her feel dizzy again. She badly wanted to sit down, but another wave of firemen had been released from their pumps and were flocking round the hatch.

'Don't matter,' the wag said sadly, retrieving a pulp of yellow tobacco and squashed cardboard from his sodden pocket.

Silently Betty reached over Hat's shoulder and passed him a cigarette. In minutes the entire packet had disappeared. More firemen jostled against the hatch, their tin helmets festooned with neck-cloths draped over them to dry in the intense heat.

A divisional officer pushed his way to the front on a ripple of angry murmurs. 'I don't like the look of that fire behind you, ladies. Dear me, it's Scarlett O'Hara, isn't it?'

Betty recognised her passenger from the dock blitz in September. 'Good evening, Superintendent Bailey. How are you?'

'Top-hole thank you, my dear. And you?'

Betty informed him she was also very well. Social niceties out of the way, he ordered her to move the van.

'Move it where?'

'Take it to the north, my dear. I don't like the way this lot's going. It could jump behind you at any moment. Even if the tide *is* turning in our favour.'

'Is it . . . ?' Hatty screwed her eyes against the ash and glare. 'It don't look no better to me, mister. I mean sir.'

'I was speaking literally, my dear, not figuratively. The Thames tide, not our luck. The blighters hit us at low tide. Never fear, we'll beat it. But sometimes it's like a rash – gets worse before it gets better.'

Moving position wasn't easy. Whichever direction Betty took the van, the roads were strewn with hoses. Some were rigid with water, others flaccid and ripped by falling debris. There were pumps pounding on every corner, their glowing bright-red exhaust pipes reflected in the water gushing back along the gutters. Tiny figures in oily black mackintoshes directed glittering streams into four-storey buildings that looked as though they might collapse outwards at any moment.

The light from the fires was so intense that it was as easy to see as if they were driving around in the daytime.

'What about down there?' Hatty pointed to a street that seemed untouched by the blaze.

'It's bit far out. But . . . all right.' Betty nosed forward. A few yards in, a narrow foot alley ran between two office buildings before opening out into an internal courtyard. They glimpsed uniformed figures moving inside and saw the black smoke pouring from top windows. Even from inside the van, they could hear the angry pounding of an axe on wood.

'Open up!'

Hatty drew a short, startled breath. 'It's . . .'

'Len,' Betty said.

A figure appeared at a top window. A wrinkled and hairless head was thrust out. They couldn't hear the words, but the gesture – hands behind his ears – was clear enough. The firemen below were waving. A shrug of incomprehension from the watcher suggested he was not only deaf but simple too.

One of the firemen came back and handed Len a hook ladder. Mesmerised, the two women saw him hook it over the first-floor sill and haul himself up. Leg locked over the sill, he leant out and hooked the next window. With quick, practised movements he climbed again. And again. Until he'd reached the watcher's window and disappeared into the blackness.

A minute later the street door opened and he re-emerged, leading an elderly man in tattered pyjamas by the hand. Two other firemen barged past them immediately, dragging a heavy hose into the narrow doorway. Len disappeared from the narrow rectangle of the women's sight.

With a loud gasp, Hatty let out the breath she hadn't known she was holding. 'Gosh, weren't he brave, Mrs Shaw.'

'Yes. I never doubted he was,' Betty said briefly, setting the van in motion again.

Hatty gave her an anxious glance. 'You're still stopping away, though. I mean, you aren't going home?'

'No.' Betty drew up beside a bomb site which had been partially cleared after an earlier raid. 'Let's get set up again.'

Hatty set to. She found she was unable to leave the subject of the Shaws' marriage. It was a bit like having an aching tooth. Your tongue kept probing even though you knew it was going to hurt.

'Do you reckon you'll find another bloke, Mrs Shaw? I mean,' Hatty hurried on quickly, realising how impertinent that might sound, 'it'd be nice, wouldn't it, if you and Mr Shaw was to find other people. 'Cos I mean, just because you ain't right together don't mean you can't be happy with someone else.'

'I can't speak for Len. But I doubt I shall. I don't think I'd trust myself again. Is there any milk left?'

Hatty stabbed two holes in a tin of condensed and passed it over. 'What do you mean, "trust yourself"?' she said doubtfully.

'I mean, I thought I knew Len. I trusted my judgement. I knew that my husband was kind, and honest, and loving.'

'He is.'

Betty smiled wanly. 'Hardly. He's certainly not honest. And as for kind and loving, well . . . do you know how he's made me feel?'

Hatty shook her head mutely.

'The worst thing is, he's made me feel . . . frightened. It's like thinking you're standing on solid ground like this . . .' Betty hit the van floor with the heel of her boot. 'And then suddenly finding it's all sand and it's crumbling under you. I just keep going over and over every day, trying to work out which were the lies. Which of his men knew? Or did they all know? You see, I've been living in this dream world and now I can't work out what was real and what was part of the dream. And it just scares me to death, discovering what a terrible judge of character I am. If I don't know my own husband, how can I trust what I feel about anyone else?'

She suddenly reached out and squeezed one of Hatty's hands. 'I'm sorry. I shouldn't be going on at you like this, Hat. It's just . . . I haven't really had anyone else to talk to since it happened.'

'Your family . . .' Hatty said uncertainly, trying to slide her hand free.

'I suppose I'll have to eventually. But admitting your husband has been making a fool of you all your married life isn't easy.'

'Not all . . .'

'Well, no. Perhaps not in the early years. But who knows?'

'I do. I mean . . .' Hatty stopped, the words she wanted to say tangled up on her tongue. She desperately wanted to reassure Mrs Shaw that she'd got it all wrong. Len hadn't been unfaithful all those years. It was just since the spring. But what if Betty didn't believe her? She really ought to hear it from Len. Hatty would speak to him tomorrow after Uncle Duggie had had his say. Explain that it would be kinder to face Betty and tell her the whole story.

Impulsively, she gave Betty a hug. 'It's not as awful as you think, Mrs Shaw. Honest it ain't. I mean, I just bet Mr Shaw loved you for years and years and I bet you'll find another bloke soon as you get divorced.'

'I rather doubt that. But you're a kind girl, Hatty. Maybe when you get your own husband you'll understand what I'm rambling on about.'

'And that day h'aint so far h'off, eh, my lovely?'

Both women jumped. The din outside masked any approaching footsteps. Now a familiar face was framed in the hatch opening.

'Snakey! Are you all right?'

'H'in the pink, my lovely. Or . . .' He took off his helmet and passed a hand over his greasy face. 'H'in the grey in my case. Any chance h'of a cup of char?'

'The tea's out, Snakey. We can offer you cocoa.'

'Nectar from the gods, Mrs Shaw. Two sugars h'if you please.'

Betty stirred up the sticky mixture and passed it over, together with a handful of biscuits. Snakey breathed half a mugful up in one enormous gasp. Under cover of the slurping, Betty asked if that was right, that Hatty was getting married?

'Yes. Later. I mean, we can't fix the date right off.'

'I didn't realise. Listen . . .' Betty gripped the tops of Hatty's arms and turned her so they were face to face. Or at least face to top button. 'Listen, Hatty, don't let what I said put you off.' She shook Hatty gently and said with emphasis: 'There are happy marriages. Just because I was unlucky doesn't mean you will be. Do you love him?'

Wordlessly, Hatty nodded.

'Then you believe this marriage is going to work out. And I really do wish you the best of luck.' Standing on tiptoe she brushed a kiss on Hatty's cheek before turning to serve the next customers. Like canary-yellow bats in their anti-gas capes they crowded round, snapping up the last of the van's supplies of chocolate and cocoa.

Hatty stepped outside the van and beckoned Snakey into the shadow at the back of the van. 'Are any more of our lot coming,

Snakey?' she whispered. ' 'Cos if they are, I'll slip something under the counter for them.'

'H'I reckon they'll be along soon h'enough to see what's happened to the water. H'I just had to shut the trailer pump down. The bug . . . the blighter's run out of petrol.'

Sure enough, ten minutes later two men appeared from a side street and shouted rude comments about Snakey's addiction to the tea wagon.

Dunking an arrowroot biscuit, Snakey called back an explanation.

Mollified, the men trudged over. 'Might as well have a brew ourselves then. G'morning, Hatty. Morning, Mrs Shaw. Two cuppas, please.'

'H'and a refill here, my lovelies.'

'You can get back to that pump, Snakey. There's a van coming round with cans of petrol. You can flag it down and get yourself a refuel.'

'H'ain't you going to give a mate a hand?'

'Soon as we've finished here.'

Muttering a few good-natured insults, Snakey strolled off.

'He's left his helmet.' Hatty took it from the counter. 'I'll not be a tick, Mrs Shaw.'

As they watched her wobbling away into a curtain of gently descending ash, Betty started to pack up. She'd just reached forward to take Snakey's empty mug from the counter when unaccountably it took off and leapt into the air. Whilst her brain tried to cope with this strange behaviour, she found herself flying backwards. The rim of her helmet collided with the urn behind her, and the vibrations of metal on metal jarred through her head. Sliding to the floor, she watched in amazement as mugs and cutlery rattled down in a shower. A roaring sound filled her ears and then she was suddenly plunged into total blackness.

It took several seconds before she could make sense of what had happened.

It was dark because the hatch had slammed shut. She was sitting on the floor of the van and . . . she flexed arms and legs cautiously . . . she was all right except for a pain in her head.

364

Standing shakily, she pushed the hatch. It swung loosely, the brackets destroyed.

'Mrs Shaw, you OK?' The two men who'd been standing in front of the van were both scrambling to their feet. Blood pouring from his nose, one held the hatch up.

'What happened? Was it a bomb?'

'Delayed action, I reckon.' Coughing, he spat a stream of black saliva into the gutter. 'Lucky you weren't up front.'

He helped her out through the hatch and showed her the van cab. A lump of piping encased in concrete had crashed through the side window and skewed itself into the steering wheel, sheering it off completely.

Betty blinked. Grit stung her eyes. She brushed it away and found her mouth was full of brick dust. Hawking into a handkerchief, she croaked: 'Where's Hatty?'

'I don't rightly . . .' The street ahead had been temporarily obscured by swirling brick and masonry dust. Now it started to clear to an accompaniment of tumbling debris and a steady sinister hiss from the crater that had appeared in the centre of the road.

'Hatty! Snakey!' Betty screamed into the darkness.

The two firemen were already running. Stumbling over the debris, she went after them. By the time she caught up, they were standing quietly, looking down at the up-ended trailer pump.

Betty's breath caught in her throat. She looked into Snakey's face. Snakey stared blankly and uncomprehendingly back at her.

'Is he . . . ?'

'Yep.' One of the men stooped and gently closed the open eyes. 'So long, mate.' Taking off his own helmet, he placed it over Snakey's face.

The sight of it brought Betty back to her senses. 'Hatty!' She looked round wildly. 'I didn't see her.'

'Might not be much to see, Mrs Shaw, best let us look.'

'No.' She stumbled back the way she'd come. 'Hatty! Hatty, if you can hear me, say something.'

The distant hungry roar of the fires and the steady thumping of pumps, which she'd almost ceased to notice, suddenly flooded her ears. She couldn't hear anything else. 'Hatty. H-a-t-t-e-e-e.'

'Hey!' One of the men gestured for silence.

Holding their breath, they waited.

This time they all heard it. 'Mrs . . . Mrs Sh . . .'

'Over there.' The first man dashed towards the opposite pavement. Part of the debris and piping from the road hole had piled against the foundation stones of an office building, forming a sort of tent.

'Mrs Shaw?' Only her head was protruding from the concrete and clay cocoon.

Betty dropped to her knees to wipe dirt from the mouth and nose. The two men flung themselves at the debris, heaving stones off with grunts and curses.

'Hold on, Hatty, we'll have you out in a minute.'

'It's all right, Mrs Shaw, it don't hurt much. 'Fact I can move a bit, see?' As proof she wriggled one hand up to her shoulder.

Betty took the fingers and gripped them tightly. Panting, the men pulled away more stones.

'Looks like the gods were watching over you tonight, young Hatty,' one panted. 'This took most of the weight.' He slapped a slab that was wedged at an angle between pavement and building. 'Let's get it shifted off you.'

Shoulders braced, they heaved. The slab wobbled and then crashed back into the road.

'Oh Jesus!'

A smooth stone, one end carved into a grinning gargoyle, lay across Hatty's legs. Or what was left of them. Her left foot was hanging off, the bone gleaming whitely from the bottom of the torn leg. Her right leg was bent and twisted under the stone, but the pool of blood trickling slowly towards the kerb told its own story.

The men tried to lift the stone. The fractional reduction in pressure let the blood flow back into the shattered limbs.

The hand gripping Betty's contracted in a spasm, and Hatty started to scream.

Chapter 36

'Miss Miller?'

Ruth's heart leapt into her throat and then settled back into its normal position, where it thundered with all the enthusiasm of a dance band percussion section. Her worst nightmare, the one that had jolted her awake every few seconds last night, had come true. The police had come for her.

'Who is it, Ruthie?' Duggie Miller came down the stairs, knotting his working tie.

'Policewoman, Dad.'

'Sergeant Sarah McNeill, Mr Miller? It *is* Mr Miller, isn't it? From the funeral place in Camden?'

'That's right, miss. Body for the morgue, is it? Don't leave the lady standing on the step like that, Ruthie.'

Ruth stepped back.

'Sorry the house's like a blooming laundry.' Duggie led the way into the kitchen, where the drying rack, clothes horse and chair backs were all draped with towels, underwear, shirts and Hatty's uniform. The whole house smelt of damp cloth, carnation talcum powder and – at present – the acrid tang of coal smoke which had just been discharged from a passing train.

Glancing back into the hall, Duggie found that most of it was drifting in through the open front door.

'Ruth, don't stand there counting clouds. Shut the door. Ye loaves and little fishes, what's the matter with you? Now, miss, body to be collected, is it?'

'No ... it's not that ... There was an incident last night, sir ...'

Sarah stopped as a small moan escaped Ruth.

'You ill, Ruthie?'

Ruth shook her head. She leant against the cooker, her mind desperately whirling as she tried to think of a plausible lie to explain what she and Stan had done. There wasn't one. She was going to hang.

With an impatient exclamation, Duggie swept a pair of woollen combinations from a chair, dried the seat with his shirt sleeve and gestured to Sarah. 'Take a seat.'

'No. Thank you. I'm not stopping. It's just . . . we had a call at Agar Street from the fire station. There's no one who can be released to inform you, Mr Miller. I'm very sorry, but . . .'

The Millers had few relatives, and only one apart from Ruth was connected to the fire service. The reason for Sarah's morning visit hit them both at the same moment.

'Hatty!'

In an unconscious gesture Duggie started smoothing his thinning hair over his bald spot with short, jabbing gestures. 'She ain't . . . I mean, we didn't hear any bombs come down over Kentish Town. Was there an accident, up the fire station?'

'I'm afraid I haven't the details. She's in the Middlesex Hospital. We were asked to contact the next of kin.'

Ruth's face brightened. Relief that she wasn't about to be arrested, and anxiety about Hatty, had revitalised her. 'Hospital. That's good, ain't it, Dad. I mean, if she were dead . . . they wouldn't put her in hospital.'

Duggie stood slowly. He looked ten years older. 'Maybe, Ruthie, I'll get down there. You go to work.'

'No! I'm coming with yer.'

'No you're not. You heard what the officer said. They're short-handed up the fire station. Now you get yourself on duty, my girl. I'll telephone soon as I know.'

Ruth put up a spirited fight and was only persuaded when Sarah pointed out that the fire station would probably have more details about what had happened to Hatty.

'Thanks, miss.' Duggie locked the front door and pushed the key back through the box on its string. 'Best she don't see if Hatty's been caught in a raid. We've had a few in Mottram's recent. Best to remember how she was.'

368

'It may not be that bad, Mr Miller.'

'Don't send for the next of kin if all she's needing is a bunch of chrysanths, do they, miss?'

They'd turned into Kentish Town Road. The ubiquitous wind howled down it, lifting a light film of powder from the goods carriage rattling over the railway bridge and swirling it in a twister that rode above the train. Beyond that, to the south and east, dozens of tangible reminders of last night's raid rose in columns of pale-grey smoke to meet the flat winter clouds.

'Worse than September, they reckon,' Duggie said. He turned his collar up. 'Thanks for letting us know, miss.'

'I'm going down to Camden Station myself.'

They walked in silence: Sarah because she'd always found the usual platitudes she was called on to utter over grieving relatives to be totally inadequate; and Duggie because he was struggling to believe that he might never hear his Hatty's voice or see her smile again.

They parted company in Camden High Street.

' 'Bye, miss. And thank you again.'

'I'm sorry we've no car. Before the war we might have . . .'

'It's all right, I'll just tell them in Mottram's then I'll get the bus down.'

He turned and straightened his shoulders, instinctively shrugging his jacket and adjusting his hat into a walking advertisement for Mottram and Cropper's – Funeral Directors of Distinction.

'Mr Miller!'

'Yes, miss?'

'Didn't you and your daughters come up Agar Street, months back? With an anonymous letter? You were at the front desk when I was called through to deal with another case. A dead baby. Oh Lord, I'm sorry . . . this isn't the time. Forget I asked.'

'Can't count on having any more time these days, miss. Best *carpe diem.*'

'I beg your pardon?'

Duggie translated his employer's favourite saying as 'do it before you start feeding the worms'. 'Someone called Ruthie a name I'll not have used about my girls. It didn't seem important after seeing that baby. Seems even less important now.'

'I see. Thank you. And good luck.'

Nodding, Duggie hurried away. He was expecting the worst, but a small part of him prayed that Hatty was still alive.

Betty Shaw was praying for the same thing. She had been ever since they'd loaded Hatty into the auxiliary ambulance. The journey had been a nightmare. She'd had to fight to make them take her in the back with Hatty, and then she'd been forced to scrunch herself in a corner whilst a nurse desperately tried to stop the bleeding from Hatty's legs. The bright, salty-smelling liquid oozed through the temporary bandages and soaked the blanket they'd thrown over the stretcher.

Mercifully Hatty had passed out, but at each bump and rattle she half returned to consciousness.

'Can't you give her something?' Betty had pleaded.

'It's best not,' the nurse had explained. 'The doctors will operate soon as we get there.'

The ambulance swayed alarmingly, flinging Hatty against the restraining straps over the stretcher. She moaned. Her eyelids flickered. 'Mrs Shaw . . . ?'

'I'm here, Hatty.' She gripped the cold, sweaty hand nearest her. 'It's all right. We're nearly at the hospital.' She prayed that was right. The ambulance was hurtling along, its bell jangling the urgency of its errand.

'Mrs . . . Shaw . . . tell . . . tell . . .' Hatty strained to speak.

'Shhh . . .' Betty stroked the damp hair. 'Lie quietly now. How much *longer* . . . ?' she murmured to the nurse.

'Soon. They're directing us to hospitals outside the fire area.'

The ambulance cornered, slowed and stopped abruptly. Hands lifted the canvas flap and slid the stretcher off its runners. It was all so fast that they'd got Hatty loaded on to a trolley in the dimly lit corridor before Betty could collect herself and scramble after her.

'Mrs Shaw!'

'I'm here, I'm here . . .'

They were running along a subterranean passage. Betty caught occasional glimpses of Hatty's terrified face, raised to find something she could recognise and understand in this nightmare, and then they were crashing through double doors and a nurse was barring her path.

'It's best you let us deal with her now. Are you a relative?'

'No. I'm . . . I was with her . . . in the van.' Through the windows she could see them cutting Hatty's clothes off in strips of material stiff with dried blood.

Gently, but firmly, the nurse directed her to another room. Later someone else had come to take Hatty's details. And Betty had realised how few she knew.

'Address?'

'Camden. One of the roads by the railway arches. I'm not quite certain . . .'

'Date of Birth?'

'She's seventeen or eighteen, I think.'

'Next of kin?'

At least she knew that. 'Her uncle.'

'It would be helpful if he could be contacted.'

Betty had done her best. Her first phone call to Good Hope had done little more than put Doing-Her-Bit into a flap. Adele over in Control had been more helpful, and she'd left it to her to find some way of alerting the Millers to Hatty's situation.

Then she'd waited. And waited. More people had arrived in the waiting room. Pale-faced and silent, they'd huddled on chairs and around the walls, reading official posters that urged them to eat more carrots and potatoes, and home-made ones urging Peace on Earth and Goodwill to All Men. Every footstep that hurried past outside caused a simultaneous flicker of hope and dread. Whenever the steps went on, the waiting relatives would subside once again into limbo. No news at least meant no bad news.

Betty found her mouth watering at the thought of tea and a smoke. She was desperate to find either but didn't dare move in case someone came in with news about Hatty.

The door opened again. A middle-aged man with thinning sandy hair stood uncertainly in the opening. His black trousers, frock jacket and waistcoat proclaimed his profession. There was a collective and sharply in-drawn breath from the room,

371

before Betty recollected where Hatty's uncle worked.

'Mr Miller?'

Plainly relieved to have found someone who was expecting him, he came inside. 'That's right, Miss . . . Mrs . . . ?'

'Betty Shaw.' She drew him down beside her to an explosion of relieved sighs from the rest of the waiting relatives. 'I was with Hatty when . . . when she got hurt.'

'Where is she? I can't get no sense out of the nurses. They just say "Doctor will see you soon".'

'That's all they'll tell me too. They're operating on her, that's all I know.'

Briefly Betty explained about the canteen van and the stone that had hit Hatty's legs. 'It was off the roof. They think it was loosened by an earlier raid.'

'It was just the legs, was it? Rest of her's all right?'

'She was protected by some concrete. Really there's hardly a scratch on her top part.'

'Praise the Lord.' He produced a large white handkerchief from his breast pocket and blew his nose noisily. 'I been thinking I'd lost her all the way down here. But legs ain't too bad, are they? Legs can be fixed.'

Recalling the mangle of flesh and bone, Betty doubted Hatty's ever would be. She squeezed Duggie Miller's hand. He gave her a grateful smile. 'Thanks for stopping with her, Miss . . . sorry, I've forgotten your name already.'

'Betty Shaw.'

An odd expression passed over Duggie's face. 'Shaw? You wouldn't be anything to do with the Shaw fellow who works up the regular fire station?'

'I'm his wife. Do you know Len?'

'Not to know in the street. My girls, they've mentioned him a bit.'

Spreading his handkerchief on his knee Duggie seemed to concentrate on refolding it before returning it to his pocket.

'My Hatty,' he said abruptly, apparently talking to the white linen square, 'she's a good girl, but she's not like my Ruthie. Sharp as a tin tack, Ruthie. But Hatty, sometimes she gets maggots in her head. Gets it fixed in there she wants something and can't be turned any more than a coster's donkey that's dug his hooves into the cobbles, if you see what I mean.'

'Really? She's always seemed very good-natured to me.'

'Oh, she is.' Duggie returned the hanky to his pocket and his eyes to Betty's face. 'Not hurt a fly, Hatty wouldn't.' He stopped, apparently having exhausted the subject of Hatty's goodness. And then suddenly said: 'The fact is, Mrs Shaw, what with her mum dying when she was just a little nipper, and then my Doris passing on before the girls were womanly, like, well, maybe I didn't explain things like I should have. But it's not easy for a man on his own. There's things that's best coming from a woman.'

She assumed he was referring to the facts of life. It seemed a bizarre subject in the circumstances. 'I'm not really sure I understand what you're saying, Mr Miller.'

'No.' He straightened his shoulders and in doing so moved fractionally away from her. 'No. I'm sorry, Mrs Shaw. I don't know what I was thinking about. But our Hatty's a decent girl, just you remember that. Lord have mercy – why don't they *tell* us something!'

Like a genie responding to the magic words, a nursing sister materialised in the doorway. 'Mr Miller, Doctor will see you in my office.'

Betty stood hesitantly. 'Shall I . . . ?'

Duggie nodded.

The doctor was young, attractive and a true angel of mercy. Seeing Betty's face when she pulled out a packet of Capstans, she offered them around.

Duggie's hand shook so much he couldn't hold the tip in the flame. 'Hatty?' he finally coughed through a lungful of smoke. 'Is she . . . the Lord hasn't taken her . . . ?'

'No. Women's Surgical has.'

'Beg pardon, miss? I mean Doctor.'

'Mrs Pardoe actually. I'm a surgeon.' Her tone became brisk and professional; facts were recited crisply and quickly before there was any chance of her becoming emotionally involved with the daily tragedies that passed over her operating table.

'We've amputated Harriet's left foot at the ankle. And the

right leg below the knee. I'm afraid there was no possibility of saving them.'

'But . . .' Duggie shook his head, as if to clear the picture these three simple sentences had evoked. 'She will get better?'

'She lost a lot of blood, but she has survived the operations very well. The next few days will tell.' A ghost of a smile flitted over the tired face. 'However, I'm pleased to say we managed a successful Caesarean. The baby is doing well.'

Duggie's mouth dropped open. It took him several seconds to ask what baby the surgeon was referring to.

'Why, Harriet's, of course. Weren't you aware your niece was pregnant?' Her accusatory glance took in both Duggie and Betty.

Duggie appeared to be having trouble breathing. 'She never said. Never said a word.'

'But surely you noticed?'

The doctor was looking directly at Betty. Clearly she'd been cast as a feckless aunt who'd failed to notice her niece was struggling through a pregnancy. She cast her mind back to the stolid, lumpish girl heaving cooking pots round the mess.

'I . . . Hatty's a big girl . . .'

'Always has been,' Duggie interrupted. 'Always well covered. Took after her mum . . . Me and Dickie . . . that's her dad . . . never had enough meat on our bones to satisfy a butcher's dog, but our Hatty . . .'

The doctor conceded that the baby was quite small and carried high up under the ribcage. It was just possible Harriet's pregnancy might not have been all that visible. 'But I would have thought Harriet would have noticed the symptoms.'

Noticed perhaps, Betty thought ruefully. But probably unaware what they meant. 'The baby . . . the explosion didn't hurt it?'

'Not that we can see. He's a fine little chap with a good set of lungs on him, I'm told. About thirty-six weeks, we think.'

'Can we see him? And Hatty?'

'For a few moments. It's unlikely she will regain consciousness until this afternoon.'

They'd put Hatty in the corner, with a young VAD nurse to watch and wait until she came round.

'She looks asleep, like she did when she was a little girl,' Duggie whispered. Keeping his eyes averted from the blanket-covered hump below waist level, he took her hand and patted it awkwardly. 'I'll see you later, Hatty. You be a good girl for the nurses, eh?'

In contrast to his mother, Hatty's son was wide awake and letting the nursery staff know that he didn't much care for this change in his circumstances. His bright-red face was screwed up indignantly beneath a mop of dark hair, and he was *angry*. Around him other babies murmured, gurgled and cried for their early feeds whilst their other ends contributed to the redolent stink of wet nappies that hung over the entire nursery.

Duggie held his great-nephew as if he was afraid he might break at any minute. 'Well – the Lord certainly moves in mysterious ways, don't he? Who'd have thought it – my Hatty a mum.'

Betty stroked the soft hair gently with two fingers. She longed to take the baby and feel its warm little body in her arms, but she didn't like to ask right now. Perhaps later, after his mum had cuddled him . . .

Duggie lowered the swaddled bundle cautiously back into the cot. 'Well now, we'd best see what your dad's intentions are, hadn't we?'

'He'll stand by her, won't he?' Betty asked.

'You know about him?'

'She told me she was getting married.'

'Don't suppose she mentioned the lucky chap's name?'

'No. Is it someone local?'

'Oh yes, you could say that. The thing is . . .' Duggie leant both arms along the cot's raised side and addressed the howling baby rather than Betty. 'The thing is . . . a boy needs a father. Needs to be able to point him out and say, "That's my dad." Got to have someone to live up to, see?'

He lifted his head and looked at Betty again. 'And the way things are with Hatty, it's best the boy has someone else responsible for him. I'm sorry, Mrs Shaw.'

'Sorry?' Betty stared. 'What are you sorry for?'

Duggie tipped his hat courteously, fixed it square on his head, and walked away without answering her.

Chapter 37

Hatty decided she must be dreaming. It was the only way things could be jumping around like they were.

Sometimes a strange girl in a white cap would be bending over her. Then she'd close her eyes and open them a minute later and the girl had moved right over to the other side, as if she'd floated over the bed. Then the girl's face changed into a woman's, and then changed again into Uncle Duggie's.

She tried to speak to him, but her mouth was too dry. Then he was gone again and this time he took the light with him.

Now she was in the dark, and she thought she might be awake, but when she tried to find the square bulk of the wardrobe that stood at the bottom of her bed, she couldn't see it. There was just an even blackness all round her. She let her eyes travel up the solid dark and saw that there was slight light up above her. Following it round, she found it stretched all around two sides and along the foot of the bed. It was very faint, like the light Uncle Duggie left burning in the chapel of rest at the funeral parlour.

A tangled memory came back: terrible pain; an ambulance bell; Mrs Shaw telling her to hold on.

Her heart started to thud. Perhaps they thought she was dead. They'd put her in a coffin and left her here alone. With a whimper she tried to sit up and tell them they'd made a mistake. She couldn't push herself up; instead her hands wavered and hit something. Glass smashed. People came. Hands were pushing her back. And then it all went black.

The next time she opened her eyes, it was light again and she could see that the coffin 'walls' were blue curtains.

'Hatty? You awake?'

'Uncle Duggie?'

His face appeared over hers. She tried to sit up and a pain like a knife stabbed through her stomach.

'Don't try to move yet, Hat.' His hand was firm on her shoulder and the other one took one of hers. 'Hat, did you know?'

'Know what?' Hatty tried to remember. Was there something she should know about? Maybe one of the shops had got something off ration in? She ought to go and queue before it sold out. Only she'd have to get up first . . . and she didn't seem to be able to. Another heave brought another slice of the knife.

'Ooow, Uncle Duggie, my tummy hurts something awful.'

'It'll be where they cut you for . . . Hatty, tell me straight. I won't be angry. Did you know you was having a baby?'

She tried to make sense of what he was saying. Of course she was going to have a baby. She was going to have lots of babies. Why should that make him angry?

'Did you know you was expecting, Hat? Past eight months, the doctors reckon.'

Hatty puzzled over this and shook her head. 'I can't be having a baby, Uncle Duggie. I can't. You said only bad girls have babies before they're married, and I'm not bad.' A look of consternation and doubt flooded her square face. 'I'm not, am I, Uncle Duggie?'

He stroked her forehead. 'No, Hatty,' he murmured. ' 'Course you're not. You trust your Uncle Duggie to make it all come right.'

Hatty smiled dreamily. Of course she trusted him.

The next time she opened her eyes he'd gone and Ruth was sitting by the bed. Hatty thought for a moment she was back in her bedroom. Except they didn't have a chair in their room.

'Ruth? Where am I?'

'Hospital, Hat. You got bombed, don't you remember?'

No, she didn't remember that. But something was niggling at her; she'd been out on duty, serving cocoa and sandwiches somewhere. 'I didn't wash out the canteen van, Ruth.'

'Don't worry about the flippin' van, Hat. It copped it too.

They towed it down the workshop over Lambeth.'

'Oh.' Ruth was sitting near the foot of the bed. Hatty tried to raise her head to see her properly and became aware of a large lump in the blankets. 'What's that for, Ruth?'

'I . . . er . . . you hurt your legs, Hatty.'

Hatty considered this. Now Ruth had said it, she could feel it was true. 'One of me ankles is hurting something awful. It's throbbing worse than when I got that big splinter in it in the playground. 'Ave a look, will you.' She pointed to her right leg.

Ruth shook her head. 'Yer ankle can't be 'urting Hatty. It ain't, I mean . . . I'll fetch a nurse.'

She fled and returned with the ward sister. Blankets were briskly folded back over the cage whilst she bent out of Hatty's sight to examine the legs. Re-emerging a moment later, she recovered them with the same quick movements and informed Hatty that the dressings were quite satisfactory.

'I'll ask Doctor to come and look at you. In the meantime, try to lie still.'

'Yes, miss.'

Behind the sister's back, Ruth stuck her forefinger under her nose and pushed it upwards. She accompanied this by pushing out her cheek with her tongue and chewing. It was their childhood code for 'toffee-nosed'.

Hatty giggled. A pain shot through her stomach. It triggered more memories. Uncle Duggie had been there. He'd said something about her having babies. Or perhaps she'd just dreamt that bit. Everything felt very odd.

Ruth held her head up whilst she drank awkwardly, dribbling dampness on to her chest.

'This isn't my nightdress, Ruth.'

'I fetched yours, Hatty. I washed and ironed it real nice too.' Ruth lowered her back to the pillow and slid her arm out awkwardly. Pulling her chair close to the bedhead, she said softly, 'Listen, Hat, there's something I got to tell yer. I should 'ave told you weeks back, but I knew you'd just get in a spate. And I never . . .'

Whatever she was going to say was interrupted by the swish

379

of the bed curtains. Ruth jumped back. 'Hello, Dad. She's feeling much better. Ain't you, Hat?'

She wasn't. In fact she was feeling sick now. And her other ankle was hurting too. But she managed a weak smile for her uncle.

'Dad, they ain't . . .' Ruth turned away slightly to mouth the rest of the sentence.

Hatty lip-read it anyway. 'Told me what?'

'I'll tell you in a minute, Hat. Something we got to get sorted first. You get off now, Ruth.'

'No. I want to stop with Hat. I ain't hardly talked to her yet, Dad.'

'Plenty of time to talk later. Two visitors a bed, that's the rule. Someone I want to see her.'

The prim-faced little man in a pin-striped suit who he ushered in was a total stranger to Hatty.

'I really do not find this appropriate, Mr Miller,' she heard him hiss at Uncle Duggie.

'Render unto Caesar that which is Caesar's,' Duggie replied, taking a bundle of notes from his top pocket and pushing it into the stranger's waistcoat. 'And you've charged me enough rendering, sir, to build your own Colosseum. So now let's get on with it.'

'Very well.' He placed a battered briefcase on the bed and removed a Bible and a printed card. 'Is this your own decision, Miss Miller?'

She hadn't decided anything. But Uncle Duggie nodded behind the stranger's back, so she said, 'Yes.'

'You are not being coerced in any way?'

Hatty had no idea what 'coerced' meant, but she guessed Uncle Duggie's slight head shake meant 'no'.

'Very well. We had better commence, then. If you will place your hand on the good book, Miss Miller.'

She didn't understand what was happening, but she repeated the words the stranger told her to say and tried not to giggle at his silly high-pitched voice.

Uncle Duggie gave her a nod of approval. 'Now the next.'

'It's not legally enforceable,' the stranger protested.

'It doesn't matter. Just so long as it looks right.'

There were more words for her to say. She was beginning to wish they'd go away and let her be. When it was over she lay back gratefully and closed her eyes. For the first time she became aware of other voices murmuring beyond the screens.

'Miss Miller.'

He was holding out a fat fountain pen. She signed two sheets of paper where he pointed and then sank back on the pillows again.

There was a smell of burning. It was like . . . like . . . Her heart started to thump violently as the memory of being crushed under the huge weight and feeling acrid ash settling around her nose and mouth forced its way through the after-effects of the anaesthetic and pain-killers.

Jerking awake, she found the stranger was holding a lighter to a stick of red sealing wax. He swirled the dissolving end on the sheets of paper.

'This really isn't *necessary*, Mr Miller . . .'

'I want seals. Amount you're charging, Mr Phipps, you can spare a lick of candle grease. Makes 'em look good and official.'

With an exclamation of impatience, the stranger delved once more into his briefcase, produced a brass stamp and banged it down into the wet wax. The movement jarred Hatty's legs. She whimpered at the unexpected raw pain. It was as though someone had pulled barbed wire round them.

'Careful.'

'I'm sorry.' For the first time he looked genuinely concerned. 'I'll wish a Happy New Year to you and . . . yours, Miss Miller. I trust you will soon be quite recovered.'

With an old-fashioned bow, he gathered up his possessions and left.

'Who was that, Uncle Duggie?'

'No matter. Just something your old uncle's got to get sorted out. Don't worry your head about it now, Hatty.' He blew gently on the cooling wax. 'Hatty.'

'Yes?'

'You know you've had an accident?'

Hatty frowned. 'I can't remember nothing much. 'Cept being in the canteen van with Mrs Shaw.' Her face cleared. 'And talking to Snakey, I remember that. Is he all right? He said he'd get me a bit extra for my wedding reception.'

'Listen, Hatty.' He moved the chair near the head of the bed and reached for one of her hands. Rubbing it gently, he explained that the doctors had had to cut away part of her legs.

Thinking about them made her try to move them. They felt, she discovered, oddly light. 'That ankle hurts something rotten, Uncle Duggie. I told that nurse, the hoity-toity one, she said she'd fetch a doctor. But she never did.'

'Hatty, your ankle can't be hurting because, well ... you remember Mr Collier?'

'The knife grinder?'

'That's him. Remember that little terrier of his?'

'The one with three legs?'

'That's right. Got along fine on those three pegs, didn't he?'

'Yes ...' Hatty found her mouth was dry again. She clutched the starched sheet to her chest and could feel her heart thundering between her heavy breasts. Surely Uncle Duggie didn't mean ... ?

She started gathering the blanket up in handfuls, frantically dragging it free of the mattress. The wire cage slid into view. And then her left leg. Except where her foot should be was a bandaged stump. And – even worse – there was no matching stump lying beside it. With a low moan, she pulled more blanket to her chest. Her right leg emerged; no more than a fat heavily bandaged lump.

'Uncle Duggie!'

He sat awkwardly sideways on the bed and gathered her into his chest, rocking her on his shoulders. 'There, there, girl. They'll soon have you fixed up with false ones.'

She wanted to cry. Her throat throbbed with the pain of wanting. But the tears wouldn't come, even though she could feel the wetness on her cheek. Pushing herself upright again, she found that it was Uncle Duggie who was crying.

'Whatever's this?' The ward sister swept in with an

expression that could have congealed ball lightning. 'We can't have this, Mrs Miller. Nurse . . . remake this bed immediately.'

A VAD scuttled over and started straightening and tucking as if her life depended on it, while Duggie blew his nose noisily, burying his face in a large white handkerchief.

The sister's face cracked into what might have been a smile. 'You have another visitor, Mrs Miller.' She beckoned to someone beyond the screens.

Hatty stared blankly at the nurse standing in the opening. Beaming, the girl walked forward and proffered the shawl-wrapped bundle in her arms. 'Here you are, Mrs Miller. Your son.' As they laid him in her arms, Hatty stared in wonder at the dark-mopped head poking through the wool.

'Mine?' she breathed. 'Are you sure?'

'Naturally we are, Mrs Miller,' the sister said. 'Nurse will collect him again shortly. I think ten minutes will be sufficient for today.' The nursery nurse took this hint to make herself scarce for ten minutes, while Sister swept off to deal with a querulous and plaintive demand for a bedpan.

Hatty held the bundle closer, feeling the baby's warm softness, and the light, almost imperceptible tickle of his breath on her chest as he slept. 'It's a mistake, Uncle Duggie,' she whispered. 'They got me muddled up with this Mrs Miller.'

The VAD nurse, who was still struggling with her hospital corners, said quietly, in a soft Welsh lift: 'They call all them with babies "missus". Ooh, isn't he a little peach?'

Her legs were forgotten. Hatty ran disbelieving hands over her son's screwed-up face. Gently she straightened each finger and examined it. Then she carefully unwrapped the bundle and did the same for each toe. 'He's just perfect, Uncle Duggie. Look, he's *beautiful*. Is he really mine?'

'Yours and Mr Leonard flaming Shaw's. Did you really not know you was expecting, Hat? I mean . . . your . . . you know . . . your monthlies must have stopped.'

Hatty shrugged indifferently. 'They don't come some months, Uncle Duggie. I don't mind.'

'Yes, but . . .' Duggie looked down at her bent head. With

the back of one forefinger she was stroking the baby's downy cheek, oblivious to anything else except the joy of her first child. What did it matter if she knew or not? It had happened.

'Richard,' Hatty murmured. 'I'm going to call him Richard Henry after my dad. You don't mind, do you, Uncle Duggie? I'll call the next one Douglas, I promise.'

'Best not if it's a girl.'

His feeble joke brought a smile to her face. Then her expression changed to dismay as the nursery nurse and ward sister reappeared in the screen opening. The baby whimpered at her tightened grip.

'Baby has to return to the nursery now, Mrs Miller. Nurse will bring him back at feeding time.'

An ingrained habit of never defying authority made Hatty relinquish the baby. Her fingers stretched out to follow him until the nurse was out of touching range.

'Richard,' she called after the girl. 'His name is Richard.'

'Well now, I think we can get rid of these, don't you?' Sister pushed away the screens, leaving Hatty exposed to the curious gaze of the rest of the ward and their visitors.

She looked down the row of iron beds, each occupant illuminated in the bleak January light by a row of blue-painted bulbs in the centre of the room. Some had telltale humps under the blankets like hers.

'Uncle Duggie, how am I going to look after him? I won't be able to boil up his nappies or bath him or nothing if I can't stand up proper.'

'I told you, Hat. The doctors will fix you up. Now don't you worry. You and young Richard will be looked after. You leave it to me.'

A loud clanging reverberated down the length of the ward.

Hatty gasped. 'It's a raid, Uncle Duggie. Go save Richard, quick.'

He patted her shoulder. 'It's just the bell for end of visiting. I'll be off. Is there anything else you want from home?'

'Can you fetch me soap, Uncle Duggie? Me special bar – Elizabeth Arden Geranium. Ruth knows.'

'I'll find it. Anything else?'

'Mr Shaw, Len. He was out on the pump. I ain't sure if he knows about the baby. Will you tell him?'

'Oh yes, Hatty. I'll tell him. I'll tell him.'

Chapter 38

'I don't see how she *could* 'ave a boyfriend.' However hard she tried to imagine it, the idea of her cousin with a man wouldn't form in Ruth's whirling brain.

'You said.' Betty finished bringing the occurrence book up-to-date and returned to the silent phones. After a few days of frantic fire-fighting activity, Good Hope Station had dropped into a lull, without even a domestic call-out to relieve the tedium. The sub-officer had driven them hard through hook ladder, hose and lifting drills; and in between he'd insisted they wash and polish every piece of equipment that was movable and scrub to its core everything that couldn't be shifted. Anything, in fact, to stop them brooding on Snakey's death and Hatty's crippling injuries.

'I mean, if you 'ave a boyfriend you go up the cinema and walks up the heath with 'im, don't yer? So even if she never brought him 'ome, someone would 'ave said,' Ruth continued, her voice pitched low and one wary eye on the watchroom door.

Neither she nor Betty had mentioned Hatty's baby to the rest of the station. Her visitors were confined to family only at present. So as far as the rest of the crews were aware, she'd lost her legs. The fact that she'd gained a son as well was something that the Millers didn't want generally known.

'Perhaps this man took her somewhere else,' Betty suggested.

'Up west, you mean?' Ruth considered this idea and shook her head. 'I don't reckon. I mean, sort of bloke who can afford posh places ain't likely to want to court a girl like Hat.'

'That's rather unkind, isn't it?'

'Is it?' Ruth doodled on the pad in front of her. 'I don' mean it to be. I know Hat's nice, but blokes don't fancy being seen out with her.'

'One did.'

'Yes . . . but . . . Mrs Shaw . . . you don't reckon she was, you know . . .'

'What?'

'Maybe some bloke made her do it.'

'Interfered with, you mean? But surely . . . she'd have said something?'

'Might not . . . she might not have liked to say. If he was someone important people might not believe her. Not if he was important.'

'Do *you* think that's what happened?'

Ruth stabbed the pencil hard into the pad until the lead point broke. 'Dunno. I was just saying.' She twirled the pencil, unsure how to phrase her next question. Finally she burst out with it. 'Mrs Shaw, how would you know if you was 'aving a baby?'

'Well . . . er . . . your monthlies would stop.'

Given Duggie Miller's awkward confession that he hadn't discussed intimate matters with Hatty, Ruth's question wasn't that strange, Betty supposed. But the bright, flirtatious Ruth had always given the impression that she was far more aware than her cousin. Obviously she wasn't quite as knowing as she'd appeared. Struggling to recall her own growing-up, Betty realised that no one had ever actually sat her down and explained; she'd absorbed knowledge unconsciously from her mother and a gaggle of grans, aunties and older cousins.

Ruth's mum was dead, of course. But surely someone . . . ? The tentative question brought an emphatic shake of Ruth's head.

'Me grans both died when I was in me pram, Mrs Shaw. And I ain't got no aunties. I asked the woman next door once, but she said there was time enough to be asking those sort of questions when I was married. Is that all . . . just your monthlies stopping?'

'No, there might be other things . . . putting on weight, being sick, especially in the mornings.'

'I don't remember Hat were sick.'

'Some women are lucky. Ruth, you're not . . . ?'

'No, course not. I just . . .'

Ruth could feel the hot flush of blood rushing into her cheeks and blessed the phone that claimed Mrs Shaw's attention at that moment. She hadn't meant to give herself away like that; but it wasn't until she'd started mulling over the mystery of Hatty's invisible bloke and her very visible kid that the possible consequences of her own rape had occurred to her. Betty Shaw's voice penetrated her whirling thoughts.

'What?'

'I said, this call's for Nell. Can you get her? She's on sandbagging.'

Ruth made her way to the yard. A blast of gritty wind hit her in the face as soon as she pushed her way through the back doors. The station sandbags were piled against vulnerable doors and windows and used to protect the open sides of the sheds housing the appliances. For the past fifteen months they had been steadily rotting away and were now reduced to a mush of hessian and wet sand. Headquarters' response to requests for replacements had been the sudden appearance of a lorry that had dumped several tons of sand and fresh sacks in one of the coldest weeks for months. Mercifully the watchroom girls were excluded from the rota to refill the horrible things.

Two male auxiliaries were shovelling sand into bags held open by Nell and another auxiliary as Ruth walked over.

'Scouts,' one said loudly. 'They had scouts doing this at my last posting. Did I sign up to shovel sand? No I did not. Why can't we have scouts?'

'Stop whingeing, you miserable blighter. And watch where you're chucking that sand, you've got more in me wellies than this sack . . .'

'Now who's whingeing? At least you have something left to put in your boots.'

They all became aware of Ruth's presence. The man who'd spoken shuffled awkwardly, grinding his boots into the soft pile of sand. 'Apologies, Ruth. Didn't see you there.'

'There's a call for you, Nell. 'Scuse me!' She felt the bile surge into her throat, fled behind a shed and just managed to reach a drain before vomiting violently.

By the time she made her shaky way back to the watchroom, Nell was replacing the phone receiver. Her face had acquired a waxy whiteness that Ruth normally associated with the corpses in Mottram and Cropper's before they'd been laid out properly.

It was Betty who asked: 'Bad news?'

'My brother's dead.'

'Oh Nell, I'm so sorry.'

Betty drew her down on to a spare chair and told Ruth to go see if she could find any tea. 'Or whisky. One of the men has a flask.'

'No. Thank you. Please don't bother, Ruth. I really don't care for any.'

Chafing Nell's cold hands, Betty asked if her brother was in the forces.

'Air force.' The words were scarcely audible. 'But he wasn't flying. I'm not quite sure . . .' She turned stricken eyes on Betty. 'That was my father. They don't have the details. Someone from Paul's office rang.'

'Paul was yer brother!' Ruth saw the surprise in the other two women's faces at her startled tone. Forcing herself to sound casual, she added: 'I thought he was yer boyfriend.'

'I had no idea you'd met him.'

'He give me a lift up Kentish Town Road once. Ages back. Dreamy car he 'ad.'

'Yes. He liked to indulge himself. Excuse me, I have another half an hour on duty.'

Ruth didn't bother to drop her voice, not caring whether the departing woman heard her or not as she exclaimed: 'Blimey, talk about stone-hearted.'

'People deal with grief in different ways, Ruth.'

'Not 'er. 'Ard-hearted as they come. Don't care for nothing or nobody. Stuck-up posh lots like 'er family don't 'ave proper feelings, I reckon. I bet yer a million quid you won't find Snooty Miss Grooty shedding no tears.'

It was as well for Ruth's bank balance that she didn't have a million pounds to hand when she tossed off her bitter summing-up of Nell's character.

Arriving home that evening after an exhausting round of checking up on various WPCs who'd been assigned beat duties, Sarah found the second flight of stairs blocked by a huddled figure.

'Hello, you had it too?' Flopping down on the tread beside Nell, she eased off her shoes and massaged her toes. 'My feet are freezing. I reckon they'll drop off from frostbite if I don't get an inside duty soon. I never thought I'd miss night patrols in the public shelters.' She became aware of the unnatural stillness of the figure sitting beside her. Touching Nell's arm, she asked if she were all right.

'Paul's dead.' Nell's lips twisted and her chest heaved.

Just managing to bite back her instinctive reaction of 'good riddance', Sarah put one arm round the other woman's shoulder and allowed her to sob out the storm. Once it had abated to the occasional hiccup, she said: 'Want to talk?'

Nell pulled her coat closer. 'I've done nothing *but* talk, all day. I telephoned his base in Kent. I thought perhaps . . . I was going to offer to collect his things . . . post any letters he'd left.'

'*Was* going to . . . you mean they've already . . . ?'

Nell sniffed noisily and fished in her pocket for a crumpled handkerchief. 'They didn't know anything about him being dead. They as good as accused me of being some sort of hoaxer.'

'But . . . didn't you get the telegram? You know . . . regret to inform you, et cetera?'

'No. Daddy telephoned me at work. Someone had called him, you see. I went to the Air Ministry. Because he'd been there on some kind of temporary attachment. They just kept passing me round and round from office to office. And asking to look at my identity card. I think they even telephoned Fire Brigade HQ at one point. You'd have thought I was a German spy!'

'I doubt it. A German spy would probably have been invited to join the office cricket team. So did you finally get any joy?'

'Joy?' Nell gave a short, hysterical burst of laughter, and then swallowed hastily and apologised. 'Didn't mean to act . . .'

'Crazy?' Sarah deliberately kept her tone light, inviting Nell to join the self-mockery. And after a moment, she did, managing a wan smile.

'I found someone – a WAAF – who knew which hotel Paul was billeted in. So I went there. They said he'd checked out last night. Even though Daddy said he'd been dead for days.' She shivered. 'It's like a nightmare.'

She stood abruptly. 'We had this call once – at the station. Woman trapped in a basement with an unexploded bomb. I know just how she felt, stuck there with nothing to do but listen to it ticking away her life. Maybe I should just get it over with. Give the blasted thing a helping kick and go off in a blaze of glory.'

She swirled away in a flurry of twirling coat and rushed into her room before Sarah could stop her. It seemed unlikely she'd got a handy UXB stored under the bed, but Sarah decided a close watch was called for.

Max was easily enlisted for guard duty. 'I propose a drink. If there isn't an alert. Or even if there is, perhaps. I'm sure Mrs O'Mara can be persuaded to imbibe the odd milk stout.'

'Or ten,' Sarah agreed. 'Especially if we're paying. Speaking of which, I'm a bit short at the moment . . .'

'I'll be pleased to treat you.'

'I'll pay you back.'

'Not on. One does not invite a lady out and then expect her to pay.'

'One didn't. One got lumbered with the lady, not to mention an Irish landlady with long pockets and arms as short as a leprechaun's. Do you really want Bridget along?'

'I thought it might make the situation a little easier. Provide more topics of conversation. If it were just the three of us, we might be tempted to speak of our last outing at Christmas. When *he* was there.'

'Are you ever going to tell Nell that you overheard us in that churchyard? You did, didn't you?'

'I think I heard Mrs O'Mara coming in. Shall we have a word with her now?'

Sarah accepted the change of subject meekly and followed him down to the hall.

Bridget bemoaned the fate that prevented her from accepting their invitation. 'Sure now, and wouldn't I have been proud to take you up on such generosity? Isn't a night in the pub with me friends just my idea of heaven? But it's Thursday, me dears.'

Max and Sarah exchanged blank looks.

Bridget enlightened them. 'It's *ITMA* night. Now I couldn't be missing that, could I? Ruby and I always share a cup of cocoa round the radio Thursday. It's her night off from the Bedford, you see. Well, it's a quiet night, everyone listens to the radio Thursdays.'

'I believe I have a pint of milk in my room,' Max hinted.

'Well now, we usually make it with hot water . . .' Bridget demurred.

'And biscuits.'

'Biscuits . . . ?'

'Broken. But a couple of pounds at least.'

They could almost see Bridget's mind weighing three spoonfuls of cocoa against free milk and biscuits. She evidently decided she was going to get the best of the bargain and an invitation to the basement kitchen was issued.

'I'll just go see my little nest is fit to be seen . . .' she beamed, bustling through the under-stair door.

'And hide anything else we might feel inclined to partake of . . .' Max murmured.

'I thought the Irish were supposed to be famed for their open-handedness,' Sarah whispered in return, following him back up the stairs.

'Probably why she got drummed out of Tipperary. See you later.' Max hesitated. 'Shall I ask Nell?'

'If you like. I'll just get out of this uniform.'

She'd barely undressed in the freezing room, and piled civvies on in a haphazard defence against the cold, when there was a rap on the door.

'She won't come,' Max said baldly. 'Perhaps you can persuade her.'

'My pleasure.' Marching across the landing, Sarah seized

392

the door handle with the intention of walking straight in.

'It's locked,' Max said unnecessarily.

Using the flat of her hand, Sarah gave the wooden boards her best official rat-tat. 'Nell. Open up.'

'Go away, please, Sarah . . . I really don't feel like listening to the radio. I . . . I have a headache.'

'If you don't open this door, Max will kick it down.'

'Will I?'

'Are you man or mouse, Max?'

Max appeared to give the question his serious consideration. 'I have always been very partial to cheese. And I have a terrible aversion to cats.'

'That settles it then. Stay out of my skirting board.'

Despite the situation, they both laughed. They were still chuckling softly when Nell's door opened a crack. Sarah didn't give her the chance to reclose it. Using all her weight, she thrust hard, pushing Nell backwards. A blast of freezing air hit her in the face. Her eyes swept round the normally neat room, taking in the crumpled blanket and pillow thrown across the bed; the wide-open window; and the sour smell that was lingering beneath the icy blasts of North London air.

'I should block up the chimney, too, if I were you. There's a terrible draught coming down it.'

At least Nell made no attempt to pretend she didn't understand Sarah's cryptic instruction. Standing half-outside on the landing, it took a moment longer for the last lingering fragments of gas fumes to reach Max's nose.

'Nell . . . you weren't . . . you can't . . . please don't . . .' Barging past Sarah, he grabbed the top of Nell's arms and held her a foot away from him, staring into her pale face as if he hoped to find some reassurance that he'd read the situation wrongly.

She looked bleakly back. 'Please, Max.' Placing her own hands over his, she pushed him gently away. 'Let me go.' Her weary tone made it plain that she wasn't referring to this evening.

'No!' He tried to catch her again, but she evaded his grasp.

'You don't understand, Max. I'm not . . . like other people.'

'There's all sorts of other people out there, Nell. Believe, me, I've met some rum ones on my travels. There's plenty with worse secrets than yours.'

'How do you know . . . ?'

The blue eyes under their startling black brows flashed at Sarah.

'Not guilty, guv.'

'I heard you, Nell. That night in the churchyard. I . . . we . . . had gone to look for you, to tell you we were ready to leave. And I eavesdropped. I'm sorry. I'm not proud of myself. But in another way, I'm glad I did. At least now I don't have to entirely blame your very understandable indifference to romance on my disgustingly ugly face.'

'Oh no, Max! You can't have thought . . .' Taking a swift step towards him, Nell cupped his long jaw in her hands. 'I think you're the nicest man I know. Have ever known. And your face isn't ugly . . . it's unusual. It's me that's the ugly one. After what I . . . after what Paul and I . . .'

Taking her hands away, Max retained his grip on them and guided them around the back of his neck, drawing her gently in to him. 'You are the most beautiful person I have ever met; inside and out.'

'Am I?' She dropped her head so that his lips were resting on the top of her fair hair. 'But if Paul *is* dead . . . if people read those letters . . .'

'Bugger them,' Max said.

'Max!'

His totally uncharacteristic use of a swear word brought her startled gaze up again. Max used the opportunity to press a kiss on her lips. After a token murmur of surprise, Nell responded to him.

They broke apart in a fluster of awkwardness as they remembered they weren't alone.

'Oi! Get that light out!'

The indignant bawl from below jerked all three of them into life and a realisation that the curtains were wide open. Sarah sprang across, banged down the sash and whipped the blackout across. When she turned back to the room, it became clear that

394

three was definitely a crowd in here, and she'd been elected as the third digit.

Downstairs, she half expected to find herself in an awkward threesome with Bridget and Ruby – minus biscuits and milk. But Max and Nell appeared just as the opening bars of *ITMA* rang out from the big walnut-cased radio on Bridget's dresser. Gathered round the oilskin-covered wooden table, they all giggled at the antics of Mrs Mopp, Funf and Colonel Chinstrap, sucked cocoa from broken biscuits, and listened soberly to the nine o'clock news.

'Oh, what a pity . . .' Ruby sighed as Bridget finally turned the radio off. 'It's so cosy down here. And far too early for bed.'

Sarah, who'd already received several ankle taps as Max's questing foot sought Nell's under the table, gave them a cynical look at Ruby's last remark and was rewarded by a stain like spilt cochineal flowing over Nell's normally white cheeks.

'Why, when I was a dresser I often had to sit up to three, four in the morning waiting for my ladies to come back. Such larks they had . . .'

'Now we don't want to be wasting precious fuel with larks, do we, Ruby?' Bridget interrupted sternly.

'Oh no . . . I wouldn't dream . . . to suggest . . .'

'Can't you keep fine and snug under a blanket . . . ?'

'Oh yes, yes.'

For the first time it occurred to Sarah that the threadbare little cinema cashier couldn't afford to use the gas meter in her room. 'What about a game of cards?' she suggested.

'Oh, yes.' Ruby clapped her hands. 'What a splendid idea . . . if the others . . .' she trailed off timorously.

'Cards would be lovely. Just for an hour . . .' Nell murmured, giving Max a slight smile.

'Well, I suppose . . .' Bridget eyed the pound of biscuits still remaining. 'But I've no pack. Now isn't that a pity?'

Ruby sprang up immediately. 'I have.'

They listened to her light footsteps ascending the internal stairs. As she reached the top the hard rap of the front door's brass knocker reverberated hollowly above their heads.

'Sure, who could that be at this time of night? Would it be that Mrs Shaw lost her key, do you think?'

'She's on duty all night,' Nell murmured, straining to sort out the muted voices.

Ruby's light steps returned. She slid round the door corner like a rabbit that half expected to find a ferrets' reunion going on in the kitchen. 'Nell, dear. A gentleman caller for you.'

'Me?'

'An RAF officer.'

He was a pilot officer – and thirty years too old for the rank. A no-hoper stuck forever with all the dirty jobs that everyone else was clever enough to avoid. In this case, apologising to Nell for her experiences at the Air Ministry that afternoon.

'Bit of a cock-up in communications, Miss De Groot. Deepest apologies and all that. Really, I don't know how . . . Thing is, your brother should have reported back to his squadron in Kent yesterday, and, well, lines got a bit tangled, really so sorry. Should never have happened . . .'

He looked blankly round the dimly lit hall, dangling a leather suitcase in one hand and plainly wishing he was anywhere else.

With a proprietorial hand on Nell's shoulder, Max said: 'I assume my fiancée's brother really *is* dead?'

A flutter of excitement passed from Ruby to Bridget at the word 'fiancée'.

The officer's ears burned red as he confirmed Squadron Leader De Groot's death. 'Bought it in the big raid. Looks like he was trying to get to a shelter. I've spoken to your father on the phone, Miss De Groot. I believe they've made arrangements for your brother to be taken home.' He seemed to become aware of the case and extended it awkwardly. 'I settled his hotel bill and packed up his kit last night. Your father suggested I leave it with you . . .'

The speed with which the case was snatched from his hands and slammed to the floor choked off the rest of the sentence. Flinging back the lid, Nell tipped the contents unceremoniously out. Shirts, underwear and a silver-backed gentlemen's grooming set spilled across the floor.

'Is that all?'

'The major part of his kit will still be in Kent, Miss De Groot. I'm sure the CO will make the appropriate arrangements.'

'Yes. Yes. Of course.'

'There is one more thing. If you wouldn't mind stepping outside . . .'

The invitation was made to Nell, but all five members of his audience chose to take it up. Parked at the kerb was a car that was familiar to at least three of them.

'Paintwork's taken a bit of a pasting, I'm afraid. And the hood's had it. But it's a spiffing little motor. Rescue services found it sitting safe and sound after the raid. Pity your brother didn't . . .' He turned what he was going to say into a sudden coughing fit. 'Well, I'll wish you goodnight, Miss De Groot. Sir. Ladies . . .' He touched his cap to each of them in turn. 'And once again, deepest condolences. Didn't know your brother long, but jolly good chap and all that . . .'

He headed away into the clear, cold night. After a few steps he turned and called back: 'Oh, by the way, Miss De Groot . . . I believe you were worried about your brother's letters? CO at the base said not to worry . . . he posted them himself today.'

He'd turned away again before Nell swayed. Max grabbed her with one hand, flicked open the car door with the other and lowered her into the passenger seat.

'Oh, sure now, has she fainted, poor thing?'

'Go and put the kettle on,' Sarah ordered.

Bridget and Ruby both surged back up the front steps, leaving Sarah to return her attention to the far from happy couple.

'What am I going to do, Max? I can't ever go back now.'

'That's up to you, my dear. But wherever we go from now on, we go together. Agreed?'

'Oh, yes.'

She let herself be half lifted back out of the car, and they made their way up the front steps entwined arm in arm.

Sarah watched them go with a twinge of envy, then realised they'd left her with the task of immobilising the car in accordance with emergency regulations for parked vehicles. Anything under the huge leather-strapped bonnet was out; she

397

wouldn't have had a clue what to do with the engine. Perhaps there was something under the dashboard that could be pulled or unscrewed? Clambering in, she lay flat along the front seats and peered doubtfully at the mysteries beneath the dash. There was nothing obviously detachable. Something white caught her eye.

It was only the fact that it stirred an uneasy memory, that she couldn't pin down for a moment, that made her reach under the seat and fish out the folded sheet of paper. The moon was only an eighth full, but it gave off just enough light for her to read the wavering capitals:

GOD REST YE MERRY GENTLEMEN – ADELE'S STINKING AGAIN AND AGAIN. AND COME . . .

Taking a leaf out of Max's book, Sarah blew out a breath of misty air – and swore.

Chapter 39

'Arms round our necks now, dear, just like before.'

Obediently Hatty grasped the back of the two nurses' shoulders. With a grunt of concentration, they heaved her up off the commode. The staff nurse held her nightdress up whilst the VAD wiped her bottom.

'There, all done. Let's get you into bed and then you've got a visitor.'

'Is it the baby?' Hatty asked eagerly.

'The next feed's at ten, you know that,' Staff said.

With practised ease they swung her up off the chair and on to the bed, smoothing the blankets to a creaseless plain that would pass Sister's inspection.

'I just thought maybe I could have him with me for a bit. He's ever so good. Hardly cries at all. Nobody'd notice.'

'Matron would. We can't have a cot in Surgical, dear. It's against regulations. Now don't fret. You'll see him again in a couple of hours.'

The little VAD whispered that she'd go see him in her break. 'If the nursery sister lets me.'

'And if we get a break,' her colleague said tartly. 'Take that commode to the sluice room. I'll send Mrs Miller's visitor in. Sister says ten minutes only, mind. He's to be gone before Doctor's rounds.' She swished the bed curtains back and bustled off towards the entrance doors.

Hatty peered the length of the beds, expecting to see Uncle Duggie. But instead a familiar figure in a fire officer's uniform was making his way down the ward. He stood aside to let the VAD wheel the commode past, wrinkling his nose at the putrid smell that arose from the uncovered seat.

'Len!' She waved, her heart pittering frantically at the sight of his strong, solid body.

Len Shaw stopped a few feet from her bed and stared. Her unwashed hair was hanging lankly round her beaming face. Her large, pendulous breasts hung against her pink nightdress, staining the flannel with spots of damp milk. The blankets mercifully hid her below the waist, but the ugly foreshortening of the lump on the right-hand side was impossible to ignore. Her skin exuded a scent of sweat, disinfectant and decay. He took a deep breath and knew he'd never make the lavatory before he was sick.

'Have you seen the baby? He's in the nursery. They don't let me have him up here. But he comes up for all his feeds. I got ever such a lot of milk but I have to put him on the bottle till me legs are better. Seems daft to me, but that's what the sister said. I called him Richard. After my dad. That's all right, isn't it? I expect we could call him Len if you like. We could call the next one Richard. 'Cept I promised Uncle Duggie we'd call him Douglas. But the one after could be that.'

Her chatter gave him the time he needed to swallow the vomit and pull himself together.

The next kid – dear God, was she serious? The idea of making love to that mutilated body made his skin crawl. He tried to picture himself lifting her on to that commode. Cleaning up her mess and pulling clothes up past those stumps. He couldn't do it. He *wouldn't* do it. But if he didn't, he'd be finished in the fire service. Duggie Miller had made that quite clear when he'd come round the house to break the news of his fatherhood. And lay out his future responsibilities.

'Be sure your sins will find you out. You might have got away with getting my girl in the family way before,' Duggie had said coldly. 'But not now. Not with her crippled for life and your son at her breast.'

'You can't prove it's mine,' Len had protested.

'Cast your eyes over that, Mr Shaw.'

One of the documents Hatty had signed was slapped flat on the kitchen table. Its wax seal gleamed like fresh blood whilst Len read a statutory declaration by one Richmal Harriet

400

Miller stating that he was the father of her child.

'Doesn't prove anything. She could have sworn she was the Queen of Poland. Doesn't make it true.'

'Anyone who knows Hat knows she'd not put her name to what wasn't the truth. There's this too.'

In the second statutory declaration, Richmal Harriet Miller formally informed the world that henceforth she wished to be known as Richmal Harriet Shaw.

'It's best for young Richard that his mum and dad have the same name. There'll be less questions to answer later. Here, I've written Hat's other details out; you can get down the town hall and register him now.'

It was the first time he'd heard his son's name. Despite the trap that was closing around him, Len hadn't been able to resist a small pang of pride at the thought of young Richard Henry – his boy. But he'd still tried to bluff his way out. 'She knew I was married. Can't claim I said any different.'

'Says you promised her a wedding.'

Len had tried a casual shrug. Ducking into the larder, he took a bottle of beer from the stone shelf and fetched two glasses from the cupboard. 'Drink?'

'At this hour?'

'I've just come off duty. Man's entitled to a drink when he comes home from work.'

He poured two beers and pushed one across the kitchen table, noting as he did so the film of dust over the wooden surface. It would never have got in that state if Betty had been here. But so much of the house was different now she'd gone. Already a miasma of coldness and neglect was creeping through the rooms, as if they sensed that no one cared about them any more.

'I met your wife,' Duggie said, breaking with uncanny perception into his wistful thoughts.

'Betty?' Len grasped the table edge and half rose to his feet.

'No, I've not told her. Although I've no doubt someone will soon. Nothing is secret that shall not be made manifest.'

'That a threat, Miller?'

'No, it's Luke. Chapter eight, verse seven. You should read

401

the good book more often, Mr Shaw. With particular attention to the Commandments, I reckon.'

'Keep your sanctimonious claptrap for them that wants it, Miller. Your niece weren't unwilling. In fact, she were downright keen.'

Duggie smoothed the strands of hair across his bald patch and murmured that he reckoned that might be his fault. 'I never explained things proper and I take the responsibility for that. And for part of the grief to Mrs Shaw, who seems to me to be a good woman who deserved to be cherished. But you didn't, and now it's my Hatty that needs to be cared for. You're the one to do it, Mr Shaw. And do it you will.'

'And if I don't choose to?'

'Then I'll take these up to your bosses in Lambeth,' Duggie tapped the two statutory declarations. 'And then I'll take 'em up the fire station and tell 'em how you've got my Hatty in trouble and now you want to wash your hands of her when she's in no fit state to look after herself any more.'

Len had known he was beaten. Given the desperate need for experienced firemen at present, it was unlikely headquarters would do anything much about disciplining him. But the station was another matter. Like Miller had said, he might just have bluffed his way out if it hadn't been for the kid. But now . . . ?

Silly, slow-witted, good-natured Hatty was well liked by the men. And she'd been crippled trying to look after them in the middle of a raid. He'd seen a station turn against a man. Hook ladders slipped from ledges; heavy spanners fell from the belts of firemen above; kit was inexplicably soaked; food became contaminated with salt and worse. If he asked for a transfer, word was passed down the line to his next station, and the baiting began all over again until there was no way out but to resign. Only thanks to the war's emergency regulations that prevented men leaving the service, that way out was no longer an option . . .

Duggie read his expression and saw him come to the only possible conclusion.

'Take the birth certificate up the hospital when you visit. Hat will like that. And get yourself fixed up for a divorce. I don't want our Hat's name written down in no court, so you'll have to find someone else. I heard you can hire women for that sort of thing.'

'Anything else?'

'Yes. Take her a present. I don't suppose you spent much on her when you was . . . well, I won't call it courting.'

He stood, adjusting his thinning and much-pressed work suit. Len had desperately wanted to smash a fist into that smug, self-assured face. But instead he drank down both his own glass and Duggie's, then made his way down to the registrar's office and collected his son's birth certificate.

Hatty was, as Duggie had predicted, thrilled with the document. Carefully she traced the spindly writing with one finger, repeating each word as if they'd been carved in stone and delivered by a heavenly thunderbolt.

'Richard Henry Shaw,' she breathed. 'Isn't that a fine name? It sounds sort of . . . strong . . . like you. I think he's going to look like you. He's got ever such a lot of black hair. Have you seen?'

'Not yet. Thought I'd fetch the certificate up to you first. See how you're going on.'

'My right leg aches a bit, which is funny when it's not there any more. And my other ankle hurts, specially at night. But it ain't too bad. The sister says when I'm a bit better they'll get me a chair so I can be pushed around. And then when I'm proper healed up I can have some false legs.'

His hand was resting on the sheet. She slid her fingers beneath it. He just managed to stop himself flinching.

'I know it will be a bit difficult at first. But I reckon I can still cook and wash when I'm sitting down. And I'll practise ever so hard on me legs. I won't be a burden, honest, Len.'

He knew he ought to say something reassuring, but the words wouldn't come. All the way down here he'd been picturing this scene. But the Hatty in his imagination had been weak, pale and barely conscious. Both legs sawn off hadn't sounded good. He'd known men with lesser injuries than that who'd died. In his heart of hearts he knew he'd even delayed his visit until this morning in the hope that the night would have pushed her a bit

403

nearer the need for her uncle's professional attentions.

The sister who'd allowed him in for ten minutes since he'd be on duty during normal visiting hours had soon put him right on the state of Hatty's health.

'She's a marvel. Why, she was sitting up in bed within a day of the operation feeding herself. And she's a fine healthy appetite.'

'I know.' Len had seen her eat.

The sister had given him a considering look but continued to reassure him of Hatty's continuing recovery. 'The full impact of her . . . disfigurement . . . hasn't sunk in yet of course. But the baby is a great blessing. It takes her mind off other things.'

Now Hatty's other hand covered his, holding him fast. 'You are pleased about the baby, aren't you, Len?'

' 'Course I am, Hatty.'

'And we will be married?'

'Said so, haven't I?'

She smiled and leant forward. It took him a moment to realise she was expecting a kiss. Swallowing hard, he smacked his lips lightly against hers. Her breath smelt of milk and toothpaste.

A kaleidoscope of all the women he'd been unfaithful with swirled around his head: blonde, brunette and red-headed barmaids; Marty Tanner's missus; the little widow who'd run a tobacconist's opposite the fire station where he'd been a leading hand; a handful of housewives who'd called the brigade to put out a fire in the chimney and suggested he might like to come back later and start one in the bedroom.

Some had been beautiful, others passable, a couple had been downright plain. He could have ended up with any of them, he supposed, if Betty had found him out earlier. But instead fate had landed him with a cripple whose touch caused an over-whelming physical revulsion. If he was a fanciful man, he could almost have believed he heard Betty's hollow laugh blowing in the vicious wind rattling the ward windows.

'I'd best go. Ten minutes, that nurse said.'

'You'll see the baby? The nursery's downstairs, away from the bombs.'

'I'll look in on my way out.'

'Will you come back soon? We can make plans about the wedding.'

'Trip starts in an hour or so. I'll not be off for a couple of days now.'

'Oh? Well, I'll be thinking about you.'

'I'll be thinking of you too, Hatty,' Len said with perfect truthfulness. *No matter how much I don't want to.*

He started to back away but she called him back with an urgent whisper: '*Len.*'

'What?'

'Mrs Shaw . . . 'ave you told her? About me?'

'Not been time. I mean, what with her and me being on different shifts . . .'

'She was ever so kind when I was hurt. I was so frightened. And it was like having me mum with me in the ambulance. You got to tell her the truth, Len. She said you made her feel scared.'

'Betty said she was scared of me!' Len didn't know which shocked him most. The discovery that his wife and mistress had been discussing him, or the fact that Betty . . . *Betty* . . . was frightened of him.

'No.' Hatty struggled to recall exactly what Mrs Shaw had said in the canteen van. 'She said she was scared 'cos she couldn't trust what she was feeling no more. On account of her thinking she knew you and then finding out she don't. But it's only because she got it wrong, Len. She thinks you've had ever so many girlfriends. If you was to tell her the truth . . . that it's just you and me . . . and . . . and that I'd really like us to be friends. Maybe you could find her another bloke.'

Her face lit up with this happy idea, giving an underlying sheen to the layer of sweat which had been gradually seeping through her pores. 'You must know ever so many blokes in the fire service who ain't got a wife, Len!'

He did. And he also knew with a cold, deep certainty that he'd kill any one of them who ever laid a hand on Betty.

'I got to go, Hatty. Don't worry about Betty, I'll sort things out.' Belatedly he remembered the present. 'Here. I fetched

405

'this for you.' He pulled a flat parcel from inside his jacket.

Hatty spread the baby's dress over the rounded mound of her stomach, examining the puffed sleeves and delicate blue ribbonwork over the bodice with delight.

'It's . . . it's . . . beautiful. Oh, you're so kind, Len. I'll put it with your other present. I'll make it smell nice for him.' Leaning awkwardly, she foraged in her locker and produced a flat tin. 'There's still loads left,' she said proudly, showing him the cake of soap. 'I only used it when I was coming to meet you. It's the best thing I've got. Apart from the photos of my family.'

He remembered now. He'd given her a bar of some fancy perfumed stuff the first time he'd got her down to his mate's house in Chalk Farm. He'd forgotten all about it until this moment. Yet it had been so important to her. The stupid, silly, naïve little cow. A wave of shame swept over Len and he was able to kiss her goodbye without feeling physically sick. Awkwardly he took her hands and told her everything would be all right. 'We'll work something out, Hatty. You just get better. I, em . . .' He couldn't bring himself to lie and say he loved her, but he managed to mutter that he was very fond of her, and was rewarded by a huge smile. Her trusting eyes, shining with love and adoration, followed him all the way down the ward.

If he'd been unprepared for the effect the sight of Hatty's foreshortened body would have on him, it was nothing compared to his first glimpse of his son.

Richard Henry had decided that a world that provided warm milk and cuddles on a regular basis wasn't so bad and had given up screaming his head off in favour of regular naps interspersed with an interested perusal of his limited kingdom. Len arrived just as he was waking with a large, gummy yawn.

Father and son regarded each other silently. Richard with a frown of puzzlement wrinkling his button nose, and Len with an inane grin as he held the small, solid body as if it might break.

'Len?'

It felt so right to be standing over a cot with Betty that for a moment he didn't react to her arrival. It was only a fraction of time, but it was long enough for Betty to take in the pride on his face and the protective way he was holding the baby.

'Hatty! You and *Hatty*!'

Chapter 40

'Wotcha!'

Sarah responded in kind and earned a cheeky grin from Sammy and a sharp reprimand from the hall.

'Mum don't like common talk. Hello's been good enough up to now.'

'Sorry,' Sarah said meekly, stepping gratefully from the cold wind into the relative warmth of the O'Days' house.

Pat paused on the bottom step. He was in his stockinged feet and uniform trousers, with a half-buttoned shirt flapping over them. 'Oh, er . . . hello, Sarah. I didn't mean you, I was talking to Sammy. Come through to the kitchen, fire's going in there. Mum's taken Annie up the dentist.'

Before Sarah could reply, there was another rap on the door and Nafnel marched in without waiting to be asked. 'Wotcha, Sammy. Coming up the heaf? They reckon they found a parachute up there.'

'Ours?'

'Dunno. Might be a spy. We could go look for him. Or get some shrapnel.'

'Yeah, OK. I'll get me fings.' Sammy shot upstairs on all fours.

'Nice scarf,' Sarah remarked.

Nafnel scowled at the striped monster that was wound several times round his neck and still managed to dust the floor on either side. 'No it ain't, but the dafty what lives in the bottom of our 'ouse knitted it for me. So I gotta wear it 'case she finks I don't like it. Even if I 'ate it. It's OK for swinging off trees, though.'

'Go in a shelter up the heath if the sirens go,' Pat shouted as the boys charged out of the house.

'I don't suppose they will,' Sarah said. 'It's ages since we've had a daylight raid.'

'Just as well. The night ones are bloody enough. Bastards.'

Sarah blinked. It didn't sound like the normal, easy-going Pat she'd got to know over the last year.

'Sorry,' he apologised once more. 'It's just one of our blokes – the auxiliaries, I mean – got it in the big one. It sort of brings it home to you when you've been sharing a locker room with the bloke. And his wife come up the station yesterday to collect his pay. We had a bit of a whip-round, made up his money for the week.'

'Don't the fire service do that?'

'Nah. Paid up to the day he died, that's the rule. They don't pay the dead, this lot.'

'There was a female auxiliary hurt too, wasn't there? A Miss Miller. I had to get her dad to go up the hospital.'

'Hatty. It was her uncle, though. Her dad's dead, I think.'

Whilst he was talking, Pat had been buffing and shining his leather uniform boots. He ran the rag over them from ankle to calf and said quietly: 'They've taken her legs off. I reckon if it was me I'd rather have got the full packet. Gone out quick and clean.'

'Eileen wouldn't have wanted that.'

'No.'

Despite the fire dying in the grate, the kitchen suddenly felt cold. 'But I think I would rather too,' Sarah admitted.

Pat pulled the boots on. 'I've got to go. But you stop and wait for Mum if you like.'

'No.' Sarah stood too. 'I was really looking for Ja . . . Mr Stamford. He's not answering his door. I thought he might be over here. Or is the street still no-man's-land between you two?'

'We 'ave the odd visit under a white flag. Mum don't like to leave Mr Stamford on his own with his arm being no better, and I reckon *he* don't want it to look like he's given up on Annie and left her with us for good.' He stood aside to let her precede him out of the front door and gave her a sly smile. 'Bet you didn't know I was such a profound thinker.' The grin stretched even wider. 'Come to think of it, I bet you didn't

409

even know I could use big words like "profound".'

What Sarah was actually thinking was how his smile transformed his face from pleasant to downright good-looking. It was almost a pity he was spoken for...

Her tongue caught up with her thoughts and she'd asked how Rose Goodwin was before she remembered the rift that had been caused by that stupid anonymous letter.

'All right,' Pat said, falling into step as they made their way down the Prince of Wales Road. 'She comes round for tea with Mum, but she's always got some excuse if I want to take her out.' He looked sideways at Sarah. 'See, it's that damn letter that done it. She thinks everyone's talking behind our backs. Saying it ain't right, with her Peter only being dead since last summer. If I could tell her it was from someone who ought to be in a loony bin, I reckon she might not take so much notice.'

Guiltily Sarah touched the edges of the folded letter in her pocket. All the way to Stamford's door this morning, she'd been debating with herself whether to tell him she'd found it in Paul De Groot's car. Discovering he was out had come as an anticlimax. Now she had to decide all over again.

They were nearly at the entrance to Agar Street and her feet slowed automatically, even though she wasn't on duty until this afternoon. 'Have you had any more letters?' she asked.

'No. Didn't need more than one, did it?'

'What about anyone else at the stations?'

'Couldn't say. Mind, we've had other things to worry about last few trips. Although now you ask . . .' He frowned. 'There's a different sort of *feel* to the place now. I can't rightly explain. It's like . . . well, it's more like before, when we was all pulling together.'

'Could you ask around?'

'It ain't that easy. But I'll try . . . if you promise to let me have first crack at knocking his block off when you catch him.'

'Sorry. Only inspectors and above are allowed to allocate teeth-loosening duties. If you see your mum before I do, wish her Happy New Year for me.'

'Not much chance of that. Not the way things are with Maury.'

The draughts that habitually skittered around the corner of Agar Street whipped strands of hair across Sarah's rapidly freezing face. Shaking them free gave her a few precious seconds to consider whether she ought to be talking about Maury's case to Maury's brother. But on the other hand, he probably knew more than she did.

'He's not come back?'

'Some of his things are gone from the bedroom. He must have sneaked in when we were all out. But we've not seen hide nor hair of him since Christmas. Not that I want to, but Mum worries.'

Sarah bit her lip. 'He's breaking the terms of his bail, Pat. Ding-Dong could arrest him.'

'Tell him not to bother. If he wants Maury, I'll fetch him up the station. Just drop me the nod.'

'You know where he is then?'

'Let's say I think I can lay my hands on him. Knuckles first if he gives me any lip.' He paused, hesitated as if he wasn't sure he wanted to know the answer, then asked if they'd heard anything more about the whisky robbery. 'This Hooper said anything yet that might put Maury in it?'

Sarah had no idea. Since Christmas she'd been more or less permanently on loan to other police areas. 'Half the WPCs are off sick with influenza. The rest of us are playing musical beats around the stations.'

'Right, well, if that's the way it's going to be . . . I'll be off.' A darkness passed over his face before he spun and set off up the hill at a determinedly fast pace.

It took Sarah a moment to realise he thought she was making up the influenza story to avoid passing on information. 'Oh, damn it.'

The desk sergeant nodded as she went through the Agar Street front entrance. 'Overtime?'

'For the love of it.'

'What other reason could there be?'

Flashing him a rare smile, she made her way to the CID office. Her intention had been to tackle Ding-Dong about Maury O'Day, but as soon as she stepped through the door she saw that fate had – for once – decided to save her some shoe leather. Beyond the glass panel of the internal office she could make out the outline of a familiar auburn head. There were others too. Except that the curling and yellowing notices stuck on the walls, plus the patina of ancient tobacco smoke, restricted the view to glimpses of an ear or half a cheek. The outer office itself was deserted, although a pipe smouldering in one of the ash-trays suggested its occupants hadn't gone far.

Whilst she was trying to make up her mind whether she *really* wanted to show the half-finished letter to Stamford, the door behind her opened and the other reason for her call at the station entered. Closely followed by the owner of the pipe.

'Morning, Ding-Dong. Sergeant Agnew.'

Both men nodded their hellos. Ding-Dong set down two cups of tea and wrinkled his nose. 'Shouldn't leave your pipe burning like that, Sarge. Wastes a perfectly good sock.'

Agnew shuffled back to his seat and indignantly informed the DC that that was the finest mixture from Cuba. 'I was forced to pay an urgent call to the lavs. Rationing has played havoc with my bowels. One of those teas for me, is it?'

'I regret not. We have important visitors, Sarge.'

'How important?'

'You'd better ask them. They were the ones told me they was important in the first place. Which was fortunate, because I fear I may not have noticed and assumed they were ordinary plainclothes mortals like you and me. Could you open the door for me?'

This last request was directed at Sarah. Leaning over, she twisted the handle whilst Ding-Dong picked up the two cups again. In the moment it took him to deliver them, she saw the visitors. They were both middle-aged, she guessed. One tall and bulky; the other medium height and slimly built, with thinning salt-and-pepper-coloured hair. For some reason she was reminded of Laurel and Hardy. Stamford was facing them both across the inspector's desk. Tightened muscles around his mouth told her he wasn't enjoying the experience. He caught her eye and nodded an imperceptible greeting before Ding-Dong backed out and reclosed the door.

'Is he back?' she asked. 'On duty?'

'Can't say really. Came in this morning. Shut himself in there. Arm still looks bad to me.'

'Arthritis,' Agnew said. 'Terrible thing. My wife has it, you know.'

Ding-Dong raised his eyes from the letter he was slitting open to enquire: 'Keeping it warm until you can find a spare spot for it, is she, Sarge?'

Agnew's reply was forestalled by a sharp rap on the internal glass above him. Stamford gestured for Sarah to come in.

'These gentlemen are . . .' he began as she closed the door behind her.

Laurel coughed loudly. 'Names unnecessary, Chief Inspector. You're the girl watching the De Groot female, are you?'

'No. I'm the sergeant watching Miss De Groot,' Sarah responded sweetly.

Since they'd taken the only two visitors' chairs, she was forced to remain standing. For the first time, she was glad of her height. Hopefully they were both going to get cricks in their necks.

'Any progress?'

'Not really,' she lied calmly.

Hardy flung back his head to swallow the last drops of unmelted sugar trickling from his cup. 'Not surprised. Takes a trained eye. Not the sort of thing you girls are used to. Still, any little detail will do. We'll take it further if necessary.'

'We . . .ll . . .'

They both leant forward. 'Yes?' Laurel prompted.

'I don't know whether it means anything . . .'

'We'll judge. Spit it out.'

'There is all the green ink she keeps buying.'

'Green ink?'

'Mmm . . . odd, I thought. Most people use black or blue, don't they? And there's the newspapers.'

'Newspapers?'

Sarah nodded vigorously. 'She keeps cutting words out and

413

arranging them on sheets of paper. She says it's some kind of therapy . . . but I just wondered.'

'Sergeant . . .' Stamford's tone was quiet, but the warning in it was plainly detectable.

Laurel smiled thinly. 'I see. A joke. You regard this as a laughing matter, do you?'

'I think this obsession with Nell is . . .'

'Misguided,' Stamford interrupted firmly. 'And frankly, so do I.' He drew something from the desk drawer with his good hand. 'The fingerprint officer's report. They've compared the ten letters in our possession against the prints from the knife Sergeant McNeill managed to remove from her lodgings.'

Don't do me any favours, Sarah thought sourly, catching a whiff of condescension.

Unaware of his offence, Stamford was explaining that they'd only been able to find one set of prints that were consistent across all ten letters. 'Mine,' he said succinctly. 'Miss De Groot's are only present on her own letter.'

'Astute,' Laurel said. Whether he was referring to Nell or Stamford wasn't clear. 'However, the fact of the matter is, whatever we think . . .' His look included both Jack and Sarah in that 'we'. 'Whatever we think, there are those higher up who don't want her pa's delicate nerves rattled at the moment. And if this lily-white young lady was to be caught red-handed at her correspondence . . . well . . . one can guess how her colleagues might choose to take their revenge.'

'Knew a girl worked in a match factory once,' Hardy said unexpectedly. 'Thief. Covered her in glue and rolled her in feathers. Looked like a five-foot pullet when they finished.'

'But I don't think she's *doing* it . . .' Sarah said, exasperated at this further sentencing without trial.

'Then prove it,' Laurel instructed. 'Stick with Miss De Groot like . . .'

'Glue . . .' Hardy suggested, for the first time showing a glimmer of humour.

'Exactly. Her pa's bound to be rattled by this business with the brother,' Laurel said.

For a terrible moment Sarah thought he'd found out about

the situation between Nell and Paul, but then he added: 'Funeral's tomorrow.'

'So soon?'

'Time, tide and horse-trading wait for no man . . .' Laurel said cryptically.

'Is that supposed to mean something?' Stamford enquired.

'Need-to-know, Chief Inspector.' Laurel tapped the side of his nose. 'Now listen, girl . . . you think you can keep the De Groot woman from scribbling for . . . let's say the next week?'

'Soon as that?' Hardy asked, before Sarah could reply.

'They reckon,' Laurel replied. He returned his attention to Sarah: 'Well?'

Sarah said stonily: 'I'll do my best.'

'Can't ask more than that.'

Slapping their hands flat on their knees, the two Special Branch officers rose in unison and, surprisingly, shook her hand before filing out.

'Shut the door but stay this side of it,' Stamford said as she made to follow them. He waved her to a chair. 'Sorry about them. I rather think I've wished them on you.' He looked at her bleakly across the gloomy, winter-lit office. 'I've resigned.'

'Oh? I'm sorry.'

She'd said it before she had time to think of the implications. She *was* sorry, of course, because he was a good officer – and one of the few she'd ever come across who was prepared to take her ambition to enter the plainclothes branch seriously. On the other hand, if he wasn't in the force . . . The possibilities of change in their relationship started to trickle into her mind.

'What will you do, sir?'

'Who knows? It will take a while to fix things up – retirement on grounds of disability. Hopefully I'll have found something useful for a one-armed man to do by then. In the meantime, I told Superintendent Dunn what he could do with his anonymous letters investigation.'

'So he did. He gave it back to those two.'

'Yes. Sorry.'

'Why are they only worried about the next week?'

'I have absolutely no idea. But if the clues continue to flood in at the previous rate, they're going to have a very tedious time.'

'Ah!'

'Ah?'

She drew the half-finished letter from her pocket and passed it across the desk, explaining as she did so about the delivery of Paul De Groot's car.

'And his sister was in the car?'

'Just before I found . . .' She gestured at the sheet. With more help than conviction, she suggested half-heartedly, 'Perhaps it was Paul all along?'

'With the depth of knowledge the writer showed about goings-on at the station, he'd have had to be in pretty constant touch with his sister. And she'd have had to pass on all the gossip. Is that likely?'

'No,' Sarah admitted reluctantly. 'They were barely on speaking terms. In fact . . .' There was, she decided, no reason *not* to tell him that all Nell's previous letters had been directed at friends and members of the family who adored her brother.

Stamford raised a surprised eyebrow. 'What was it? Spite?'

'Something like that.' There was, however, no need to tell him *everything*.

Stamford pointed out that Nell might have been feeling spiteful towards her workmates. 'I got the impression she wasn't well liked at the fire station. A bit too aloof for most tastes. Still, not my problem now. I just came in to tidy up loose ends. Maybe you'll find out something at the funeral. People sometimes let their guard down on emotional occasions. Say more than they mean to.'

'I don't suppose Nell will be going . . .'

'Why not?'

'Well, she'll be on duty, and she had extra time off at Christmas, and, em . . .'

'And, em, you know more than you're telling me?' He held up his good hand before she could entangle herself in more lies. 'It's all right, I've been known to tell the odd Betty Martin to senior officers myself. But I got the blush under control first . . .'

'I'm not blush . . .' Sarah began hotly. Then saw she'd fallen straight into the trap.

She expected him to probe further, but once again he managed to surprise her by simply saying quietly, 'Be careful, Sarah,' before standing to show her out.

'What about the letter, sir? Should I pass it on to Special Branch?'

It was still sitting in the middle of his desk. They both looked at the solitary sheet of paper that was the only definite link between the De Groots and the case.

'Leave it with me,' Stamford said. 'Is that the only fresh evidence that's come to light since we last talked about the case?'

The memory of what had happened the night they'd discussed the letters was hastily pushed to the back of Sarah's mind as she said quickly: 'I found out Ruth Miller got a letter. Called her a tart, I suspect.' She told him about the Millers' appearance at the same time as the faceless baby. 'I was dealing with the other, so I only heard second-hand about the Millers' letter from the desk sergeant. Anyhow, they tore it up in the end. 'Bye, sir.'

Ding-Dong was on his knees in front of the rarely used fire grate of the outer office. 'Radiators are off. Boiler's gone,' he explained, laying sticks of splintered wooden crate in a criss-cross pattern.

Sarah looked at the metal fragments he was adding to the pile. 'What on earth's that?'

'Chopped-up shell case. It burns up a treat, I'm told. We haven't got any coal, but that's just a minor problem.' He chuckled at his own joke. Which was odd, since the DC usually kept his sense of humour well hidden at work.

'New Year resolution, Ding-Dong? Crack a smile at least once a month?'

'Crack a case, more like.'

Climbing awkwardly to his feet, he leant past her and took up the letter he'd been opening when she'd gone into Stamford's office.

'It would appear Eddie Hooper has seen the light. He wants

417

to see me and make a full statement about his accomplice in the warehouse robbery.'

Chapter 41

'Man that is born of woman hath but a short time to live, and is full of misery...'

You can say that again, Vicar, Sarah thought silently. Surreptitiously she tried to move her feet up and down to restore the circulation. The cold in the unheated church had seeped up from the stone floors and reduced her toes to ten stubby icicles. Now the numbness was working its way towards her ankles and making her thankful she'd decided to wear her uniform shoes. At least the stout lace-ups were keeping some of the wet out, and she'd managed to retain her balance on the slush of damp grass and trodden leaves in the graveyard. Unlike some of the mourners, who'd opted for fashionable rather than practical and now looked as though they wished they were somewhere else. *But then don't we all?* Sarah mused.

Nell certainly had last night.

'I'm not going,' she'd said baldly. 'I shouldn't even be off duty. But the sub-officer got to hear about the funeral somehow and ordered me home immediately. I really can't think who told him. Even I didn't know the details until I telephoned Daddy.'

'Well, don't look at me. I just heard myself, didn't I?' Sarah lied. She'd had a call from her own woman inspector that afternoon, confirming that her shadowing of Nell De Groot was to take precedence over her other duties. Which was fine in theory, but lacked any practical suggestion as to how she was supposed to lurk around the fire station. From her point of view, accompanying Nell to the funeral would be a darn sight easier than impersonating a fire hydrant!

'But you must face them sometime, my love,' Max said.

'And it's like falling off a bike. The longer you leave it before you climb back on again, the harder it will be.'

'They don't arrest you for falling off a bike,' his beloved had said. She and Sarah were seated on the bed whilst Max took the chair in Nell's room.

'Arrest?' Max's eyes flew to Sarah, seeking . . . what? Reassurance? Confirmation.

She wasn't really in any position to give either. 'Those letters . . .' she said hesitantly. 'Well, they do contain details of a crime . . . incest is a misdemeanour. But they couldn't arrest you at the funeral . . . the case has to go before the Director of Public Prosecutions. And since your brother's dead anyway . . .'

'You could say you made it all up.' Max beamed.

'I never said that . . .' Sarah protested.

'Of course you didn't. I'm sure you have far too much respect for the law, Miss McNeill. Fortunately I have no such scruples and will be quite happy to support your pose as an exceptionally precocious young lady with a lurid imagination, my love. Let the law try to prove otherwise if they wish.'

'I don't care what they prove or disprove,' Nell exploded. Flinging herself back against the pillows, she hugged her knees in an uncharacteristic tomboy pose. 'Don't you understand? Everyone will *know*. People I've known for years, reading my letters. Seeing what I did. And the worst part is . . . I won't even be sure which ones they are.'

She started to rock herself back and forth, still clutching her knees.

'Every time someone serves me in a shop; every time I go to church; every time I walk down a street; I'll be watching and wondering. Which ones know? Who's laughing behind their polite smiles? Is that one crossing the road because they haven't seen me or because they're so disgusted they can't bear to be near me?'

Her voice had risen to near hysteria. Max came swiftly across and took her shoulders. 'Stop it. Stop it this minute!'

Sarah saw the mounting storm start to ebb again as Nell regained control of herself. The long, slim fingers came up to cover Max's on her shoulders. 'I'm sorry. I want to be brave, I really do. It's just . . . what should I do, Max?'

'Go home,' Max said firmly. 'I'll be with you. Everything together from now on, remember?'

Her knuckles whitened as she gripped his hands. 'If you think it's right, Max.'

'I do.'

They made such a strong, solid duo that once again Sarah felt decidedly intrusive. Remembering her orders, she intruded a bit further and said: 'I'm on leave tomorrow. I'll come with you if you like.'

If they hadn't liked it, it could have been a little tricky. But fortunately Nell was pleased to accept a bit more moral support.

Which had caused further problems with Paul's two-seater car.

'There's a bit of a gap behind the seats now the hood's up,' Max said, as they huddled inside their mourning clothes, trying to ignore the spiteful wind skittering beneath coat hems and probing down collars and into gaping sleeves. 'I could squeeze in there.'

But Nell would have none of it. 'I'm the smallest. You drive, Max, and Sarah can take the passenger seat. 'You *can* drive, can't you?'

'I can, my love.'

'Oh good. There's so much I don't know about you, Max.'

Lifting one of her leather-gloved hands to his lips, Max said quietly: 'Well God willing we'll have the next fifty years to find out.'

Nell managed to clamber over the seats with some difficulty and ease herself to the floor. Her head appeared over the seat back like a jack-in-the-box. 'There's a blanket back here I can sit on.' She wrinkled a fastidious nose. 'It smells terrible. Smoke and . . . some kind of cheap perfume.'

'Never mind. The ventilation system will soon sort that out,' Max said, thrusting his arm through a large charred hole in the hood above her head. 'Whatever did this must have missed him by inches.' He fed Paul's case in beside Nell, and then invited Sarah to hop in.

421

She hopped as instructed. Max started the engine. Nothing happened. Belatedly Sarah recalled her attempt to comply with the Motor Vehicles (Control) Order the other night. 'Immobilise stationary cars, you know . . . I, em, pulled something out under the bonnet.'

Once they'd undone the leather strap from the bonnet, and Max had located and replaced the 'something' she'd detached, they clambered back in and the ignition started.

Nell pointed to a dial. 'The tank's nearly empty. What are we going to do? We haven't got any petrol coupons.'

Bridget rose to the occasion with a knowing wink in Sarah's direction and the promise of a friend who could oblige. 'For a bit of a wet, you understand?'

'More like Noah's flood,' Max murmured, when he ended up handing over two pounds for one can of pool.

Wondering whether her orders to stick close to Nell super-seded any obligation to arrest black-marketeers, Sarah heaved the can up, tilted it over the tank and discovered she was breaking yet another law. The liquid was bright red and should only be used in a commercial vehicle.

'Oh well . . .' Sarah added the last pint, rescrewed the cap, returned the can to Bridget and clambered into the passenger seat once more.

They'd finally arrived in St Albans just as the cortège was preparing to leave for the church.

The vicar had stopped speaking and was looking expectantly at the De Groots.

Holding hard to her husband's arm, Margot picked up a handful of earth and threw it on to the coffin. Globules of wet clay stuck to her gloves. She tried to free them with a washing movement over the gaping grave.

'Out, damned spot,' someone murmured *sotto voce*.

Her husband stepped forward and gently but firmly pushed her arms down. Taking her elbow, he drew her back.

'Paul . . . my poor boy. We can't leave him here, Charles . . . it's so far away.'

'I'm afraid we must, my dear. Part of him will still be with us . . . you'll see.' He captured her hands and rubbed them comfortingly.

Nell came next. Her face was impassive as the soil spattered over her brother's coffin.

The vicar's wife stepped forward, plainly regarding herself as next in the pecking order of mourners. Max touched her arm briefly, stooped, and sent a shower of gravel bouncing off the brass plate. It announced his relationship to Nell more effectively than inserting a notice in the local paper. The ripple of speculation swayed amongst the mourners like a breeze in a field of wheat. Only his future in-laws were too wrapped up in their own grief to notice.

Others followed. Mostly locals, apart from a wing commander who seemed to be representing the Air Ministry and a middle-aged flying officer who'd coughed and spluttered through the entire service with a ferocity that had caused the undertakers' eyes to light up with a mercenary gleam. The lack of official ceremony was odd, Sarah reflected, stepping back to allow others to file past the open grave. Apart from the two RAF officers and a Union Jack draped over the coffin, there was little evidence that this was a military funeral.

The puzzle was partly explained by the wing commander's murmured apologies to Dr De Groot. 'Such short notice. If the ceremony had been nearer your son's base, we could have arranged a better turn-out. But can't let a whole section go, even for a few hours . . .'

'Please. Apologies are unnecessary. My wife and I wanted a private service.'

Stepping awkwardly backwards, the wing commander made to salute, nearly lost his footing and would have fallen into the open grave if the doctor hadn't grabbed him.

'It's the wrong 'ole,' a voice beneath Sarah's elbow grumbled. 'Always brings bad luck, that. People should stick to the 'oles that's been dug for 'em.'

Looking down she found a wizened, nut-brown old man glaring at the departing guests.

'This isn't the squadron leader's hole, then?'

'Agnes Susannah Sligoe, last of this parish, I dug this 'ole for.

423

Graveyard's full of Sligoes. Always good breeders, the Sligoes.'

'And they used the grave for Squadron Leader De Groot instead?'

The sexton bobbed his head. With his long, lined neck and balding head, he looked like an aggrieved tortoise in a battered tweed jacket and cord trousers. 'Now I got to dig another 'ole for old Agnes. It's a mercy she's dead or she'd be creating merry hell about being kept stood in this wind.'

With a scowl he shuffled off round the side of the church, leaving Sarah to wonder about the hasty burial.

She glanced round. The mourners had split into small groups. Their subdued voices rose and fell, releasing odd snippets of local gossip into the cold air and leaving the few outsiders like herself and the RAF officers to drift awkwardly from knot to knot.

Nell and Max were still standing silently by the open grave. Their heads were close together in an intimacy that said they wouldn't welcome her just at that moment. She drifted over to the edge of the churchyard, hoping it wouldn't be long before they could set off for the De Groots' house and tuck into the promised funeral tea and drinks. The stiffer the better, Sarah decided, turning her collar up. The bleak, bitter coldness of December 1940 had flowed into January 1941. She found herself feeling sorry for the solitary landgirl struggling to fork straw and manure across a frozen field behind the church.

'Crumpets and log fire weather, isn't it?' a voice said behind her. The explosion of hacking coughing that followed this remark allowed her to identify the flying officer before she turned round. He'd arrived in a rush at the same time as they had. Falling out of a local taxi, clutching a large wreath that had moulted leaves and flower heads across the pavement outside the De Groots' house.

'Don't think we met, did we? I'm Sarah McNeill.'

'Wilcombe. Clive.'

'You're the one from the Kent squadron, aren't you? The place where Paul was based?'

He nodded. 'Bad form I know, being late for the funeral. But couldn't be helped. I came by train. Nearly didn't make it. Jerry strafed us. Didn't expect it.' He looked up at the bare-branched trees and hedgerows framed against the graphite-coloured sky. 'It's not flying weather, they tell me.'

'Tell you? Aren't flying officers supposed to know that sort of thing?'

'Oh, I don't fly. I'm the intelligence officer. That's why I could be spared for this funeral. Flyers are essential for a Spitfire squadron. Intelligence isn't.'

He grinned and she smiled back. Then they both became aware that hilarity was out of place.

'Did you know the Skipper well?' Wilcombe asked, suppressing a cough in his handkerchief.

'Let's walk,' Sarah suggested. 'Before we freeze. And no. I didn't. I'm a friend of Nell's.'

'His sister? That's her over there, taking a turn round the headstones, isn't it? He had a picture of her in his locker. I, em, helped clear it out.'

'Really?' Sarah took his arm and steered him in another circuit of the drive.

During the service she'd been alert for any signs of nods and nudges in Nell's direction, but hadn't been able to pick up on any. And the De Groots, from what she'd seen, had exhibited no signs of disgust or discomfort in their daughter's presence. In fact, Margot had leant against Nell as they'd climbed into the car for the journey to the church.

'I wonder,' she said, keeping a grip on the flying officer, 'I wonder if you noticed any letters when you were clearing out the locker? Nell was told that they'd been posted, but they don't seem to have turned up . . .'

'Oh dear.'

She waited patiently until the next spasm of coughing had passed. 'Oh dear?' she prompted.

'The CO did ask me to post them, but this bug rather brought me down . . .'

'So you didn't put them in the post . . . ?'

'No. Actually, I brought them up today. They're all local addresses. Don't suppose a couple of days made much difference, do you?'

You'll never know, mate, Sarah thought triumphantly. She was tempted to fall on the poor man's neck and kiss him but decided she didn't fancy his bugs. And she was pretty sure the bugs reciprocated.

'Anyway they've got them now.'

'What!'

Flying Officer Wilcombe took a nervous step backwards. 'I said they have them now. I just handed them out.'

Sarah glanced round wildly. She was in time to see the vicar's wife turning over an envelope in her gloved hands. She held her breath. The vicar said something. His wife looked up, nodded and walked across to him, pushing the envelope in her coat pocket.

'Listen.' Sarah grabbed Clive Wilcombe's arm again. 'This is very important. Can you remember exactly who you gave them to?'

'Well . . . em . . .' He dissolved into another paroxysm of coughing. Sarah thumped him none too gently between the shoulder blades.

Two minutes later she was walking as fast as she dared without attracting unnecessary attention. Nell and Max had abandoned Paul's grave and were now browsing amongst the older plots. They'd stopped before a large set of white marble steps crowned with a cross. It was dedicated to the memory of *Hannah Margaret Ramsbottom 1850–1921, wife of the late Paul Edmund Ramsbottom and beloved mother of Margot De Groot (née Ramsbottom).*

'My grandmother,' Nell said as Sarah came up. 'She left most of her money in trust for Paul. He was quite well off, you know. He never had to rely on Daddy for money. Perhaps if he had . . .'

'He'd have been a nicer human being. Although frankly I doubt it . . . Listen, Nell. You see that woman by the grave?'

Nell glanced across. A stout, grey-haired woman in black was reading the cards on the flowers that the undertakers had laid in a line by the piled earth. 'Mrs McGregor from the tea shop. What about her?'

'She's got one of Paul's letters.' Rapidly Sarah explained

about Flying Officer Wilcombe's personal delivery service.

'So no one has had a chance to read them yet?' Max said. He looked round. The small groups were starting to drift towards the cars. 'How many . . . ?'

'Only three, according to Wilcombe,' Sarah replied. 'This McGregor woman, the vicar's wife, and your father.'

'But there were lots more than that . . . a dozen at least,' Nell protested.

'Paul probably didn't hang on to them all . . .' Sarah made a rapid reconnaissance. There was a good chance the De Groots would wait until they could read their son's letter in private. 'If I get Mrs McGregor's, can you deal with the vicar's wife? She put it in her coat pocket. Right-hand side.'

'Will do.' Max headed off with a purposeful step. Nell hesitated, then followed him.

Sarah sauntered across to Mrs McGregor. With her feet planted wide apart and her coat straining across several yards of spreading backside, the woman bent over each floral tribute, muttering to herself: 'T-r-ragic; t-r-r-agic.' She straightened up as Sarah's feet came into view, pushing back the hat that had fallen over one eye. 'T-r-ragic,' she repeated, the rolling 'r' confirming that her Scottish connection wasn't confined to Mr McGregor.

'Quite terrible,' Sarah agreed. 'Were you a close friend?'

'Oh yes. Known him since he was a wee lad. Oh, but he loved ma seed cake. He wouldna go back to school unless he had a big slab of ma seed cake in his tuck box. There's no one makes seed cake like you, Greggy, he used ta say. I baked him one special for Christmas. It's sad ta think it was the last time. Oh, but he was a lovely boy. And a handsome man. If I'd been thir-r-ty years younger, ma dear.'

The last remark was accompanied by a coy smile and a pat on Sarah's arm. Apparently she'd been taken for one of Paul's girlfriends. Not one to waste a good cue, she stifled a sob and started patting her pockets and fishing up her sleeves. 'Sorry . . . hankie . . .'

'Oh, here y'ar, dear-r-rie.' Mrs McGregor fiddled with the gilt clasp on the capacious leather bag over one arm and extracted a minute lace-edged scrap. It gave Sarah enough time to glimpse a white envelope tucked in the central pocket.

'Thank you,' she gulped. With a few more sobs, she flung herself into Mrs McGregor's arms. As she did so she slid her foot behind the older woman's. She'd only intended to knock her off balance and give herself a chance to grab at the bag and flick the clasp as she steadied her. But she overcompensated for the woman's heavier weight, leant harder than she should have, and felt them both toppling.

Sarah landed on her knees but was too late to grab the other woman. To her horror she looked up just in time to catch a glimpse of pink knee-length bloomers, thick lisle stockings and sensible brogues as Mrs McGregor slid backwards into the open grave.

Chapter 42

'Oh, hell . . .' Sarah said loudly, completely forgetting where she was. Scrambling over the edge, she peered down and found that Mrs McGregor was lying sideways across the coffin. 'Are you all right?'

'Oh dear . . . oh dear-r-rie me. Fancy that. Th-r-owing myself at a man in uniform at ma age . . . ma dear mather would have had a fit . . .' To Sarah's relief she broke into a deep chuckle as she struggled to extricate herself.

'Hang on.' Sarah dropped down beside her. She landed by the brass plate screwed to the lid. It was a simple engraved statement: *Paul Edmund De Groot: 1912–1940*. A deep, almost primitive horror shuddered through her. Just a few inches below her all that vitality and sexuality had started to rot away to nothing. Despite everything she knew about him, a small flicker of that attraction she'd felt on the park bench on Christmas Day flared for a brief second. The smile that lit up his eyes; that rather mocking way he lifted one eyebrow; his voice. No one would ever see or hear them again . . .

Giving herself a brisk mental shake, she leant over to help Mrs McGregor. 'If you stand up, I could boost you up over the edge.'

Still laughing, the other woman did her best to lever herself upright.

A nut-brown tortoise popped its head over the side. 'The wrong 'ole. I said the wrong 'ole was unlucky.'

'Oh, hush your blether and pull me outta here, man.'

It would have been like an ant trying to heave a walrus up. But fortunately several other people had seen what was happening and come running across. Between them they pulled her out, to chuckling assurances that she was quite all right, thank you. 'I t-r-r-avel with ma own cushion,' she panted, slapping her substantial rear.

Sarah extracted a sodden hat that had slipped down one side of the coffin and passed it up. 'Hang on.' She bent again and pulled the leather bag from where it had become wedged down the other side. 'Here you are.'

It was Max who took it from her and offered a hand to help her out. As they came face to face, she dropped him a quick wink. He responded by raising a thumb.

Two down, one to go.

It proved the most elusive. For the simple reason that they couldn't be sure where the doctor had put it. Once he was safely back in his own house, he had plenty of opportunities to lock it in a drawer or bureau, and it was impossible to watch him amongst the ebb and flow of guests helping themselves to the rather meagre food.

Liquid refreshments were in more generous supply, since guests had contributed the remnants of Christmas and New Year bottles. Tea, sherry and whisky were on offer, and as the last two went down, the level of noise went up. The hushed, reverent tones of the graveyard were replaced by animated chatter about relatives posted abroad, elusive rationed goods and the fact that the De Groots had taken down their Christmas decorations before Twelfth Night.

The doctor, fortunately, was occupied with supporting his wife. Their positions seemed to have become reversed. Her down-to-earth bustle had been replaced by a vague confusion, as if she didn't quite recognise her own house. Whereas the doctor's woolly academic air had given way to a decisive practicality. He moved from group to group, seeing everyone was suitably refreshed, accepting condolences and joining in reminiscences of his son's past exploits.

It gave Sarah the opportunity to slip into the study and check his desk. She'd been half-afraid the drawers would be locked. They weren't. Neither did they contain anything, apart from a few worn stubs of pencil, bent paper-clips and a rusting pen nib. Puzzled, she looked round and realised that the shelves that had been crammed with books on her last visit were now half-empty. Other details started to impress themselves on her mind. The photo frames in the dining room had gone. She surreptitiously slid one of the drawers of the bureau out. It came easily; about half the cloths and napkins had been removed.

The chattering groups were still coalesced in clumps downstairs. Murmuring 'Toilet, excuse me' to anyone in earshot, she slipped upstairs. The doctor's overcoat was hanging behind their bedroom door. The pockets were as empty as his study drawers. With one ear straining to the stairs, she opened the wardrobe. Half the hangers were empty. A large leather trunk, strapped and marked 'PLANE', was standing on the floor.

The bedroom door opened before she could reach it. Her mind whirled, concocting excuses, and settled back into neutral when she saw it was Nell.

Her anxious eyes asked the question. Sarah shook her head. 'No luck yet. Are your parents going away somewhere?'

'They haven't mentioned they had any plans . . .' She spun round as the door opened again. 'Oh Mummy, I was just showing Sarah the curtains. I think a pattern like that would be perfect for her room.'

It was a pretty feeble excuse, but Margot was in no condition to notice if they'd started a Morris dancing troupe in here. 'I need an aspirin.' Wearily she opened a bedside cabinet. 'Oh dear. I forgot. I've packed them.'

'Packed? Where are you going?'

Margot stared at her daughter from eyes ringed with purple shadows, then, inexplicably, she burst into tears.

'I don't want to go and leave you and Paul back here in the middle of the bombing. But I have to go with Daddy, you do see that, don't you? He needs me, else he'll be working all hours, forgetting to eat or change his shirt . . . Well, you know what he's like . . .'

'Yes. I know.' Nell joined her mother on the end of the bed and put her arm round her shoulders. It was an awkward gesture, confirming that there had never been much open

431

affection between mother and daughter. 'But where are you *going*, Mummy?'

'Minnesota.'

'Minne . . . *America*!'

Margot sniffed and used the hem of her eiderdown to dry her eyes. 'I'm not supposed to say. It's a secret. But I don't see why I shouldn't tell my own daughter. Daddy has a new job. Some American company that's been doing the same research. It's a very good job. You wouldn't believe the wages these people pay. And they're giving us a house too. Daddy says we'll be gone for several years at least.' She took Nell's hand. 'If only you hadn't joined up, you could have come with us.'

'But how?' Nell asked. 'I mean . . . Daddy's doing vital war work, isn't he? Surely he won't get an exit visa?'

'We have. We leave as soon as Daddy gets his files up-to-date. That's why we had to bury Paul so quickly.'

A light clicked on in Sarah's mind. 'Horse-trading', the Special Branch officer had called it. Officially the United States was neutral in this war, and whilst their government's support had been generous, there were still those in the States who opposed *any* form of involvement in a European war. But the British Government was allowing a scientist vital to the war effort to leave the country – complete with working files – and join a commercial firm in the States. So what was slipping across the Atlantic in the opposite direction? Different research? Arms? Money?

No wonder the Government had been so keen to keep Charles De Groot in a stable frame of mind during these last few weeks. A man on the verge of a nervous breakdown might have been regarded as damaged goods. Presumably once he was safely delivered and the swap complete, Nell could run amok with a fire axe if she liked.

'Oh, Nell . . .' Her mother took both her shoulders and looked her full in the face. Margot's lips twisted in an effort to hold back the tears again. 'Oh Nell, I do wish you'd found a nice man to take care of you.'

'But I have.'

A little of the colour came back to Margot's face. The tears were forgotten. 'You mean you . . .' The fingers of her left hand slid over her daughter's.

'We haven't had time to get a ring, Mummy.'

'Oh well, never mind . . . Who is he? Have I met him?'

'It's Max.'

'*Max!*' Margot's mouth dropped. 'But Nell, you can't. I mean, there are so many more . . . some of Paul's friends . . . RAF officers . . .'

Nell withdrew her hands. 'I,' she said slowly and distinctly, 'am marrying Max. I hope I do it with yours and Daddy's blessing. But I'm of age and I shall do it anyway.'

'Yes . . . but . . . oh Nell . . . you'll be *Mrs Death*! And what on earth will my grandchildren look like! When I think what pretty babies you and Paul were . . .'

'Looks aren't everything, Mummy.' Defending Max had given Nell courage. Her eyes sparkled dangerously. 'None of you could ever see beyond Paul's good looks, could you? I'd rather have a thousand Maxes than one Paul!'

'Nell! How could you say that? And today . . .' The tears were returning, spilling into the caked make-up below her eyes. 'Paul adored you. You were his baby sister. He left you everything.'

'What!'

'Didn't you know? All his money comes to you.'

'No!' Nell sprang up. 'I don't want it! I won't have it! Give it to charity!'

'Nell!' Margot gaped at her daughter's whirlwind exit from the room. With a small apologetic smile for the fact that she hadn't tactfully made herself scarce when this conversation became personal, Sarah left too.

Nell's bedroom door was partially open. She poked her head in, thinking perhaps she'd gone in there, but the room was empty and dust-sheeted. Beyond the window, she could see a drift of hazy smoke from the back garden. Charles De Groot was standing by a small bonfire, apparently feeding papers into the blaze. She watched Nell march up the garden, hand in hand with her intended. Charles lifted his head and said something.

Continuing in her role of the visitor who didn't know when

433

she wasn't wanted, Sarah made her way out to join them.

Nell greeted her with a brilliant smile that was totally at odds with her earlier tantrum in the bedroom. 'Sarah. Something wonderful. Daddy's spoken to his bosses here and they're going to offer Max a job. A proper position: chemical research. It's a reserved occupation, so he won't be called up.'

'But aren't you too . . .' Sarah bit off what she was about to say.

Max finished for her. 'Old? As a matter of fact, no, I'm not. In fact I've been expecting a letter for the past few weeks. They've reached my age for call-up. I'm very grateful, sir.'

'Charles, please. After all, we're family now.'

'He can live here.' Nell snuggled up to her fiancé's arm. 'And I'll see if the London brigade will let me transfer to the local auxiliary service here.'

I should think they'll chauffeur you down here, Sarah thought cynically, given the trouble Nell had unconsciously caused the brigade recently.

A puff of smoke billowed upwards from the fire, making them all cough.

'Forgive my rudeness,' Charles said, indicating the bonfire. 'But I suddenly recalled some more papers I couldn't leave behind. I do hope your mother is taking care of our guests.'

'I don't think they need taking care of any more. They're doing quite well by themselves.'

'Oh no! How stupid . . .' The doctor started making ineffectual snatches at the flames.

'Daddy, don't, you'll burn your hands.'

'But the letter . . . the letter . . .' The doctor waved his hands over the fire, which had the effect of fanning the flames even higher. 'Paul left a letter. That flying officer gave it to me at the church. I put it with these papers . . . oh, heavens, how could I have been so stupid . . . ?'

They watched the blackened envelope edges curl in on themselves and burst into flames. The doctor blinked, took off his glasses, polished them on his waistcoat and replaced them as if he couldn't quite believe what he was seeing. 'Now we shall never know . . .'

'No.' Max took something from his own pocket, ripping it into shreds as he did so. 'Reminds me. I have a bit of rubbish I wished to dispose of.' He cast the vicar's wife's letter into the fire.

Sarah promptly did the same with Mrs McGregor's.

'Well, that's that, I suppose.' The doctor frowned towards the house. 'I think I should be getting in. It would seem rude not to see guests off. It's fortunate I didn't mention the letter to your mother.'

He made his way over the slightly slippery grass to the back door. Sarah sent a silent salute after him for a brilliant performance. Obviously only she, from her position at the bedroom window, had seen him reading the letter just before Nell and Max joined him.

Nell slid her arms round Max's chest and hugged him. 'I'm free, Max.'

'Not quite, my love.' He returned the hug. 'I've got you for the next fifty years, if you'll recall . . .'

'Yes . . .' Nell raised her mouth for a kiss. 'On two conditions . . .' As Sarah prepared to be the perfect guest at last, Nell turned to her. 'No, don't go, Sarah. One of these concerns you. Max . . . tell me what you really do. I don't believe for a minute you travel in cosmetics . . .'

'Yes I do.' Max looked between them. 'In a manner of speaking.'

'Speak!' his beloved commanded.

'I have a specialist market . . .'

'Yes?'

Max saw he was trapped. 'Undertakers.'

'Pardon?'

'What?'

'I supply make-up to funeral parlours. Crème powder for carcasses; mascara for mummies; blusher for bodies . . .'

The two women started laughing. Nell's peal was the most light-hearted sound they'd ever heard coming from her.

'It's a very specialised market, I'll have you know. There's no body heat to blend the ingredients . . .'

'You mean they were a dead loss as customers?' Sarah suggested.

Nell giggled even harder, and Max silenced her with a kiss. 'Now, my love, what's the other condition?'

'That Sarah finds out who's sending those anonymous letters to the fire station.' She fixed an appealing stare on both of them. 'You see, I don't think it's me, but I need to be *sure*. I couldn't put Max through what I put my parents through . . .'

'But I don't care. I mean, I'm certain it isn't you . . . but if it were . . .'

'As a matter of fact, I've had an idea about that. Can I use the phone, do you think?' Sarah said.

Chapter 43

'Sorry I'm late.' Ruth slid into a chair by her cousin's bed. 'I was waiting for Dad to come home from work. But he ain't. Must be doing overtime.'

'Are you?' Hatty turned her head wearily on the pillow. 'I hadn't noticed.' She ran a cupped hand over her son's dark hair. 'They let me have him up here for visiting time. Ain't he wonderful, Ruth? And he looks just like 'is dad, don't he?'

Ruth gave her new nephew a less than affectionate look. 'You ought to 'ave told me, Hatty. About you and Mr Shaw. You really ought ta!'

'I couldn't. Len said I wasn't to. Not till he'd told Mrs Shaw. Is she ever so upset, Ruth?'

'Well of course she flamin' well is! Honestly, Hat, Dad's right, you have got cotton wool between your ears.'

'That ain't nice. And it ain't none of your business anyhow, Ruth Miller.'

'Oh yes it flamin' well is,' Ruth hissed, keeping her voice down below the general chatter of the ward. 'I gotta work with her. She had a right go at me in the watchroom last night. Said I must 'ave known. Reckoned I'd been laughing at her behind her back. She slapped me face. The sub-officer reckons one of us will have to be transferred. Everyone up the stations knows now.'

'I don't care.' Hatty kissed the downy head. 'He's ever so good, Ruth. I can't wait to push him out in 'is pram.'

Ruth's eyes flicked involuntarily to the stumps under the blanket. It would be a long time before Hatty walked again; if she ever did. She wondered if perhaps Hat was deliberately forgetting. She was good at that: stubbornly refusing to see things that didn't fit in with her own ideas.

The sight of those mutilated legs made her feel guilty about her own grievances. 'Listen, I got a bit of good news for yer. And . . .' she produced a package clumsily wrapped in old newspaper, 'I got you some pears. They're a bit hard but you can leave 'em for a bit.'

'I'll have to. I ain't allowed to eat anything. See.' Hatty pointed to the notice over her bed saying *Nil by Mouth*.

'Why not?'

'It's because me leg ain't getting better.' Hatty pointed to the longer stump. 'The doctor wants to cut a bit more off.'

Ruth felt even worse. Here she was moaning on just because Betty Shaw had belted her, and poor old Hat was going to be cut about again. She looked at her cousin closely and saw that her complexion had a greyish tinge that hadn't been there before. She seemed to be sweating quite a bit as well. And – Ruth's nose twitched fastidiously – there was a funny smell like rotting apples.

'What's wrong with it then? Yer leg?'

'I ain't exactly sure. The doctor said something got in when I was lying in the dirt. Anyhow he said it would be better if they made them both the same length. Make it easier to learn on me metal ones. I expect it'll be like that bloke we saw once up the fair on Hampstead Heath. On the big stilts, remember, Ruth?'

'Yes.' Ruth found she was crying. This was awful. How could Hatty be so brave about it? If it had been her, she was sure she'd have found some way to drag herself to the window and throw herself out.

Hatty peered at her. 'You don't look too good yourself, Ruth. You feeling poorly?'

'I've been sick. I . . . I was sick this morning too.'

'Oh. 'Spect it was something you ate. It's a pity I didn't know I was 'aving a baby, Ruth. We could 'ave got a green ration book and we could have gone to the front of the ration queues. Saved ever so much time. What's this good news then?' Hatty's face brightened briefly. 'Is Len coming?'

'What? No, his watch is on duty till tomorrow.'

'Did you hear that, Richard? Your daddy's coming to see you tomorrow, that'll be nice, won't it?' And Hatty started to croon a wordless song into the baby's head.

Ruth watched uneasily. She had a sense of something slipping away. She'd always thought she'd be the one to go. But now Hat was moving on and leaving her behind.

'Listen,' she tried again. 'There's something I gotta tell you.'

She was interrupted again, this time by a trolley clanking to the bed. The VAD pushing it smiled and cooed at the baby. 'Ooh, isn't he a lovely one? Ooh-chi-coochee . . .'

Young Richard seemed to have got the idea that he was supposed to gurgle in response to these inane sounds. After a brief period of mutual admiration, the VAD straightened up and announced she had to shave his mummy now.

'Shave me?' Hatty ran a large hand over her sweating face.

'Not there. Further down. They didn't have time when you come in. You being an emergency an' all. But it's to be done proper this time, Sister says. Shall we pop the baby back in his cot for a minute?'

'No. Ruth can hold him, can't you, Ruth?'

Doubtfully Ruth received the bundle. She wasn't too keen on babies, and unlike Hatty had never felt the need to mother her dolls. However, once her nephew was snuggled in her arms, she found the experience quite enjoyable. Jiggling him gently, she paced up and down the ward. The baby watched the dim glow from the hanging lights with wide-eyed fascination. Ruth offered him a little finger and he sucked vigorously. It gave her a strange feeling. Perhaps she might like to have babies after all; one day, perhaps, when she could bear the idea of a man touching her again. But at present she woke up every morning praying for the crippling stomach cramps that would tell her she'd come on and wasn't carrying Paul's child. So far her prayers had remained unanswered.

The staff nurse clanged the bell loudly to announce the end of visiting. Richard yelled in protest. Turning him awkwardly into her shoulder, Ruth patted his back and made 'there-there' reassurances. It worked. She felt quite proud of herself. The curtains were still drawn around Hat's bed. She took another turn along the ward, joining the visitors who were obediently streaming out. Through the circular glass panel in the door, you could see into the sister's office. She glimpsed a familiar head nodding and speaking to someone out of sight.

'There's your uncle . . . no, great-uncle,' she corrected herself. She held Richard up so he could see as well. Not liking the position, the baby cried vigorously. The sound attracted Duggie's attention. He said something to his hidden companion and then came out into the ward, followed by a young doctor.

Ruth whisked the baby into her shoulder again with a skilful twist of her wrists and was flattered when he stopped crying immediately.

' 'Lo, Dad. Did you have to stop at work?'

'Carriage broke down. Rear axle . . .' Duggie said dismissively. 'You heard Hatty's not too good?'

'She said she had to have another bit off. But you said the doctors reckoned she was doing ever so well.'

'Your sister took a turn for the worse, Miss Miller. It happens sometimes.'

'Hat's me cousin. What's up with her then?'

'Her left leg. I'm afraid gangrene has set in.'

'Oh?'

'They've got to cut it out before it gets a hold and poisons her blood good and proper, Ruthie.'

'Oh!' Ruth found her eyes filling with tears again. 'Poor Hat. She will be all right, though, won't she?'

The doctor rattled a tray. 'She has a good chance if we catch it in time. I'm going to prep her now. They'll take her down in half an hour or so.'

'Can we stop with her?'

'We . . . ll . . .' With a wary glance at Sister's empty office, he suggested they might if they kept out of the way.

Hatty greeted them with the information that the razor didn't half tickle. Lifting the sheet she peered underneath and asked why they'd shaved her there. 'They're not going to cut me right up there, are they, Uncle Duggie?'

'No, Hat. It's just what they do in hospital. Procedures, like. How's my girl then?'

He leant over the bed and kissed her. Hatty squeezed him back and held out her arms for her son. Ruth laid the baby on his mother's chest, where he was pillowed between her heavy breasts and soothed by the steady rhythm of her heartbeat.

With a wide yawn, Hatty said: 'I feel ever so tired.'

'It's what the doctor give you, Hat. You just lie back and get a bit of sleep. And when you wake up it will be over, all right?'

'Yes, Uncle Duggie.' Through another yawn Hatty asked if he'd be there when she woke up.

' 'Course I will. Wouldn't leave my girl, would I?'

'Oh good. Because I am a *bit* scared, Uncle Duggie. I wish Len was here. He makes me feel safe. He's so big and strong.'

Duggie's lips tightened, but he took her hand and held it on the sheet, gently rubbing his thumb over the knuckles.

Hatty twisted round and tried to reach out with her other hand. 'Ruth, can you get me presents out . . . in the locker . . .'

'You can look at them after your operation, Hat.'

'No. I want them now . . . *please* . . .'

'Get them for her, Ruthie.'

Under Hatty's guidance, Ruth located a white baby robe with blue ribbonwork, and the tin that contained Hatty's best soap that only she was allowed to use.

Hatty gathered them into the crook of her free arm. 'They're from Len,' she explained. She gave another enormous yawn and her eyes closed for a moment, then opened again. In a sleepier tone, she asked if they'd taken the Christmas decorations down at home.

Ruth and Duggie exchanged a look over her body. Neither of them could recall noticing the decorations for some time. Presumably they'd just blended in with the rest of the furniture.

'Well, you know, Hatty, we'd not that many to take down. It was always you had a knack for that kind of thing. Making the house seem like a home. I don't know how we'd have managed without you after your Auntie Doris died. Best thing I ever did bringing you to live with us. Your mum and dad would have been real proud if they could have seen how you turned out, Hat.'

'Do you really think so, Uncle Duggie?' Hatty turned her

441

head on the pillow with difficulty, as if it had suddenly become too heavy for her neck. 'Only I been thinking about them a lot since I been lying here. I wish they could have seen Richard.' She took her hand from his to cuddle across her son. 'Wish my gran had sent me a picture of my mum, too. She'd not have missed just one. And I'd have liked to have remembered what she looked like.'

'Just like you . . .' Ruth said suddenly. 'She looked just like you, Hat. I know she did.'

'Ruth's right. You're the spit of your mum, Hat. And soon as you're better we'll go down and see the old lady and *make* her hand over one of them blessed photos.'

Hatty smiled sleepily. Her eyes closed again. For a moment they thought she was fast asleep. Then, with her eyes still shut, she mumbled: 'Uncle Duggie? You know the silver threepenny that goes in the Christmas pudding? I can have it to take with me, can't I? You promised.'

' 'Course you can, Hat.' He patted her hand and she twisted it round so her fingers linked into his.

'That's good. I don't feel so scared now, Uncle Duggie. I'll make a nice Christmas for us all next year. We'll have a proper tree from up the market. And stockings like we always have . . . with 'range . . . an' appl . . . and a little one for Rich . . .'

Gradually her breathing became more even, and Richard rose and fell on her breast to the sound of her snoring until the little VAD came to take him back to the nursery and place the baby robe and soap tin back in the locker. Then the staff nurse and a couple of porters lifted Hatty gently on to a wheeled trolley and took her down to theatre.

Thirty minutes into the operation her heart failed and she died.

442

Chapter 44

They managed to catch the last bus back to Camden Town.

A soldier offered Ruth his seat because she was carrying the baby. Richard was wrapped in one of his mum's nightdresses since they didn't have a shawl. Duggie had to stand all the way with the rest of Hatty's belongings bundled up in her other nightdress. There was a Saturday-night feeling amongst the passengers. Their breath exuded alcohol, their chatter was loud and light-hearted, with much discussion of the film they'd just seen, the partners they'd just danced with or the plans they had for the rest of their leave.

Ruth sat staring blankly at them. She didn't understand why the world was still going on as normal when Hatty was dead. It was worse than when her mum had died. Because then there had been Hat, bustling around, polishing and cooking and chivvying them along in an imitation of her Aunt Doris's cheerful tones, so that in a way it had seemed as if her mum hadn't died, just become younger.

And now there was just her and Dad. She looked up at her father, seeking some sort of reassurance. He was staring at the back of the next strap-hanger's neck with a glazed expression. Somebody had put the pears she'd brought for Hatty into the pink flannelette bundle and they were spilling out through the gaps by the knot and rolling amongst the passengers' feet. Duggie didn't seem to notice. There was no comfort to be had there. Her dad was as lost as she was. She shivered despite the fuggy atmosphere inside the bus and grew up a little bit more.

The bus dropped them in Camden High Street and they walked the last few yards through the blacked-out streets in near silence, apart from the occasional murmur from the baby, who didn't like this first taste of the world outside the hospital.

They'd had to argue before the hospital agreed to hand him over. There was no medical reason for Richard to stay in the nursery; he was a healthy baby who'd only been kept in so that he could be with his mother. But the doctor in charge of the maternity section had pointed out that the child had a father, and that surely he was the legal guardian now.

'If Len Shaw wants him, he knows where we live, he can come fetch him. In the meantime, I'll be taking our Hat's son home. It's what she'd have wanted.'

In the end, they'd let Duggie have the baby on the grounds that he was still listed as Hatty's next of kin on her admission forms.

'Do you think Mr Shaw will want him?' Ruth asked, sitting in the dark kitchen with the baby in her arms, whilst her father fixed the blackout.

'I can't say, Ruthie. Since his name's on the birth certificate I suppose he's got the right. But I don't see how he'd manage being at work for forty-eight hours at a stretch. Unless he puts him out to a foster mum.'

'Hat wouldn't like that, Dad. We can keep him.'

Duggie picked up the bucket and went out to the coal shed before replying. Coming back, he crouched in front of the small grate, laying a fire. 'We're in the same boat, Ruthie. We've to work too.'

'But I could stop home, Dad!'

'I'm not sure they'd let you resign the fire service, Ruthie. It's not like it's your own kid. But sufficient unto the day, eh? Let's get him settled tonight.'

They made a cot by padding a drawer with a folded blanket, and cut a towel in half so they could change his nappy. And then discovered they were out of milk.

'Didn't you take the bottle in off the step this morning?' Duggie asked.

'There wasn't any.' Ruth bit her lip and asked if he'd paid the milkman recently.

444

'Me? No. Hat always . . .' Duggie stopped. There were so many things that Hatty had taken care of.

'What we going to do, Dad? We haven't got a bottle or nothing. And he'll want feeding in the night, won't he?'

'If he's anything like you were he will. I could ask next door for a borrow, I suppose.'

But it would mean explanations, and they hadn't told anyone in the street about Hatty's baby yet. By mutual silent agreement they decided to put the moment off a little longer. They didn't want people saying Hat was no better than she should be. Not tonight.

Duggie took an enamel jug from the cupboard. 'Rest centre down the veterinary college has been fitted up for those that's been bombed out. I reckon they'll have a few bits and pieces for the kiddies. I'll see if they'll let me have a loan of a feeding bottle and some milk. After all, his mum was got by enemy action, weren't she? I'll be quick as I can. You'd best cut up another towel; we'll need more than one nappy.'

After he'd gone, Ruth put the baby's cradle on the kitchen table and sat by it, carefully dissecting their thinning towels. Fortunately most were still clean from her washing onslaught on the night she'd killed Paul. The memory of how calm and strong Stan had been filled her mind as she cut steadily along the fraying material. 'I wish I'd been nicer to Stan,' she informed her nephew.

Thumb in his mouth, he blinked sleepily at her. His long, curling eyelashes fluttered on his cheeks and he slept. Ruth wanted to cry for his mum; but the tears just wouldn't come.

The front door knocker reverberated in the small hall. Assuming her father had forgotten to take his key, she pulled the door open saying: 'It was on the latch . . . oh!'

It wasn't her dad at all. For a second she had a terrible sense of time spinning backwards to the night she'd opened the door to Paul. Then her eyes focused and she saw the man on the step wasn't in uniform.

'Good evening, Miss Miller.' He took his hat off. 'Remember me?'

'You're that policeman who came up Good Hope Station

445

with Pat O'Day's little brother and that other kid.'

'Chief Inspector Jack Stamford. I called earlier, but you were out. May I come in?'

He already was in. Ruth supposed he meant could he come into the kitchen, so she led the way. 'You said the kids wanted to look round the fire station, but they didn't really, did they? Betty Shaw told me about you being on some investigation. I know she weren't exactly supposed to, but . . .'

'But people do gossip in a fire station, don't they, Miss Miller? I don't imagine there's much else to do in the slack periods.'

'The blokes play cards and darts and things . . .'

Stamford took a seat at the table without being asked and took a peek in the makeshift cradle. His expression softened for a moment. 'Boy or girl?'

'A boy. He's Hatty's son.'

Ruth waited for the conventional expressions of regret. None came. Once again she realised that the whole world neither knew – nor cared – that Hatty was dead.

His next question knocked the breath out of her. 'Do you know a Squadron Leader De Groot? His sister works at your fire station.'

It was on the tip of her tongue to deny everything, when she recalled telling Nell that Paul had given her a lift once. Maybe he already knew the answer and was trying to trick her?

'He gave me a lift. To work.'

'I think you knew him rather better than that, didn't you, Ruth?' The voice was quiet but firm. It was phrased as a question, but the tone said he already knew the answer.

'I . . . em . . . went out with him. Just the once. But me dad don't know.'

Richard whimpered in his sleep. To her surprise, the policeman reached over with his good arm and stroked the baby's cheek gently with one finger until he was quiet again.

The gesture made him seem more human and gave her confidence. 'Why do you want to know about me and Paul?' she asked boldly.

'He's dead.'

446

Ruth's new-found courage evaporated. He knew she'd killed Paul. 'How . . . I mean . . . ?'

She'd meant to say: 'How did you find out?' But he misunderstood her and replied: 'He was caught in the big air-raid. They buried him today.'

Ruth's thundering heart slowed again, a wave of dizziness hit her and she had to grip the table edge to stop herself sliding off the chair in a dead faint. He didn't know. Nobody knew except her and Stan. Paul's body was safely hidden under several feet of earth. They'd got away with it! She realised the policeman was still talking. Something about a policewoman being in Paul's car.

'There was a blanket in the back with a particularly distinctive smell. Sarah . . . Sergeant McNeill . . . smelt the same scent the morning she came here to ask your father to go to the hospital. Carnation, she thought.'

'Talcum powder. I spilt some.'

'Bit cold for a blanket this weather, wasn't it?' Stamford said, raising one eyebrow.

He thought she and Paul had been tussling on the floor of some empty street shelter presumably. Well, she could hardly tell him what she'd really used the blanket for, so she tried to force a blush and look coy.

Stamford took a folded paper from his pocket. 'She also found this on the floor of the car. It must have got caught up in the blanket.'

Ruth's heart skipped again. She replayed the past few weeks. It wasn't from the blanket. The half-finished letter must have dropped out of the jacket Paul had returned.

He spread the sheet flat with his good hand and said quietly: 'So why did you write them, Ruth?'

She opened her mouth to lie her way out, and found she hadn't either the will or the strength. A tear trickled down her cheek.

'I didn't mean to, honest. Not all of them.' Her voice rose as the ache in her throat grew stronger with the strain of holding back her tears. 'Adele . . . one of the girls over at Control . . .'

'I know Adele.'

447

'Yeh ... well ... she said something nasty about me. So I sent her a letter saying she smelt. Which she *does*. Sometimes. I only meant to send the one. But then ... she had to come over and help out in Good Hope watchroom for a day because one of the girls went sick. And she was reeking of this awful carbolic soap and she kept going in the washroom and scrubbing and scrubbing ... and it was ever so funny. So a few days later I sent her another one, to see if I could make her do it again ... and then I started wondering if I could make other people do things.'

'How did you know what to write?'

'I didn't exactly. I mean, the men tell me things, but mostly I just sort of guessed. I'd send a letter and then watch and see if the person did anything. And if they looked put out, I knew I'd guessed right and I'd send another one. It was fun, knowing I could make people do things without them knowing it was me. It got sort of like I couldn't stop ... And then when Mrs Shaw said as how it was to do with national security – well, it was really exciting, like being a secret spy or something.' A flicker of pride lit her face for a moment. 'I was clever though, wasn't I? I remembered about fingerprints.'

'Have you *any* idea of the damage and misery you've caused, Miss Miller?'

His voice was even, but she sensed that inside this self-contained, grim-faced man there was a steely anger that was far worse than anything she'd ever encountered before.

'I'm so sorry,' she whispered. 'I did stop. I haven't sent any for weeks.' Not since Paul had raped her and she'd started to understand that the world wasn't the exciting adventure she'd always pictured it to be, and that it wasn't just bombs and things that could hurt. 'Are you going to arrest me?'

'Not at present. However, interfering with the work of persons involved in essential services – such as the fire service – is an offence under Defence Regulation 1A, so there may be charges brought. But you haven't told me the whole story, have you, Ruth?'

A coal fell in the grate, sending up a shower of sparks. It

briefly glinted off his auburn hair and showed her the hard lines of his face.

'I'm not sure what you mean . . .'

He drew out a list of dates and pointed to the one at the top of the list. 'This is the earliest letter I can trace. Your father brought it into the police station in early September. I believe he initially intended to report the matter, and then something happened to change his mind.'

'There was a baby . . . When Dad saw it he said the letter didn't matter no more . . . It was horrible . . .' The headless child. She'd thought that day she'd never forget it, but already she almost had. Would she forget Hatty like that one day?

'I know. Sergeant McNeill told me.' Surprisingly his voice sounded kinder. 'But you see, Ruth, I find it hard to believe you started off by sending an anonymous letter to yourself. I really don't think you're that devious.'

That clever was what he really meant. But she didn't care any more. 'It was Dad's fault. Going on and on about me letter and making me show it to him. Well, I didn't have time to write much, and anyhow he'd have known it was my writing. So I printed big capitals.'

'And called yourself a whore?'

Ruth nodded. 'It's the sort of thing people put in those letters, isn't it? We had a film like that up the Gaisford once.' She bit her bottom lip. 'I thought Dad would chuck it on the fire. I didn't know he was going to go up the police station.'

'Why couldn't you show him the real letter?'

'Because it wasn't for me. It was for Hatty.' Her blue eyes opened wider in an automatic gesture of innocence. 'I didn't steal it, honest. See, Hatty's real name is Richmal Harriet . . . and the letter said Miss R. Miller . . .'

Stamford assured her he understood the mistake. 'Who was it from?'

'Her gran. Her mum's mum. The one who never wanted nothing to do with Hatty.'

In a somewhat tangled and breathless recitation, she explained about Hatty's mother coming from a middle-class family and marrying Uncle Dickie against her parents' wishes.

And Hatty's later attempt to get a picture of her mother which had led to a formal disowning of both her and her mother.

'Hatty said she wouldn't have nothing to do with the old horror after what she'd said about her mum. And she meant it too, because Hatty can be stubborn like you wouldn't *believe*.'

'I take it you've seen the old lady? Since you know she's an old horror?'

Ruth nodded. 'It . . . the letter, I mean . . . said she might be prepared to forgive Hatty on certain conditions and reconsider the terms of her will.'

'I see.'

'Well, why shouldn't we have her money?' Ruth's chin went up. 'She'd only changed her mind because the nephew she was going to leave it to got himself sunk on the Atlantic convoys. And she didn't have anyone else left except Hat. Serves her right if you ask me, nasty old bat.'

'You went to see her pretending to be Hatty?'

Ruth nodded vigorously, sending her black curls dancing. 'I used to say I was going to see my mate Lulu in Bedford. The old horror's house is in Flitwick so I just had to get off the train a couple of stops early.'

'And she never suspected?'

'Why should she? She'd never seen Hat, had she? Anyway, she was half-blind. I used to have to sit by her bed and read to her from the Bible and agree how ungrateful and undutiful my . . . I mean Hatty's . . . mother had been to defy her parents and how awful it was of her to disgrace the family name by going into service . . . She just went on and on about that. Hatty wouldn't have said all those things about her mum . . . not if she was promised a million pounds . . .'

'But you did . . . ?'

'Yes. I sat in that horrid smelly room for hours and hours saying everything she wanted me to. And it was all for nothing.' Her face twisted and the tears fell in large peardrops to splatter the wooden table.

'You mean the old lady found you out?' Stamford asked.

Ruth shook her head. She opened her handbag and dragged out an official-looking letter. 'It's from her solicitors . . .' she said in gasps. 'She's dea . . . d. Three days ago. She's left the lot to Hat. And I ne . . . ver got to tell her. Because Hatty's dead!' The grief came then in one huge Niagara of tears and words. Hatty was dead and she'd never see her again. Stan hated her. She'd never live in a big house or have a handsome husband now because it wasn't what she wanted any more . . .

The noise woke Richard, who screamed in sympathy.

Walking in on the scene five minutes later, Duggie found his great-nephew bawling his head off in the drawer whilst his daughter sobbed her heart out on some strange bloke's shoulder.

Chapter 45

They gave Hatty a service funeral. Superintendent Bailey gave the address at the church and all crew members who weren't on duty climbed aboard a hired bus to follow the hearse and relatives' carriage on the long journey up Junction Road and the Archway to St Pancras cemetery.

'She'd have appreciated that,' Duggie murmured, nodding through the car window to the silent group of firefighters who stood with heads bowed as the carriages passed between the main and auxiliary stations.

'She wouldn't have known where to put her face, Dad,' Ruth said. 'You know how she couldn't say boo to a goose if there was a lot of people around.'

'Yes, you're right. She wasn't one for a fuss, my girl.' Duggie reached out blindly for his daughter's hand and squeezed. 'You take care yourself in this new station of yours, you hear me, Ruthie? They're a funny lot south of the river.'

'Yes, Dad.'

There had been no real nastiness from the stations since her authorship of the poison-pen letters had come to light. The approaching funeral and respect for Hatty's memory had kept recriminations to a formal request from the sub-officer that Miss R. Miller would not report for duty again until directed to do so. This morning's post had brought a letter informing Firewoman R. Miller that she was transferred to Lambeth HQ, where she should report for parade at 08.00 hours on the following Monday.

'I'll come see you on my days off, Dad. And Richard too, if Mr Shaw gets him minded somewhere local.'

Len Shaw had arrived on their doorstep two days ago and

452

demanded his son. He'd left with the baby and the promise ringing in his ears that if he didn't do right by their Hat's son, he'd have Duggie Miller to deal with.

'That's right, Ruthie, we'll still be a proper family.' Duggie squeezed her hand ever tighter. 'You are all right, are you? You look a bit pale. Not feeling faint?'

'No, Dad. I'm OK. It's just . . .' She slid a hand over her stomach. 'I started this morning.'

Embarrassed at having intruded on a female problem, Duggie made vague noises that could have been sympathy or apology. Ruth lay back against the car upholstery and allowed the waves of stomach cramps and sickness to pass over her. For once she welcomed them. It was the only good thing that had happened since that awful night with Paul. At least she wasn't going to have his baby.

At the cemetery gates Mr Mottram himself stepped from the hearse and beckoned the four firemen who were to act as pall-bearers. Dismounting from the bus, the fire crews shuffled to line up behind. With Ruth and Duggie going first, followed by the senior officers, the firewomen and finally the firemen, the procession wound its way to the dark hole in the near-freezing earth and laid Firewoman Richmal Harriet Shaw (formerly Miller) to rest.

As a final gesture Duggie threw something in. The silver threepenny bounced and twirled over the surface of the oak coffin and spun to rest on the brass name plate.

'There you are, Hat. I didn't forget, see.'

In subdued groups they started to make their way back to the transport and the funeral tea which was being provided in a private room over the Oxford Tavern.

Betty Shaw caught up with the Millers. 'Mr Miller, I'm not coming back with the rest. But I just wanted you to know that I'm very sorry about Hatty. She was . . . a nice person.'

Duggie stopped. His hand went up in that automatic hair-smoothing gesture of embarrassment. It caught his hat and knocked it to the ground. Stooping and mumbling at the same time, he retrieved it and thanked her for her kindness. 'I know what our Hat done wasn't right, but she never meant no harm to anyone in her life. She just . . .'

'She just trusted the wrong man,' Betty finished for him. 'Well, that gives us something in common, doesn't it?'

Duggie blew his nose noisily. 'You're a good woman, Mrs Shaw. I told your husband that. I hope you stay safe.'

She offered her hand and he shook it awkwardly. Ruth, who'd been hovering in the background, received the smallest nod of recognition. There were limits to Betty's forgiveness, and those anonymous letters still rankled. Then she followed the straggling groups winding amongst the gravestones. A figure in front of her had stopped in front of a granite headstone, apparently fascinated by the engraved message in which Violet White somewhat immodestly urged her husband to rest in the bosom of the angels until he found greater happiness with his beloved wife again.

'Betty. Please wait.'

'I don't think we've got anything left to say to one another, Len.'

'I have. Damn it all, Betty, I'm still your husband, I've got *some* rights, haven't I?'

Out of the corner of her eye, Betty could see other figures swerving and veering off as if she and Len had an 'Unexploded Bomb' sign pinned to their backs. Mind you, she thought ruefully, that was probably a pretty good description of them. The idea brought a brief smile to her lips.

Misreading it as encouragement, Len stepped eagerly forward and tried to take her arm. She twisted free angrily. 'Just say what you've got to say, Len.'

What he had to say was everything he'd already said. That none of the others had meant anything. That Betty was the only woman he'd ever loved. 'You must believe me, love.'

'Oh, I do believe you, Len. But that doesn't make it any easier. Have you any idea how humiliating it is to have everyone know that you preferred to go to bed with a great fat thing like Hatty?'

'But I didn't prefer . . . it was just . . . being sick of steak and kidney and fancying a bit of scrag end for a change . . .'

'I don't suppose it should make any difference really, what

454

she . . . they . . . looked like,' Betty continued as if he hadn't spoken. 'But it *does*. It hurts that much more because she was such a plain lump. The funny thing is, I can't seem to hate Hatty. But you . . . Len . . . you . . .'

She whirled away, surprising several groups of firemen who'd found excuses to hover just out of earshot, ostensibly taking quick drags on cigarettes or removing imaginary turds from boots.

'Betty, wait. This is your last chance. I'll not ask again, I'm warning you . . .'

Head high and spine straight, his other half called back over her shoulder that she had a wedding to go to.

Nell became Mrs Max Death by special licence in a quiet register office ceremony. The bride looked radiantly lovely in a powder-blue suit with matching veiled hat and a corsage of hothouse orchids. The groom wore his one and only black suit and managed not to crack any mirrors.

Only the bride's parents and the other inhabitants of the Vorley Road boarding house were invited. Bridget O'Mara, resplendent in a purple suit, fox-fur stole and a hat that looked as though several inhabitants of the parrot house at London Zoo had given their lives in its cause, acted as one witness. Sarah McNeill, in a pale-grey suit and saucy black hat, stood as the other.

'Oh, isn't this exciting? So *romantic* . . .' Ruby trilled for the fiftieth time, flitting round Bridget's basement kitchen in a swirl of ancient damson velvet that exuded a strong scent of mothballs.

'Oh sure, will you find a perch, Ruby, and take a glass,' Bridget instructed. She dispensed one of the two bottles of champagne provided by Dr De Groot with a liberal wrist, which became even more liberal as it passed over her own glass. 'Will you be cutting the cake now?'

The white cardboard 'icing' was lifted off the plain fruit cake and a single cut made by the bride and groom before Bridget whisked it away to slice into neat squares.

The doctor invited them to toast the happy couple and Max

responded by thanking them all for coming: 'Particularly Nell.'
He slid an arm round his new wife's waist. 'I know it is
traditional to say that she has made me the happiest man in the
world . . .' He paused. 'And I see no reason to break with a
perfectly good custom. I don't know if I can give her a fraction
of the joy I am feeling at this very moment, but I swear I'll
spend the rest of my life trying to do so.'

He kissed her soundly to loud applause and lamentations
from Ruby that Dr De Groot's box camera couldn't take a
picture down here.

'I fear we shall have to leave you to get the pictures
developed, Max,' his father-in-law said, placing the camera on
the kitchen table.

Nell disengaged herself from her husband's arms. 'So soon?'

'A taxi is to collect us in . . .' The doctor checked his pocket
watch, 'ten minutes. Our luggage is already at the station.'

'Are you going on a little trip then? Sure now, isn't that nice?
I love to travel myself. Mr O'Mara took me to Galway for our
honeymoon. He'd the family there to stop with, you see.'

Max responded to the blatant fishing on Bridget's part by
remarking that *they* wouldn't be going quite that far. 'One night
at the Ritz is all I can offer, I'm afraid, my love. Perhaps your
taxi could give us a lift into the West End, Charles?'

'What! Oh, Max, why didn't you say? I've nothing to wear!'
There was a flurry of activity as Nell flew upstairs to pack a
case.

Bridget drew Sarah to one side and suggested she might
change rooms with Max. 'That way they can have a cosy little
flat up there on the top floor, and I'll not charge them a penny
extra for it.'

'I'm afraid we may be giving notice shortly, Bridget,' Max
interrupted.

'Leaving? Two rooms empty!' Bridget's round eyes became
ever wider at the impending tragedy.

The arrival of the taxi saved them from her full repertoire of
hardships. In whirls of laughter, tears, hugs and promises, the
foursome piled into the taxi and rolled away in a cloud of
Ruby's home-made confetti.

'Oh dear . . . oh dear . . .' Ruby tottered back to the kitchen, drunk on half a glass of champagne and a whole afternoon of friendship. 'I must go. The box office.' She hiccuped and giggled.

Sarah collected her square of cake. 'I'll walk out with you if you wait until I've changed . . . I'm on night duty.'

Bridget looked towards Betty.

'I'm not on duty again until tomorrow morning.'

'Ah well . . . it's hardly worth opening a bottle for the two of us.' And the unopened bottle of champagne disappeared into Bridget's store cupboard.

Sarah wished the drunken little cinema cashier goodnight and got off the bus at the top of Kentish Town High Street, leaving Ruby to trundle down to Camden.

Her excuse for leaving Vorley Road early had only been half-true. She wasn't due on parade for several hours yet, but today was the day that had been set for Ding-Dong's interview with Eddie Hooper in Pentonville Prison. And she desperately wanted to know if Eddie had implicated Maury O'Day in the warehouse robbery.

Apparently she wasn't the only one. The first person she saw as she reached Agar Street Police Station was DCI Stamford.

'He's not back yet,' Stamford said simply.

Sarah nodded. There was no point in pretending either of them was here for any other reason than the coming explosion in the O'Days' house.

'Canteen's still open. May I buy you a cup of tea?'

'Thank you, sir.'

For once Sarah didn't give a damn about the speculative looks that were cast in her direction because she was sharing a table with Jack Stamford. Elbows on the table and sipping two-handed from the cup, she stared at the dismal emulsioned walls and wondered how on earth she'd ever face Eileen again if Maury was sent to prison.

'Have you noticed anything?' Jack asked her.

Puzzled, she looked around. There didn't seem to be

457

anything – or anyone – new in the canteen.

'Not there. Here.' Jack picked up a teaspoon and stirred his cup with exaggerated swirls.

'Your arm, it's better.'

Wincing, Jack flexed the shoulder. 'Better is perhaps a bit optimistic. But it's undoubtedly mobile again.'

'When? I mean, how?'

'Well, oddly enough, I think I've got Ruth Miller to thank. When she started howling on my shoulder, I put my arm round her.'

'You didn't say,' Sarah said accusingly.

She'd seen him briefly after her return from St Albans in order to find out the result of her phone call regarding the telltale scent in Paul De Groot's car. And to fill him in on the reasons behind Special Branch's obsessive interest in Dr De Groot, since she hadn't dared discuss the American swap on an open telephone line.

'I wasn't sure. I think I'd just become so accustomed to holding the arm in this position that I didn't realise it was only stiffness keeping it locked there now. Anyway the MO says I'm to exercise it whenever possible.' As proof that he was doing as he was told, he rolled the shoulder joint several more times. 'He also said the arthritis could strike again at any time, but in the meantime . . .' He executed a final victory roll, picked up his cup with the injured arm and toasted her. 'Cheers.'

'Here's to a happier year,' Sarah responded. 'I can't believe they aren't going to charge that wretched Miller female. What on earth did she do something so . . . so . . . *spiteful* for?'

'I think she started to enjoy the power. The feeling of being able to manipulate other people. I doubt she'll do anything like that again. Her cousin's death made her grow up fast.'

'I still think she got off lightly . . .'

'I daresay. But Special Branch lost interest the minute they realised the De Groots weren't involved. And the fire service would rather just forget the whole thing – bad for morale to drag her through the courts. Not to mention airing a whole graveyard of skeletons they'd rather keep safely hidden, I suspect.'

Sarah snorted. 'What's going to happen to the money . . . the cash Hatty Miller's gran left her? Ruth's not going to get that, is she?'

'No, you can put your hackles down. It's going into a trust for the baby.'

Stung by the crack, Sarah retreated into her cup and pointedly stayed silent until Stamford said: 'I called in at the Yard after I'd seen the medical officer.'

'Oh yes, sir?'

'Don't sulk . . . it doesn't suit you.'

'I am not . . . Well, yes, all right, I was. Is there anything interesting happening at the Yard then, sir?'

'Depends on your point of view. They need to bring the CID staff level up to strength on this station.'

Sarah's face brightened with hope.

'No. Not you, I'm afraid. They still take the view that a permanent female officer isn't necessary. Sorry.'

Sarah gave what she hoped looked like a casual shrug, though she suspected it came out as a childish pout.

'And they want to make a permanent appointment to head up the department. It's never rated a chief inspector before, but . . .'

'But you've resigned . . . !'

'Apparently not.'

When he'd reported back from the doctor to Superintendent Dunn's office and wondered whether it might be possible to reconsider his medical discharge, Dunn had opened his desk drawer, drawn out Jack's resignation letter and murmured that he hadn't quite got around to forwarding it yet.

'Damn busy recently,' he'd said airily, dropping the envelope into his waste-paper bin. 'Now, about this job in Agar Street . . .'

'So you'll be staying . . . ?' Sarah wanted to say she was glad. And part of her truly was. But the other part was digesting what this would do to their personal relationship . . . Stick it straight back on the slow burner, that was what! She opened her mouth to congratulate him . . . and froze.

Surprised, Jack looked behind him to see what had thrown her.

Ding-Dong dabbed droplets of evening mist from his moustache, rubbed his cold hands together and made his way to the serving hatch. He'd have taken his cup to a separate table if Jack hadn't practically ordered him to join them.

'Well?'

'Tolerably, thank you, sir. The lady wife has a touch of bronchitis, but . . .'

'Christmas, Detective Constable, is over. Put away the comedy turn until next year and tell me what happened with Eddie Hooper. Has he admitted the robbery?'

'Didn't have much choice really, did he? Not after the sarge here caught him red-handed with the pickings.'

'So he's going to plead guilty?'

'Made a statement in the presence of a solicitor. All fair and above board.'

'And his accomplice? Did he name him?'

'Oh yes.'

Ding-Dong drew a paper from his pocket and unfolded it with infuriating slowness. He scanned the closely written sheet until he found the paragraph he wanted: ' "It was Roger Colefoot talked me into it. Robbing the warehouse was his idea and it was Roger hit the watchman. I never wanted nothing to do with hitting the bloke and I want it to be known how I bitterly regret my slide from the path of virtue." '

Jack and Sarah exchanged blank looks, before Stamford voiced what they were both thinking: 'Who the hell is Roger Colefoot?'

'Old drinking partner of Eddie's, sir.'

'Have you picked him up?'

'Tricky that, sir. Unless you can spare me a dozen or so coppers.'

'Pardon?'

'Colefoot did a bit of casual night work himself. Helped out at a printer's near St Paul's . . .'

'You mean . . .'

'That's right, sir. The late Mr Roger Colefoot was scattered over a large part of the City a week ago . . . courtesy of the Luftwaffe.'

'Ah!'

'As you say, sir ... ah!'

'There's still the two bottles from the chicken shed,' Sarah said, slipping into the role of Job's comforter.

'Not traceable to the stolen batch. And if young Mr O'Day chooses to stick to his story that he bought them fair and square ... well, we can't prove different, can we?'

Jack stood up. 'I'll go and tell Eileen the good news ... if you've no objections, Constable?'

'None at all, sir. The lady wife is making toad in the hole tonight, air-raids permitting. The bombs play havoc with her batter.'

He returned with apparent calm to his tea. Jack opened his mouth to point out that it was still a very good collar, and then thought better of it. Catching Sarah's eye, he jerked his head towards the door.

Pat answered the door to them. His face fell at the sight of the two visitors. 'Thought you were someone else,' he admitted, closing the door and whisking the blackout curtain across. He led the way back to the kitchen, where Sammy and Annaliese were playing with what appeared to be a dismantled mangle, and Eileen was prodding and muttering over boiling saucepans.

Sammy gave them a wide grin. Annaliese, to Jack's pleased surprise, skipped across, touched his hand briefly, gave him a shy smile and returned to her play.

'You'll stay for your dinners?' Eileen said firmly, her eyes sparkling with relief when they delivered the news that Maury was off the hook.

'I can't keep eating your rations, Eileen,' Sarah protested. 'Anyway, I have to go on shelter duty at ten.'

'It ain't rations. One of the blessed hens died. I've boiled her down with some rice and onions. And you'll be finished long before ten.'

'If you put it like that ... Here ... for the children.' She held out half the wedding cake, which she'd purloined before Bridget could get her hands on it.

'Never mind the children ...' Eileen said, whisking the package from under Sammy's nose. 'It will do for pudding. I'll

461

fry it up in a knob of marge. Sprinkled with sugar and smear of jam. Where are you going?'

Pat was pulling on boots. 'Shan't be long, Mum.'

'But Rose is coming round.'

'I'll be back in an hour, two at most.' He left them looking at the closing front door.

'Are he and Rose Goodwin . . . ?' Sarah enquired.

'Rose had a letter yesterday from some girl up at the fire station. Said she was sorry for writing all those things about her late husband and she hoped she *would* marry my Pat on account of him being a smashing bloke.' Eileen's knife slashed down with a surgeon's precision, cutting the rich cake into eight segments. ' 'Course, I'm not saying Rose's going to marry Pat on some nasty little madam's say-so. But she's coming round for her dinner with him. I gave the front room a clean – just in case they were wanting to use it for a bit of courting. I hope he ain't gone too far.'

Pat had gone as far as a dingy hotel in Theobald's Road. Nodding to the barman, he made his way through a door at the back of the bar, up several flights of stairs and walked into an attic room without knocking.

Maury jumped from one of the beds with an aggressive ' 'Ere, what's your . . . oh, it's you. What you want?'

Briefly Pat explained about Eddie Hooper's confession.

Maury smirked. 'Just what I always said, ain't it? I'm innocent.'

'And Winston Churchill's a ballet dancer. Get your things, you're coming home.'

Maury put his hands behind his head and stretched. 'Maybe I don't want to. How'd you find me anyway?'

'There's not many places you can hide from a fireman, Maury. The world's full of us nowadays, ain't you noticed? Now move yourself. Mum wants you home.' He lifted the corner of the grubby blanket. 'How many people renting this bed?'

Maury shrugged. 'Just me and another bloke. He works nights.'

462

'So do I, Maury. I ain't wasting my night off arguing with you. Get up.'

Maury still looked inclined to argue. Leaning over, Pat lifted him, locked one arm round his neck and spoke softly next to his ear.

'You're planning to be a pretty big shot when you grow up, aren't you, Maury? Well, just think how it will be if every time people out there see Mr High-And-Mighty Maurice O'Day, they start remembering the day his big brother dragged him up Kentish Town High Street with his head clamped under his arm.'

There was a moment's silence, broken by a burst of laughter from the bar downstairs and the frantic bell of an ambulance in the distance.

'I'll stick me stuff in a bag,' Maury said. 'I was coming home anyway.' He'd missed his mum – and his mum's cooking. Not to mention the free laundry service she provided. And his own bed was better than the smelly flea-pit he'd been part-renting recently, even if he did have to share it with the squirming Sammy.

Nonetheless, despite the alert-free night, it was dawn before he finally fell asleep. Mr Stamford's quiet words as he'd wished them all goodnight kept ringing in his ears: 'You may have got away with it this time, Maury. But the likes of Eddie Hooper don't forget what they're owed. And believe me, if I owed Hooper as much as you do, I'd be very, very worried.'

Well, he was right about that, Maury thought, staring at the grey ceiling as Sammy breathed noisily beside him. Eddie's price for getting Maury off the hook had been a signed confession from Maury that would be left in the safe keeping of Eddie's friend until such time as Eddie chose to collect on it. Well, Eddie would be inside for the next few years. And before he got out, Maury was pretty certain he'd have found some way to get that incriminating piece of paper back – at his own price, not Eddie's.

On this heartening thought, Maury turned over and slept soundly.

Epilogue

The wind blew sharply on the corners, with a vicious tingle in it that promised snow very soon. Betty told herself that was why she was drawing up her coat collar and pulling her hat down as she hurried along the road. And it was for the same reason that she clasped the edges of the collar even tighter over her mouth as she hurried past her own house with her head bent.

The door to number seven was closed but unlocked as usual. Making her way up the oilcloth-covered stairs, she paused on the top landing and stood listening. A whirring sound came from beyond the left-hand door. Rapping on the panel she called: 'Clara?'

The sound stopped immediately. Furniture was moved hastily and something heavy slammed. A key was turned in the lock and the door opened. Relief flooded over the face of the thin, pale-faced young woman when she saw Betty.

'Mrs Shaw, Gawd, I thought you was from the Assistance. Come in.'

She ushered Betty into the overcrowded sitting room, at the same time ordering a toddler who was throwing painted bricks around: 'Mind yer manners this instant, Georgie, and come say hello to Mrs Shaw.'

Recognising a reliable source of treats, the little boy came eagerly and lifted a grubby face for a kiss. He was rewarded with a pear-drop and contentedly retired to a corner to dribble large amounts of spittle down his chin.

'Here.' Betty handed over the paper bag. 'For the other three.'

'Ta ever so much. I'll give 'em when they come back from school. Sit down. I'll put the kettle on.'

An ancient treadle sewing machine was clamped to one side of a scarred and scratched table. Betty took a seat on the other side and declined the tea. 'I don't want to take your rations. You stretch them thin enough as it is.'

'It's all right. Tea's about the only thing the kids don't eat or drink. You see Lord Woolton reckons they might cut the meat ration down to one and threepence?' She lit a burner on the gas cooker in one corner of the room then stooped and took a bundle of material from where she'd hidden it in the oven. 'I got a bit of outwork. Making flags.' She held a Union Jack out as proof.

'Very patriotic,' Betty said with a tight smile.

Clara measured out two flat teaspoons of tea into a chipped pot. 'It's good to see you again, Mrs Shaw...' She paused awkwardly, then added: 'Mr Shaw said as how you weren't working up the local station no more.'

'No. I've transferred to Euston.'

'Got a place up Vorley Street now, ain't you?'

'It's just a room.' Betty accepted the offered cup.

'Bet you've made it homely, though.'

'No, not really,' Betty admitted. 'There's not much point when you're on your own. Anyway, I'm on duty a lot of the time.'

' 'Spect them big raids at the weekend kept you busy, eh?'

'Fairly... we've lost appliances to the Portsmouth convoy this time.'

'Oh.' Clara fiddled with the cup on her lap. Georgie sucked and banged bricks noisily in the corner. A gust of wind rattled the window.

'Looks like it might snow soon,' Betty said.

'Yeah, it's cold enough.'

'Have you heard...'

'Do you reckon...'

They spoke together and stopped in confusion.

'Sorry. What were you going to say, Clara?'

'Nuffing. After you, Mrs Shaw...'

'I just wondered if you'd heard from your husband?'

' 'Ad a couple of letters. He ain't one for writing much.

This lady from Red Cross come round. Says you can send prisoners of war up to two quid a month if you want. Well, I told 'er 'e'd be lucky! Where am I gonna get two quid to spare!'

'Bardia's fallen. The radio says we're going really well in Libya. Perhaps it won't be that long before he's home.'

'Yeah. Hope so. They reckon the Americans is gonna give us more help. That's good of 'em, ain't it?'

The awkward silence fell again. Clara's eyes flickered around; she twisted her cup in the saucer, setting the china screeching.

'Have you . . .' Whatever she was going to ask was interrupted by a rising wail from across the landing.

For a moment they stared at each other across the table. Then Betty said: 'Is that Len's baby? Hadn't you better see to him?'

Anxiety drained from Clara's scraggy face like water running from a sink. 'I weren't sure you knew I was minding 'im.'

'Someone said,' Betty said airily. Which was only partially true. She'd seen them out together, Clara pushing the baby in a hood pram, with only his knitted bonnet visible above a great mound of blanket. Several times she'd been on the point of going over and boldly looking in the pram, but pride had held her back.

'May I see him?'

' 'Course you can.' Clara made for the screams, which were becoming more demanding with each second he was ignored. Georgie flew across the room and pushed past her, flinging himself at the far door knob and hurtling into the room. Scrambling on to the double bed, he trampolined energetically, sending the springs twanging in rusty protest. 'Leave off,' his mother ordered, without much hope of him taking any notice.

This room was as overfurnished as the other. In addition to the double bed, there was a large wardrobe and dressing table, a clothes horse draped with airing nappies, a single mattress lying partially under the bed, and the baby's cot.

'You've a bit of a squeeze in here, Clara,' Betty remarked, pushing her hands into her pockets to control an irresistible impulse to whisk the baby up and cuddle away his miseries.

'It ain't so bad. My four go in the bed and I have the mattress. Unless there's an alert. Then it's all down the Anderson. Come on, then.' Stooping, she put the baby on the single mattress on the floor and dragged a clean nappy off the horse.

'Can I help?'

'There's a bucket . . . by the cooker . . . Can yer . . . ?'

The wet nappy was added to a pile already soaking. Betty came back and stood silently watching as the fresh one was pinned to the kicking baby. When she had finished, Clara climbed off her knees and went to lift him.

'Let me help.' Betty swooped in and scooped the baby up. She held him on her shoulder, feeling the firm legs pressing into her chest and the rapid pit-pat of his pulse on her chin. 'He's a fine-looking baby. Is he good?'

'Good enough. And a right little greedy-guts. Got an appetite on him like his . . .' Clara broke off and blushed redly.

'Like his dad?' Betty finished. 'Yes, Len always liked his food.'

'Yeah . . . well . . .' Clara bit her lip.

'Does Len see the baby at all?'

'Oh yes!' Clara nodded vigorously. 'I take him over every time Mr Shaw has a day off. And he don't stint him. Gives me money to get everything new.'

'Len's watch is off duty today.'

'Yeah, I know. I was going over soon as I'd finished me flags. It's piece work, see. The bloke's coming to pick it up soon.'

'Could I take him over?'

'You?' Clara hesitated. 'Well, yeah. I mean . . . it ain't for me to stop yer really, is it? . . . I . . .'

Georgie gave an exceptionally vigorous bounce and shot himself into the wall. He cannoned off it and landed on the floor with a loud howl. His mother was still kissing him better and threatening him with a clip for not minding her as Betty pulled a blanket from the cot, wrapped it round the baby and made her way carefully down the stairs.

There was no answer to her knock at the front door. She'd

dropped her own key down a drain in an angry gesture of finality the night she'd found out about Hatty, so she had no choice but to walk round the back. Len was digging in the thick clay, turning the heavy clods over for the frost to work on. He didn't hear her coming, and for a few minutes she stood as he thumped and twisted the spade, watching the familiar way his muscles flexed and slid under his shirt. Finally Richard got bored with the view over her shoulder and mewed his irritation.

Len straightened, thrusting the spade in. 'Take him in the kitchen, Clar . . . Betty!'

'Hello, Len.'

'Betty?' He stared as if he couldn't believe she was real.

'Can I come in?'

'Yes. Of course. I mean . . . yes.'

The fire burning in the kitchen grate was newly lit, and it spat and sparked with loud cracks that fascinated Richard. He lay in the crook of Betty's arm, wide-eyed and alert as each spark leapt on to the small hearth. The original shock of black hair he'd had at birth had come out, but in its place he was growing a softer cap of dark brown to match his eyes.

'He's a fine little lad, isn't he?' Len said uncertainly.

'Not so little . . .' Betty said, running a hand down the sturdy legs and arms.

'Well, us Shaws have always been on the well-made side. Don't do for a lad to be skinny. Needs a bit of beef on him so's he can look out for himself.'

Despite the situation, there was a note of pride in his voice as he regarded his son and heir.

He took a kitchen seat opposite her. 'It's good to see you here again, Betty. How have you been?'

'All right, thank you. How about you? Have things settled down at the stations?'

'Yeah. Everyone's pulling together again. Got some new blokes. New girls too. That blonde one . . . Nell . . . she left. Transferred to St Albans. Got herself a husband who works out that way, apparently.'

'I know. I shared a house with them . . . remember?'

'Oh. Right. Still in the Highgate place, are you?' Before she could answer, he burst out with: 'This house is bloody awful without you, Betty.'

The loud voice jerked Richard's attention from the fascinating fire. He wrinkled his nose and considered whether it was worth a good bawl. Seeing the signs, Betty cooed and rocked him gently. He beamed and chuckled.

'It looks tidy enough to me.'

'Clara cleans it a few hours a week. You know damn well that ain't what I meant . . .'

'Don't swear in front of the baby, Len.'

'Sorry.' He stared at her uncertainly as she bounced and swung the baby, singing softly to it. 'I've really missed you, Betty.'

'Why? Haven't any of the new women taken your fancy?'

He flushed. 'I never meant . . . it's not that. Not just that. I miss the other things. The sight of you when I come in from work – like it used to be before you joined up. And the smell of you around the place . . . and just, well, being able to think about you when I'm out on a shout . . . knowing you're here waiting . . . all soft and warm and sweet . . .' He looked at her pleadingly. 'Haven't you felt any of that, Betty? Don't you miss me?'

Of course she missed him. She hated the aching loneliness of turning over in bed and not being able to cuddle up against his broad back. She loathed not being able to sit across the table from him and watch him eat a meal she'd cooked specially for him. Her days were full of incidents that she stored up to tell him about – only to remember that he wasn't there to tell any more.

'You're not the man I thought I married, Len. You never were,' she said sadly.

'Well, even when I weren't, I still made you happy, didn't I, Betty?' he said softly.

'Ignorance is bliss, Len. There wouldn't be much bliss in wondering what you were up to every time you were out of my sight.'

'Not that, Betty . . . I swear I'll never . . . Come back please, love. We could be a proper family. You, me and the lad. I'll fix up the back bedroom as a nursery just like we always planned. You could give up work. Or just do a few hours like the other women with nippers. What do you say, love?'

She looked down at the baby. Richard stretched and kicked vigorously, apparently enchanted by the sight of his own booties.

'Poor Hatty,' Betty said softly. 'She'd have loved him so much.'

'Yeah . . . well . . .' Len's lips tightened. The last person he wanted to discuss was Hatty.

She leant forward, gathering the baby tighter into her arms. The movement caused the medallion the fortune-teller on Hampstead Heath had given her to slip between a gap in her blouse buttons. The cheap metal caught the firelight in the gloomy kitchen and glittered like molten gold. Richard's eyes widened. He reached up to pat this fascinating thing and sent it spinning round.

He looked up at Betty and she looked down into his long-lashed eyes. A silent message passed between them. A deep, fierce, possessive love like nothing she'd ever felt before swept through every particle of her body. Lifting him up, she tucked his head into the soft hollow of her throat and whispered into his downy hair: 'My son, my son.'

'Betty?' Len leant forward, eagerness and hope mingling in his face. 'You'll come back? You'll give me another chance?'

Locking her arms round the baby so that she could feel his heart beating against hers, Betty said: 'Yes. Oh, yes.'

Where the Mersey Flows

Lyn Andrews

Leah Cavendish and Nora O'Brien seem to have little in common – except their friendship. Nora is a domestic and Leah the daughter of a wealthy haulage magnate but both are isolated beneath the roof of the opulent Cavendish household.

When Nora is flung out on the streets by Leah's grasping brother-in-law, the outraged Leah follows her, dramatically declaring her intention to move to Liverpool's docklands, alongside Nora and her impoverished family. But nothing can prepare Leah for the squalor that greets her in Oil Street. Nor for Sean Maguire, Nora's defiant Irish neighbour . . .

'A compelling read' *Woman's Realm*

'Enormously popular' *Liverpool Echo*

'Spellbinding . . . the Catherine Cookson of Liverpool' *Northern Echo*

0 7472 5176 2

HEADLINE

Maggie's Market

Dee Williams

It's 1935 and Maggie Ross loves her life in Kelvin Market, where her husband Tony has a bric-a-brac stall and where she lives, with her young family, above Mr Goldman's bespoke tailors. But one fine spring day, her husband vanishes into thin air and her world collapses.

The last anyone saw of Tony is at Rotherhithe station, where Mr Goldman glimpsed him boarding a train, though Maggie can only guess at her husband's destination. And she has no way of telling what prompted him to leave so suddenly – especially when she's got a new baby on the way. What she can tell is who her real friends are as she struggles to bring up her children alone. There's outspoken, gold-hearted Winnie, whose cheerful chatter hides a sad past, and cheeky Eve, whom she's known since they were girls. And there's also Inspector Matthews, the policeman sent to investigate her husband's disappearance. A man who, to the Kelvin Market stallholders, is on the wrong side of the law, but a man to whom Maggie is increasingly drawn . . .

'A brilliant story, full of surprises' *Woman's Realm*

'A moving story, full of intrigue and suspense . . . a wam and appealing cast of characters . . . an excellent treat' *Bolton Evening News*

0 7472 5536 9

HEADLINE